AND

THE DOCTOR'S REASON TO STAY

BY
DIANNE DRAKE

Praise for
Fiona Lowe:

'MIRACLE: TWIN BABIES is a wonderful story, full of heart, pathos and humour, that will make you laugh and cry. Fiona Lowe never fails to write enchanting, heartwarming and realistic Medical™ Romances, with wonderful three-dimensional characters you'd love to know (and, in the case of her heroes, love to love!). A spellbinding and emotional tale. Talented Australian author Fiona Lowe has penned another enjoyable romantic tale that will make your heart sing!'
—*Cataromance.com*

A new trilogy from
Dianne Drake:

With THE DOCTOR'S REASON TO STAY Dianne Drake welcomes you to the first story in her *New York Hospital Heartthrobs* trilogy

Three gorgeous guys return home to upstate New York. It's a place they love to hate—until they each find a bride amidst the bustle of a very special hospital.

CAREER GIRL IN THE COUNTRY

BY

FIONA LOWE

First published in Great Britain 2011
by Mills & Boon, an imprint of Harlequin (UK) Limited,
Eton House, 18-24 Paradise Road, Richmond, Surrey TW9 1SR

ISBN: 978 0 263 88600 9

Harlequin (UK) policy is to use papers that are natural, renewable and recyclable products and made from wood grown in sustainable forests. The logging and manufacturing process conform to the legal environmental regulations of the country of origin.

Printed and bound in Spain
by Blackprint CPI, Barcelona

Dear Reader

Poppy Stanfield is a successful surgeon who's on the cusp of being made Chief of Surgery: her ultimate goal and everything she's spent years working towards. So when she's suddenly sent to Bundallagong not only does she think she has landed on Mars, she thinks life as she knows it has ended too. All she can see is plains and red dust, and not even the sparkling Indian Ocean is enough to win her over. From the first moment she steps onto Bundallagong soil she is making plans to leave.

But sometimes what we think is the worst thing possible turns out to be the best thing that ever happened to us. Poppy has no clue that this is going to be her story, and she's not quick to realise it either as she rails against everything Bundallagong throws at her.

Dr Matt Albright had the perfect life until it was stolen from him, and now he doesn't care where he lives or who lives with him—which is why he's totally ignoring the goanna that has moved into his roof! He goes to work each day and goes through the motions of living, hating that the town he loves now walks on eggshells around him. When he first meets Poppy all he can see is a starchy, uptight woman who is going to drive him absolutely spare.

The isolation of the Outback, with its fiery heat, will either send you mad or heal you; I'll let you read on to find out what is in store for Poppy and Matt! ☺

I hope you enjoy their story! For photos of the area that inspired the story, head to my website at www.fionalowe.com I love to chat to my readers, and you can also find me at Facebook (Fiona Lowe author), Twitter, and at eharlequin's Medical Romance Authors' blog or via my website. I'd love to hear from you!

Happy reading!

Love

Fiona x

Always an avid reader, **Fiona Lowe** decided to combine her love of romance with her interest in all things medical, so writing Medical™ Romance was an obvious choice! She lives in a seaside town in southern Australia, where she juggles writing, reading, working and raising two gorgeous sons with the support of her own real-life hero!

Recent books by the same author:

SINGLE DAD'S TRIPLE TROUBLE
THE MOST MAGICAL GIFT OF ALL
HER BROODING HEART SURGEON
MIRACLE: TWIN BABIES

Dedication

**To Sandra,
with many thanks for keeping us neat and tidy!**

CHAPTER ONE

FEMALE SURGEON TAKES BAMPTON AWARD

> Ms Stanfield's meteoric rise in the male-dominated field of surgery was recognised last week. Journal's 'on the ground' photographer snapped Ms Stanfield wearing last season's black suit (right), and we're left wondering if rather than taking the 'Old Boys' Club' by storm she's actually joined it. Rumour has it she's in negotiations with two prestigious hospitals for Chief of Surgery.

POPPY STANFIELD'S 6:00 a.m. sip of Saturday coffee turned bitter in her mouth as she read the five-line article on the back page of the Perth newspaper. She didn't give a damn about the bitchy comment on her cinch-waisted black suit but how the hell had the gossip columnist found out about the job interviews? One job interview especially—the one she'd very carefully and deliberately kept quiet because it was hard enough being female in this business, let alone having the temerity to want a top job. A top job she was determined to get one way or another, which was why she'd applied for the post of Chief of Surgery at Southgate as well as Perth City, the hospital she currently worked for.

And now 'one way' was her only remaining option.

Her disappointed gaze caught sight of the envelope with the Southgate crest that had arrived yesterday containing a letter with the words 'unsuccessful candidate'. She hadn't read past them because there'd been no point. Poppy Stanfield didn't lose, she just regrouped and planned a new strategy. It would have been a huge coup to land the Southgate job ahead of the Perth City one, but the interview panel had been hostile from the moment she'd walked in.

The Bampton win had ruffled more than a few feathers in surgical ranks, and the media attention had been unexpected. The memory of the ditzy and penless journalist, with hair flying, who'd arrived late to interview her, sent a sliver of irritation down her spine. Poppy reread the article and the bald, incriminating words. Hell, why hadn't she spent more time with the journalist instead of rushing through the interview?

The faint echo of mocking laughter sounded deep down inside her. *You spend all your time at work and when have you ever really spent time with anyone?*

Steven.

Her phone chirped loudly, making her jump. Given it was 6:00 a.m., the call was most likely the hospital needing her for an urgent consult and absolutely nothing to do with this tiny article buried in the centre of the paper. Yes, an emergency consult would be the best scenario. The worst scenario would be— *Stop right there.* She refused to contemplate the worst scenario, but still she checked the screen before answering it.

She groaned into her hand. The name of the hospital's executive medical officer and her current boss blinked at her in inky and unforgiving black. *Damage control.* Tilting her head back and bringing her chin up, she answered the call with a firm, crisp greeting. 'Hello, William.'

'Poppy.' The professor spoke her name as if it pained his tongue to roll over the combination of letters. 'I've just seen the paper.'

Show no weakness. 'You must be pleased.' She ignored the vividly clear picture of him in her mind—tight face and stern mouth—the way he always looked when he believed a staff member had let him down. She infused her voice with enthusiasm. 'It was an excellent article about your groundbreaking in utero surgery.'

'It was, and surprisingly accurate, but that's not the article I'm referring to.'

No way was she admitting to anything so she let the deliberate silence ride, biting her lip not to say a word.

William continued. 'In your thank-you speech at the Bampton awards you said you were committed to Perth City.'

She pushed the Southgate envelope under the paper and out of sight. 'Absolutely. City's given me every opportunity.' The words of her speech flowed out smoothly, in stark contrast to the reality, which had involved her fighting to get into the surgery programme, working harder and longer hours than her male counterparts and ignoring the advice that surgery took beautiful young women and turned them into ugly old ones. She'd stopped thinking of herself as a woman long ago and with it had gone the dream of marriage and a family of her own. 'Should the board see fit, it would be an honour to serve as the Chief of Surgery.'

'An honour?'

His tone bristled with sarcasm, which Poppy ignored. 'Yes, indeed, and as I outlined in my interview with the board, I can start immediately and provide a seamless transition period before Gareth leaves for Brisbane.'

'The board's still deliberating on the best person for the position.' His voice dripped with disapproval. 'But I'm reassured by your commitment to the hospital, and by knowing how much of an honour you consider it to be working for the WA Healthcare Network.'

She let go of a breath she hadn't realised she'd been holding. 'Excellent.'

'So it stands to reason that you were the *first* person we thought of when Bundallagong Hospital requested a visiting surgeon.'

'Excuse me?' Of all the possible things she might have anticipated him saying, that wasn't one of them.

'Bundallagong Hospital.' William repeated the name slowly, a hint of humour skating along the cool steel of his voice, as if he was party to a private joke.

Her brain stalled, trying to think why the name of the town was vaguely familiar, and with a start she frantically flicked the pages of the paper open until she found the weather map. Her gasp of surprise was too quick for her mouth to stifle. 'But that's fifteen hundred kilometres away!'

'Or nine hundred and thirty-two miles, which is why they need a visiting surgeon for three months.'

Years of well-honed control started to unravel. 'William, this is ridiculous. Sending me out into the boonies is only going to make the day-to-day running at City even tighter than it is.'

'We've allowed for that.'

Her stomach clenched at his terse tone. 'We've been

chasing staff for over a year and what? Now you've just pulled a surgeon out of a hat?'

'One of the east coast applicants will fill your position while you're away.'

The staccato delivery of his words shot down the line like gunfire and she rocked back as if she'd been hit. The board was deliberately sending her away so they could observe her opposition in action without her being around to counteract any fallout. Incandescent fury flowed through her. 'And let me guess, that surgeon would be male.'

A sharp intake of breath sounded down the line. 'Poppy, you know I can't disclose information like that. Besides, as you've always pointed out, gender is irrelevant and it's all about expertise.'

He'd used her words against her to suit his own ends.

'Let's just be totally honest, shall we, William? You're seriously ticked off that I applied to Southgate and now you're punishing me for doing what any other surgeon in my position would have done.'

'Now you're being irrational, which isn't like you at all. Go to Bundallagong, Poppy, do your job and let the board do theirs. My secretary will be in touch about flight details but start packing because you're leaving tomorrow.'

The phone line suddenly buzzed and she realised he'd hung up on her. Blind anger tore through her and she shredded the newspaper, venting unprintable expletives at the journalist, William, the hospital and the system in general. Who the hell was this interloper from the east coast? She had contacts and she'd find out because learning about the enemy was a vital part of the strategy of winning.

But as the final strips of paper floated to the floor, her anger faded almost as fast as it had come and uncharacteristic tears of frustration and devastation pricked her eyes. Suddenly she was whipped back in time to when she had been a gangly ten-year-old girl valiantly trying to hold back tears after a drubbing in the first set of a tennis final, one of the few matches her father had actually turned up to watch.

He'd crossed his arms and stared down at her, his expression filled with derision. *'Don't be such a girl. Do you think boys cry? They don't. They just go out there and win.'*

Shaking her head as if that would get rid of the memory, she stomped into her bedroom and hauled a suitcase out of the wardrobe. If Bundallagong Hospital needed a surgeon then, by God, they were getting one, and the staff there wouldn't know what had hit them. She'd clear the waiting list, reorganise the department, overhaul the budget, meet every target and make William and the board sit up and take notice. Nobody put Poppy Stanfield in a corner.

Dr Matt Albright was on an island beach. The balmy tropical breeze skimmed over his sun-warmed skin and a book lay face-down on his naked chest, resting in the same position it had been for the last half-hour.

'Daddy, watch me!'

He waved to his daughter as she played in the shallow and virtually waveless water, then he rolled onto his side towards his wife, who lay next to him, reading. At that precise moment he knew his life was perfect in every way.

She glanced up and smiled in her quiet and unassuming way.

He grinned. 'You do realise I've loved you from the moment you hit me with play dough at kinder.'

Her tinkling laughter circled him and he leaned in to kiss her, knowing her mouth as intimately as his own. He reached out to curve his hand around her shoulder, trying to pull her closer, but his fingers closed in on themselves, digging into his palm. He tried again, this time cupping her cheeks, but they vanished the moment he tried to touch them.

'Daddy!'

He turned towards his daughter's voice and saw her evaporating, along with the water that tore all the sand from the beach. Panic bubbled hot and hard in his veins and he sat up fast, hearing the sound of his voice screaming 'No!'

His eyes flew open into darkness, his heart thundering against his ribs and sweat pouring down his face. His hands gripped something so hard they ached and he realised his fingers were digging deep into the edge of the mattress. He wasn't on a beach.

He was in a bed.

Slowly his eyes focused and he recognised the silhouette of his wardrobe, and he heard the thumping and scratching of the goanna that had at some point in the last few months, without any protest from him, moved into the roof.

Bundallagong. He was in Bundallagong.

He fell back onto the pillow and stared blindly up at the ceiling. His heart rate slowed and the tightness in his chest eased and for one brief and blessed moment he felt nothing at all. Then the ever-present emptiness, which the dream had momentarily absorbed, rushed back in. It expanded wide and long, filling every crevice, every cell and tainting every single breath.

Sleep was over. He swung his legs out of bed, walked into the lounge room, stared out into the night, and waited for the dawn.

'And how long have you had this pain, Sam?' Poppy pulled the modesty sheet back over the young man's abdomen.

He shrugged. 'Dunno. I think I saw Dr Albright about a month ago but then it just went away.'

'And is today's pain worse than a month ago?'

'A lot.'

'The nurse tells me you've been vomiting?'

'Yeah, sorry about that.'

Poppy tried not to smile. Dressed in tough mining workwear, and looking like not even a bullet could take him down, Sam's politeness and air of bewilderment reminded her of a young boy rather than a strapping and fit man of twenty.

'I'll be back in a bit, Sam.' Poppy pulled the screen curtains shut behind her as she stepped out into the compact emergency department, running the symptoms through her head—fever, high white blood cell count, rebound tenderness and an ultrasound that showed nothing unusual, although that in itself wasn't unusual. The process of diagnosis soothed her like the action of a soothing balm and she relaxed into the feeling.

The shock of landing two hours ago on the Mars-scape that was Bundallagong still had her reeling. The green of the river-hugging suburbs of Perth had not prepared her for the barrenness of the Pilbara. When she'd exited the plane, her feet had stuck mutinously to the roll-away airport stairs as her gaze had taken in the flat, red dust plains that stretched to the horizon in three directions. Then the ferocious dripping heat had hit her like an impenetrable wall and it had been like walking into a raging furnace with an aftershock of wet, cloying steam. The irony wasn't lost on her—William had sent her to hell.

The only way to reduce her 'sentence' was to start work so she'd asked the taxi driver to take her directly to the hospital. The fact it was a Sunday afternoon mattered little because the sooner she started her rotation, the sooner she could finish. She'd planned to spend a couple of hours studying medical histories and drawing up her first week's surgical list but as she'd arrived, so had Sam. The nurse on duty had happily accepted her offer of help with a smile, saying, 'Thanks heaps. It'll give the on-call doctor a break.'

Now Poppy walked briskly to the nurses' station and dropped the history in front of Jen Smithers, whose badge read 'Nursing Administrator'. 'Sam's got appendicitis so if you can arrange everything, I'll meet him in Theatre in an hour.'

The nurse, who Poppy guessed was of a similar age to her, looked up, a startled expression on her face. 'So it's an emergency case?'

'Not strictly, but he'll be better off without his appendix and there's no time like the present.'

'Ah.' Jen spun a pen through her fingers, as if considering her thoughts.

Poppy rarely took no for an answer and the 'Ah' sounded ominous. She made a snap decision: she needed the nursing staff on her side but she also needed to show she was the one in charge of the team. 'Jen, I call a spade a spade and I don't play games. I'll be straight with you and you need to be straight with me.

I want to operate on Sam this afternoon and I expect you to do your job so I can do mine.'

Jen nodded, her demeanour friendly yet professional. 'Fair enough. I can get nursing staff in to staff Theatre and Recovery, but that isn't going to be enough. It's the anaesthetic registrar's weekend off and he's not due back from Bali until this evening's flight.'

Gobsmacked, Poppy stared at her, not knowing whether to be more stunned that a person could fly direct to Bali from the middle of nowhere or the fact that it left the town without an anaesthetist. 'Surely there's someone else?'

'Well, yes, technically there is, but…'

A tight band of tension burned behind Poppy's eyes. Hell, she really *had* come to Mars. She didn't have time for staff politics, especially if they got in the way of her doing her job and proving to William that she deserved the chief of surgery position back in Perth. 'Just ring the doctor and get him or her here, and leave the rest to me.'

Jen gave a wry smile. 'If you're sure, I can do that.'

'Of course, I'm sure.' Poppy headed back to her patient, shaking her head. It seemed a very odd thing to say but, then again, she was a long way from Perth. She busied herself inserting an IV into Sam's arm, administered Maxolon for his nausea and pethidine for the pain.

'This will have you feeling better soon.'

'Thanks, Doc.'

'No problem.'

She clicked her pen and started scrawling a drug order onto the chart when she heard voices coming from the direction of the nurses' station. She couldn't make out Jen's words but could hear her soft and conciliatory tone, followed quickly by a very terse, deep voice asking, 'Why didn't you call me first?'

'Because Ms Stanfield was here and I thought I could save you—'

As Poppy hung the chart on the end of the trolley, Jen's voice was cut off by the male voice. The anger was unmistakable and his words hit painfully hard. 'Save me? I don't need you or anyone else in this town making decisions for me, do you understand? I'm the on-call doctor today and that means I get called.'

Sam's head swung towards the raised voices, his expression full of interest.

Staff politics. She'd asked Jen to call in this guy so she needed to be the one to deal with him. 'Back in a minute, Sam.' Poppy grabbed the cubicle curtains and deliberately pulled them open with a jerk, making the hangers swish against the metal with a rushing ping to remind Jen and the unknown doctor that there was a patient in the department. She marched briskly to the desk.

'Oh, Ms Stanfield.' Jen glanced around the man standing with his back to Poppy. Her organised demeanour had slipped slightly but instead of looking angry or crushed at being spoken to as if she was a child, her expression was one of resignation tinged with sadness and regret. 'Poppy Stanfield, meet Dr. Matt Albright, Head of ED.'

The tall, broad-shouldered man turned slowly, his sun-streaked chestnut hair moving with him. It was longer than the average male doctor's and the style was either deliberately messy-chic or overdue for a cut. A few strands fell forward, masking his left cheek, but his right side was fully exposed, and olive skin hollowed slightly under a fine but high cheekbone before stretching over a perfectly chiselled nose. A dark five-o'clock shadow circled tightly compressed lips, leaving Poppy in no doubt of his masculinity.

With a jolting shock she realised he wasn't handsome—he was disconcertingly beautiful in a way that put everyone else into shadow. In ancient times he would have been sculpted in marble and raised onto a pedestal as the epitome of beauty. Poppy found herself staring as if she was in a gallery admiring a painting where the artist had created impossibly stunning good looks that didn't belong on battle-scarred earth.

He was heart-stoppingly gorgeous and she'd bet anything women fell at his feet. Once she would have too but thankfully, due to years of practice, she was now immune and not even a quiver of attraction moved inside her.

Nothing ever does any more.

Shut up. Work excites me. She extended her hand towards him. 'Matt.'

His hand gripped hers with a firm, brisk shake, and a faint tingling rush started, intensifying as it shot along her arm. *Immune, are you?*

Compressed nerve from a too-firm grip, that's all.

'Poppy.' He raised his espresso-brown eyes to meet her gaze. She expected to see at least a flicker of interest in a new colleague, almost certainly a calculating professional sizing-up, and, at worst, a derisive flare at the fact she was a surgeon and a woman. None of it worried her because she knew exactly how to handle the men she worked with—she'd had years of experience.

But what she saw was so unexpected that it sucked the air from her lungs, almost pulling her with it. A short, sharp flame flickered in his eyes for a split second, illuminating hunger, but as it faded almost as fast as it had flared, she caught deep and dark swirling shadows before clouds rolled in briskly, masking all emotion.

She swayed on her heels as his hunger called up a blast of her own heat but as she glimpsed the misery in his eyes, she shivered and a jet of arctic cold scudded through her. Fire and ice collided; lust and pain coiling together before spiralling down to touch a place that had been firmly closed off and abandoned since—

She abruptly pulled her hand out of his, breaking his touch and moving her gaze to his left shoulder. *There you go, simple solution: no eye contact.* She didn't want to care about what hid behind that flawless face and now that his heat wasn't flowing through her, she marshalled her wayward thoughts and valiantly recomposed herself. This was no time to be discomfited. She needed to be in control and in charge, her future depended on it.

'As Jen will have explained, I need you to anaesthetise Sam Dennison.'

Long, lean fingers on his right hand crossed his wide and casually clad chest, flicking at the sleeve band of his white T-shirt. 'This is my department and I need to examine *my* patient before any decisions are made.' He turned and walked towards the cubicle.

Poppy matched his stride. 'And as Bundallagong's resident surgeon for the next ninety days or less, it's my considered opinion that—'

'You've had time to examine Sam and now you need to extend that courtesy to me.'

He didn't alter his pace and before she could reply, Matt Albright stepped through the curtains and closed them in her face.

CHAPTER TWO

MATT could hear the new surgeon pacing, her black heels clicking an impatient rhythm against the linoleum floor. Well, she could just wait. He wasn't a stickler for protocol but Jen had overstepped the mark by not calling him in to examine Sam first. God, he was sick of the town walking on eggshells around him and trying to protect him when all he wanted was normality. *Yeah, and what exactly is that these days?*

'You OK, Doc?' The young miner lay propped up against a bank of pillows, his eyes slightly glazed from the opiate pain relief.

Hell, if a spaced-out patient noticed he was shaking with frustration then things were really spinning out.

Matt, how can you always be so calm? Lisa's slightly accusing voice sounded faintly in his head. But that conversation had taken place in another lifetime, before everything he'd held dear had been brutally stolen from him. He hadn't known calm in over a year.

'I'm fine.' *Pull the other one.* 'But you're not. That appendix rumbling again?'

'Yeah, although whatever that other doctor gave me is good stuff.' Sam grinned happily.

Matt smiled as he examined him. 'Have you got any family up here?'

Sam shook his head. 'Nah, came for the job and the money.'

'I'll arrange for a phone so you can talk to your mum because there's a very high chance you'll be parting with your appendix. We'll fast you from midnight and observe you overnight.'

'OK.'

'Any questions?'

'Nah, you explained it all last time and then it got better.' Sam's eyes fluttered closed as the drugs really kicked in, tempering any concern over the surgery that he might have.

Matt decided he'd explain it all again to him later. He pulled the curtains open and the new surgeon immediately ceased pacing, but she held her wide shoulders square and tight. It struck him that there was nothing soft about this woman except for her name.

And her mouth.

Guilt kicked him hard. His initial top-to-toe glance of her had stalled unexpectedly on her mouth and a flash of lust-filled heat had sparked momentarily, shocking him deeply. There'd only ever been *one* woman for him, and until ten minutes ago no one else had ever registered on his radar, let alone elicited such a response. But there'd been something about Poppy Stanfield's plump mouth that had held him mesmerised. Lips that peaked in an inviting bow were the colour of crushed strawberries and hinted at tasting like an explosion of seductive sweetness. He'd almost licked his own in response.

It was a totally ridiculous and over-the-top reaction given the contrast between the softness of the lips and the precise and no-nonsense words they formed. Everything else about Poppy Stanfield was sharp angles and harsh lines. Her long black hair was pulled straight back exposing a high and intelligent forehead. Black hair, black brows, black suit, black shoes; the monotone was only broken by her lush mouth and the most unexpectedly vivid blue eyes.

Eyes that were fixed on him, full of questions and backlit with steely determination.

He deliberately sat on the desk and put a foot up on a chair, the position screaming casual in stark contrast to her starchy demeanour. For some crazy reason he had to concentrate really hard to get her name correct because, apart from being the colour of her lips, Poppy didn't suit her at all.

Her fingers tugged sharply at the bottom of her suit jacket, which was ludicrously formal attire for Bundallagong, and she seemed to rise slightly on her toes so she wasn't much shorter than him. 'Dr Albright.'

'You're in the bush now, Poppy.'

Her gaze drifted to the red dust on his boots before moving up to his face. 'Oh, I'm *very* well aware of that.'

Her tone oozed urban superiority and for the first time in months something other than anger and despair penetrated his permanent sadness—the buzz of impending verbal sparring. No one had faced up to him or even questioned him since Lisa. Hell, half the time his friends and colleagues had trouble meeting his gaze and, like Jen, their well-meaning attempts to help only stifled him. But he had a citified stranger in front of him who knew nothing about him and he realised with unexpected relish that he was looking forward to this upcoming tussle.

He met Poppy's baby-blue eyes with a deadpan expression. 'Excellent. Oh, and by the way, we use first names here even when we're ticked off.'

Her eyes flashed but her mouth pursed as if she was working hard not to smile. It was the first sign that a sense of humour might lurk under all the superficial blackness.

'Thank you for that tip, *Matt*. So you agree with my diagnosis that Sam has appendicitis?'

'I do.' He tilted his head ever so slightly in acquiescence. He didn't have any problem with her diagnosis, just her modus operandi. 'The pain he was presented with last month has intensified.'

Poppy schooled her face not to show the sweet victory that spun inside her. 'So we're in agreement. He's been fasting due to his nausea so Jen can prep him for Theatre and—'

'I said I agreed with your diagnosis.' He raised one brow. 'That doesn't translate into agreeing with your treatment plan.'

The coolness of his tone didn't come close to soothing the hot and prickly frustration that bristled inside her, and she silently cursed William for sending her to the middle of nowhere where men ruled and women had no choice but to follow. 'So you're going to sit on it until his appendix bursts and we're faced with dealing with peritonitis?'

Emotionless molasses-coloured eyes bored into her. 'Not at all. He requires surgery and he'll have it—tomorrow.'

So this is a power play: my turf versus your turf. 'But he could deteriorate overnight and we'd have to come in anyway. Tomorrow is an unknown quantity, whereas right now it's quiet, we're both here, so why wait?'

'Technically you don't even start work until 8:00 a.m. tomorrow.'

'That's semantics.'

He lowered his gaze and stared at her bright red suitcase stowed by the desk and then he moved the stare to her. 'Is it? It's Sunday and I would have thought seeing as you've only just arrived, you'd want to get settled in the house, hit the supermarket and fill your fridge.'

Something about his unflinching gaze made her feel like he saw not just the persona she showed the world but way beyond it and down deep into the depths she hadn't allowed anyone to enter since Steven.

But he really didn't want to—

I am so not doing this now!

She shut the voice up, hating that her hand had crept to the pendant that sat just below her throat. She forced her arm back by her side and her voice came out stiff and authoritative. 'You don't have to concern yourself with my domestic arrangements.'

'Very true.' He radiated a controlled aura that was an odd mix of dark and light, although the dark dominated. 'But I do concern myself with my staff's. They have lives outside work, Poppy.' His expression intimated that he thought perhaps she didn't. 'This is not an emergency and therefore we are *not* interrupting their family time, their fishing and sailing time, and, for some, their afternoon naps.'

'Afternoon naps?' Her voice rose in disbelief as her brain tried unsuccessfully to wrap itself around such a foreign concept. 'You're joking.'

Matt gave a snort that sounded like a rusty laugh as his face creased stiffly into lines that bracketed his mouth and for a moment his lips broke their tight line. A streak of something close to warmth followed, giving life and character to his face, which up until this point had been almost a caricature of unmarred features.

Her gut lurched as a flicker of delicious shimmers moved through her and she wished he'd stop. Perfection she could resist. Deep life lines around those dark and empty eyes, not so much.

His expression neutralised as the shadows returned. 'Life is slower here and, as you'll discover, the humidity at this time of year really saps your energy.'

She thought of the chief of surgery job back in Perth and went back into battle. She knew this game and she didn't plan to give an inch. 'Nothing saps my energy. I'm here to work, not to relax.' She reached for her briefcase and pulled out a folder. 'In regard to staff, I have a surgical budget and my own staffing ratios, and it's my call when to operate, not yours.'

'It is, and come tomorrow, your first official day, when David, the anaesthetic registrar, is back on duty, you can order him about to your heart's content. Today, as the ED doctor and the back-up anaesthetist, it's my call. We're not operating on Sam just so you can rush in, set a precedent and get some runs on the board.'

'This has *nothing* to do with me and everything to do with patient care.' She protested too quickly as his words hit far too close to home. Sam's case technically wasn't an emergency but it wasn't strictly elective surgery either. She hated that he'd guessed at her need to operate so she could stake her claim as the incumbent surgeon, competent and in charge.

He slid to his feet, the movement as graceful as a gazelle's but with the calculation of a panther. Everything about him screamed, *I don't believe you.*

'Should Sam's condition change, I'll call you

straight away. Meanwhile, go stock your fridge and turn on the air-conditioning so you can sleep tonight.'

Her body vibrated with rage. 'Don't patronise me.'

Genuine surprise raced across his face and he gave a sigh filled with fatigue. 'I'm not. I'm actually trying to help. Your life here will be a lot easier if you don't get the staff off-side before you've officially started.'

She wanted to stay furious with him, she wanted to cast him in the role of obstructive male, but his gaze wasn't combative and amid the darkness that hovered around him, she detected a sliver of goodwill. It totally confused her.

'I see. Well, we may not agree about Sam but I take on board what you're saying.' She made herself say, 'Thank you.'

'No problem.' His fingers pushed through his straight hair, the strands sliding over them like water on rocks.

With a shock she caught the glint of gold on his ring finger. How had she missed that? But it didn't matter how or why—what was important was now she knew. Married men didn't interest her.

It's been a long time since an unmarried one interested you.

Get off my case!

She had a gut feeling that she and Matt Albright would probably spend the next ninety days disagreeing but now it would be without fear of those strange and unwanted shimmers. Working with Matt would be uncomplicated and all about the job, and that was what she did best.

She pulled out a business card and held it towards him.

'This is my mobile number should Sam deteriorate,

and meanwhile I'll let you get back to your Sunday afternoon and your family.'

The goodwill vanished from his eyes as his lean body ceased all movement, and an eerie stillness hovered around him.

So much for her attempt at being polite. She couldn't work him out.

The card hung between them for a moment and then he slowly raised his arm and plucked it from her fingers. 'Right. See you around.'

'I guess you will.' What else was there to say?

'Wait!' Jen hurried over as two bloodied men supported and half dragged another man into the department.

'What happened?' Matt hauled his way back from the black despair Poppy's innocent comment had plunged him into, hating that it had, and was glad to be able to focus on the patient.

'Patient involved in a brawl, suspected head injury and possible fractures.'

He grabbed a gown and stifled a groan. In years gone by, drunken brawls had been exclusively Saturday night's domain but the mining boom had brought more people into the town and some of them had more money than sense. This patient could have anything from a broken toe to a subdural haematoma, with a million possibilities in between.

He threw Poppy a gown. 'I think you just got a reprieve from filling your fridge but just so we're clear, this is my emergency and you're assisting.'

'Oh, absolutely.' But deep sapphire blue shards scudded across her enormous baby-blue eyes, making a mockery of her supposed compliance. 'It's your emergency right up to the point when you realise he needs surgery and you're totally out of your depth.'

No one had been that blunt with him in a long time. A noise rumbled up from deep down inside him and for a moment he didn't recognise the sound. With a shock of surprise he realised that for the first time in months he'd just laughed.

Matt moved into action, work being one of the few things in his life he didn't question. He called out to the two men, 'Help me get him onto this trolley.'

They half hauled and half dropped the injured man onto the mattress and as soon as the sides had been pulled up, Matt asked, 'Do either of you have any injuries or is that your mate's blood?'

'We're OK.'

Matt wasn't convinced. 'Sit over there and wait. As soon as we've checked out your mate, someone will examine you both. No one is to leave until you've been examined, do you understand?'

Both men looked sheepish. 'Yeah, Doc.'

He pushed the trolley into the resus room. 'What's his pulse ox?'

Poppy slid the peg-like device onto the end of the patient's finger. 'Eight-five.' She unravelled green plastic tubing and turned on the oxygen. 'Mr…?'

'Daryl Jameson.' Jen supplied the information.

'Mr Jameson. I'm Poppy Stanfield, this is Jen Smithers, and on your left is Dr Matt Albright. You're in good hands. We're just going to give you some oxygen and help you to sit up.'

Matt tried not to show his surprise that Poppy had failed to mention her qualifications and that unlike many surgeons she was actually quite personable with an awake patient. 'Daryl, how's the breathing, mate?'

'Hurts.'

'Where does it hurt?' Poppy adjusted the elastic to hold the nasal prongs in place.

'It's me chest and arm that's killing me.'

'Do you know what day it is?' Matt flicked on his penlight.

'Sunday. I remember everything up to the moment the idiot hit me.'

Matt flashed the light into his patient's eyes. 'Pupils equal and reacting.'

Jen tried to ease Daryl's shirt off but resorted to scissors when Daryl couldn't move his arm without flinching. The soft material separated, revealing purple bruising all over the thin man's chest. The nurse gasped.

Matt looked up from the IV he was inserting, hating that he knew exactly what would have caused such trauma. 'Steel-capped boots. Welcome to the seedier side of Bundallagong, Poppy.'

She attached electrodes to Daryl's chest, and at the same time Matt knew she was examining the rise and fall of his chest given the complaint about pain on breathing. 'Sinus tachycardia. Jen, organise for a chest and arm X-ray.'

'On it.' The nurse started to manoeuvre the portable X-ray machine into position.

While Poppy wrapped a blood-pressure cuff around their patient's uninjured arm to enable automatic readings, Matt swung his stethoscope into his ears and listened to Daryl's breathing. He could hear creps and he palpated a paradoxical movement of the chest wall. 'Flail chest. I'll insert prophylactic chest tubes.'

A frown furrowed her smooth, white brow. 'Good

idea but it's the damage under the fractured ribs that worries me.'

Matt nodded. 'We're in agreement, then.'

'There's a first time for everything.'

The words sounded precise and clipped, but her plump, berry-red lips twitched. Like the siren's call, he felt his gaze tugged towards them again and wondered what they'd feel like to kiss.

The blood-pressure machine beeped loudly, ripping into his traitorous thoughts and grounding him instantly. He pulled his shame-ridden gaze away, reminding himself that he loved Lisa and he had a patient who needed his total concentration. 'Pressure's dropping.'

'He's bleeding somewhere.' Poppy's hands went direct to Daryl's abdomen, her alabaster fingers, with their neatly trimmed nails devoid of polish, palpating expertly. 'Any pain here?'

Daryl barely managed a negative movement of his head.

'No guarding. It's not his abdomen.' Poppy's frown deepened, making a sharp V between her expressive black brows. 'His O2 sats aren't improving. What about a haemothorax?'

'If he does have that, it's not massive because there's no mediastinal shift or tracheal deviation.'

But the blood-pressure machine kept beeping out its worrying sound as Daryl's heart rate soared and his conscious state started to fade. Matt stared at the green lines racing across the screen. PQRST waves scrawled the heartbeat but he thought he saw something unusual. He hit the printout button and studied the paper strips, detecting a change in the ST segment. Combining it with Poppy's musings, he had a sudden idea. 'Check his jugular vein.'

Matt shoved his stethoscope back in his ears and listened carefully to Daryl's heart beat. Instead of a loud and clear lub-dub, the sound was muffled.

'Cardiac tamponade.'

They spoke in unison, their thoughts and words meshing together for the very first time. 'He's bleeding into the pericardial sac.'

Poppy ran the ultrasound doppler over his chest, locating the heart. 'There you go.' She pointed to the dark shadow around the heart that squeezed the vital muscle.

Matt snapped on gloves and primed a syringe, knowing exactly what he had to do. Under ultrasound guidance, he withdrew the fluid from around the heart. 'Hopefully that will stabilise him until you work your magic.'

Her teeth scraped quickly over her bottom lip; the slightest of hesitations. 'A pericardial sac repair without the back-up of bypass isn't quite what I'd expected.'

He understood her concerns and he had some of his own. 'The anaesthetic will stretch me too.'

'It's going to be touch and go.'

'I know.' He met her direct and steady gaze, one devoid of any grandstanding or combative qualities, and wondered not for the first time about the many facets of Ms Poppy Stanfield.

CHAPTER THREE

IT HAD been a hell of a piece of theatre. Matt couldn't help but be impressed by Poppy's expertise. Except for requests for unanticipated instruments, she'd been virtually silent throughout, but it hadn't been an icy silence that had put the staff on tenterhooks; the case had done that on its own. Given the complexity of the surgery, she'd done the repair in a remarkably short space of time, giving Daryl the best chance of survival. It had been a lesson to Matt that she knew her stuff and did it well. Although many visiting surgeons had her air of authority, not all of them had the skills to match.

It had been one of the most challenging anaesthetics he'd ever given due to the patient being haemodynamically unstable, and maintaining his pressure had been a constant battle. Thankfully, Daryl had survived the emergency surgery and was now ventilated and on his way to Perth.

Once the flying doctor's plane had taken off and the night shift had arrived, Matt no longer had a reason to stay at the hospital. As he took the long way home it occurred to him that even Poppy had left the hospital before him, finally taking with her those bright red cases that matched her lips.

Again, shame washed through him. He hated it that

he kept thinking about her bee-stung lips. He didn't want to because they belonged to a woman who was so different in *every* way from his wife that it didn't warrant thinking about. When he thought of Lisa the words 'fair, soft and gentle' came to mind. Poppy Stanfield wouldn't understand the description.

He pulled into his carport and as he reluctantly walked towards the dark and empty house, memories of past homecomings assailed him.

'Tough case, honey?'

'Yeah.'

'Well, you're home now.' Lisa leaned in to kiss him. 'Annie's already in bed and our room is deliciously cool.'

His key hit the lock and the door swung open, releasing trapped and cloying heat, which carried silence with it in stark contrast to the past. God, he hated coming back to this house now.

Yeah, well, you hated not living in it.

He dropped his keys in a dish he'd brought home from the Pacific and which now sat permanently on the hall table, and thought about the months he'd stayed away from Bundallagong. Being back hurt as much as being away.

He turned the air-conditioner onto high, poured himself iced water and briefly contemplated going to bed. Picking up the remote, he turned on the television, rationalising that if he was going to stare at the ceiling he'd be better off staring at a screen. He flicked through the channels, unable to settle on watching anything that involved a story and eventually stared mindlessly at motor racing, the noise of the vehicles slowly lulling him into a soporific stupor.

He was back on the beach again, with dry heat

warming his skin and coconut palms swaying in the breeze, a peaceful idyll that promised so much. Set back from the sand line was a grass hut, its roof thatched with dried sugarcane leaves, and he strode towards it quickly, anticipation humming through his veins. His family was waiting for him. He stepped up onto the lanai but instead of cane chairs there was a stretcher. Bewildered, he stepped over it and walked into the fale, expecting to see the daybed, but instead he was in an operating theatre that looked like a set from *MASH*, with patients lined up row upon row, some with sheets pulled over their heads. Voices shouted but he didn't recognise the words, and he turned back, wanting to run, but the lanai had vanished, leaving splintered timber as the only evidence of its existence.

Deafening noise roared and his arms came up to protect his head and then his eyes were suddenly open and the television was blaring out so loudly the walls vibrated. He must have rolled on the remote, taking the volume to full blast, and he quickly pumped it back to a bearable level, but the ringing in his ears took a moment to fade. He shook his head, trying to get rid of the buzzing, and thought perhaps bed was a better option than the couch—not that he wanted to sleep because the dreams would terrorise him.

As he swung his feet to the floor, a woman's scream curdled his blood. He quickly shoved his feet into his shoes, grabbed a torch and ran outside.

He heard a wire door slam and he moved his torch round to the house on his left, the house owned by the hospital. With a start he saw a tall, barefoot woman dressed in a long T-shirt standing on the steps, her arms wrapped tightly around her.

He jogged over as the outside lamp cast her in a pool

of yellow light. 'Poppy? What the hell happened? Are you all right?'

She shuddered, her height seeming slightly diminished. She swallowed and it was if she had to force her throat to work. 'Mice.'

He knew his expression would be incredulous. The woman who'd stormed into his department with an approach similar to a man marking his territory had been reduced to a trembling mess by a mouse. For months he hadn't been able to laugh and now he had to try hard not to. '*You're* scared of a mouse or two?'

Her head flew up and a flash of the 'take no prisoners' woman he'd met nine hours ago surfaced. 'Not generally, no. But I opened the wardrobe to hang up my clothes and *mice* streamed out, scurrying over my feet, into my case and…' She took a steadying breath. 'I defy anyone, male or female, not to let out a yell of surprise when confronted by fifty of them.'

His mouth curved upwards, surprising muscles stiff from lack of use. 'That has to be an exaggeration of about forty-eight. Are they in the kitchen too?'

'I don't know!' Her voice snapped. 'I didn't stop to enquire if they'd taken over in there as well.'

Don't get involved. But he couldn't resist a dig. 'I did suggest you settle in to the house earlier in the day.'

Her chin shot up and she gave him a withering look. 'I am *not* exaggerating, and if that is the extent of your useful advice then I suggest you shut up now and leave.'

She crossed her arms and he suddenly noticed she had breasts. Small but round and… He hauled his gaze away. 'It's been a few months since anyone's lived here, although I would have thought someone would've checked out the house before you arrived. Who did you talk to in Administration?'

She stepped back inside, her gaze darting left and right and her long legs moving gingerly. 'No one.'

He followed. 'No one?' Usually Julie was very efficient.

'Me coming up here was—' She stopped abruptly for a moment. 'I rushed up here because the town was desperate. The fax telling you I was coming probably only arrived a few hours before me.'

They'd been desperate for weeks so her hasty arrival without the usual planning didn't make a lot of sense and he was about to ask her about it when a mouse raced out from under the couch.

Poppy leapt into the air, her long T-shirt rising up to expose creamy white thighs.

Matt tried not to look and instead marched like a foot soldier on patrol, punching open the kitchen door. Every surface was covered in mouse scats.

He heard Poppy's shocked gasp from the doorway but by the time he'd turned, her face was the usual mask of control, although she had a slight tremble about her.

'Just fabulous. This really is the icing on the cake of a stellar few days, and yet the poets wax lyrical about the bush.'

A startling fragility hovered around her eyes despite her sarcasm and he had an unexpected moment of feeling sorry for her. He shrugged it away. 'Living with a few creepy-crawlies is all part of the Bundallagong allure.'

'Not from where I'm standing it isn't. I think we have definition conflict on the word "few".'

Again he found himself wanting to smile yet at the

same time a feeling of extreme restlessness dragged at him. He flung open cupboards and found mice squeaking and scurrying everywhere amidst bags of pasta, cereal, oats and biscuits, all of which had been chewed and their contents scattered. He slammed the doors shut. 'OK, you were right. It's a plague and with this many mice it probably means you don't have a python.'

Her eyes widened like the ongoing expanse of Outback sky and her hands flew to her hips. 'No snake? And *that's* supposed to make me feel better? Hell, and they give surgeons a bad rap about their bedside manner.'

This time the urge to smile won. 'Actually, a python would have meant fewer mice. I haven't seen an infestation like this in years. Your predecessor must have left food and I guess the cleaners figured it was non-perishable and left it for the next occupant. Thing is, time marched on and the mice moved in. Julie can get the exterminator to come in the morning.'

'The morning.' The words came out as a choked wail loaded with realisation. Another mouse shot past her and she stiffened for a second before hastily retreating to the lounge room.

Matt crossed the kitchen and leaned against the architrave, watching her. She had her back to him and was standing on tiptoe, reducing her contact with the floor to the bare minimum. One hand tugged at the base of the T-shirt in an attempt to make it longer, and the other pressed her mobile phone to her ear as she spoke briskly.

'Yes, I need the number for motels in Bundallagong. I don't have a pen so can you put me through direct?'

He thought about the suit she'd worn when they'd met and how it had been followed by surgical scrubs.

Both garments had given her a unisex look, but the baggy shirt she wore now hid little. Poppy Stanfield might sound like a general but she had the seductive curves of a woman.

Heat hit him, making him hard, followed immediately by a torrent of gut-wrenching guilt. He loved Lisa. No woman could match her but for some reason his body had disconnected from his brain and was busy having a lust-fest. He hated it and every part of him wanted to get the hell out of the house and away from Poppy Stanfield and that damn T-shirt. But he couldn't leave, not until he knew she was settled in a motel. So he moved instead, putting distance between them by crossing the room and tugging his gaze away from the sweet curve of her behind that swelled out the T so beautifully that his palm itched.

He stared at the blank walls and then at the couch with a ferocious intensity he'd never before given to decor. He noticed a significant-size hole in the material covering the couch and realised the inside was probably full of rodents too. It would take days before baits and traps took effect, making the house liveable again.

He started making plans in his head to keep his mind off those long, shapely legs. As soon as he knew which motel she'd got a room at, he'd set the GPS in the hospital vehicle for her so she wouldn't get lost at this late hour. There'd be no point driving her because she'd need the car to get to and from the hospital.

Yeah, that, and you don't want to be in a car alone with her.

Poppy's voice suddenly went silent and the next moment, with a frustrated yell, she hurled her phone with a great deal of feeling onto the soft cushions of the couch. It was her first display of 'surgical temper'.

The outburst—so very different from Lisa's quiet approach—made him feel less guilty about getting hard, and yet it was so full of energy and life that it swirled around him, both pulling him in and pushing him away. After months of not feeling anything this maelstrom of emotions confused and scared him, and when he spoke, the words shot out harsh and loud. 'No instruments to throw?'

She didn't even raise a killing look. 'I have *never* thrown anything in Theatre, although I did train with a master thrower and once had to dodge a chair.' She plonked herself down hard on the couch, threw her head back and closed her eyes. 'This is a nightmare.'

Grey shadows hovered under her eyes and she looked exhausted.

'Actually, it's probably not a good idea to sit on that.' He pointed to the gnawed hole.

He'd expected her to fly off the couch but she merely shuddered and stayed put. Eventually she opened one eye and stared accusingly at him. 'You could have told me that the Australian billfish competition is on!'

Was it? Had that many months passed? 'Sorry, I didn't realise it was that time of year.' Once he'd had his finger on the pulse of his hometown and been part of the committee for one of the biggest events on the calendar, but not any more. Now days just rolled together into one long and empty period of time.

She frowned at him as if she didn't quite believe him. 'Every motel between here and a hundred k up and down the coast is fully booked out with anglers hoping to catch a two-hundred-and-twenty-kilo marlin. God, I hate this dust-impregnated town.' She picked up her phone and stared at it as if willing it to ring with news of a bed.

A mouse scuttled between his feet.

She can't stay here.

She's not staying with me.

Why not? You don't care about much any more so why care if she stays a few nights?

She sighed. 'I don't suppose you know if my office at the hospital has a couch?'

Her tone was unexpectedly flat, as if all the fight had gone out of her, and a tiny crack appeared in the blackness of his soul. His mouth started to work before his brain had fully thought it through. 'You can stay at my place until this joint is clean and mouse-free.'

Her smooth brow creased in uncertainty. 'That's kind of you but don't you think you should discuss it with your wife first?'

Your wife. He felt the darkness sucking at his heart and soul, threatening to drown him over again the way it had so many times in the last year and a half. His heart thumped faster, pumping pain with every beat, but he somehow managed to growl out, 'No need. Come on, grab your stuff. It's late.'

He turned and strode out of the house, not waiting for her, not offering to carry her case, and not looking back because if he did he might just change his mind. Not even Poppy deserved that.

Poppy lugged her unopened and mouse-free case the short distance to what she assumed was Matt's house—lights on, front door open—and wondered what on earth this man's deal was. He lurched from sarcastic to ironic, friendly to downright rude and a thousand emotions in between. Why offer her a bed if he clearly wasn't happy about her staying? She assumed he'd gone on ahead to let his wife know they had an unexpected guest. She thought of her gorgeous apartment in south Perth with a view of the river and silently cursed William and the hospital board.

She stepped into the empty foyer of a house considerably larger than her hospital residence, and unlike the minimalist furnishing of rental accommodation she could see the hand of a woman in the decor. Silence hovered and given it was close to midnight she didn't want to call out and wake anyone. For all she knew, there could be children asleep.

A closed door on her left was probably a bedroom so she left her case by the front door and padded down the well-lit hall, which opened into a formal lounge-dining area. Despite its stylish couches and polished wood table, it had an air of 'display only', lacking the personal touches like ornaments or photos that created living spaces. She kept walking and passed through a doorway into another huge space, which wasn't well-lit but she made out a kitchen and assumed beyond was a family room and bedrooms.

She spoke softly. 'Matt?'

He appeared through a door off the kitchen, his arms full of bed linen and his face set in unforgiving lines. 'Your room's this way.'

She expected him to turn towards the yet unexplored part of the house but instead he headed back from where she'd come from and entered the bedroom at the front of the house. A stripped white-wood queen-size bed dominated the room, which had a feature wall wallpapered in alternating cool blue and white stripes. Matching white-wood bedside tables held reading lamps with gold stands and white shades, although Poppy noticed the plugs had been pulled from the sockets. No books or boxes of tissues adorned any surfaces but gauzy curtains hung softly in front of a white blind, which was pulled down. The room should have said, 'restful haven for adults' but instead it looked abandoned.

Matt threw out the bottom sheet and Poppy moved to grab her side. She was almost certain this room had been designed to be the master bedroom. 'Are you sure this is OK?'

Matt deftly made a hospital corner with the top sheet and didn't meet her gaze. 'The en suite and walk-in wardrobe is through there.' He waved towards a doorway. 'The hot water's solar and it's really hot but it takes a minute or so to come through. Catch the water in the bucket unless you like to wake up to a cold shower.' He shoved a pillow so hard into the pillowcase it bunched up and he had to thump the feathers back into place before throwing it on the bed.

He strode to the door, his hand gripping the handle and his gaze fixed firmly on the cornice where two walls met. 'We leave at 7:30 a.m. and you'll find something for breakfast in the kitchen. Good night.'

The door closed firmly behind him, the click loudly stating, 'this is your space so stay here.' Poppy fell back onto the bed, her relief at being out of the infested house short-lived, and she wondered if she'd have been safer sharing with the mice.

Perhaps it had been sheer exhaustion but, despite Poppy's misgivings, she'd slept soundly. Now, as she dressed, she could feel the temperature climbing despite the early hour and her suit, which she donned automatically, felt hot. Still, if she had her way she'd be in scrubs soon enough. She opened her door, expecting to hear a household in full Monday morning action mode—radio or television news blaring, the drone of a kettle as it neared boiling and the ping of the toaster—but although she could hear the harsh squawk of cockatoos outside, she couldn't hear anything much inside. She made her way to the kitchen, which was empty, but with morning light streaming in she saw that, unlike the front part of the house, which held an unlived-in air, the kitchen showed more than the occasional sign of occupation.

Newspapers were piled so high on one end of the long granite bench that they'd started to slide onto the floor. Used cups and glasses sat abandoned close to, but not in, the dishwasher. A supermarket bag filled with tins took up more space rather than being stored in the adjacent pantry and every other surface was covered in clutter from half-opened mail to nails and paperclips.

A casual eating area off to the left had a table and chairs but instead of the polished jarrah having place-mats it held a laptop and was covered in screeds of paper. She glanced into the family room and saw a similar chaotic mess that jarred with the decor, which had obviously been undertaken with care and a great eye for detail. Poppy wasn't a domestic queen by any stretch of the imagination but even she managed better than this. She was amazed the Albrights didn't have mice!

She filled the kettle and while she waited for it to boil for her heart-starter morning cup of coffee, she emptied the dishwasher, guessing where items went, and then reloaded it with the dirty cups and glasses. She located the coffee and then opened the fridge. Milk, a loaf of bread, three apples and a tub of yoghurt hardly made a dent in the cavernous space that was big enough to store food for a family of six.

'Morning.'

His voice startled her but at the same time it reminded her of a Cabernet Merlot from Margaret River: deep, complex and with a hint of tannin. She turned around and stifled a gasp as her body betrayed her with a shot of delicious, tingling lust.

He stood on the other side of the bench, his hair still slightly damp and rumpled from the shower, the ends brushing the collar of his open-necked shirt. His long fingers tackled the last few buttons and his tanned and toned chest fast disappeared under the placket. His wedding ring glinted in the sunshine through the window and when he raised his gaze, the Kelly green in his shirt lightened his dark eyes but the shadows remained, and fatigue hung over him like a threatening cloud.

What are you doing? Get yourself under control; he's married, off limits, and even if he wasn't he's too damn moody and you've sworn off men for all time.

The moody man spoke. 'Did you sleep?'

His question sounded almost accusatory. 'I did, thank you.' *But you don't look like you did.*

He seemed to be staring at her suit and she thought she detected relief in his eyes, which made no sense whatsoever so she was probably totally wrong. She had no clue why she was letting Matt Albright unnerve her. If anyone unnerved her it was usually other women. Men she understood because she worked in a man's world but the whole women and friendship thing she'd always found challenging and unfathomable, and that dated back to primary school.

You're conveniently forgetting Steven, are you?

He didn't unnerve me, he just broke my heart.

And now you avoid men.

I work with men all the time!

That's not what I mean and you know it.

To distract herself she picked up a cloth and started to wipe down the bench. 'No one else up yet?'

'You don't have to do that.' He swooped, his fingers brushing her skin as he tugged the cloth out of her hand.

Trails of desire shot through her. This was crazy on so many levels and she had to act. 'Look, Matt, I'm sorry I had to prevail on your family for a bed, although you were the one who offered. Obviously me being here is a problem and I'd like to apologise to your wife for the inconvenience.'

He lowered the dishcloth onto the sink, the action slow and deliberate. When he raised his head she experienced a chill.

'My wife isn't here.'

And you're an incredibly gorgeous guy that women viscerally react to even when they're sensible and know they shouldn't. 'And she's not OK with me being here. I get it.'

He grimaced. 'No, you don't get it at all, Poppy.' The ping of the kettle sounded bright and cheery, in sharp contrast to the strain in his voice and the emptiness in his eyes. 'She died.'

His grief rocked through her, sending out waves of shocked surprise, and her fingers immediately crept to the pendant at her neck. *Death*. She hadn't expected that. Suddenly everything fell into place: the vacant master bedroom; the messy kitchen; Jenny's lack of anger towards him yesterday; and his aura of immense sadness. 'I'm sorry. I shouldn't be here. I'll find somewhere else today.'

He scooped ground coffee beans into the plunger and dashed the hot water over them. 'It makes no difference to me if you stay or not.'

And she realised he spoke the truth. His perfectly handsome face that could have graced the cover of any magazine was a façade. Underneath it, pain burned inside him, making caring for anything difficult.

You should leave. 'When does the billfish thing finish?'

He consulted a wall calendar that was two months out of date, and turned the pages. 'Next Sunday. Everything will be booked solid until then.'

Hope sank in her gut like a lead weight. 'That's probably how long it will take them to get the house under control.'

'Could be.'

'So you're saying it's a waste of time even trying to find somewhere else?'

He shrugged as his hand closed around the coffee-pot. 'It's your call.' Lifting two clean mugs from the cupboard, he poured the coffee and held up the milk carton.

She shook her head at the milk and reached over, lifting the black ambrosia to her nose, and breathed in deeply. The aroma sparked up her synapses, firing her brain into action. Was it such a bad thing if she had to stay here? She'd be working long hours so she'd hardly be in the house and when she was, she had her own room and bathroom so they'd hardly have to see each other. She had no doubt in her mind that Matt Albright was still very much struggling with the death of his wife so her occasional errant feelings, which she was certain she could squash, wouldn't be reciprocated at all, leaving everything as it should be: colleagues only.

'I came to operate, not to spend time trying to find a room, so, thanks, I'll stay.'

His blank expression and lack of response reinforced her decision and she brought the mug to her mouth, closed her eyes and drank in the brew. With a sigh of bliss she licked her lips and savoured every drop. She finally opened her eyes to find Matt's *chocolat-noir* gaze fixed intensely on her mouth and a spark of something broke through their blackness.

A shot of heat way beyond the definition of delicious tingling, and fully loaded with longing, rocked through her so hard and fast her knees sagged.

Get out now. 'I better get to the hospital and meet my staff.'

He gave a curt nod as the shadows scudded back in place. 'Don't give 'em hell.'

She bristled. 'I'll give them what they need.'

'I imagine you will.' His tone held resignation but his mouth curved slightly and the hint of dimple hovered in the darkness of his stubble, foreshadowing how heart-stoppingly magnificent he'd look wearing a full smile.

Poppy fled.

CHAPTER FOUR

POPPY flicked the switch on her Dictaphone to Off, having finished her last surgical report for the day. Her first couple of official workdays had arranged themselves into a routine of rounds, surgery, reports, phone calls to her spies in Perth to get an update on her opposition, and then arriving back at the house very late and falling exhausted into bed. Work consumed her, as it always did, only this time she appreciated that it left no space in her brain; no space to think about the way her body had gone into sensual overload when Matt Albright had looked at her through his heavy-lidded eyes.

She rubbed her forehead and wondered what on earth was wrong with her. Sure, he extended the handsome scale by about ten numbers but he was grumpy and short with everyone except patients, and obviously still grieving for his dead wife. Just like her, he wasn't fit for a relationship and she surely didn't even want one so there was absolutely *no* reason for her to be even thinking about him.

So why did thoughts of him sneak under her guard at random moments in the day? It made no sense and many times she'd needed to shake herself back into full-focus work mode because she had far more important things to think about, like the chief of surgery position in Perth.

'Ready, Poppy?'

The words broke into her thoughts and she glanced up, expecting to be asked for an emergency consult. Instead, Jen stood in the doorway dressed in casual clothes. 'Um, ready for what, exactly?'

Jen grinned. 'All work makes Poppy a dull girl.'

She straightened a pile of folders on her desk. 'All work is what I'm here to do.'

'Sure, but day is done and there's drinks at the pub.'

'Thanks but I'll pass.' Making small talk wasn't something that came easily to her; in fact, she was shockingly bad at it.

The nurse shook her head. 'Not an option, Poppy. It's a Bundallagong tradition that the nurses buy new medical staff a drink.'

She must have looked horrified because Jen hurriedly continued on with, 'Think of it as a girls' night out and a way of getting all the goss on the place.'

Her horror intensified. Poppy had no clue what a girls' night out entailed, having never been on one. *Getting the goss.* The words pierced her horror and she realised with a buzz of clarity that this might just be the solution to her problem of random thoughts about Matt interrupting her concentration. It was a normal human reaction to have natural curiosity when you heard unexpected news; healthy even, and Matt's statement about his wife being dead had been totally unexpected. She was pretty certain Matt wouldn't tell her any details and although she was known for her brusque, straight-shooting style, asking someone 'When and why did your wife die?' wasn't something even she would do. But if she found out the story from

Jen then knowing would end the curiosity and banish all her unsettling feelings.

Decision made, she stood up, slung her handbag over her shoulder and joined Jen in the corridor. 'So how far away is the pub?'

'Next door.'

'There's a pub next to the hospital?' She couldn't hide her incredulity. 'Why haven't I seen it?'

'Its position is historical. Mining towns back in the day were pretty rough and I guess putting the two together was a short walk for the drunks. Today things are more PC so there's limited signage advertising the pub. It's mostly used by the hospital and college staff, so a fun crowd but not too rowdy.'

They stepped outside into the dusk and the ever-present heat enveloped them. Streaks of vermillion slashed the sky as the sun sank low against the horizon and the bright white light of the first star pierced the rising darkness. 'This sunset belongs on a postcard.'

'Yeah, it does from this direction, but turn one-eighty degrees and the port's infrastructure gets in the way. Mining dominates everything but I guess without it the town wouldn't exist.'

The sunset unexpectedly mellowed Poppy. 'Does the pub have a garden? Now you've planted the idea of a drink, a glass of champagne while watching this sunset might go down very well.'

Jen roared laughing. 'You can have any drink you like as long as it's beer or rum and Coke. Welcome to the north-west.'

The pub was busy and Jen made a bee-line for a table with a banquette seat on one side that had a reserved sign on it. The waitress appeared with a tray of glasses, a jug of beer and bowls of peanuts. Poppy, not normally a beer-drinker, accepted a glass of the icy-cold amber fluid. As it trickled down her throat she was surprised at how good it tasted, and put it down to the heat.

Jen raised her glass. 'Welcome.'

'Thanks. It's been an interesting start.' And the perfect segue into the information she wanted. 'I'm sorry if I got you into trouble with Matt on Sunday.'

'No worries. Matt has good days and bad, and they're hard to pick so we just roll with them.' Jen fiddled with a thick cardboard coaster already damp from condensation. 'It's been an awful eighteen months. It's hard to know what to do or say when someone goes through something like that, you know?'

Something like what? Cancer? Car accident? 'How did—?'

'Hi, sorry I'm late!' Sarah Fielding, Poppy's theatre nurse, slid into the bench seat, all sparkling green eyes, wild red hair and a handbag the size of the Outback. She looked very different from the competent woman who'd made the morning's theatre session run so smoothly. 'Justin got home earlier than I thought and as the kids were already in bed we took advantage of it.' She winked and raised a glass. 'To fast sex.'

Jen laughed and clinked glasses with Sarah and threw Poppy a conspiratorial grin. 'To long-distance phone sex. David's out in the Kimberley for another month.'

The hairs on Poppy's arms stood up. God, this was why she never went out in a group. Joking about sex with women she barely knew wasn't something she was comfortable doing.

Let's face it, you're not comfortable doing sex, full stop.

Shut up.

But she wasn't fast enough and the memory of Steven's voice echoed through her. *Sexually, a fridge is warmer.*

She realised with a jolt that the two women were staring at her, expecting a response to the toast. She gripped the edge of the table to keep her hand from touching her pendant. 'Actually, I'm not planning on having sex here.'

Jen's eyes blazed with interest. 'So it's phone sex for you, too. Have you left a gorgeous man behind in Perth, pining for you?'

'Uh, no.' He left me.

Jen's brows rose in surprise. 'So you're unattached?'

Poppy sipped her beer against a tight throat, wishing she could mutter a magic word and conveniently vanish. She didn't do this sort of chitchat well, and she was even worse when the focus was on her. 'I am, and I came here to work. Given the amount there is to do, I won't have time for sex.'

'You can't go three months without sex!' Sarah's expression combined abject horror with good-natured scheming and she glanced around the bar as if she was looking for someone.

'Oh, I can *easily* go three months.' Poppy drained her glass.

But it was as if Sarah hadn't heard her and she turned back, her face fill of dismay. 'Damien isn't here tonight but, Poppy, you have to meet him. He's the new flying doctor pilot. He's totally gorgeous, unattached and he'd be the perfect diversion for you.'

She was having trouble trying to align this sex-obsessed woman with the one who'd been so professional this morning, and it took a lot of effort to keep the biting tone out of her voice. 'I don't need diverting.'

'We all need diverting. Life in this town is tough.' Sarah gave a sincere and friendly smile with no agenda, while she refilled Poppy's glass.

Poppy stuck to her mantra. 'I came here to do a job, pure and simple.'

'But why not have some fun at the same time?' Sarah tucked her curls behind her ear. 'Damien would be the perfect reward for being stuck out here, although you will have a bit of healthy competition from every other single woman in town and probably the occasional married one as well. Any single, professional man who arrives is immediately considered as a ticket out of here, or a way of making the town work for you.'

Poppy smiled stiffly. 'Well, I don't need a ticket out because I've got a huge job back in Perth.'

Not necessarily. She tried to close her mind to the undermining thought and at the same time wrestle back some control in the conversation. She spun the spotlight back on Sarah and raised her brows. 'So, did marrying Justin make this town work for you?'

Sarah laughed; a big, congenial chuckle. 'Touché, Poppy. OK, I get it—you don't want to be matched up. But to answer your question, Justin and I met in Canberra during his intern year. He came out here as a med student, fell in love with the Outback and wanted to come back. As I loved him, I said I'd come out for a couple of years and see if I could love it too.'

Love *and* career support. The answer slugged Poppy, totally demolishing her preconceived ideas and stabbing her with a combination of jealousy and remorse. Sarah had what she'd never been able to achieve. 'And?'

Sarah shrugged. 'It's a man's town and there needs to be more of a focus on the women. I'm on the neighbourhood house committee and we're setting up groups based on interests that we hope will spin off into support, mentoring and friendship groups.' Her face suddenly lit up. 'Hey, what else are you good at besides surgery?'

She tried to focus on the unexpected question. 'What do you mean?'

'Hobbies, interests, things like that.'

Her mind was a blank space because for years all she'd done was haul herself up the surgical ladder with long and punishing hours, leaving no time for anything other than sleep. Often there'd been scant time for that. 'The last few years have all been about work.'

'What's on your "to-do" list? What do you crave to do when you have the time?' Jen leaned forward, her eyes filled with unexpected sympathy.

Poppy bristled at the look. Why on earth would a nurse be feeling sorry for her? But her usually quick and logical mind struggled to think of an answer to the question. Desperate to banish Jen's air of pity, she dug deep but nothing surfaced. 'I've always wanted to…' God, what had she always wanted to do?

Win.

Win Dad's love. Steven's love.

She grasped at straws, needing to give them something, needing to show them she was a successful woman in control of her life *and* with interests. Interests she didn't have. For some reason, she thought of how she enjoyed singing in the shower and belting out a tune. Shower singing was something she did most mornings and it reminded her of how she'd sung in the choir at school and at uni. Singing would do as an answer. 'I'd go back to music and rejoin a choir.'

Sarah squealed and clapped her hands together. 'You sing? That's fantastic.' She high-fived Jen.

Another prickle of apprehension washed through Poppy, this time stronger than the last. 'Have I missed something?'

Sarah beamed. 'I've wanted to start a women's choir because it's so much more than just singing and so many women here would benefit. Jen plays piano and now you've arrived with choral experience so we have a musical director. It's just perfect!'

'Musical director?' She heard her voice rise and she shook her head hard. 'I don't have time for something like that.'

Sarah's eyes narrowed and her carefree aura vanished, replaced with a very professional and determined one. 'Poppy, you're a successful woman in a field dominated by men and that makes you a mentor. We have women here who are isolated, living in tough conditions, dealing with their partners' shiftwork and dislocated from their families because they've followed their partners out here for work. It can all add up to depression and low self-esteem.' The passion in her voice carried clearly out above the noise of the room. She leaned forward. 'I know you're busy but seeing as you're so adamant about not having sex while you're here…' she winked '…that frees up time for some community service. Think of it as improving women's health, and as a doctor you can hardly walk away from that.'

Checkmate.

Poppy wanted to plead too much work and no time but she knew both these women were intimate with her workload and would juggle rosters to create the time for her if she didn't find it herself. Sarah, with her air of good fun and no cares, had her over a barrel with her well-developed sense of social justice.

Poppy sighed. 'We start small, right?'

Sarah gave a long, slow smile. 'We'll start with whoever's interested.'

Poppy reluctantly raised her glass. 'To the Bundallagong's women's choir.'

'To the choir and friendship.' Jen titled her glass towards Poppy's and gave her a wide, open smile.

'To fun, friendship and service.' Sarah joined the toast.

A flurry of movement caught Poppy's eye and she turned towards the door. A tall man had entered and was crossing the room towards the bar, where he pulled up a stool and sat down next to another man. The chatter of the room dropped for a moment as all the women turned and followed his movements.

She instantly recognised Matt as the guy already sitting, his wild hair gleaming like a dark and rumpled halo in complete contrast to the golden fire of the man next to him. Side by side the two men looked like light and dark, storm and sunshine. Her gaze should have been tempted by the freshness, youth and sheer vitality of the unknown man but instead it was stalled on Matt. Stalled on the way his hair curled around his ears, stalled on his toned shoulders that filled out his shirt, giving it a precise and square fit; stalled on him full-stop.

'The blond delight is Damien and you have the right to change your mind about sex but not the choir.' Sarah leaned back with a conspiratorial smile on her lips. 'Rumour has it he can take a woman flying in more ways than one.'

Matt had been quietly getting drunk when Damien had arrived. He hoped that after one drink, the pilot would be taken away by one, two or more of the many women who'd been waiting so patiently for his arrival. That would mean he could resume his relationship with the barman, and wipe himself out for the night.

It had been a very long time since he'd got drunk, but during the first few weeks after returning to Bundallagong, alone, it had been a regular event. It had been the only surefire way to stop the dreams that broke his sleep and took him back to the heart of his grief, never allowing him any time to breathe without it. But the morning he'd woken up on the back steps after sleeping rough because he hadn't been able to work out how to put the key in the lock had been the day he'd stopped drinking hard. That, and the fact he knew it was a very fine line between himself and the alcoholics he treated in Emergency.

He'd been sober for weeks. He'd even started running again at dawn now he was able to get out of bed without a thundering headache, but Poppy Stanfield's arrival had changed everything. The only way he was going home tonight was completely buzzed so he could fall into the black oblivion of deep and uninterrupted sleep.

He threw back a shot. God, he hated himself. He despised the way he couldn't get Poppy out of his mind when he should be honouring Lisa's memory. He couldn't believe that on Monday night he'd left the hospital on time and cooked a meal in anticipation of Poppy's arrival home. All day she'd jumped in and out of his thoughts and he'd found himself looking forward to sitting down at a table with her, hearing about her day and sharing his own with a living person rather than the silent walls of the house.

But he'd eaten alone. By 10:00 p.m. he'd thrown out the food and gone to bed—to bed but not to sleep. His silent monologue had veered between cursing life in general that he no longer had Lisa and Annie, and cursing himself that he'd been so pathetic as to think he could try and have a normal evening, although he had no clue what normal was any more. He'd heard her car pull in at midnight and when he'd finally fallen asleep, his dreams had been filled with a woman who had looked like Lisa but whenever he'd got close, he could only see vibrant blue eyes. Poppy's eyes.

He spoke to the barman. 'I'll have another Scotch and…' He turned to the pilot. 'What can I buy you, Damien?'

'Soda water, thanks, I'm on call. Your night off?'

'Yep.'

'Hey, Doc, third drink in an hour—time for your keys.' Lewis, the barman, held out a container with a couple of sets of car keys at the bottom.

'I walked, Lew.' He had a standing arrangement with the barman so he avoided doing anything really stupid. A couple of times soon after Lisa's death, when being alive had almost been too much to bear, he'd got way too close to stupid.

'Good to hear it.' Lewis slid the two drinks across the counter.

Damien sipped his and surveyed the room. 'So

how's that guy I flew down to Perth the other night getting on?'

'Not bad. You'll probably be transporting him back here in a couple of weeks.'

Damien raised his hand in a wave and Matt glanced around to see who'd caught his attention. With a shot of surprise he recognised Sarah Fielding. Why on earth was Sarah beckoning Damien?

She and Lisa had been firm friends from the moment the Fieldings had arrived in town and as a result the two young families had socialised together a lot. Since coming back to Bundallagong, he'd only seen Justin at hospital functions and at the GP in-service he conducted every few months. He hadn't been able to face a social gathering with Sarah and the kids.

He stared at her and then made out Jen's profile behind her, before realising there was a third person at the table.

Surprise rolled through him. Poppy sat on a chair, looking awkward and completely out of place.

Sarah arrived at the bar, her gaze cautious, and she seemed to breathe in before she spoke. 'Justin was sorry you didn't make golf the other day, Matt. He's on for next Wednesday and looking for a partner, so call him?'

He didn't want to play golf. 'Sure.'

She nodded, her expression worried, and then she turned and gave Damien a flirty smile. Sliding her arm through the pilot's, she urged, 'Come and meet our new surgeon. She has the most amazing eyes you've ever seen and is in town for three months with no one to play with.'

Damien looked over Sarah's head towards the table of women. 'Ebony and ivory?'

Matt didn't like the way the pilot was scoping out Poppy and his voice came out on a growl. 'That's her, but be warned: just like a praying mantis, she'll play with you and then she'll eat you.'

But instead of being put off, the pilot grinned. 'I love a challenge.' He slid off the bar stool and strode towards the table.

The thought of Damien hitting on Poppy had Matt up and off the stool. *What are you doing? She'll probably tear strips off glamour boy and even if she doesn't, what do you care?*

But he picked his drink up anyway and let his feet carry him to the table. He arrived just as Damien was suggesting to Poppy that the only way to really appreciate the Pilbara was from the air.

Poppy's fine black brows rose in a look Matt was starting to recognise as pure sarcasm. 'If flying means not missing out on every single millimetre of the thousands of kilometres of endless, flat gibber plain and red dust, yes, I suspect you're right. Fortunately I flew in on a clear day so I don't feel the need repeat it any time soon.'

Damien looked slightly taken aback that his usual invitation had failed and Matt hid a smile before sitting down next to Poppy. Her fresh floral scent hinted at the newness of spring and it spun around him, urging every cell in his body to lean in close and breathe deeply. 'Actually, the only way to appreciate the unconventional beauty of this area is by four-wheel drive and getting a hands-on perspective.'

'Unconventional is right.' Poppy's fingers closed around the base of the pendant at her neck.

Jen's quizzical expression moved between Poppy

and Matt. 'Matt's right. You should make sure you visit Walker's Gorge while you're here.'

'It's a fair distance from here, though. I could fly you in,' Damien countered. 'Just let me know when you have a free day.'

Poppy's hand fell back to her lap and she gave a short laugh. 'That's very kind but given that my surgical list is endless, and Sarah's already shanghaied me into starting a women's choir, I think my time in Bundallagong is pretty much full.'

A choir. Matt did a double-take, not able to imagine her in a musical role, but was that just another piece of the puzzle that was Poppy? His eyes met hers and he watched the vivid blue of her irises almost disappear into rapidly dilating inky discs. A flash of undisguised attraction burned bright for a heartbeat and then faded, but not before a wave of her heat crashed into him. Like a chain reaction, every part of him vibrated with hungry need.

She pulled her gaze away and rose to her feet, her movements jerky. 'Thanks, everyone, for the welcome drinks. It was really kind but it's time to call it a night.'

Damien moved towards her. *No way, mate.* For the second time, Matt found himself shooting to his feet and he spoke without thinking. 'I'll come with you.'

Her fingers tugged at the fine, silver pendant and her expression mixed hesitation with determination. 'Really, there's no need.'

But he wasn't letting her leave alone or giving glamour boy an opening so he shrugged casually. 'I need the ride.' Instinctively, he slid his hand into the small of her back and guided her around the group, through the crowd and out into the night, ignoring the stunned looks of his colleagues.

The heat from Matt's hand flooded Poppy, streaming through her veins like hot vapour and culminating in a tingling pond of undeniable lust. Her breath came too fast and the muscles in her legs threatened to melt as the sensations spun through her with their intoxicating promise of pleasure.

Pull yourself together. It's just the touch of a well-mannered man. Steven had exemplary manners and remember what happened? The thought grounded her momentarily. Gathering her tattered self-control, she passed through the doorway into the starlit night and stepped away from his touch.

She hadn't been surprised that Matt had been drinking alone at the bar, given the way he held himself aloof from people and coupled with the townsfolk not seeming to know how to treat him, but the fact he'd joined them at the table had caught her off guard. His offer to leave with her had totally floored her. From the moment he'd sat down next to her she'd struggled to keep up with the conversation as every part of her had been absorbed by his closeness.

Now his gaze stayed fixed on her, and she shivered. *Find your strength, defuse the tension.* 'Where's your car?'

'At home.' He had no trouble matching her stride. Unlike her stiff and jerky gait, his was fluid. 'I walked because I'd planned to drink more than the legal driving limit.'

He didn't look drunk and she wouldn't call him relaxed but something about him was different. Less guarded perhaps? 'And have you?'

'Probably.' He leaned casually against the car, waiting, with his toned arms crossed over his T-shirt-clad chest and the light from the streetlamp spilling over him. It gave him the quintessential look of a bad boy.

Her mouth dried and her well of strength drained away. Flustered, she dropped her gaze and fumbled in her handbag, searching for her car keys. She breathed out in relief when her fingers closed over metal and she quickly activated the lock release button and swung up into the vehicle. She just had to get through a short drive. How hard could that be?

He sat down next to her, filling the cabin with his fresh scent of laundry soap and everything male. She let it fill her nostrils, pour into her lungs, and suddenly her hands trembled.

Intelligent brown eyes zeroed in. 'You OK to drive? We could always walk.'

'I'm fine.' *Liar.* She wasn't drunk but she was a long way from fine. With Matt so close her brain had closed down under the assault of her body's wayward pleasure-seeking mission and she couldn't think straight. She hit the on button of the radio with the palm of her hand, filling the cabin with music, and then she planted her foot. She tried valiantly to focus on the music but even that was against her with a raunchy song about make-up sex. Her hand wanted to leave the steering wheel, reach out and press her palm against the stubble on his cheek. She turned left at the first intersection and right at the second, and then drove straight.

'Uh, Poppy?'

'What?' It came out far too snappy as her body mocked her every good intention to stay aloof by sending rafts of hot and cold streaking though her.

He tilted his head, a lock of hair falling forward. 'I'm not so drunk that I don't notice where we are.

You're going the wrong direction and the house is back that way.'

She squinted through the windshield. Oh, God, he was right. With her mind complete mush, she'd taken the wrong turning at the first intersection and now she had no clue where she was. 'It all looks the same at night.'

'Sure, it pretty much does except for the bright lights of the port, which gives you a whopping big navigational tool.' His voiced teased as he turned towards her, his face clear in the moonlight. His mouth was curved up into a broad smile, a smile that banished the usual hovering sadness as it raced to his eyes, creasing the edges and making them dazzle with fun and wicked intent.

She almost drove off the road.

She'd wondered what he'd look like when he truly smiled and now she knew—completely devastating. Hauling her gaze back to the road and loathing herself on so many levels for her total lack of control over her body, she tried desperately not to sneak another look at his sexy grin. Usually when she was proved wrong she got defensive, but there was something about the unexpected softness that had momentarily surrounded him that made her laugh. 'I'll concede you have a point.' She slowed in preparation to do a U-turn.

'Keep going. We're pretty close to Estuary Road and you get a great view of the town from there. It looks pretty at night.'

She changed gears. 'What, no red dust?'

'The key to Bundallagong is to focus on the ocean. The turtles and the whales will amaze you.' He stretched out his arm. 'Turn here.'

The headlights beamed onto a break in the trees and

she slowly navigated the vehicle down a narrow track. 'Are you sure this is a road?'

He leaned back in his seat. 'You're such a city girl. Live a little.'

'I live plenty.' *You love deluding yourself, don't you?*

The track opened up into a wide parking area with a boat ramp and she parked. Matt jumped out of the car and quickly walked round the front of the vehicle, reaching her door before she'd finished unlatching her seat belt. Surprise piggybacked on every other rampaging emotion.

He opened her door. 'Come on, you need to see this.'

She followed him across the stony area until they stood on the curve of the bay. Across the moonlit water, the massive port with its heavy equipment that looked like a scar on the landscape during the day sparkled white, yellow, blue and orange. 'I concede it has its own charm.'

He laughed—a rich, deep sound that made her think of the bass notes of a clarinet. 'Careful, Poppy, you're in danger of gushing.'

He stood so close to her she could feel his heat, hear his breathing and smell his spicy scent—all of it swirling around her, taunting her to reach out and grab it for herself. 'It's nothing like I expected.'

His head leaned in, his eyes smoky and intense. 'Nothing ever is.'

'No.' She barely got the word out as his breath caressed her face and her heart bruised itself against her ribs. She spoke almost as much to ground herself as to reply. 'I belong in Perth.'

'Who really belongs anywhere?' His warm hand slid along her jaw, and then long, strong fingers tilted her head. His dark hair fell forward, stroking her cheek, before his lips brushed hers—soft, hot, partially testing but mostly firm and sure.

He tasted of malt, tropical heat and arousal. He was kissing her and, God help her, she wanted it like her body needed air. Her hand wrapped around the back of his head and she pulled him into her, feeling the hard muscles of his thighs pressing against her and his heart thundering against her own. He murmured a groan and his tongue flicked at her closed lips, seeking entry, and she opened them to him, needing to have him inside her, wanting him to explore, lick, taste and take. Wanting him to treat her like a woman.

Every part of her burned as Matt's expert mouth dismantled any lingering doubts that kissing him was a bad idea. She kissed him back. She kissed away the past, banishing Steven's cold, hard voice and releasing the barrier on her femininity, letting it flood her and then flood Matt.

He gasped, his hands tangling in her hair and then gripping her head to gain access to her throat. He trailed spine-tingling kisses along her jaw before dropping his head lower, tracing the hollow of her neck with his tongue. She sagged against him as she heard a mewling sound in the back of her throat.

She hauled his mouth back to her own, needing that intimate contact and tasting salt and her own heady desire. Nothing mattered except losing herself in the heat of that hot, throbbing place, and she turned herself over to its power, allowing her mind to spin out on bliss and her body to burn.

She was boneless, wet with need, weak with longing yet strong with the power of her body and she gloried in it. His hand covered her breast, the thin material of her blouse and bra feeling like a concrete slab between them. She wanted to feel the heat of his palm against her skin, let the weight of her breast fill his hand, and she ached for the graze of his thumb on her tightening nipple. She popped her shirt open and guided his hand. 'Touch me.'

His body stiffened against hers, rigid from head to toe, and suddenly his hands were on her shoulders, pushing. He ripped his mouth from hers, stepping back, breaking the kiss, breaking all contact.

'This is a mistake.' His words shredded the night air—harsh, ragged and uncompromising.

You're a machine, Poppy, not a woman. The memory of Steven's voice taunted and the fire in her body chilled to ice. Her legs shook, followed by the rest of her, and she desperately wanted to evaporate like water against parched ground. Instead, she lifted her chin, locked down every emotion and pulled her blouse shut tight. 'That's what they all say.'

She strode to the car, slamming the door against his voice, and gunned the vehicle out of the car park, not caring how the hell he got home.

CHAPTER FIVE

'EXACTLY *where* is Victor Chu's fluid balance chart?' Matt's head pounded and the backs of his eyes ached.

Jen frowned but her mouth moved into an anxious smile. 'It's clipped to his chart board.'

'If it was there, I wouldn't be asking.' He spun the chart board so it skidded across the desk. 'His pulmonary oedema is worsening and he's now on a strict fluid intake, which I'd write on the chart, if I could find it.'

She pulled the sheaf of charts out of the folder and started going through them one by one. 'You don't look very well. Do you need some of my winning combination of complex B and C vitamin drink?'

'I'm *not* hungover.'

She smiled overly brightly as if she didn't believe him and produced the elusive, pink, fluid balance chart.

'I'm not.' He sighed and tried to swallow his defensive tone. 'I had a terrible night and no sleep.' He wrote his orders on the chart and added a new drug regime in an attempt to dry Victor's lungs and maximise the effectiveness of the weak beats of an old and tired heart. 'I just need coffee.'

'There's a fresh pot in the lounge.'

He nodded his thanks and backed away from her sympathetic glance. He didn't deserve it. Not this time when his lack of sleep had nothing to do with grief and everything to do with Poppy. God, why on earth had he kissed her?

But he knew why. He'd had plenty of time to think about it as he'd walked the three kilometres home. He poured himself a large mug of the aromatic brew and closed his eyes, instantly seeing Poppy's plump, lush lips. He forced his lids open but it didn't help—he could still see the after-image of their shape and colour, and that, combined with those startling eyes, had him almost permanently hard. It had rendered his restraint so thin it was friable. Last night, standing so close to her under that bright, white moon, with her intoxicating perfume spinning around him and her body heat rolling into his, it had all combined to demolish the tattered shreds of his self-control. All he'd known was that he'd ached to touch her, craved to taste her, and hungered to savour her.

So he had.

And she'd flooded him with unforeseen and unrestrained passion. Passion that had roared through him, feeding his desire with so much fuel that he'd almost combusted on the spot. His body had taken over, emptying his mind of everything except the white-hot pleasure of sex. And he'd revelled in it. It had been so long since he'd felt alive like that and nothing had existed except two hot bodies seeking each other.

Touch me. Her tremulous and breathy voice had sliced through him, penetrating his lust-fogged mind like a knife and dumping reality upon him as he'd realised who he'd been kissing.

Not Lisa. Hell, he'd had his tongue down the throat

of another woman and it hadn't been enough: he'd wanted so much more.

So he'd pulled away, despising himself for betraying Lisa.

What about betraying Poppy?

He stifled a groan and slugged more coffee. He hadn't seen her since she'd stormed away from him and he'd been in no state then to even try and call her back. Even if his mind and voice had worked, he knew she would never have stopped to listen and he'd been incapable of telling her the truth.

'Matt, ambulance is pulling in,' Jen called out as she hurried towards the ambulance bay.

Matt joined her, glad to be distracted from the mess he'd created, and he pulled on gloves, ready to treat the young man writhing in pain on the ambulance's stretcher. 'What happened?'

'His apprentice said he'd been lifting concrete slabs and went down screaming. I gave him some nitrous but he's still in pain.' Doug Finlay, the senior paramedic, gave a brief handover.

'Hernia?' Jen muttered, before moving to transfer the man onto the trolley, but as she reached his side she paused in surprise. 'Liam?'

Matt instantly recognised one of the town's builders and based on what the ambulance officer had said thought an abdominal or spinal disc hernia were very possible. 'Where does it hurt? Your back?'

Liam shook his head, his expression a combination of pain and embarrassment. 'It's *not* my back.'

Matt caught the look. 'Ah, Jen, can you go and start the paperwork.'

'Sure.'

As the door closed behind her, Liam started to dry-retch and Matt grabbed a kidney dish. 'As soon as I've examined you, I can give you something for the pain.'

'I remember being kicked in the balls when I was aa kid but this—' He seemed to have trouble breathing against the pain. 'This is absolute agony.'

Matt nodded sympathetically. 'I want to rule out a couple of other possibilities.' He palpated Liam's abdomen and groin but he couldn't feel a hernia. 'I need to examine your testicles.'

Liam barely nodded as his white-knuckled hands gripped the silver railing of the trolley.

'I think you've got a torsion of the testicle.'

Liam looked blank. 'What?'

'It's twisted.' He pulled the ultrasound over and examined the area. He pointed to the screen. 'There's the problem.'

Liam looked like he could hardly focus. 'It's absolute agony.'

'That's because the blood supply is being restricted.' He saved the picture, wiped the Doppler and returned it to its holder.

A knock sounded on the door and Matt tossed the modesty sheet over Liam as he called, 'Come in.'

Jen entered the room, followed by a woman who appeared to be a similar age to his patient. She rushed towards Liam, picking up his hand. 'I came as soon as Tim called me.'

Jen slung the clipboard over the end of the trolley and said quietly to Matt, 'Should I page Poppy?'

Matt tilted his head in agreement.

Jen returned it as she spoke. 'This is Emma Waterson—Liam's fiancée.'

Emma, still holding Liam's hand, looked up,

her forehead creased with worry. 'What's wrong with him?'

Matt filled her in on his diagnosis and watched her face pale.

'Why…? I mean, how did it happen?'

'It's not an uncommon condition in men under twenty-five and I'd say Liam probably has a genetic or structural weakness. Combine that with heavy lifting, and it would be enough to cause the twist.'

She turned accusingly to her fiancé. 'You told me you were getting the bobcat in to lift that concrete.'

Liam blanched as another wave of pain hit him. 'Em, I'm sorry. I couldn't get it today and I was trying to get everything done so we could have a two-week honeymoon.'

Emma let out a wail. 'Oh, God, the wedding. Can you untwist it?'

Matt tried to suppress a shudder. 'Liam needs surgery. The good news is that we have a surgeon here.' *Good news for Liam, anyway.*

'Good news?' The soon-to-be bride swayed on her feet. 'That means there's bad news too. Will it mean we can't have children?'

'If the testicle has to be removed, the other one won't be affected.'

'And the honeymoon?' Liam grimaced as he moved.

Matt gave a wry smile. The guy was in agony but still thinking about sex. *It's all you've been thinking about today.*

He rubbed his temple. 'You'll be a bit tender for a day or so but the second week you should be just fine.'

Liam sunk back on the pillows. 'In that case, do your worst—just stop the pain.'

'I can do that.' Poppy strode into the room, her blue eyes flashing brightly.

With her green theatre scrubs floating around her and concealing the soft curves Matt knew nestled underneath, she gave him an almost imperceptible nod before studying the ultrasound screen.

Liam choked. 'You're the surgeon?'

Poppy gave a restrained smile. 'I understand you'd probably feel more comfortable with a man but think of it as taking one for all the women in the world who find themselves being treated by male gynaecologists.'

Emma laughed. 'I like her.'

'You're not the one going under the knife,' Liam grumbled.

'Poor baby, I'm sure she'll be gentle.'

Matt didn't disillusion either of them with his thoughts.

After Poppy had explained the procedure and obtained consent, he followed her out of the room, thankful they had a patient to discuss. 'I'll put in an IV, take some blood for FBC, U&Es and cross-matching, and then he's all yours.'

She raised her well-shaped jet brows. 'As long as you're sure. I'd hate it if you made a mistake.' Hurt shimmered around the sarcasm.

He swallowed a groan. It was time to make some sort of restitution. 'I wanted to talk to you this morning but you left before dawn.'

She folded her arms, scrunching the scrubs tightly over her breasts. 'Ah, the apology. No need, heard it before.'

Apology? What apology? But his gaze snagged on the outline of her bra and he swallowed, hard, forcing his mind to stay on track with the conversation. 'How can you have heard it before? I haven't ever apologised to you.'

She rolled her eyes, azure deepening to midnight. 'You're a man, I'm a woman. Believe me, I've heard it and I've heard every single excuse in the book of sorry. I don't have time for this, Matt. I'm due in surgery.'

He trapped his angry retort and watched her walk away. *Believe me, I've heard it.* What the hell did that mean? Did she think she could throw off some line and just keep walking?

Well, what did you really expect? He had no clue. Damn it, he hadn't actually planned on apologising. She'd been an equal participant in the kiss and this was 2011. Surely people had a right to change their minds.

You touched her breast; it had gone way past a kiss.

He tried to recall the sequence of events last night after his head had roared so loudly with the realisation of what he'd been doing—when betrayal and lust had collided and he'd pulled back.

This is a mistake.

That's what they all say.

Who the hell were 'they'?

This time Matt didn't cook. He didn't go to bed at 10:00 p.m. Or eleven. He opened the door to Poppy at eleven-fifteen.

Shocked surprise crossed her face and she quickly glanced towards her house before staring straight back at him. 'Two houses, both have rats.'

Anger scorched his intention to invite her to sit down and calmly talk this mess out. 'Oh, and that's really mature.' He ran his hand through his hair, trying to find the calm he'd once been known for. 'Look, we have to work together and right now we're sharing a house, so what do you need me to say so we can go back to being semi-civil with each other?'

'Nothing.' She tried to move past him.

He blocked her. 'That's rubbish. If it was nothing you wouldn't have left me out at the point last night to walk home.'

She shrugged. 'You told me you were planning on walking home anyway.'

'From the pub!' He heard his voice rise. 'Which is three minutes away, not three kilometres.'

Her stony expression wavered slightly with the tiniest mark of contrition, and he pounced on it as a sign of a chance at reconciliation. 'Do you want a drink?'

Her brows rose. 'Isn't that what got you into trouble last night?'

'I was *not* drunk.' For the second time that day, he ground out the indignant words. 'Six months ago you could have levelled that accusation at me but not last night.'

The faintest tremble wove across her bottom lip before she snagged it with her teeth. Teeth that had nipped at his lips last night in the frenzy of *that* kiss. The memory sent a bolt of heat through him and he realised he was staring at her mouth.

Her chin shot up. 'So you were sober. That makes it worse. I have to say, this is one hell of an apology.'

'I'm not apologising.' The yelled words shot around them both, loud and uncompromising.

She blinked and then spoke quietly. 'No, you're not.'

She walked past him, leaving him standing in the hall, stunned.

Your manners always made me feel special.

Lisa's voice chided him. He'd never yelled at a woman in his life so what the hell was wrong with him? He leaned against the wall and slowed his breathing before walking into the kitchen. Poppy had poured herself a glass of sauvignon blanc from the bottle he'd put in the fridge earlier, and was staring out into the night.

'I'm sorry, I shouldn't have yelled. I don't usually yell.'

She didn't turn round but her shoulders stiffened so much that balls could have bounced off them. 'Yeah, well, I've been known to have that effect on men. That and not being woman enough. Congratulations. You've gone two for two and you're up there with the best.'

He felt like the floor was tilting under his feet and he was left scrabbling for purchase while careering inexorably into a black sinkhole. 'What are you talking about?'

She spun to face him, her face pinched as conflicting emotions broke through her usually impenetrable armour. 'You want me to spell it out to you?' Her voice rose and she dragged in a breath. 'I'm an exceptional surgeon but a lousy kisser. I'm sorry it was such a disappointment for you.'

Her words hit with the velocity of a missile, stunning him. 'That's what you think?' He picked up his bottle of water, trying to assemble coherent thought. 'You think you're bad at kissing? Why on earth would you think that?'

A shudder whipped across her shoulders, round her torso and down her long, long legs. 'Oh, let me see. It started at high school with my name scrawled all over the boys' toilets, then my ex-husband mentioned it as often as he could and, hmm, last night you told me it was a mistake.'

That's what they all say. Her words from last night

lanced him and then all-encompassing anger at an unknown man erupted so fast it turned his breath fiery. 'Your ex-husband doesn't know squat.'

Her pupils dilated, drowning her shimmering cornflower-blue irises, and she swallowed, the ripple of movement centred in the hollow of her throat. The place he'd branded last night. The plastic bottle of water crunched loudly under his tightening fingers.

She shrugged. 'Yeah, well, let's not go there.'

'Poppy, believe me, you can kiss.' The husky words somehow passed through his tight throat and he downed some water, trying to douse his burning need for her.

She bit her lip as her hand crawled to her pendant. 'Don't do this, Matt. I'm not a child and you can't muddy the truth. It stands and it has done for a long time. It stood loud and clear last night out at the point. For whatever reason, you were moved to kiss me. I kissed you back and you pulled away. End of story. We'll both live.'

Despite everything, he knew their kiss had fired life into parts of his body that had been numb for a long time. Poppy had done that with her mouth, her tongue, her teeth and her taste. He couldn't let her continue to believe she was a lousy kisser. *So tell her why you pulled back.*

But he couldn't do it. He didn't want to have *that* conversation, and see and hear her pity. With a growl he forced out, 'You've obviously been kissing the wrong men.'

She gave a derisive laugh, her face tight with the pain of her past. 'Yeah, well, last night was a case in point.'

No, it wasn't. In two strides he stood next to her,

cupping her cheeks and pressing his mouth softly to hers. Taking a gamble to prove a point, a point she needed to understand.

She stiffened, her lips closed to him. Gently, his tongue ventured along the outline of those wondrous bee-stung lips, lips that drove him crazy on an hourly basis, and he tasted a hint of gooseberry and restraint born of hurt. But she didn't push him away so he slowly nibbled her generous bottom lip, coaxing it to open and unlock the ambrosia he knew waited within.

He heard a strangled moan and recognised the moment her inherent sexuality defeated her control. Her mouth—hot, moist and seeking—met his with a scorch of fire, lighting a blaze that tore though him, revisiting places and invading untouched parts of him. He buried his hands in her hair and her fingers dug into his scalp, as if it was the only way she could stay standing.

His skin, slick with sweat, tingled with something he barely recognised because the memory of it had faded to fuzzy faintness—hedonistic pleasure. He lost himself, amazed at how decadent yet occasionally sweet and tender her mouth could be. His tongue met hers in a dance of wonder that ignited into a fevered duel, each of them angling for control and driven crazy by need.

The power surge of her desire lit up the back of his mind.

When did you ever kiss Lisa like this in this house?

The thought shocked him so hard his mouth slackened and he almost fell.

Poppy's eyes, glazed with ecstasy's bliss, instantly focused. She pulled away, her breasts rising and falling with fast, shallow breaths. 'What the hell is happening? You're doing it again.'

This time, with the light of the room, he glimpsed raw and pulsating pain in the electric blue of her eyes before her steely control shut it down.

He closed his eyes against his own pain, shame, guilt and utter despair. *She doesn't deserve this.* Forcing himself to look at her, he knew with gut-wrenching certainty what had to come next. 'It's not you, Poppy, it's me.'

Poppy stared at him, barely able to catch her breath and hardly able to believe her ears. Her heart pumped desire-fuelled blood through her, making her skittish and demolishing her usually logical thought processes. It took more than effort to clear her head. She scraped her mussed hair out of her eyes and clamped it by tightening the now loose band, the action giving her precious moments to pull herself together. 'I don't understand.'

His hand ploughed through his hair as his expression became imploring. 'Please believe me when I tell you that you're not *just* an exceptional surgeon.'

A kernel of belief almost sprouted inside her, but words counted little against crystal clear actions. He'd pulled away from her twice and both times had ended the most bone-melting kisses she'd even known. He'd rejected her, like all the men in her life. 'I get the feeling there's a "but" coming.'

His eyelids hooded his dark eyes, masking his emotions, but his body betrayed him when his left hand fisted so tightly his knuckles gleamed white. When he finally spoke it sounded like it was coming from the depths of his soul. 'You're the first woman I've kissed since Lisa died.'

Poppy's legs gave way and she sat down hard on the couch. Oh, dear God, how had she been so dumb? She wanted to bury her face in her hands at her thoughtless and completely selfish neediness. Last night, when he'd stopped kissing her, her past had come rushing back so hard and fast it had obliterated any other possible reasons as to why he'd stepped back. By default, she'd made it all about herself, when in reality it was about him.

She had no idea what to say except the obvious. 'You loved her very much.'

'I do.'

And right then, with the blinding clarity of the hindsight, she understood. 'Kissing me is like cheating on Lisa.'

He sat down on the opposite end of the couch, his expression tinged with apologetic regret. 'Yeah.'

She wondered what it would be like to be loved by someone so much that they considered it an act of faithlessness to kiss someone else even when you were dead. Steven hadn't loved her enough in life to be faithful and yet she wasn't certain she'd want a lover to be racked with this much guilt after she'd gone. Had she done something to trigger memories? 'Do I remind you of her?'

'God, no!'

She took the hit, feeling it reverberate through her with a dull ache, which was dumb because of course he loved his wife.

Show no hurt. She tilted her head in irony. 'Just as long as you're sure.'

He had the grace to look abashed. 'Sorry.'

'Don't be.' She grabbed her wine and took a gulp, trying to dig down to find the mature adult. His emphatic reply spoke volumes: she was nothing like his wife and no matter how that made her feel it gave her the opening to ask the question that had been on the tip of her tongue from the moment she'd discovered he was a widower. 'So what was Lisa like?'

Her name. Matt stared at Poppy for a moment, realising that no one in town ever said Lisa's name to him any more. He turned away, doggedly looking out through the patio doors, uncomfortable about the comparison he was about to make. 'She was blonde to your black and short to your tall.' *Her mouth wasn't as full as yours.* He banished the thought by trying to focus on Lisa but his mental image of her face clouded around the edges. 'She had a way with people, an ability to find something uniquely special about them. It made you feel like you were the only person who mattered to her at that moment in time. She made friends easily but she also kept them. There was something about her that made you want to try and be the best person you could.'

'She sounds…exceptional.' Poppy's voice was strained and she cleared her throat.

'She was.' He kept staring out into the night as memories sucked at him, threatening to drown him, and he fought not to go to that dark place.

Poppy placed her glass on the side table and the noise of glass on wood brought him back to the present. She rose to her feet, the movement fluid yet extremely controlled, right down to the way the last hair on her head settled into place. He remembered the first time he'd met her and thought her all sharp angles and harsh lines. But that had been before he'd kissed her and discovered how wrong he'd been. Her air of command hid a raw sexuality that when unleashed had rocked him in ways he'd never imagined.

She jutted her chin in that precise way that meant she'd made up her mind about something. 'It's late.'

'It is.'

'See you in the morning, Dr Albright.'

He stared at her, realising she'd just played the colleague card, putting the boundaries firmly back in place, cutting the attraction off at the knees. Wasn't that what he wanted? Restoration of equilibrium? 'Coffee at seven, Ms Stanfield.'

'Seven it is.'

He ignored the scud of disappointment that gnawed at his gut.

CHAPTER SIX

'SO HAS he put a foot wrong yet?' Poppy held her phone hard to her ear as she took the call in Matt's kitchen while making a late night 'catch-up' sandwich with chicken and salad.

Luke Davies, her favourite anaesthetist, filled her in on Alistair Roland, her competitor in Perth. She'd made the call after coming home from the first choir practice, needing to get her head firmly back in the game of her career rather than letting herself be sidelined by Bundallagong and a man with the smokiest gaze she'd ever encountered.

Not that it mattered that Matt could reduce her to a quivering puddle of need with one gaze, because he didn't want her. Her rational self didn't want him either but her body craved him so badly it sobbed continuously. If past history had taught her anything it was that she doomed relationships, familial and sexual. Even if she had any relationship skills, she couldn't compete with the memory of a dead woman who, unlike her, had made friends with ease and been admired by all she'd met. Matt had made that more than clear three nights ago.

So she'd been very sensible and pragmatic over the last few days, as had he. Whenever they consulted at work they were polite, professional and courteous. No one observing them would have any reason to think they'd once kissed each other senseless. As a result, it was getting easier with every day.

Is that so?

Yes!

You are so deluding yourself.

Luke's voice rumbled down the line, bringing her back to the point of her call. 'You might be in trouble. Alistair's got the nursing staff eating out of his hand.'

'That's not good news.' She opened the fridge, scanning the now considerable contents she'd purchased, and looked for her favourite mayonnaise.

'You wanted facts. I'm just the messenger.'

It was just the sort of information she didn't want to hear. 'Exactly how has he achieved that in such a short time?'

'Sorry, PICU is paging me. I have to go. Hang in there.'

The phone beeped as the call disconnected and Poppy felt the hitch in her gut. She didn't have the XY chromosome to make a predominantly female nursing staff 'eat out of her hand' but she'd always prided herself on being fair. Why didn't that ever seem to count for much?

Frustrated by the report and the paralysis of distance, she snapped her phone shut with one hand, grabbed the mayo with the other and bumped the door closed with her hip.

'What's not good news?'

The mayonnaise and her phone clattered onto the bench as her heart thundered hard and fast. *Matt.* She couldn't be certain how much of her reaction was due to fright and how much was the result of her body's natural response to seeing him.

Her heart hiccoughed.

Question answered.

It was a lot safer to hide behind fright and find indignation. 'First there's the goanna thundering in the roof at 3:00 a.m. whenever a cat disturbs it and now this.' She righted the mayonnaise bottle. 'Didn't anyone ever tell you not to sneak up on a person?'

He gave her a wry smile. 'Sorry. I thought you heard me call out when I came through the door. Is there a problem?'

Never show weakness, Poppy. Her father hadn't been around a lot but when he had, he'd hammered that message home hard, loud and clear. 'No.' *Deflect.* 'Well, there *is* the goanna. It's like an elephant in the roof. How do you sleep?'

His jaw tightened for a fraction of a second. 'The goanna and I have an understanding and you're changing the subject.' His perceptive gaze shone with questions. 'You're wearing a frown as deep as a mineshaft and it isn't goanna related.

Admit nothing. 'I've got a lot on my plate, that's all.'

Matt lowered himself onto the stool by the bench, his manner interested but slightly detached, just like it had been at work ever since they'd buried the entire kissing incident. 'I'm happy to listen.'

'You wouldn't understand.' The words shot out, defensive and self-protective, with the intent of warning him off. Steven had never understood.

Instead of looking offended, Matt just shook his head slowly as if he felt sorry for her. 'Try me. You might be surprised.'

His long fingers reached out and she watched mesmerised as he snagged a piece of chicken, tilted his head back and dropped it into his mouth. The mouth that had created such delicious havoc the other night and in the process had been branded on her memory for ever.

It had been years since she'd confided in anyone, having vowed never to again after the debacle with Steven. Usually she blocked people with snappy replies and if that didn't work, she crossed her arms. She didn't know if she was overtired, surprised by his interest or just a sucker for *chocolat-noir* eyes, but before she could second-guess her decision, she blurted out, 'I'm fighting for the chief of surgery job back in Perth.'

'Good.'

Indignation roared through her and she slapped mayo and mustard onto wholemeal bread. This was the sort of patronising response she'd got from Steven and the *exact* reason she never opened up to anyone. 'Good? Exactly *how* is it good?'

'You'd be great in that position.'

Surprise barrelled through her, dismantling her righteous anger and leaving behind a trail of confusion. 'Oh, um, thank you.'

Matt raised his brows as he sliced an avocado. 'Now, was telling me that so hard?'

Stop whining, Poppy, and just do the job. 'Yes.'

This time he laughed.

'Seriously, you have no idea.' She pushed her father's and Steven's voices out of her head but thoughts about work took their place. She waged a constant battle—emotionally and physically—to get the same deal as her male counterparts, which meant staying one step ahead at all times. She'd given up so much and she deserved the Perth job, but it was hard to keep fighting for it when she'd been taken out of her own work-place.

His laugh faded. 'Well, you did it, you told me, and life as we know it is still happening, so keep going. What's the specific problem?'

She loaded bread with moist chicken, avocado, thin slices of peppered tomato, fresh basil leaves and lettuce, before adding the top layer of bread and slicing the squares into neat triangles.

'Poppy?'

She knew she was stalling. She pushed one plate towards him and saw intense interest underpinned with support. 'My competitor is currently doing the job, shovelling charm by the bucketload and winning over the staff, while I've been sent up here to languish in the backblocks.'

'Ah.' He bit into the sandwich.

'Ah, what?' She pulled a piece of avocado out from between the slices of bread, her appetite vanishing.

'Who did you upset?'

Her hands hit her hips despite the truth. 'Why do you automatically assume I upset someone?'

'Come on, Poppy, you have to admit that sometimes you have a "take no prisoners" approach that steps on toes.'

She bristled at his criticism. 'You're not perfect yourself.'

'I'm very well aware of that, but right now we're talking about you.' A quiet smile wove through his dark stubble. 'Great sandwich, by the way.'

She leaned against the bench and sighed, partly at her inability to withstand his smile but mostly because she realised she was totally unable to sidetrack him away from the topic. 'I was covering all bases and I applied elsewhere too and was unsuccessful. News got out and now it's being used against me.'

'But you want the job at Perth City?'

'I do. It's *my job*.' She tapped her chest vehemently. 'I've worked too hard for it to go to some interloper from the east.'

Understanding crossed his face. 'If it helps at all, everyone at the hospital is in awe at how much you've achieved in such a short time and I haven't heard too many grumbles about staff feeling overworked.' His cheeky wink softened his words. 'OK, you might not have the charm quotient like Mr East Coast but you've generated grudging respect.'

Her stomach clenched and she pushed her plate away, virtually untouched. 'Oh, fabulous—grudging respect. That good, huh? That's going to look sensational on my review…not! The only way I can counteract my competition is if I do an equal or better job so I need the staff to like me!'

'That will come with time, Poppy.'

She would have preferred simmering sexuality to this 'father knows best' air and she wanted to shake him. This was *her* career on the line and her voice rose in frustration. 'I don't have time on my side.'

His calm expression didn't change. 'So make it work for you instead of against you.'

'What the hell is that supposed to mean?'

'Be a surgeon at work and a person at play.'

'Play?'

'Yes, Poppy, play. Get out there and go fishing with the theatre techs, call into the nurses' clothing and product parties, comment on the holiday photos of the clerks, cluck about the cleaner's new grandchild and make sure you show up to drinks at some point *every* Friday night.'

An unfamiliar sensation she didn't want to call panic zipped along her veins and her hand sneaked up to her pendant. 'But that's not me. That's not how I've *ever* done things.'

Matt's gaze showed no mercy. 'Do you really want that chief of surgery job?'

'Hell, yes.'

He grinned. 'And there's the drive we know and love.' He walked round the bench to plug in the kettle. 'Use your drive but redirect it. Show them there's another side to Poppy Stanfield.'

She'd spent years only showing the world the surgeon in charge because it was so much safer. The surgeon had steel-plated armour but the woman buried inside her did not. She crossed her arms in self-protection and her teeth snagged her lower lip. 'What if there isn't another side? What if what you see is all there is?'

'I don't believe that.' A husky edge clung to his voice and the collegiate mentor vanished under the heat-charged words.

Her stomach flipped. Memories of their kisses swirled and eddied around them, mocking everything she'd done to convince herself they were only colleagues. He stood so close to her she could smell the peppermint scent of his shampoo. She wanted his lips on hers, his arms around her waist and his body pressed hard against her, but when she glanced into his eyes, seeking the heat to match his voice, she could only find professional concern and perhaps a hint of friendship.

He doesn't want you. Men don't ever want you. She hated the empty feeling that settled over her and she ducked away from him, briskly covering the uneaten sandwich with cling wrap and covering her own irrational disappointment. 'By the way, I got the all-clear on the house. I'm moving in tomorrow as soon as the new furniture's delivered.'

A muscle close to his mouth twitched and he gave a brisk nod. 'I'm sure you'll be pleased to be in your own space.'

But Poppy read the subtext. He wanted her out and was pleased she was going. For her own peace of mind, she should be pleased too.

At 10:00 p.m. Matt saw the lights go on next door and tried to ignore them. Tried to ignore the fact Poppy was home. He tried to think about work, focus on how they'd both gone out of their way to be polite professionals, but all he could do was picture her in the kitchen, making one of her enormous 'catch-up' sandwiches after a day of grabbing food on the run.

Like the one she'd made him on the night he'd tried so hard not to let his hunger for her take over. The night she'd actually accepted some advice. It had been a good evening and they'd shared a companionable half-hour right up until the moment she'd nibbled her full, lush bottom lip.

He could have taken her right then—in the kitchen, on the bench, against the wall, anywhere. He had no idea how he'd managed not to. How he'd pulled himself back into line so she'd had no clue what he'd been thinking. Then she'd hit him with moving out.

God, he had to stop thinking about her, but the house was too quiet and offered up no distractions. Shadows danced across the walls and the strident, singing cicadas under the deck had gone silent on him.

Even the goanna was undisturbed. The sensor light on the deck flickered on, probably triggered by a cat, and a slither of light caught something red behind the barbecue. He squinted and his heart cramped.

Annie's ball. He'd thought he'd collected all her toys but this one had refused to be found, lying in wait to layer on another fresh round of pain. He turned away from the glass and slumped down on the couch. Before Poppy's arrival he'd thought he was finally getting used to the emptiness of the house, if not the silence.

The huge silences were why he hadn't done anything about the goanna, because any sound was at least noise. But post-Poppy he'd realised that just by having another person in the place, even one who argued the point on almost every subject, had lessened the void that had taken over a home. Once it had known so much buzz but now silence had reduced it to a house. Four walls of loss.

Poppy had moved her two red suitcases out three days ago. Three long, quiet and lonely days. His loneliness had shocked him. Since Lisa's death he hadn't wanted company but tonight he ached for it. He'd spent the last three days arguing down every urge to go and visit her. He'd fought off the guise of the friendly neighbour bringing over a house-warming gift, wrestled down the doctor who thought he should 'follow up' on a case, and he'd shut up the eager mentor who kept insisting he should 'check up' and see how she was going with her campaign to warm up the staff.

So far he'd been successful at not going over, but it was consuming every moment of his day. And night. His phone beeped; a blessed distraction, and he read the reminder that flashed up on the screen. *Jen's b'day 2morrow bring food.* He smiled. Jen must have put the reminder in his phone when he'd left it at the nurses' desk.

He knew he hadn't contributed to a staff celebration in a long time and when he did he always bought something from the bakery, but right now, on this particular night, he wanted to make something, and the more he thought about it, the more it seemed like the perfect thing to do. He jumped to his feet and headed into the kitchen. He could only make one thing; a simple, no-cook chocolate slice his mother had taught him when he'd been a kid. She'd called it 'hedgehog'. Opening the kitchen cupboards, he reached to the very back and found a packet of plain biscuits. Amazingly, they were within the 'best before' expiry date.

He started whacking them hard with a rolling pin, enjoying the sensation of doing something normal and everyday. He rummaged through the drawer where Lisa had kept the spices and found cocoa and coconut and added them before opening the fridge for butter and eggs.

A cold, empty space greeted him.

Fresh ingredients? Who are you kidding?

Damn it, he hadn't shopped. *You never shop.* Had he lived in a city, he could have grabbed his keys and hit the supermarket at 10:00 p.m., but he didn't. He slammed the door closed, frustration licking along his veins. For the first time in for ever he'd actually wanted to make something and now he was stymied.

He turned slowly, looking out across the deck, and saw the lights next door were still on. *Poppy.* She'd have butter and eggs and, unlike all his created excuses to visit her, the ones he'd talked himself out of, this one was real. After all, Jen worked really hard and she deserved a birthday morning tea.

Oh, yeah, it's all about Jen's morning tea.

He ignored his sarcastic self. This visit was all about eggs and butter. He strode out of the house, across the garden and straight to Poppy's door, where he pressed the doorbell.

Waiting impatiently, he paced on the small porch. He pressed the bell again, this time holding his finger in place.

'Hang on, I'm coming.'

Poppy's voice sounded deep inside the house, followed by running feet slapping the bare floorboards. A moment later the door opened and Matt swallowed. Hard.

She stood in front of him, her long, black hair cascading over her shoulders like a silk shawl. His eyes followed the line of her hair, across shoulders almost bare except for the slash of the pink spaghetti straps of her camisole top. His gaze skimmed across her round breasts and down to the edge of the top. Here an expanse of tanned belly with the gentle swell of healthy roundedness was met by the band of a skimpy pair of royal-blue pyjama shorts, which clung low on her hips and high on her thighs. And then her legs; her long, long legs stretched on for ever.

He lost the power of speech.

'Matt?' Her blue eyes spun with confusion and concern.

Eggs and butter, remember? 'I need…' The words sounded way too husky. He cleared his throat. 'I need an egg and some butter.'

Her eyes widened and filled with surprise. 'You'd better come in, then.' She turned and walked towards her kitchen, the fabric of her pyjama shorts outlining the sweet curve of her behind.

Heat slammed through him, making him hard, and somehow, with superhuman effort, he managed to keep walking. *Talk about normal stuff.* 'It's to make something for Jen's birthday morning tea.'

'Oh.' She snagged her bottom lip with her teeth and disappointment sounded clear in her voice. 'I didn't know or I would have made something too.'

He stifled a groan. 'Seeing as you're donating the butter and egg, I'll say the hedgehog came from you.'

'You don't have to do that.' She opened the fridge, handing him an egg from the container in the door.

The egg felt thankfully cold in his hot and itchy palm. 'Sure I can. It's not like anyone's going to believe I cooked it.'

She laughed—a deep and throaty sound. 'Yes, but will I want to put my name to it?' She bent over, reaching for the butter, her pants riding up and exposing a glorious expanse of skin.

Heat fired through him, replacing air with all-encompassing need. He dropped the egg.

'Damn it.' He grabbed for a cloth and kneeled down at the same moment Poppy did, her hands filled with paper towel. Their foreheads banged.

'Ouch.' She laughed, her eyes sparkling with life.

Life. She was here, warm, real and, oh, so sexy. For months he hadn't wanted sex but every time he saw her he wanted her. Wanted her badly, and right now he couldn't think of anything else but sex.

Sex with Poppy.

He waited for the gut-wrenching guilt that had pulled him back every time but it didn't come and he didn't understand why but he wasn't going to question it. Poppy was nothing like Lisa and perhaps that was why it didn't feel like a betrayal. All he knew was that his hands burned to cup her bottom and her breasts, his mouth ached to trail kisses along her neck and across her glorious bare skin and he wanted to lose himself in her hair and breathe in her scent of being alive.

He slid his palm along her cheek, tilted her head and kissed her.

Poppy felt his hot lips on hers, felt her body melting, but the protective part of her brain screamed, *Stop!* Somehow she managed to grip his shoulders and pull back. 'Wh-what are you doing?'

Unfocused eyes, loaded with the haze of lust, stared at her. 'Kissing you.'

The words came out thick and hoarse, sending tingling need strumming through her and sucking at the edges of her control. 'What about the hedgehog?'

'I'll buy a chocolate cake.'

She wanted to smile but instead she rose slowly, dignity demanding she speak. 'You've kissed me twice before and pulled back.'

His face tensed and a sad smile curved his mouth. 'I promise you, I'm not going to stop this time. I want to keep kissing you until neither of us can stand.'

She bit her lip as she saw the turmoil of the lust of now and the pain of the past in his eyes, and felt her own hurt. 'I'm not Lisa.'

His hand played in her hair and he spoke softly. 'This has *nothing* to do with Lisa.'

She didn't know if she should believe him or not. 'Then what is it to do with?'

'Us. This living, breathing "thing" that swirls constantly between us every time we're together, and even when we're not.' His eyes almost pleaded. 'You know what I'm talking about.'

She nodded silently. God help her, she did.

'So we need to have sex to defuse it and bring this "thing" back under control or we're both going to go insane over the next few weeks.' He pressed his mouth to the hollow of her neck.

Stars spun in her head and she clung to rational thought by a thread. 'Sex to defuse it?'

'Exactly.'

She could hardly think straight to follow his so-called logic. She had her own issues to face and she sucked in a deep breath. 'The thing is, I'm not very good at sex.'

'I don't believe that for one minute.' His mouth pressed nipping kisses along her jaw. 'I plan to show you just how good you really are.'

She swallowed hard, trying to stay strong against the delicious rafts of pleasure pouring through her, but she could feel herself slipping under the waves of desire and drowning in their headiness.

His finger tilted her chin so she looked directly at him. 'Sex for the sake of sex. No promises, no regrets, no future and no past, and absolutely no apologies.' His hands gripped her shoulders. 'Are you in?'

Just sex. Nothing more, nothing less.

Why not? It wasn't like she believed in 'happy ever after', and she knew she sucked at relationships and was never going down that torrid path again. She filled her life with work but right now her career hung in the balance, she was a hell of a long way from home and her body constantly hummed for this man. He wanted her body, which was more than any man ever had. Really, what did she have to lose?

Everything and nothing.

She circled his neck with her arms and sank into him with a moan that came all the way from her toes—the bliss of giving in to the longing that had consumed her for days and days. His mouth invaded hers: furnace-hot and with unleashed, potent desire that pulsated through her. She lost herself in his mouth, filling herself with his taste of mint and anticipation, exploring with teeth and tongue. With each foray he met her with one of his own, deepening the kiss, urging her to do the same until all thoughts vanished, the past imploded and nothing existed except his mouth and this kiss.

This time there was no holding back. This time Matt's hand sought her breast, slipping easily under her top, and while his thumb abraded her aching nipple his tongue sabotaged her mouth with bliss. The star-filled night sky had nothing on her body and mind as she lit up, every part of her igniting and burning for his touch. Gasping for breath, she pulled her mouth from his.

He groaned and could barely speak. 'Are you… changing…your mind?'

Her body screamed in protest that everything might come to an abrupt stop right now. 'God, no, but what about protection?'

Matt ran his hand through his hair as an expletive hit the air. Then he kissed her hard and fast and came up laughing. 'Every hospital house has a medical kit. Where is it?'

Her brain spun with bliss and she fought to think. 'I put it in the bathroom.' He grabbed her hand and tugged her down the hall. 'Matt, it won't have condoms.'

He grinned. 'We're in the middle of nowhere and we have everything.' He flicked the latch and lifted the top tray.

Dipping her hand in, she pulled out a sheet of distinctive square foil wrappers. 'Plenty.'

'Speak for yourself.'

His eyes darkened, sending shivers of anticipation scudding through her. She tugged at his shirt, pulling it over his head, and her eyes feasted on a broad chest, slick with the sheen of the sweat of desire. Desire for her. She could hardly believe it as she reached out her hand, pressing it against hard muscle, feeling his heart thundering against it. 'You're magnificent.'

'So are you.' With a flick of his fingers the three silk-covered buttons of her top opened and he slid the material down her arms to the floor. 'That's so much better.'

His mouth closed over her breast and she cried out with sheer amazement as sensations cascaded over her. Sensations she didn't ever want to stop and she sagged against him as pleasure stole the strength from her legs.

He raised his head from her breast and trailed tantalising kisses back along her breastbone to the hollow in her neck. 'Time to move this to the bedroom. I want room to move and room to see you.' He linked his fingers through hers as he scorched her mouth with another kiss.

She sagged against him. 'I won't make the bed if you keep doing that.'

He tore his mouth away and grinned. 'Can't have that.'

He pulled her down the hall, stopping twice to kiss her. The second time she pressed her back against the wall, her body melting into a puddle of paradise as she clung to him, wrapping her legs around his waist.

He met her moan of need with one of his own and then staggered into the bedroom, carrying her. She fell backwards onto the bed, pulling him with her, never wanting to let him go, needing to feel his hands and mouth on her. She'd never known such rising pleasure, pleasure that tingled and taunted at the same time, and she wanted more of it.

He pulled back to unbuckle his belt and shuck his pants and she whimpered.

A moment or two later, condom in place, he leaned over her, his eyes as dark as rich chocolate, and slowly scanned her body, from her now burning cheeks across her aching pink-tipped breasts and down to her damp panties. He trailed a finger along the lace band before stroking downwards, inexorably slowly.

Her hips bucked as she throbbed with desperate emptiness and delicious promise, both of which were driving her insane. Her fingers gripped his wrist, trying to control his movements, trying to hurry him up before she spun out from unmet need.

'You're so amazingly hot.' His velvet-deep voice floated over her hot, flushed skin and then his mouth took hers for a moment before he slipped his finger under the lace and onto the one place that made her call out his name.

With delicious but maddening touches, he wove a path in ever-diminishing circles until she was beyond coherent thought and begging him. 'Now. Please, now.'

But he didn't do what she asked and instead slipped his finger inside her. She immediately tightened around him as her head thrashed against the pillow, and the tingling zeroed into one intense ball. She tried to pull him down, urge him inside her before she ruined everything, but the ball was soaring through her, sucking her with it, and she let go; let herself be carried into the whirling maelstrom until she was flung out in an explosion of wickedly wondrous and deliciously sweet convulsions that rained through her.

When the last wave ebbed away, leaving her limbs feeling like they were filled with molasses, she gazed up at him, not able to believe her body could do that. She almost sobbed. 'I'm sorry. I've never, that is, I mean…' But words couldn't explain it. 'Thank you.'

'Don't apologise or thank me.' His voice sounded rough and hoarse and he nuzzled her neck, his five o'clock shadow scraping gently on her skin. 'Watching you was almost as good as being there with you.'

She stared at him, studying him hard, trying to find the buried message that she'd done the wrong thing by climaxing before he'd entered her, but all she could see was heat and excitement. Heat for her. *You're so amazingly hot.* Was she? Really?

His tongue found her ear and her post-orgasm bonelessness instantly vanished. Flames licked at her again, building heat, building need, and this time she ached so much it hurt. She wanted to give to him what he'd given to her and she pushed at his shoulders, rolling him onto his back. 'Just lie there, I've got something for you.'

His hands gripped her arms. 'Don't even think about using your hands.'

She laughed and straddled him, her hair making a curtain around their heads. 'I wouldn't dream of wasting this.'

He grinned. 'And you thought you weren't good at this.'

She laughed as exhilaration poured through her and she eased herself over him, marvelling at his beauty. Then she closed her eyes and took all of him, almost crying with relief as he filled her. Moving in a rhythm as old as time, she opened her eyes and saw the combination of wonder and pain etched on his face.

She felt the jab right through to her solar plexus—he was thinking of his wife. *Just sex, no regrets.* She didn't want him to go to that dark place of grief so she kissed him with all she had and then threw her head back, gripping him hard. With more bravado than she felt, she hooked his gaze. 'I'm amazing, remember. Don't let me down now, Matt, or you'll put me in therapy for years.'

Lust drove every other emotion off his face and his hands gripped her buttocks. Rising with her, he drove them both higher and higher, taking them away from everything they'd ever known and hurling them out into a place free of pain and suffering, where they hovered until gravity pulled them back and reality encased them again.

CHAPTER SEVEN

'You look different.' Sarah gave Poppy a long, interrogating look when choir practice finished.

'It's just the hair. You're used to seeing it pulled back at work.' Poppy briskly tapped the pages of her music into a neat pile before sliding them into her folder.

Jen lowered the lid of the piano, smiling. 'No, it's more than that. You've had a secret smile for a few days now and we all know what a secret smile means.'

Poppy schooled her face into a blank expression despite the fact she was really starting to enjoy Sarah and Jen's company. However, she wasn't quite ready to confess to having had mind-blowing and universe-altering sex with Matt every night for a week, although she wasn't totally certain who she was protecting most by staying silent.

She threw her music satchel over her shoulder. 'Well, I did win the slab of beer for catching the biggest fish when I went out with the theatre techs the other day.'

'Oh, yeah, that would do it.' Sarah rolled her eyes and linked arms with Jen. 'I think she's holding out on us.'

'So do I. Especially given there's some new graffiti in the staff toilet that says, "P is a make-out bandit."'

Really? A ridiculous rush of gratitude rushed through her that Matt had actually done that. 'You so know that isn't me. That P has to be Penny Duffield.' Poppy didn't feel too bad about creating that rumour given she'd seen Penny locking lips with her anaesthetic registrar early last Wednesday morning.

Before Sarah could quiz her any more, Poppy's phone conveniently beeped and she checked the text message. *Hungry for food but hungrier for you. M.*

This time nothing could restrain her smile or the rush of anticipatory heat rising in a flush, racing up her neck and burning her cheeks.

'I knew it.' Sarah reached to grab the phone and Jen moved to corner Poppy.

But Poppy had played basketball and could weave and duck, so she used her height to hold the phone high and reached the door before they did. 'Have to go, girls, but great practice.' She stepped out of the door, using it as a barricade. 'Next week I think we'll start an *a capella* piece because the choir has been singing so well. Night.'

Good-natured jeers floated across the car park. 'You know we'll find out.'

'You can't hide for long—this is Bundallagong.'

'I'm not hiding, I'm flying high.' Laughing, Poppy got into her car as she heard Jen mention Damien's name. Hopefully her throwaway line would keep them off the scent for a bit longer.

She could hardly concentrate on driving for excitement. She and Matt didn't see a lot of each other during their workday, and today had been emergency-free so she hadn't seen Matt at all, but they always got together at night. Late at night. Both of them had kept the deal of no past, no future and no regrets. They were living for the moment and ignoring everything else. That was the way it had to be.

What if it could be different?

A tiny daydream started weaving its way through her mind but she immediately applied a wet rag to it, dismissing the thought. Once she'd let dreams of marriage and motherhood derail her and they'd taken her to the bottom of a very black pit. Now she knew that her job was the one thing she could rely on; unlike dreams, her career was concrete. She'd spent years sacrificing everything to climb the career ladder and now she was so close to the top job she couldn't let it go. *Your time here is just a minor detour.*

Five minutes later she parked in her carport and a fizz of surprise washed through her as she noticed that her interior lights were on. As she walked up the short path, her front door opened and Matt stood in the doorway, wearing a white-collared shirt with fine purple and green stripes. He looked neat, pressed and very much the eminent country doctor. But she knew appearances counted for little and the man in those clothes had more in common with his dishevelled hair that covered his collar and brushed his cheeks. Neat on the outside but anguished on the inside.

His aura of sadness didn't seem as dark as when she'd first met him but she wouldn't kid herself that if had anything to do with her. Both of them were conveniently forgetting their real lives for a few weeks and where was the harm in that? This was perfect. *Too perfect?* She banished the traitorous voice in her head, telling herself that with all the depressing news coming up daily from Perth about how Alistair Roland was 'owning' her job, being with Matt gave her something fun to focus on.

She walked straight into Matt's strong, welcoming arms and breathed in deeply, loving his scent and still not quite believing she could hold him like this whenever they were alone. 'Hey.'

He smiled and kissed her thoroughly.

She lost herself in the pleasure of his mouth and her hands were reaching for the buttons on his shirt when he unexpectedly cupped her cheeks, kissed her on the nose and said, 'I thought we'd eat here.'

She leaned back slightly to focus on his face and at the same time focus on the change in their routine. Every other time she'd been the one to open the door to him and they'd kiss and that led to sex. Always. Granted, he normally arrived at around 11:00 p.m. because one of them had been caught up working, so tonight was unusual because it was only 8:00 p.m. and he was opening the door for her. *Her door.*

She tilted her head. 'By eating here, you mean my fridge has food in it. Food that's required to make something.'

He winked as they walked inside. 'That's part of it but I did bring wine.'

'So you've been waiting here for me to arrive home and cook?' A spurt of irritation washed through her and Steven's voice, which had faded to almost nothing recently, sounded deep and loud in the recesses of her mind. *Is it so unreasonable to expect you to cook?* She stomped towards the kitchen, annoyance growing into anger. She'd had a huge operating day followed by choir practice and the last thing she wanted to do was have to create a proper meal from scratch. The door swung open and the two glasses of white wine and two plates of salad with grilled chicken sat waiting on the bench.

She spun around to see him standing in the doorway, eyebrows raised and a questioning look on his face. Her hand shot to her pendant. 'Oh, God, I'm so predictable, aren't I?'

He stepped in close and kissed her cheek. 'Actually, you're not. Given any other combination of food in the fridge and dinner wouldn't be waiting for you, but the one culinary thing I can do is barbecue.'

'And supposedly make hedgehog, although I've yet to see any.' She smiled, returning his kiss. 'I must remember to always stock meat, then, so you can grill.' She glanced at the tiny kitchen table and then out the window. The sun was dropping fast and the sky was streaked in the vibrant colours of red and orange that Bundallagong offered up almost every night, and that she was coming to love. Right then she lamented the fact she didn't have a deck. 'It's gorgeous out there. Why don't we eat on your deck and enjoy the sunset?'

A tremor of tension rolled across his shoulders. 'The outdoor furniture's covered in bird poop and it needs cleaning. Here's fine and we can enjoy the sunset through the window.' He placed the plates on the set table and then brought over the wine. 'Cheers.'

She tried to shrug off her disappointment. *'Salut.'* She clinked his glass distractedly, realising with a start that every time they'd been together it had been here, at her place. Still deep in thought, she cut into the fragrant and moist chicken and absently put a piece into her mouth. They'd fallen into a routine of him arriving late and usually leaving her bed around 3:00 a.m. to return to his place. She understood that he wouldn't want to have sex in the house he'd shared with his wife but did that preclude social stuff? Deep inside an ache sent out a niggle of distress that she could never compete with a dead woman.

You don't want to compete. This is short term, remember? You don't want long term. Steven burned you for that.

'Earth to Poppy?'

His words broke into her reverie and she jerked her head up to see his gaze full of questions. 'I'm sorry, what were you saying?'

'I was asking you about your pendant.'

'Oh.' Her hand automatically fingered the tiny diamonds at the bottom of the fine silver. 'It's a Tiffany P.'

'I gathered that.' He smiled. 'Who gave it to you? Family?'

She thought of her father and his endless array of trinkets that turned up by express post at birthdays, always with a note explaining why he couldn't visit. 'My father tried to give me a lot of jewellery but not this one.'

He frowned, his dark brows pulling down. 'Your husband, then?'

She flinched. 'My *ex*-husband and, no, he didn't give it to me. If he had, I wouldn't be wearing it.' She stabbed at her salad. 'Why would you assume someone gave it to me?'

'Because I've noticed you always touch it when you're feeling out of your depth.'

She stared at him, horrified. 'I thought we were just having sex, not analysing each other.'

He leaned in towards her. 'We're having fabulous sex but that doesn't mean I don't notice things. And the fact you're getting defensive means I'm right, doesn't it?'

She took a large sip of her wine, wishing he wasn't

perceptive and feeling like she was more exposed than when he gazed at her naked. 'I gave it to myself when I got divorced.'

'New start?' He drizzled balsamic dressing over his salad.

She shook her head. 'More of a reminder to be true to myself. My marriage, unlike yours, was very much a mistake.'

A pensive look crossed his face. 'How so?'

She sighed. 'For all intents and purposes, I married my father.'

He shrugged. 'Was that such a bad thing? I married my childhood sweetheart and statistically that shouldn't have worked either, but it did.'

Childhood sweetheart? It was the first time he'd voluntarily offered up any information about his marriage. She hadn't asked him any more about Lisa because this thing between them didn't mean spilling their guts to each other and dredging up painful memories.

Be honest, you're protecting yourself. You don't want to be held up against the perfect wife and citizen that you can never be. She wanted to put her hands against her ears to drown out the noise in her head or yell *I'm a damn good surgeon*, but both those options would have Matt doubting her sanity.

Instead she said, 'Given my relationship with my father, it was a bad move and not thought out at all. Very unlike me.'

He ran his finger around the base of his wine glass. 'Love is never rational.'

'Now, that *is* handy to know.' She heard the waspish tone that came out automatically to close down the conversation but it only seemed to make him smile.

'OK, point taken. We'll change the subject. Tell me the story behind your name.'

She immediately relaxed. 'Stanfield?' We go back to the Norman Conquest.'

He grinned. 'How very apt. But I meant Poppy.'

Relaxation vanished. 'Of course you did.' She put her knife and fork together on the plate and decided to just blurt it all out and get it over with in one fell swoop. 'My father wanted a son and I was to be named Hugh after him, his father, his father before him and back another three generations. When I arrived and couldn't be Hugh, he gave the naming rights to my mother. She was a florist and my fate was sealed. I was Poppy to Mum, and Dad called me "mate".'

With a pang of immense sadness, Matt thought of his laughing Annie and all his affectionate pet names for her. He felt his brows draw down. 'Mate?'

Her shoulders rose and fell, and resignation rolled off her. 'He wanted a boy and, you know what? I did a damn good job trying to be a son for him. I learned pretty early on that if I played sport, he noticed me, so I became very good at tennis and basketball and I even got to the point where I occasionally beat him at one on one. Things got sticky when I started to develop breasts.' She refilled her glass. 'Around that time he also left my mother for his secretary and finally got the son he'd always wanted.'

Matt's parents had enjoyed a happy marriage so he could only imagine what losing her father's affection must have been like for her. 'Tough to compete with a baby boy?'

'Impossible. Even harder when a second son arrived.' Her usually firm voice cracked for a moment and then steadied. 'I sometimes wonder if it would have been better if Dad had cut himself off completely from my life but instead he'd send money and gifts for every birthday, every academic prize and sporting trophy, leaving me constantly hoping one day he'd actually turn up.'

Matt saw the remnants of a young girl's pain on her face, and caught the moment the steely, determined woman caught up.

She rolled her shoulders back. 'Still, the flip side is that I drove myself to impress him, which got me into medicine, and for *that* I can never have regrets.'

Her words illuminated her work ethic and the constant striving to win, and he realised what had started out as a bid for affection had become ingrained behaviour. 'And your husband was a father figure to you?'

His question shot out on an urge to find out more about the unknown man he actively disliked with an intensity that surprised him. He didn't really expect her to answer it.

Her amazing mouth formed into an ironic pout. 'Not that I was aware of at the time, although the counsellor I saw once post-divorce did point that out.' She took in a quick breath as if gearing up to get something nasty out of the way quickly. 'Steven was fifteen years older than me, divorced and an "empty-nester" with grown-up children. We met when I was a surgical registrar and his brother was one of my first solo procedures. Sadly, his presentation of a perforated bowel turned out to be undiagnosed cancer and he was riddled with secondaries. He died on the table.'

Poppy's fingers laced, her knuckles shining white. 'Perhaps it was my inexperience in dealing with relatives after losing a patient, perhaps it was his charm that was so similar to my father's, I don't know, but we started dating. For a few short weeks he made me feel like the centre of his world and when he proposed, I accepted. We hit the wall within weeks when he realised I wasn't going to be the sort of wife he'd expected. It got angry and ugly, and we divorced.'

Don't let me down: you'll put me in therapy for years. 'The ugly being him telling you that you weren't woman enough for him?'

Her head inclined slightly and then her eyes glittered with resolute grit. 'So, now you know all my sordid details. Aren't you lucky we're living in the moment and me and my emotional baggage will be heading back to Perth in a few weeks?'

He stood up and walked around to her, pulling her to her feet and into his arms, not really wanting to think about the fact her time here was finite. He stroked some inky-black hair back behind her ear. 'Did you happen to see the graffiti that you're a make-out bandit? I think we've managed to unpack and throw out the stuff about you not being woman enough.'

She smiled, a hint of hesitation spinning around her. 'Maybe.'

'Just maybe?' He thought about what they'd done in her bed, how every time the darkness threatened to suck him under she managed to keep him in the moment, and how losing himself in her kept the past at bay in a way hard drinking, exercise or work had never been able to. He wanted their sex to help her too.

'If it's only a maybe then you need to practise more because I know how much you like to be the best at everything.' He knew she could never resist a challenge but just in case he pressed his mouth to her ear, tracing the outline with his tongue, knowing that always made her melt against him and kiss him hard.

Her fingers reached for his belt buckle, unlacing the leather with expert ease, and then bluer-than-blue eyes shimmered with wicked intent. 'Prepare to be exhausted.'

He grinned. 'Sounds good to me.'

'Mr Simmonds, there's a spot on your lung that I want to do a biopsy on.' Poppy sat in a chair opposite the Vietnam veteran, watching his expression carefully.

'Cancer?' He sounded resigned. 'I've been waiting for the thing to catch up with me. Mates I served with have died from it.'

Poppy moved to temper the leap to that conclusion, although most of her agreed with him. 'Or it could be something else, which is why I want to do the biopsy so we know exactly what we're dealing with.'

'This cough's been with me for six months and the antibiotics haven't done a damn thing. Doc, I'm a realist. The war never leaves you and this is just another reminder.' The sixty-three-year-old's gaze stayed steady.

Poppy was the one who dropped her gaze first. 'I can only imagine what you went through and it probably doesn't come close.'

He shifted in his chair. 'Yeah, but I was one of the lucky ones. Janice and the girls, they've kept me going.'

Poppy knew Janice from the choir. 'She's a delightful woman, your wife. Being able to share your experiences with her must have helped.'

He shook his head vehemently. 'I've never told her or the girls any of it. Why would I want to taint my home with horrors like that? No, that's what army mates are for. With Janice I can forget.'

His reply astounded her. How could he have been

married for thirty-odd years and completely avoided a topic that had had such an impact on his life? 'And it's important to forget?'

'Yeah, love, it is.' His head dipped in reverie for the briefest of moments before he looked back at her. 'So when do you want to put me under the knife?'

Poppy showed her patient the thin, flexible bronchoscope, explained how he would be sedated and how the sample of tissue would be taken. 'I can do it tomorrow. See Sarah on your way out for the paperwork.'

Her pager bleeped loudly. *Need you in Emergency if you're not scrubbed. Jen.*

Mr Simmonds rose from his chair and extended his hand. 'Thanks, Doc. I'll let you get on with your day.'

She walked him to the door and then hurried towards Emergency. Jen met her as she pushed through the Perspex doors.

'Great, I was hoping you weren't in Theatre.'

'What's the problem?'

'There's a child in the resus room with a broken leg and the pain and stress has triggered an asthma attack.'

Poppy pulled on the proffered gown as she walked towards the room, thinking the break must be pretty bad for Jen to call her. Usually young kids experienced greenstick fractures, which didn't require surgery. 'So, Matt's in with the patient already?'

Jen frowned and shook her head. 'No.'

Poppy's hand stalled on the doorhandle, thinking about her very first day in Bundallagong. 'But he's on his way, right?'

'No. I only called you.'

Poppy felt like she was missing something. 'I'm happy to consult but this is his department and you can't bypass him. You know how he hates that. You have to call him.'

Conflicting emotions played across the nurse's face. 'But the patient's the spitting image of Annie.'

OK, now it was definite. She was totally missing something. 'Who's Annie?'

Jen's eyes dilated in shock. 'You don't know? She was Matt's three-year-old daughter. Lisa and Annie died together.'

His daughter. A wave of nausea hit Poppy so hard she thought she'd vomit on the spot. *Oh, God!* She'd thought it bad enough that he'd lost his beloved wife but she'd no clue he'd lost a child too. Lost so much. No wonder the town had no idea how to behave around him. 'Page him.'

Genuine distress slashed Jen's face. 'But, Poppy, it will kill him.'

She shook her head, knowing that Jen's intentions were good but sadly misguided, and wouldn't help Matt one bit. 'It's not our place to make this decision for him. If he doesn't want to treat the child, that's fine. I can do it. But only he can make that choice.'

'You don't know him like we do or know what he's been through. Sure, he'll bark, but in this case, I know I'm right.'

The unfamiliar exclusion from Jen hit her with a chill, taking her straight back to high school, where she'd never fit in with the girls at school. Part of her wanted to side with Jen, to care for the fledgling friendship she was starting to value, but most of her knew this 'protection mode' was the worst thing in the world for Matt.

She tried to keep her voice even. 'That's very true.

I don't know him like you do but this is a hospital, and protocol needs to be followed.'

'Protocol over people?' Jen muttered, before reluctantly picking up the phone.

Poppy bit her lip as she pushed open the door of the resus room, knowing she'd just lost a much-needed ally in Jen and, by default, the Perth job had taken another critical hit. But she'd worry about that later. Right now, she had a patient.

A distressed little girl rested against a bank of pillows with a vaporising mask on her face. Jen had correctly commenced a salbutamol nebuliser but the child was still visibly struggling to breathe, her chest heaving as she tried to force air into constricted and rigid lungs. Her left leg was encased in an air splint and a woman Poppy assumed was her mother sat next to her, holding her hands through the side bars of the emergency trolley.

'Hello, I'm Poppy Stanfield and I'm going to insert an intravenous drip into…' she picked up the chart '…Ashley's arm and give her some drugs that will help her breathe.'

'Thank you.' The worried mother wrung her hands. 'She hasn't been this bad in a long time.'

Poppy nodded her understanding and turned her attention to the little girl. 'Hey, Ashley.' She picked up a cuddle bear that Jen had provided. 'Can you give this bear a big hug for me? He's a bit scared and I know you can show him how to be brave while I put a needle into your arm, OK?'

The little girl's eyes widened in fear. 'Will it hurt?'

'Not as much as your leg does.' Poppy slid the brightly coloured tourniquet around the child's small, pudgy arm and prayed she could find a vein on her first attempt. Surgeons didn't insert IVs very often—that's what anaesthetists were for.

As she swabbed Ashley's arm with alcohol and popped the cover off the cannula, she heard raised voices outside. Matt's rough-voiced yell at Jen didn't surprise her in the least—that she could have predicted. What she couldn't foretell was how he'd react to Ashley.

Matt strode into the room with blind rage, boiling and ready for a fight. First Jen and now Poppy. Not since her first day had she made an arbitrary decision about a patient and he'd thought they'd worked all that out. So much for collegial respect. He couldn't understand it because just lately she'd actually been doing pretty well and gaining ground with the staff, but it was stunts like this that made him wonder if she'd ever learn.

Certainly, after hearing her talk about her father, he totally got why her need to win was so deeply ingrained and work was her world but, damn it, in this instance she knew better. He triaged and if she was required for a consult he called her. It didn't work the other way around.

Poppy's left hip rested on the edge of the trolley and her hair, which caressed his face every night when they had sex, cascaded down her back in a sleek, silky ponytail. She was leaning forward, deep in concentration, and he saw her hand reach for the pre-cut strips of tape on the dressing trolley. The angle of her body blocked his view of the patient but, no matter; he'd see him or her in a moment when he asked Poppy to step down.

'I'm sure you're required elsewhere, Ms Stanfield. I'll take over here.'

She turned and something in her cornflower-blue gaze sent a shiver of disquiet through him. He'd seen those eyes steely with the determination of a woman on a mission, shadowed by the memories of inflicted hurts, filled with the burning fires of lust, and sated with the fog of complete satisfaction. Not once had he ever seen sympathy in their depths, and although it made no sense that is exactly what he saw.

'Ashley, Beth, this is Matt Albright, our emergency specialist. I'm sorry he wasn't here to greet you—there was a slight miscommunication with the nursing staff.' She adjusted the flow of the IV and then moved aside.

His chest tightened so fast air couldn't move in or out of it. A little girl with a riot of blonde curly hair and clutching a hospital bear stared at him through huge, violet eyes.

Daddy, look! I've got a doctor bear with a white coat just like yours.

No. No! This isn't possible. His heart thundered hard and fast, pushing blood through a body that was both icily numb and throbbing in pain. Sweat dripped into his eyes and he blinked rapidly, as if that would help change the image in front of him. But when his eyes refocused, his daughter's double was still there on the trolley, struggling to breathe but, unlike his Annie, still breathing.

'I've started Ashley on IV methylprednisolone.' Poppy pulled a stethoscope out of her pocket and held it out towards him.

He snatched it like a lifeline. 'I'll page you if I need you.'

'I can stay.' The quiet tone of her voice matched her eyes.

His stomach churned and bile seared his gut. God,

she knew. How the hell did she know? The town had gone silent, never mentioning the two people he'd loved as much as life itself, and he damn well hadn't told Poppy about Annie because he didn't want her to know. He'd never wanted to see 'that look' in her eyes.

'Get out.' He heard Beth's shocked gasp at the aggression in his voice but he didn't care. No way was he having Poppy in here with pity in her eyes, offering to take over or watching him struggle to keep it all together. Worse still, fall apart. He got enough of that from all the staff.

Her hand crept towards her pendant but stopped short. She rolled her shoulders back and stripped off her gloves. 'Ashley is in excellent hands, Beth, and hopefully the break is a clean one that only requires a cast.' She took a quick step forward and touched Ashley's hand with genuine caring. 'You look after that bear for me, won't you?'

The scared little girl nodded behind the mask as if she was petrified by the thought of Poppy leaving.

At that point Matt didn't know who he hated most—himself, Poppy or the universe.

CHAPTER EIGHT

ALTHOUGH Ashley didn't require surgery, a burns victim from the day before did, and that had tied Poppy up in Theatre until past six. She'd been thankful to have been kept busy because thinking about how much Matt was hurting was just too painful. She hurt too, even though she didn't want to, but the fact he'd never told her about Annie ate at her, making a mockery of everything they'd shared.

What did you expect? The deal you made was no-strings sex. That's want you want, remember, because it's safe.

Except you've been sharing meals and sharing stories, laughing together, and he's become a friend.

The thought chafed like a rash of doubt; hot, prickly and decidedly uncomfortable. Turning her doorhandle, she realised they probably weren't likely to be sharing anything any more. Not when he'd ordered her to leave ED in a voice that could have cut steel, and the look in his eyes had packed the velocity and damage of a bullet ripping through flesh. She stepped inside and the low glow of a lamp greeted her.

'Poppy.'

With a start she turned towards the sound of the deep but expressionless voice and instantly recognised those familiar and tormented eyes. Surprise became tinged with concern and her heart beat faster. 'Matt? I didn't exp— Are you all—?' But his taut face stole her words, silencing her.

Go for neutral. 'You finished up earlier than I did.'

With his mouth grim and tense, he strode straight to her, his hands gripping the tops of her arms. Silently, he hauled her up onto her toes, pulled her against him, and then took her mouth in a kiss, plundering it with a frenzy close to desperation.

Surprise spun through her at the fact he was there at all, and intensified at the knowledge he still wanted her given what had happened in the ED. She opened her lips under his, wanting and trying to claim her place in the kiss and struggling to find it. She'd never been kissed quite like it, urgent need spinning together with what she guessed was misery.

With a gasp he pulled his mouth away and, still silent, grabbed her hand, tugging her up the hallway to the bedroom. Her feet stumbled at the speed and she should have been angry, perhaps even on one level scared, but all she could feel was his pain roaring through her like a hot wind.

Then his mouth was on hers again, hot, hard and frantic, and she was tumbling back onto the bed. 'This is in the way.' With clumsy movements he pushed her dress upwards but his hands fumbled with her bra.

'Let me do that.' She quickly undid the clasp and unbuckled his belt, and when the clothes were gone, she wrapped her arms tightly around him. Holding him close, trying to give him comfort, and then she kissed him. Softly.

He returned the kiss and for one brief moment his shuttered eyes opened and she saw ragged pain and torment. Her heart cramped so hard she felt the spasm tear clear through her, sending his searing hurt into every cell. She knew then he needed her to be there just for him.

His mouth pressed against her neck, marking a line of ownership as if she might vanish underneath him. Her hands soothed him by caressing his back while he kissed her, but it was like there was an invisible wall between them. But then his mouth took her breast in the way he knew she loved, and her body started to rise on a familiar stream of pleasure. As her mind slipped into bliss and her hips rose to meet his, he entered her, burying himself deeply.

Sensations built, spinning through her, and she wrapped her legs around him, feeling all of him and giving all of herself to him. She touched his face as she always did, seeking his gaze that filled her with joy. But like a man in a trance he looked right through her and all she could see was the reflection of a man trying to outrun his demons. A man who still loved his dead wife.

She swallowed her gasp of hurt. She wanted to wave a wand and change everything. For her. For him. She'd do anything to take away his pain and hurt but she had no power to do that. So she did the only thing she could. She held him tight and sheltered him until he sank with a sob against her, exhausted and spent.

Matt felt Poppy move under him and like a shock of electricity ripping through him he jolted back to earth, realising what he'd just done. He'd taken and not given much in return. He rolled off her, immediately stroking her hair. 'Hell, Poppy. I'm sorry.'

Her clear gaze hooked his and she put a finger against his lips. 'So you got it wrong once. Just don't make a habit of it.' She shot him a cheeky smile. 'Of course, if you're feeling guilty at not totally meeting my needs, you can always buy me flowers, chocolates, champagne and fill my freezer with delicious meals from Lizzie's Kitchen.'

An uncomfortable relief settled over him and he released a breath he hadn't realised he was holding. A breath of thanks. Pressing a tender and appreciative kiss to her forehead, he said, 'Is that all? Nothing in a pale blue box?'

She fingered her pendant. 'No, thanks, I buy my own.'

And that was Poppy to a *P*. Completely independent. Deep down something ached. He knew he owed her a full and detailed explanation about what had just happened but he couldn't do that until he'd made amends. He trailed a finger gently along the curve of her jaw. 'Can I start to make it up to you now?'

Black brows rose. 'What did you have in mind?'

'A neck massage. I know surgeons spend a lot of time looking down, which is tough on the neck muscles.'

She reached out and pressed her hand against his chest, in the same way she always did, with fingers splayed wide. 'Hmm, that might be nice, but I don't have any massage oil.'

Damn. Why hadn't he ever thought of buying some? He covered her hand with his. 'Well, I could massage you in the shower, using soap.'

'Perhaps.' She pouted, her lips slick with the sheen of desire. 'Surgeons also get aching shoulders and backs.'

He grinned, loving the way this was heading.

'That's very true, not to mention all that standing takes its toll on your legs. I could massage those as well.'

'Could you?' She raised herself up; her pink nipples tightly budded against her creamy breasts. 'An entire body massage? Now, that might just go a long way towards clearing your tab.'

He kissed her with a rush of heat that tangoed with heady affection, and carried her into the shower.

The mattress moved underneath Poppy and a cool draught zipped in around her naked back. Barely awake, she rolled over as part of her brain accepted it was about 3:00 a.m., the time Matt always left her bed. The fact the room seemed lighter didn't really penetrate and sleep quickly pulled her back under. The next moment a shock of white light made her closed eyes ache and she moaned as her arm shot to her forehead to shield her eyes.

'Whoa.' She managed to crack one eyelid open and realised Matt was standing in the room, fully dressed. 'Is it morning?'

His hands circled her wrists and he gently pulled her into a sitting position before sitting down next to her. 'It is. Good sleep?'

She stretched languidly. 'It was an amazing sleep. Best one I've had since arriving.'

'Excellent.' He brushed his lips against her forehead. 'I got up half an hour ago and I've made breakfast.'

Half an hour ago? She could hardly believe it. Thirty minutes meant he'd stayed all night. She'd had her best sleep in—for ever, and he'd been in her bed all night. She didn't want to let herself connect any dots about those two events but already her mind was doing it. 'Is there coffee with breakfast?'

'There is.' He tossed her a pair of shorts and a T-shirt.

She tugged the top over her head. 'Can't I have it in bed, seeing you've woken me up at…' she squinted at the clock '…stupid o'clock?'

'No. Breakfast is at my place.'

His place? She pulled up her sagging jaw as he walked out of her room. They never spent any time at his place. She fell into her shorts, wondering what was going on, and stumbled into the bathroom.

Five minutes later she slid, grumbling, into a chair at Matt's kitchen table and found herself in front of a steaming mug of coffee. 'You'd better have food as well as coffee.'

'Are you always this delightful first thing in the morning?' Matt sat down next to her, coffee in one hand and a photograph album in the other. 'I'm short on fresh food but I'll buy you something from the bakery on the way to work.'

'You're always short on fresh food because you never shop. Why are we here when I have fruit and yoghurt at my place?'

'Because my coffee's better and I need to show you this.' He put the album on her placemat and opened it up. A little girl with eyes the colour of grape juice stared up at her. 'I'd like you to meet my daughter.'

Her heart hiccoughed and she touched his hand as she continued to turn the pages of the album looking at photos of a loving wife and mother, a proud and loving husband and father, and a child they both clearly adored. She wondered about that kind of love; a love that encompassed everyone in the family, the sort of love she'd never known. A bright green streak ricocheted through her. What sort of a shocking person was she to be jealous of a dead woman and child?

One that wants the same thing?

No. Thoughts of the dark days of her childhood and her marriage shored up her momentary lapse.

'All those curls. She's gorgeous.'

'Yeah.' He ran his hand through his hair, the strands falling back and masking his face, and then his body shuddered. 'Annie and Lisa died on a beach in Samoa when a tsunami struck. I was spending the day at an inland village and survived.'

She immediately wrapped her arms around him, resting her forehead on his, wishing she could take away all his pain and knowing she couldn't touch it. 'I can't even imagine what this is like for you.'

He absently kissed her cheek. 'I know.'

She needed him to really understand. 'I had no clue you had a daughter until yesterday when Jen and I argued over why she hadn't called you to the ED.' She tried to keep the hurt out of her voice. 'Why didn't you tell me, Matt?'

He shrugged. 'Perhaps I wanted *one* person not to define me by what I'd lost. One person who could stare me down, argue with me and treat me just like any other bloke.'

She bit her lip and tried not to tear up, tried to be the same person she'd been yesterday. 'I can argue the point.'

A quiet smile tugged at his lips. 'You can, and you do it very well.'

She thought of Mr Simmonds and how he'd never told his wife about the war because he didn't want to have to think about the horrors he'd been through when he was with his family. A shaft of clarity hit her and she realised why Matt was showing her photos of his family in his house and not hers. 'I still plan to argue with you.'

'I hope you do.' He dropped his head into her hair and sighed. 'Poppy, about last night. Seeing Ashley, who looks so much like Annie, and realising that you knew about her, well, I lost it. I haven't lost it in a long time. I'm truly sorry.'

She cupped his jaw and raised his head to hers, fighting an irrational sadness about her role in all of this, which was crazy. She had no reason to feel sad because she wasn't sticking around. She'd learned a long time ago that work was safer then relationships with all their inherent pitfalls and she knew Matt certainly wasn't looking for one. Yet she couldn't quite shake the feeling that perhaps together they could have something more. 'It's OK, I get it. Me and my house are a place for you to come and forget.'

Matt raised his head slowly and met Poppy's eyes filled with tacit understanding and something else he couldn't define. 'You're an amazing woman, Poppy.'

A ripple of tension shot along her mouth before she smiled. 'That's me. Brilliant surgeon and sex goddess.'

The quip reassured him that things hadn't changed between them, that their loose arrangement would continue while she was in town and she wasn't going to go all touchy-feely on him and want him to bare his soul even more. That was the beauty of Poppy: she didn't do emotions very well, either. With her he could still pretend his life hadn't been turned upside down and pulled sideways, and when that got too hard, he lost himself in her.

She drank more coffee. 'Have you been back to Samoa?'

He shook his head. 'I stayed there for a few months after it happened and then I thought it was time to come home.'

'How's that working for you?'

He didn't want to analyse that at all so he gave her the bare minimum. 'I think I mentioned the initial drinking binge but that's long over and now, well, I get through each day. I know I can treat children again, even ones who look like my daughter, so that has to be an improvement, right?'

A thumping noise sounded from the roof and Poppy's eye's rolled. 'And yet you let Rupert live in your roof?'

Unease shot through him that she was way too close to the truth. 'Why are you so obsessed by the goanna?'

'I'm not. I'm merely pointing out most people wouldn't want something like that living in their roof, causing damage to the house.' She stood up, taking her cup to the sink. 'Are you sure living here is the right thing for you?'

He gripped his coffee mug, hating that she'd just asked the question he often asked himself. 'Of course I'm sure. This is my home.'

Two small creases appeared at the bridge of her nose. 'This house or this town?'

'Both,' he said, but knew he lied. He stood up, knowing the exact way to cut this conversation off at the knees. 'You'd better hit the shower or you're going to be late for work.'

She yelped as she caught the time on the clock. 'Oh, hell, is it really seven-thirty? I've got pre-op consults in fifteen minutes.'

He saw a blur of colour, heard her feet on the bare boards and then the door slam. He grinned. 'Poppy has left the building.' He went to close the photo album and saw Lisa's face smiling up at him. He braced himself for the sear of guilt—guilt that he was still living, guilt that he'd found pleasure with another woman—but it didn't come. He released a long breath, left the page open and headed to the shower.

Sweat poured off Poppy as she gesticulated, controlling the choir with her arm movements, and backed up by her silent mouthing of the words. The clear, true sound of *a capella* rolled over her as the words of 'Amazing Grace' soared along with such a wave of feeling that she felt tears sting her eyes.

With her fingertips touching, she slowly drew her hands apart, holding the last note until she fisted her hands to indicate 'stop'. She grinned at the women's awestruck faces. 'Yes! You really did sound that fantastic. Well done. I think Sarah has posters about the concert she'd like you to put up so please take one with you before you leave, and on that note I'll call the formal part of choir over for the night. There's the usual tea and biscuits if you can stay.'

Shrieks of delight followed with the choir members breaking to give each other high-fives and Poppy turned as Sarah's hand touched her shoulder. 'Amazing.'

'Grace.' Poppy smiled.

'Take a compliment, woman!' Sarah hugged her. 'They're going to rock the town at the concert.'

'You mean the five people who might actually come out on a Sunday afternoon.'

'Yeah, well, there's that, but Justin's selling tickets at the surgery with the odd bribe, and I heard Matt Albright's reply to a recovering Daryl Jameson when he was trying to thank him for saving his life. He said that all the thanks he needed was Daryl attending the concert.'

Poppy groaned. 'These women deserve more than a pity audience.'

'You worry about the music and let us locals get the audience.'

Us locals. An odd feeling settled in Poppy's belly, and she tried to shake it off. It was ridiculous that she was letting two little words, two absolutely accurate words, make her feel uncomfortable. Sad almost. It didn't make a lot of sense—in fact, it made none at all because it wasn't like she planned on staying.

You're just tired and emotional. This is nothing a good sleep won't fix. Remember, this is a godforsaken place that's just a blip on your career radar.

A small voice protested. *The sunsets are amazing. So are the people.*

People like Matt.

Her stomach flipped, scaring her, and she dragged her mind back so fast from the man who was turning her world upside down that she risked mental whiplash. It was time to focus on the choir.

She'd met some incredible women out here, women whose lives were far from perfect but they kept going, trying to improve their situation and those of their families. Local or not, she wanted to honour them and be involved.

'I want this concert to be a success. How about we have a planning meeting at my place now? I got a hamper sent up from Perth yesterday with a fabulous Margaret River white wine, Swiss chocolate and a gorgeous runny Camembert that needs to be eaten.'

Sarah laughed. 'First of all you give me the "no-sex" talk and now this. Are you asking me out on a date?'

She smiled, enjoying the teasing. 'You found me out.'

Jen wandered over. 'Found out what?'

Things had been a bit strained between Jen and herself since the incident in the ED and perhaps this was a way of building bridges. 'Drinks at my place now—can you come?'

Jen visibly started. 'Really? OK, why not? Can I catch a ride with you?'

'Sure. We can ask Janice Simmonds to lock up, can't we?'

Sarah nodded. 'Janice will do anything for you now you've cured Harry. Your eyes were like saucers when you saw that sprouting pea in his lung.'

This time Poppy high-fived. 'Well, it was a pretty amazing find and so unexpected, but in a good way.' And not just for Harry Simmonds. The uniqueness of the case meant it had made it into the 'odd spot' in the Eastern papers and the Royal College of Surgeons had asked her to write it up for their journal. It was win-win for the patient and for herself, as well as a shot across the bows to Alistair Roland, William and the board. They might have sent her to the outer Barcoo but she was still a force to be reckoned with.

Sarah kept them entertained on the quick drive home with a story about a very tired Justin being called out of an antenatal clinic to stitch up a nasty wound when the patient had lost a battle with a bush saw. 'He was stitching John Ledger's hand.'

'I don't think Poppy's had the pleasure of meeting John,' Jen chimed in.

'If you think most of the blokes in this town are

tough then John is reinforced steel. Anyway, Justin's going through the motions, asking all the important questions, but instead of asking John when he last had a tetanus injection, he asked the question he'd been asking all afternoon at the pregnancy care clinic, which was, 'When did you last have a pap test?"

Jen started to giggle. 'Poor Justin.'

'John gave him one of his famous "you're a moron" looks and said, "At the same time I had my last tetanus shot." John went straight from the surgery to the pub and Justin's never going to live it down.'

The laughs continued as they shared embarrassing work stories and Poppy poured wine and Jen opened chocolate and cheese.

'OK, how are we going to sell this concert as a "must attend" event?' Poppy tapped a pen against a note pad. 'Offer food?'

Jen sliced the cheese. 'Serve beer and the men will come.'

Sarah sat forward, wine glass in hand. 'Poppy, remember your first week here when you operated on the head of transport for the mining company?' She clarified, 'The bowel obstruction.'

Poppy nodded as his name came to her. 'Ed Papasoulis?'

'That's him. The miners who "fly in, fly out" get collected and taken to the airport. I'm sure with a word to him the bus could be early that day and come via the concert. It's only going to be half an hour and it would double our audience. Any unsupportive husbands who weren't planning on coming will be there on company time, and have the added benefit of being blown away by their wives' performances.'

Poppy stared at her. 'I'm in awe of your scheming.'

Sarah shrugged and gave her a grin. 'Perhaps I'm learning from you. By the way, great sound bite and visual on the Perth news the other night about Harry. So how's the battle for the Perth job going?'

'I wish I knew. It's just so hard being this far away and not being able to see my opposition in action and lobby.'

'He can't see you either so that levels the playing field a bit, doesn't it?' Jen remarked as she sipped her wine.

The support in the words both surprised and reassured Poppy. 'I guess I never really thought about it that way. Thanks.'

'No problem.' Jen paused for a moment. 'Listen, Poppy, I'm sorry about the other day with Matt. The thing is, just lately he seems to be coping better, looking less tormented and even cracking jokes and smiling, and I didn't want seeing Ashley to bring the trauma back again and send him backwards.'

An apologetic look touched her face. 'But you were right and I was wrong. He managed to hold it all together but I hated watching him have to do it.'

Poppy thought about how he'd fallen apart in her arms a few hours later. 'It was a tough day all round and no choice was easy, but it had to be his choice.' She offered the nurse a chocolate. 'Truce?'

Jen frowned. 'There was never a war, Poppy, we just differed in opinion. Friends can do that, you know, and then they talk it out.' She popped the ball of rich praline chocolate into her mouth and murmured a sound of delight. 'Oh, my God, Sarah, you have to try these.'

Sarah chose a chocolate and joined Jen in equal rhapsodising about the taste and texture, and Poppy leaned back and watched.

Friends. She realised with a start that these two strong women really did consider her a friend. The feeling settled over her like a new pair of shoes that fitted but would become truly comfortable with some extra wear. She was looking forward to it.

The front door opened with its usual squeak and Jen and Sarah looked up as Poppy's gut clenched. *Matt.* She'd been on such a high after the choir practice and enjoying herself with the girls, she'd forgotten to text him.

He walked in, talking. 'I thought we— Ladies, good to see you.'

The change in his conversation was almost seamless and if Matt was surprised to see Sarah and Jen, his face didn't seem to show it. He held up a bottle of wine. 'I brought wine for the choir meeting.'

Shock rendered Poppy speechless but Sarah stood up and accepted the bottle with a smile. 'Thanks, Matt. This is really thoughtful and will add to our spur-of-the-moment meeting. By the way, didn't know you were psychic.'

He didn't skip a beat. 'It's one of my many skills. I'll leave you girls to it. Have a good night.' He closed the door behind him.

Sarah spun around with a squeal and pointed straight at Poppy. 'You are so having sex.'

Jen punched her gently on the arm and beamed. 'No wonder Matt's been looking better lately.' She looked at Sarah. 'How did we miss this?'

Sarah sat down. 'Because Poppy is cagey.'

Poppy tried to deny it, shaking her head. 'I'm not cagey and I'm not having sex.'

Sarah crossed her arms. 'The game's over, Poppy,

and now it's time to spill. But before you do, can I just say thank you?'

'Thank you? I don't understand.'

'Matt and you as a couple—it's just so great after what he's been through.'

A ripple of panic set off through her and Poppy's hands flew up like stop signs. 'No, please, don't make that leap. I've been married once and never again. This is just sex. I'm only here for a few more weeks and, like you said that night in the bar, why not have some fun? See, I took your advice.' The words spoken with true conviction sounded strangely hollow.

Sarah frowned. 'Does Matt know?'

'It was *his* idea.' She moved to reassure their worried expressions, finding it harder than expected. 'Neither of us wants anything permanent and he still loves Lisa. We're both adults who've gone into this with eyes wide open. There's nothing for you to be concerned about.'

Liar.

The creases in Jen's brows faded slightly. 'Well, you have to admit, he's been a lot happier, so that's a good thing, right?'

Sarah didn't look quite so convinced but she smiled and leaned forward. 'Just sex, eh? So how good is it?'

Poppy leaned back, raised her glass to her friends, unable to stop a wicked smile racing across her face. 'Let's just say good is a far too prosaic adjective to describe it.'

CHAPTER NINE

POPPY kicked up from the depths of the water hole, breaking the surface, and felt Matt's arms wrap around her. She leaned back against him and stared up at the clear Outback sky. A strange feeling washed over her and she realised with surprise that this was what happiness felt like.

A while later, she lay in the shade cast by the massive, red-walled gorge, soaking in the unexpected coolness, when a mere forty steps away the sun was unrelentingly hot. 'It's so amazing that in the middle of all this arid, red-rocked, gibber-plain nothingness, there are ferns and a permanent water hole.' She rubbed her arms, flicking off the water from her swim, and laughed. 'I'm almost cold. How weird is that?'

Matt wrapped a towel around her shoulders. 'The Outback has its secrets, you just have to open yourself up to them.'

'And here I am.' She gave him an arch look. 'Although I thought the guy who asked the girl out did everything.'

He grinned. 'Division of labour. I drove and you arranged the picnic.'

She smiled against a looming frown. 'I'm not sure that's actually a fair division, considering driving here happened on your day off and yesterday I had to shop and then put the food together.'

He winked. 'Yeah, but it made you finish work a bit earlier. Besides, you needed a day off and I've wanted to bring you out here for ages.'

She flicked him with the towel, half in jest and half serious as the scars of her marriage reddened. 'This week I've been home by eight three nights and no paperwork. I really think I've broken the back of the waiting list and things are getting more manageable and into a routine. Besides, you're the one who told me to go fishing and accept invitations to clothing parties, so today was my first totally free day.'

'How dumb was I? Still, that advice was before I got you into bed.' He kissed her on the nose. 'If you asked today, I might tell you something different.'

'I'm not so sure about that.' She looked hard into his eyes, trying to read more. She could see affection but it ran into something else. Something that prickled at her. 'All I'm saying is that I came here with a job to do, and I'm getting it done.'

'And all I'm saying is that *balance* in life is good.' He stretched out next to her. 'Your phone doesn't work out here and doesn't it feel good not to be obsessively checking emails?'

A defensive flicker clenched her gut. 'I don't obsessively check emails.'

He cocked a knowing brow.

'OK, but to be fair, I've been sending William biweekly reports. How unreasonable is it to expect a reply?'

'Poppy, he holds the power in this so accept that he's toying with you and make it work for you.'

All her fears collided. 'This is my career you're so casually talking about. My life.'

He sighed. 'I know it's not easy for you to take advice but if I've learned anything in the last year and a half it's that life isn't all about work.'

She thought about how her father had consistently let her down, and how Steven had zeroed in on her need to be loved, turning it into a battlefield of 'you change and then I'll love you'. Now Matt was hinting along similar lines. The one constant in her life, the one safe thing that didn't let her down, was her career. 'And I've learned that my work is far more reliable than anything else.'

He opened his mouth to reply but she didn't want to spoil the day by arguing any more about work or workloads so she leaned over and pressed her mouth against his, kissing him deeply and hoping that was enough to distract him. 'Thanks for bringing me out here.'

He stroked her hair as she rested her head against his chest. 'You're very welcome. Walker's Gorge is always worth the drive. When I was a kid, Mum would choose the beach for picnics but Dad and I loved it out here. It was a favourite with Lisa's family, too. I remember getting into serious trouble when I was five after I pushed her into the water hole.'

Five! She could scarcely believe it. 'You really were childhood sweethearts.'

He crooked his free arm behind his head. 'It's hard to think of a time when she wasn't in my life.'

'What about uni?'

'Lisa came to Brisbane with me.'

It was spoken so casually, as if it was totally unremarkable that two people had lived all their lives together, but Poppy's surprise swooped to her toes. Had they never been apart until her death? 'So you were at uni together?'

'No, Lisa didn't want to go to uni. She was an artist and made the most amazing jewellery. She worked in the office of a law firm and made jewellery at night.' His mouth curved into a smile full of pleasant memories. 'We had a tiny flat with bookshelves made out of bricks and wood, beanbags for furniture, and it was decorated with Lisa's artwork. Her parents weren't happy about any of it and would visit often, mostly so her father could give me a really hard time about how I was a kept man because Lisa was earning more money than I was as a student.'

His chest rose and fell under her cheek. 'The moment I qualified we got married, and I took great delight at outearning her so she could quit her job and do jewellery full time. When Annie arrived, we moved back here and she cut back the jewellery to commission pieces only because she loved being a stay-at-home mum and being involved in the town, volunteering.'

He'd never talked so openly and Poppy knew she should be pleased for him that he'd now reached a place in his grieving where he could do this, only the green monster that had been slumbering of late raised its head. Lisa had been family-oriented and naturally giving, everything *she* wasn't.

Does it matter? It's not your future. Your future is Perth.

Is it? A hollow feeling filled her gut. The words so easily spoken when they'd first started their affair were getting harder and harder to believe, but her heart knew the alternative wasn't an option. Having it all—

career, marriage and kids—was a big-time con and she'd learned that the hard way.

If he'd noticed her silence he didn't show it. 'If I'm honest, Lisa's choices made my life a lot easier because, given the hours I sometimes work, coming home to an oasis of calm was a gift.' He tensed. 'Ironically, it was her push to go to Samoa that changed everything.'

'No one was to know a holiday would end like that.'

He shook his head. 'We weren't there on holidays. Lisa had read about an organisation working with indigenous women to help them achieve sustainable futures and thought she could offer her skills and knowledge about turning crafts into income. She had it all worked out: we'd go for half a year and I could do medicine while she did business models.'

Poppy propped herself on an elbow and thought about how he'd mentioned staying in the Pacific for a while after the tsunami. 'So you stayed and fulfilled her vision?'

He frowned and the sadness that had left him returned. 'I stayed because I couldn't leave. I tried to leave, believe me, but I just couldn't separate myself from the island because it meant I had to accept Lisa and Annie were gone. Initially, I was part of the relief effort and the frantic pace kept the real world at bay, but once the Red Cross realised who I was, they pulled me out of the field because, as the paperwork described it, I was one of the victims.' His chest heaved. 'God, I hate that word.'

'So don't use it.' She pressed her hand to his chest, wanting him to see himself in a new light. 'You're someone directly affected by the event and it changed the direction of your life irrevocably. It's not OK that it happened but it doesn't make you a victim.'

Matt traced a finger down Poppy's cheek, marvelling at her inherent strength. 'I like that reframing.'

'It's yours. What brought you back to Bundallagong?'

'Time, and Lisa's father eventually came over and said the town needed me back.'

'Did you want to come back?'

He shrugged. 'I had to do something and coming home was at least familiar. Same town, same job.'

'Same house.' She wrinkled her nose. 'I think it must be unbelievably hard to try and live the same life you were living two years ago but without Annie and Lisa. I don't think it's really helping, is it?'

Her words echoed harshly yet truthfully in his head. He thought of the town's tentativeness around him, of how the only place he'd ever felt close to normal was at work and how he now hated a house he'd once thought was the only place he'd ever want to live.

'Nothing I do will bring them back so it really doesn't matter what I do or where I live.'

A shot of white anger sparked in the depths of her eyes, shocking him. 'That's not true. You have choices, Matt. You don't have to try and live the life you had before they died but why not finish the chapter you were living in when the tsunami hit? Lisa had a vision that she can no longer achieve but you can make it happen in her name.'

Fury, powerlessness and panic skittered through him. 'I know nothing whatever about jewellery, Poppy!'

She sat up straight, her face both earnest and irritated. 'But you probably know people who do, and if you don't, you can find them. Who you actually know are the people in this town who loved and cared for

Lisa and Annie, so start there. Do some fundraising and create a foundation in their name so the work can be funded long into the future.'

A foundation? He tried to shrug off the thought, cross that Poppy was being her usual steamroller self, but it insisted on taking a tenuous hold. Why hadn't he thought of something like that? *Because the time wasn't right and you weren't ready for it.*

Was he ready now? The more he thought about it, the more the idea appealed. A foundation would do two special things—remember Lisa and help in a way she would have totally approved of.

And of all the people to think of this perfect idea, it had been Poppy, who hadn't even known Lisa. In a way it connected them and he found that oddly consoling. A tide of mixed emotions poured through him and when he spoke, his words came out roughly. 'Have you always been this damn bossy?'

She blinked and then a slow smile strolled across her cheeks before smouldering in her eyes. 'Yes. Bossy and in this case absolutely right.' She rummaged in her backpack. 'I'm sure I've got a pen and paper in here and you can start brainstorm—'

He shot his hand out to touch her arm. 'It's all about balance, remember. I can and I will do that later, on the long drive back. But right now we're on a day off and…' He pulled her into his arms, nuzzled his face against her neck and smiled as she relaxed against him. His blood hummed when he heard her delicious moan of consent.

'My dad does that to my mum.'

Poppy's eyes flew open in wild and shocked surprise as Matt's mouth trailed kisses along her collarbone while his hand caressed her left breast. She frantically leaned sideways to hide her partial nakedness and try and see who was talking. Matt almost toppled forward into the newly created space.

A little boy, who looked to be about five or six, stood in front of them, and she struggled to find a coherent reply as she pulled the shoulder strap of her bikini back into place. 'D-does he?'

The child gave a serious nod.

Matt, having righted himself, now squatted at eye level with the child, a smile on his face. 'Well, that's good to know because it means he loves your mum.'

Love? Panic and joy stalled Poppy's heart for a moment before common sense prevailed. Matt was merely explaining why he'd been more than just kissing her, in terms a child could understand.

'They close the bedroom door.'

'Obviously not always,' muttered Matt, throwing her a look that combined laughter with chagrin. 'I'm Matt. Who are you?'

'Lochie, and I five.'

'Five, hey? That's getting big. And where did you come from, Lochie?' He shielded his eyes with his hand and peered beyond the child and down the stony river bed, looking for people.

The little boy pointed behind him. 'There.'

Poppy, now decent, scrambled forward, wondering why this child was alone in the middle of nowhere. 'Where are Mummy and Daddy?'

'I runned here first.'

Matt's mind was obviously going to the same place as hers and he put his hand out to the little boy. 'How about we go back the way you came and meet them? Because even though you know where you are, Mum and Dad don't.'

Lochie shrugged. 'OK.'

Poppy grabbed their towels and stuffed them inside the backpack. 'I'll come, too.'

Matt nodded, his face full of concern. 'Good idea. There are two water holes in this area so I've got no clue which one his parents are heading for. The track, if you can actually call it that, divides. Best bet is to return to the car park and we either meet them on the way or we wait there until they come back to sound the alarm.'

She touched his arm. 'Am I missing something about an Outback childhood or is the fact he's separated from his parents really dangerous?'

'No, you're right, but not everyone realises the dangers in this place until it's too late.'

They started walking and Lochie immediately streaked out in front, which was obviously what had got him separated from his parents in the first place.

Poppy called out, 'Hey, Lochie, slow down,' but the little boy didn't alter his pace.

Matt sprinted up to him, catching him by the back of his T-shirt, and Poppy caught up to them just in time to hear Matt say, 'Want to play a game, mate?'

Lochie's eyes lit up. 'What is it?'

'You stand between Poppy and I, and hold our hands. We all walk together counting out loud, and something special happens on three.'

'OK.' The child's warm hand slid into Poppy's as Matt mouthed over his head, 'We swing on three.'

Poppy knew Matt the lover, Matt the grieving widower and the professional doctor, but this was the first time she'd seen the father in him. Deep down inside her an old, faded and discarded dream moved.

'Let's go.' Poppy started walking briskly to push

away the unsettling feelings. *Chief of Surgery is what you want and where you belong. You gave up the dream of motherhood a long time ago. Work is far more reliable than men.* 'One, two…' she gripped Lochie's hand firmly in her own to avoid any slipping '…three!' Her arm swung forward, as did Matt's, and Lochie's legs swung sky high.

As the child's feet touched the ground again, he gave a whoop of delight. 'Again.'

Poppy laughed at his joy and looked across at Matt, knowing he would have done this very thing with Lisa and Annie, and a combination of concern for him and envy for herself sat heavy in her gut.

His expression was a revelation. Instead of the raw pain she'd seen so often in his eyes, his dark gaze held warm delight with a glimmer of resigned sadness. Sadness she knew would understandably stay with him for ever in some shape and form when he remembered his beloved daughter. Seeing him in action with Lochie, she knew he'd been a wonderful father.

The dream shifted again, tugging hard, morphing into something tangible and real. *You, Matt, a child on a picnic out here.* It tempted her so much that it terrified her. This time she deafened it with a loud yell of 'One, two…*wheeeeee*!'

The sun was dropping low in the sky and the air temperature dropped with it. Matt jogged back from the second water hole track, now seriously worried. He could see Poppy in the distance, wrapping Lochie up in one of the towels to keep him warm. Where the hell were his parents?

Relief filled Poppy's eyes when she saw him. 'Are they on their way back?'

'I didn't find them.'

Her face blanched and he gave her arm a squeeze. 'It's time to contact the police.' He leaned into the truck and got onto the radio as he heard Lochie asking for food.

'What about a lucky dip?' Poppy sounded overly bright as she opened the top of her backpack. 'Stick your hand in there and see what you can find.'

Lochie looked sceptical but Matt smiled, knowing Poppy had a secret stash of food in that pocket of her backpack. She had a natural affinity with children, which had been another surprise to him. It shouldn't have been. He'd learned over the past weeks that once people got past the smoke and mirrors of her no-nonsense, crisp façade that she hid behind, they found a woman with a huge capacity to give.

'Chocolate!' Lochie held up the distinctive purple-foiled bar.

'Jack, it's Matt Albright. We're at Walker's Gorge with a five-year-old and his parents are missing. Vehicle has New South Wales plates. We've been back at the car park for well over an hour and I've walked the two tracks the little bloke said he'd been on but there's no sign of them.'

'Five-year-olds are not that reliable, Matt.' The experienced police officer took the registration number and went on to suggest he break into the vehicle for any clues.

Cursing central locking, he yelled to Poppy and Lochie. 'We need a big rock to break a window.'

'Now, that's not going to be hard to find.' Poppy took two steps, picked one up and threw it through the driver's side window.

'You're really bad!' Lochie threw himself at Poppy's

legs and she immediately bent down. 'Sweetie, I'm sorry but we need to see if Mummy or Daddy left a map or a plan of where they were going and they're not going to be cross, I promise.'

'I want Mummy.' The small boy's wail rent the air.

'I know you do, Lochie.' She gave him a quick hug and then opened the car door, carefully brushing away the shards of glass with a towel before looking for any identifying information.

Matt hung onto the radio, waiting for Jack. 'Have you found anything, Poppy?'

She held up a National Parks brochure. 'There's a map of the park and both water holes have been highlighted.'

'Matt.' Jack's voice crackled down the line. 'Car's registered to a Lance Wilkinson and we've just had a report that a personal location beacon's been activated in the area. Do you have a map?'

He leaned over and grabbed the laminated and detailed hiking map he always carried when he came out here. 'Got it.'

'Find your location. On the west side of the car park there's a rough side track that heads along the ridge. The GPS in the PLB is coming from there. You can get in by vehicle if you drive to Koonunga picnic ground.'

'How the hell did they end up there?' But it was a rhetorical question because to an inexperienced walker all scraggly gum trees and red rocks looked the same and taking the wrong direction was sadly far too easy. 'We're on it, Jack.'

He turned to call Poppy, only to find her sitting in the dirt by the other vehicle, cuddling a sobbing Lochie. Her right arm held him close and her left hand stroked his hair while the little boy clutched a well-loved soft toy bear she must have found for him in the car. Her dark hair rested against the boy's jet locks.

Mother and child. Poppy as a mother. The image stuck him hard in the solar plexus. He had to clear his throat before speaking. 'We've got co-ordinates, hop in.'

Half an hour later, after bouncing along a rocky escarpment no one in their right mind would call a road, and using their GPS, Jack's guidance and their eyes and ears, Matt stopped the truck for the fourth time and hopped out. Bringing his hands up to cup his mouth, he yelled, 'Cooee.'

Then he listened. He'd been straining to hear anything for so long that at first he thought the returning 'cooee' was his own voice.

'Did you hear that?' Poppy's face filled with hope.

He called again, and this time Lochie and Poppy joined in.

A male voice replied, 'Cooee. Help us.'

'We're on our way.' Matt grabbed the medical bag and was starting to walk in the direction of the voice when a bearded man, supporting a woman, stumbled into the clearing.

'Mummy, Daddy!' Lochie pulled out of Poppy's grasp and ran to them.

'Thank God, Lochie.' The woman sobbed out her child's name as she was lowered to the ground, gripping her left arm close to her chest.

Lance grabbed his son, hugging him close until Lochie wriggled and said, 'Daddy, it hurts.'

Poppy ran to the distraught woman, and Lance, on seeing Matt, gripped his shoulder. 'Thank you. Thank you for finding him, for finding us.'

Matt suggested Lance sit down. 'Actually, Lochie found us and your PLB is how we found you.'

Lance rubbed his head, relief clear in his eyes. 'One minute we could see him and the next he was gone. Then I lost our bearings searching for him because all this red rock looks the same.'

'I'm just glad you're safe.'

'Matt, I need the medical bag.' Poppy was crouched down next to the woman, who was pale and sweaty and had removed her shirt. 'Joanne fell on an outstretched arm and she's got a shoulder separation, but you've probably seen more of these than me.'

Matt introduced himself to the patient. 'I'm going to be as gentle as I can but this will probably hurt.'

Joanne flinched. 'It can't be worse than it already is, can it?'

Matt didn't want to promise anything. His fingers explored the top of the humerus and then followed the clavicle. A red tinge flushed the skin, indicating bleeding, and a distinctive bump marred the normally smooth line over the AC joint. 'I'm going to treat this with a cuff and collar sling and give you some strong painkillers to keep you comfortable on the long trip back to Bundallagong. We'll X-ray and ultrasound it when we arrive at the hospital and check for any other fractures, displacement, muscle and ligament damage. Does it hurt anywhere else?'

'Just our pride that we did something so ridiculously stupid.' Joanne leaned her head against Lance's shoulder as Lochie nestled between them. 'I'm never letting this child out of my sight again.'

'Good idea.'

Matt and Poppy spoke at the same time and he caught her vivid gaze full of intense feeling. For the briefest moment he experienced a moment of pure simpatico unlike anything he'd ever known.

Poppy pulled her theatre cap off her head and dropped it in the bin, wondering what on earth was going on in Bundallagong on this particular Thursday with two middle-of-the-night emergencies. She'd only just finished removing a lacerated spleen from a young man after a car accident when Matt's registrar, who was on night shift this week, had rushed up a guy with a bleeding gastric ulcer. It had been touch and go, with the patient bleeding so much that the blood bank was now in dire straits.

As she created a reminder on her phone to ring the radio station's breakfast show at seven to get the word out so Bundallagong residents would make a special effort to give blood today, she saw the time and sighed. 6:00 a.m. It was a really lousy time to finish as there was no point going home to sleep because she'd barely have got settled when she'd have to get up again. Yet she had ninety minutes to fill before she could do pre-surgical rounds. She thought of Matt; gorgeous and rumpled, sleeping spread-eagled across her bed. Even though she knew she wasn't going home right now, the fact he was there, in her bed, waiting for her, wound around her heart.

Careful. She gave herself a shake and walked quickly to her office.

She turned on her computer and brought up the email program as she did routinely every morning now, since Matt had pointedly said that bed was a work-free zone. She'd tried to argue that point but had deliciously lost, conceding defeat as he'd brought her to the brink of orgasm and then suggested he needed to stop right there to go and check his emails.

She'd even amazed herself by not sending William the surgical report this week. It had taken considerable strength of will and she'd almost capitulated, especially when her secretary had reminded her, but Matt's suggestion had been worth a try, given that everything else she'd tried hadn't made much difference in getting any response from her boss.

As thirty emails downloaded, the ping of her 'countdown' widget alerted her to the blinking number fourteen at the bottom of her screen. Ten weeks down and two weeks remaining in Bundallagong. Two weeks left with Matt.

The thought screamed through like a missile. *You'll miss him.*

'Ms Stanfield?'

She looked up distractedly, her brain stalled on how fast her time in Bundallagong had flown and how soon it would be over. One of the cleaners stood in the doorway of her office, and with wobbly legs she stood up and greeted him. 'Morning, Joe.'

He pulled a photo out of his overalls front pocket. 'My Louisa, she had the baby, and my son-in-law, he email me this.'

She'd been hearing about this long-awaited baby who'd been very slow to put in an appearance for ten days now, and as she stared down at the photo of a black-haired baby with fathomless eyes, her throat tightened. 'Congratulations, she's adorable.'

Joe beamed. 'Maria and I, we fly to Perth today to visit, but don't you worry. Franco will be looking after your office and I tell him to start your coffee at seven.'

A prickle of embarrassment made her feel uncomfortable. 'That's very kind, Joe, but, really, I can make my own coffee.'

The cleaner nodded as he put the photo back in his pocket. 'Yes, but if we look after you, perhaps you stay here in Bundallagong.'

Two and a half months ago Poppy would have scoffed at such a suggestion, but with every patient she'd treated, with every staff member she'd got to know and with every choir meeting, tiny roots had sprouted, connecting her to the community. She'd enjoyed her time here.

And if you don't get the job, would you stay?

The unexpected thought spun around her heart like the silky strands of a web, tying her to Bundallagong. Tying her to Matt.

A spasm hit, freezing her muscles, making it hard to breathe and hard to stand. Somehow she managed to smile, wish Joe a safe trip to Perth and sink back into her chair. She pushed her hands against her forehead and up into her hair.

No, no, no. You can't be that stupid.

Panic skittered through her, sending her reeling. Falling for Matt, a man who still loved his dead wife, would be beyond dumb—it would be her worst nightmare. She sucked at relationships at the best of times but there was no way she could compete with Lisa, who'd been perfect alive and was now immortalised as a saint.

Have you learned nothing from your disastrous relationships? Her guiding Amazon rose up to her full height and brandished her sword and shield. *Woman up!*

Poppy pulled up memories of her father and Steven—betrayal, hurt, rejection—each recollection shoring up her resolve, but every time she thought of Matt she could only picture him laughing with her, teasing her, talking, listening and wrapping his arms around her each night until she fell into a deep sleep.

You love him.

Oh, God, no.

No, not love, please, not love. She dropped her head into her hands as the thought branded her with its full impact. She loved him. Little by little, day by day, she'd fallen in love with him so slowly she hadn't even realised it.

How had she left herself so unprotected?

She knew better than this. She knew from bitter experience that love wasn't enough and never had been. Love left a girl open to hurt and heartache, and to being let down in the worst way. Nothing good could ever come from being in love, and exploring this bit of self-realisation was pointless.

No promises, no regrets, no past and no future.

Matt's words rose up in her mind. She'd made a complete mess of something that should have been fun and short term. Once again, she'd let herself fall in love with a man who wasn't able to love her. She was too foolish for words.

Biting her lip, she welcomed the jolt of physical pain and rolled back her shoulders, pushing the feelings down deep to languish with the other relationship mistakes in her life and the ashes of her ill-fated marriage.

She tuned into work like she always did, keeping all her emotions at bay, and ploughed through the list of mail, deleting, forwarding and replying as required, while she sipped coffee and listened to the cacophony of sound that came with the dawn. She smiled as the sky filled with pink and grey as the native parrots rose from their sleep—another Bundallagong ritual she'd come to enjoy.

As she hit Send on the last email, her phone beeped its reminder. 7:00 a.m. She silenced it and immediately heard a ping from her computer, heralding a new email.

William.

A chill ran through her as her gut rolled on a wave of acid. She put her phone down and her hand hovered over the mouse for a few seconds before she moved the cursor over his name and clicked.

CHAPTER TEN

MATT woke with a start and stretched out to feel for Poppy but his arm and hand only connected with cool sheets. A vague memory slowly formed and he recalled Poppy's phone ringing, her quietly murmured conversation, his grunted 'Do you need me?'

And her lips on his cheek as she'd said, 'Go back to sleep.'

But now he was awake and the green light of the bedside clock said 5:00 a.m. With a groan, he closed his eyes and as his head hit the pillow he gratefully accepted that at least it wasn't three. He hated 3:00 a.m., when there was still so much night left and no more ability to sleep. It became a long slog, waiting for the dawn, and so as not to disturb Poppy, he'd get up and go and pace the floors at his house.

His eyes shot open so abruptly that the muscles ached. He hadn't woken up at 3:00 a.m. all this week. *It's been longer than that.* He worked backwards and realised with a start that he couldn't recall an early wake-up since he'd told Poppy about Annie, and that had been three weeks ago.

With a contented sigh, he rolled over, tugging at the sheet, intending to grab one extra precious hour of sleep, but his brain, already jolted awake, buzzed with ideas for the foundation. He accepted defeat, got up, walked into the pre-dawn chill—the only time Bundallagong was cool—and let himself into his house.

The long hallway echoed as he walked towards the kitchen and the house smelled musty, like it needed a good airing. He filled the kettle and then picked up the folder marked 'Lisa's Way', which he'd left on the table next to his laptop two nights ago. Grabbing a pen, he quickly scrawled down the name of Lisa's bead supplier that had been eluding him, along with some ideas to run past Sarah for a fundraising night at the neighbourhood centre. That done, he made coffee and set the plunger to rest on the top of the carafe while it brewed, and then opened the fridge for the milk.

A malodorous scent greeted him, the milk having become yoghurt and a lone lettuce now a ball of slime. He hastily dumped both in the bin and searched the pantry all the way to the back for some long-life milk. There was none. How could that be? He knew he was a poor shopper, but UHT milk was a staple that even in his darkest days he'd always had.

You're virtually living with Poppy.

The thought rocked him. He poured sugar into his coffee, stirring it fast as he grappled with his thoughts. Running back over the events of the last few weeks, the truth stared him in the face. He'd hardly been here. The reality was that he'd only been using his place to shower, change clothes, do laundry, and when Poppy was held up at work he'd come back here to do some foundation work.

Not even then.

He sat down hard in a chair as his legs trembled. Last week he'd spent an evening at her place working on Lisa's Way while Poppy had been at choir practice because being over there was so much more pleasant than being here.

He heard the dawn thumping of Rupert but instead of being much-needed noise, he suddenly saw in his mind's eye the damage the reptile was likely inflicting on the roof. He looked around the room as if seeing it with new eyes, and for the first time the house didn't seem to be mocking him with its silence or its memories. He stood up and slowly walked the length and breadth of the house. Starting by opening the door to Annie's room, he systematically visited every other room in the house until he stood in the stripped-bare master bedroom. A room he'd avoided with the exception of the night Poppy had arrived.

He girded himself for the expected onslaught of pain, sadness and grief, the way it had been when he'd first arrived home from the Pacific, and the reason he'd moved to the guest room. But the house no longer spoke to him about loss—it didn't really speak to him at all.

Lisa and Annie were no longer part of the house.

The news should have broken his heart but instead it soothed it and an odd peace settled over him. His love for Lisa now resided in the creation of the foundation and his love for Annie poured into his work whenever he had scared and sick kids in the ED.

He ran his hand through his hair. He was no longer part of the house, either.

It's time.

He blew out a long breath laden with relief. He'd loved his wife and daughter dearly but now the time had come for him to move on with his life. Shoving his hands in his pockets, he glanced out the window at the house he'd come to think of as Poppy's place, despite the fact many people had lived in the house over the years.

Poppy.

Her lips matched her name and she was a bright spark of colour in what had been a very black time of his life. God, he enjoyed being with her. She made him laugh, she challenged him and at times frustrated the hell out of him, but she was the first person he thought of when he woke up in the morning and the last person he thought of when he closed his eyes at night.

That's love.

His chest tightened on his sharp intake of breath and he gripped the architrave. *Love.* The spasm faded, followed by a wave of warmth and the tendrils of belonging.

It *was* love.

He loved her.

He started to grin like a fool, his cheeks aching with happiness. She'd stormed into his life all attitude and vibrant energy and turned his grieving world upside down. Somewhere along the way he'd moved into her house and she'd moved into his heart. Now he couldn't imagine his life without her.

With a plan forming in his mind, he stepped out of the house and gently closed the door behind him.

Poppy stepped out of the theatre change rooms into the main hospital corridor and suddenly found herself being twirled around, pulled into strong arms and kissed so soundly her legs gave way.

Matt's sparkling brown eyes stared down at her as his fingers caressed her cheek. 'Hello.'

'Hel—' Her mouth stalled as her brain received the

image from her eyes. Her hands flew to his hair, her fingers unaccountably aching as they tried unsuccessfully to lose themselves in the now short strands 'Oh. Your hair, it's…' She finally found her voice. 'You've had it cut.'

He grinned. 'I have. It was time.'

She'd always loved the way his hair reached his jawline, reminding her of a pirate. 'Why?'

But instead of replying, he just gave her a secret smile and pulled her into the on-call room and locked the door. A small white-cloth-covered table held a platter of freshly made sandwiches along with two bottles of fruit juice and a plate of what looked like peppermint slice. 'Lunch for two, courtesy of the kitchen.'

She smiled and kissed him, reminding herself of her plan to treasure every last moment with him. 'Lovely idea. I'm starving.' She greedily picked up a sandwich and started eating. 'Hmm, this is so good. Why haven't we done this before?'

'I guess we didn't have a reason to celebrate before.'

Her hand fell from her mouth and she stared at him in surprise. How did he know William had offered her the post of Chief of Surgery at Perth City? She hadn't told anyone. She'd read the email five times and had waited for the rush of joy that she'd finally got the job of her dreams, the one she'd been working towards for years. But instead of a rush it had been more of a slow trickle, as if she couldn't really believe she'd finally nailed it. But she had. The job was hers and the end-point to her time in Bundallagong had arrived, as she'd always known it would. What hadn't arrived was the excitement she'd expected to experience on leaving the dust-filled town.

Matt stood in front her, his face full of warmth,

friendship and pleasure for her, and the fact she'd achieved her long-held dream. Nothing about him showed that he was in any way sad about her leaving.

Why would you expect that? He still loves Lisa.

No promises, no regrets, no past and no future, remember?

But given all that, he'd thought to organise this lunch so they could celebrate now rather than waiting until the end of the day. No one had ever done anything like that for her before and she swallowed around the lump in her throat.

'Thank you.' She threw her arms around his neck with such enthusiasm that he staggered backwards, falling onto the bed. She lay against him and kissed him the way she knew made his head spin and his body hard.

He rolled her over. 'Had I known you were this easy to impress, I'd have done lunch a long time ago.' He stroked her hair. 'Marry me.'

Her gut went into freefall and she sat up fast, not able to believe what she thought she'd just heard. 'I beg your pardon?'

He sat up too, gently cupping her cheeks with his hands. 'Marry me.'

He knows about the job, he told you weeks ago you'd be great at it, and he still wants to marry you. Say yes.

But the question was so unexpected that she searched his face, his eyes, even the line of his mouth for clues. Although everything seemed familiar, *nothing* was the same. A tremor of panic scuttled through her, mirroring her feelings early that morning when she'd realised she loved him. 'Are you sure you really want to marry me?'

'I do. I love you. I was floundering but you've changed everything and brought me back into the world. With you there's light.' His sincerity wrapped around her. 'I want to live with you until we're old and grey, and running around after ten grandchildren.'

Grandchildren. The aching longing that had been part of her since their day at the gorge surged and she let her head fall onto his shoulder, feeling the security of his breadth and the protection of his arms. *I love you.* The marvel of his words wove through her, tempting her with a promise of an amazing future. 'You see us with children?'

He kissed her hair. 'Why sound so surprised? You're great with kids and you'll be a sensational mother.'

She let the dream float over her and dared herself to believe. This wonderful man loved her and wanted to be the father of her children. *This time love and marriage will be different.* Her heart expanded, bursting open the self-imposed lock she'd chained to it years ago. 'We *will* be great parents.'

His lips touched hers with an almost reverent kiss, the touch imbued with a promise of things to come. 'Children are amazing and they change your life. I can picture a house, a garden, a deck, a pool. *Our* home.'

She could see it too and her hand pressed against his chest, feeling the beat of his heart. 'Somewhere by the river.'

His fingers played in her hair. 'I think you mean the beach.'

'No, I don't want to live in Fremantle because it's too far from the hospital. I suppose we could look at Cottlesloe if you think you'll miss the sea too much, but you might be surprised—the river's really pretty.' Still talking, she hugged him hard, excitement finally hitting her, bubbling through her like the bubbles of champagne. She had it all. It really was possible to have a man who loved her, a top job and in the future a family of her own.

'I wanted to tell you in person but somehow you found out and then you did this special and amazing thing for me and—' She stopped babbling, realising he'd gone completely still and was staring at her intently.

'What are you talking about?'

She joke-punched him on the arm. 'Don't be such a tease. You know exactly what I'm talking about.'

Confusion lay heavily on his cheeks and he shook his head slowly.

'But the celebration lunch...' And she realised the lunch wasn't connected with her new job at all but with his proposal. He didn't know her news. She grinned, loving how much pleasure it gave her to be the one to tell him as she'd originally planned. 'You're not only looking at your fiancée, you're also looking at Perth City's new Chief of Surgery.'

She opened her arms, expecting congratulations and an enormous embrace, but he just stared at her, his expression both stunned and surprised.

'You got the job?'

His words came out quietly without any acknowledgment of her massive achievement. The young Poppy who'd always strived yet failed to impress her father stirred deep inside her, sending out an aching ripple. 'William emailed me early this morning and followed up with a phone call. The board has been really impressed by the work I've done, especially with the way I had the full support of the staff.'

She reached out her hand, needing to touch him, needing to see some sign from him that he was happy for her. 'I couldn't have done it without your advice and support.'

Finally he smiled and hugged her tightly before kissing her gently on the cheek. 'Congratulations, I'm so proud of you.'

She breathed again, not realising she'd stopped.

His warm and loving gaze turned serious. 'But now we're engaged, are you certain this is the job you want?'

Every muscle in her body clenched. 'It's been everything I've worked towards for the last ten years.'

'Absolutely.' He nodded, his expression sincere. 'But things have just changed, haven't they? It's best if we live, work and raise our family here in Bundallagong.'

Steven's voice rose up like a spectre from the past, taunting her with pain and bitter memories. *Poppy, we're living at my place. It's really not up for discussion.*

When Annie arrived, Lisa and I moved back here.

Her heart quivered and her voice sounded overly bright. 'So we just relocate and do it all in Perth instead.'

He frowned. 'We move to Perth and you take the job?'

'Of course I take the job.' She smiled. 'Ten years, remember? All that hard work and now this is the reward. It's incredibly prestigious.'

He sighed, a long, low, ominous sound. 'In Bundallagong your surgical hours are almost workable, but how on earth are you going to balance family life with being Chief of Surgery?'

You're never home and I only asked you to do one thing—to collect my dry-cleaning and you couldn't even manage to do that.

It made you finish work a bit earlier.

Nobody has ever loved you without wanting to change you. First your father, then Steven and now Matt. A surge of anger obliterated her sob. She should have realised, she should have known this was all too good to be true. She should have recognised the massive signs from their conversation at Walker's Gorge.

She crossed her arms to stop herself from shaking. 'Worried you're going to have to learn how to shop and cook, are you?'

His jaw tightened. 'Believe me, cooking and shopping are the least of my concerns.'

Fool, fool, fool! He's no different. 'Oh, and let me guess what those concerns might be. You hate it that I won't be home every night before you, that I'll earn more than you, and that I'm not going to be barefoot and pregnant when you come home from a hard day at work.'

He threw up his hands. 'Now you're just being ridiculous.'

For heaven's sake, Poppy, you're my wife so act like one. Steven's voice faded as Matt's moved over it.

Lisa's choices made my life a lot easier. She remembered so clearly Matt saying that out at the water hole.

Her world tilted sideways, tipping out the fantasy of marriage and a family that she'd foolishly allowed herself to believe in for a few deluded moments. She so wanted to trust that he loved her for who she was but, like her father and Steven, he could only love her if she changed for him. If she gave up everything for him. Her chest tightened so much she could barely breathe as the past choked her.

Matt didn't really love her, he just thought he did. He only wanted a replacement for Lisa. His love, just like that of the men before him, came with conditions that would destroy them both. She stood up, moving away from him, and forced herself to do what she should have done the moment he'd proposed.

'I can't marry you, Matt. I can't make your life easier by being a stay-at-home wife. I can't be Lisa's replacement and live in the same house and help you live the life you had with her.'

Poppy's words plunged into Matt's heart like a knife, leaving him completely bewildered. 'God, Poppy, this has *nothing* to do with Lisa.' But he could tell by the look on her face she didn't believe him.

He tried to explain it. 'Lisa *chose* to stay at home and I supported her in doing that. I'm not asking you to give up working—of course you need to work. I want you to work. All I'm asking is that we live and work *here* so we can protect what we have.'

The starchy Poppy he hadn't seen in weeks materialised, her voice sharp and brisk. 'What we *have* is a short-term affair with an end date. We've been in this sensual bubble where it's just been us and the sex, but that isn't real life.' Her hand touched her pendant. 'Today real life intruded and already it's tearing us apart and it's only going to get worse.'

'It doesn't have to.' He walked towards her, wanting to touch her, wanting to remind her that what they had was worth saving. 'I'd consider moving to Perth if you took another job there. Look, if we compromise, we can make this work.'

Her eyes flashed. 'Not when one of us wants something at the expense of the other.'

'I'm not stopping you being a surgeon!' Trying to rein in his frustration, he ploughed his hand through his hair, only to discover with a shock just how unsatisfying it was with short hair. 'Give me some credit here, Poppy. I know how much time it takes to make a relationship work and if you become Chief of Surgery, you'll disappear into that job and it will kill us.'

She shook her head, her lips compressed into a thin line. 'Obviously I can't be married to you and be the surgeon I want to be.'

His heart slammed against his ribcage and slithered down, a bleeding, battered mess. 'You really believe that? You're going to walk away from this amazing thing we share for a job?'

'A job?' Her eyes glittered with a collage of emotions that swirled together with no defined edges. 'You really don't get it at all.'

Anger born of desperate hurt spewed bile. 'Oh, I get it. I get it loud and clear. My God, I thought you'd grown while you were here. I thought you'd worked out what was important in life, that it was people and relationships and love that counted, not pushing yourself to win at any cost. You're putting this job ahead of everything else. You really don't have a clue, do you?'

She tilted her chin up, her eyes flashing and her shoulders sharp, reminding him of the very first time he'd met her. 'I have more of a clue than you do, Matt. This conversation is just the start of what will happen to us if we get married, and the arguments will only get worse until we're tearing each other apart and wondering why the hell we once thought we loved each other. I'm doing this for us.'

'That's total garbage, Poppy. You're doing it for yourself and I only hope being Chief of Surgery keeps you warm at night.'

She flinched. 'I think we're done now. Goodbye, Matt.'

The door slammed behind her, shattering his hopes and dreams and leaving him devastated and alone.

CHAPTER ELEVEN

'MAIL for you, Ms Stanfield.'

Poppy glanced up from her spreadsheet to see the Perth City internal postwoman holding out a sheaf of mail. 'Thanks, Leanne. By the way, how did that biology assignment go?'

Surprise raced across the young woman's face before she smiled shyly. 'Wow, I can't believe you remembered that I was doing the course. I got an A.'

Poppy smiled as she picked up her outbound mail from the tray. 'Of course I remembered. It sounds like you're well on the way to getting the mark you need to get into nursing.'

'Hope so.' Leanne took the proffered mail. 'See ya, Ms Stanfield.'

'Bye, Leanne.'

As she walked out, William walked in, clutching a manila folder. 'First-name terms with the clerks, Poppy?' His brows rose. 'What the hell happened to you in that godforsaken place?'

'And hello to you too, William.' She pasted a smile on her face for her acerbic boss. 'Perhaps you should visit Bundallagong one day.'

He either missed or ignored the jibe. 'Harrumph. Far too busy for that and so are you.'

He wasn't wrong. She'd thought her first two weeks in Bundallagong had been long and arduous but they'd been almost relaxed in comparison to her start at Perth City. Not that she minded working hard, she didn't, which given her current circumstances was a good thing. But unlike in the past, when work had excited her, now a lot of it seemed like a chore.

When she'd first arrived back in Perth she hadn't cared how busy she was because work had filled her brain to capacity, leaving no space to think about Bundallagong, Matt and heartache. But just recently, when most nights she was only home for barely enough time to sleep, she'd started to think William's expectations of his department heads might be excessive. For the first time in her life she was pining to sit on her couch and just 'be'. Yesterday afternoon she'd even found herself wondering who she knew in Perth who might want to catch up for a drink and a chat, and much to her surprise she'd checked the notice-board for any posters about product parties. *You're lonely.*

William dropped the file on her desk. 'Applications for the surgical registrars and consultant operating rights. You also have to pick someone to go to Bundallagong next month. Interviews start at seven on Thursday evening. Happy reading.'

She stifled a groan. She'd been determined to have one night at home reading this week but job applications didn't count. 'I can't do Thursday.'

He fired her one of his penetrating looks. 'You *are* full of surprises today. I thought your life was the hospital but don't tell me you actually have a private life?'

She bristled, even though he was pretty much correct. 'I've organised a movie night fundraiser in the hospital auditorium for that night. I can interview earlier in the day.'

'Oh, yes, I think I saw a poster about that—something to do with women in Samoa? Can't you just do your speech at the start and then leave?'

Somehow she held onto her temper. 'No, William, I can't. I need to be there, sell raffle tickets, answer questions and thank people for their support.'

He nodded slowly, as if absorbing the news. 'I'll get my secretary to contact you with the new interview date but, Poppy, next time you act out of character, let me know.'

Quietly seething, she watched his retreating back and pictured daggers. Just because she wanted to have *one* night off, it didn't mean she'd changed.

You never got involved in anything out of work before Bundallagong.

True, but just because she was raising money for a worthy cause, it didn't mean she'd changed. *Lisa's Way is not just any worthy cause, though, is it? You're doing it to feel close to Matt.*

Blocking the perceptive voice in her head and throwing off her William-induced ill humour, she started flicking through her mail and her hand stalled on a small square box. She sliced open the tape with her letter knife and drew out a CD and a card written in Sarah's bold script.

Hi! Wanted you to have the first copy of the choir's CD, recorded at the concert! Sorry it's taken this long to get it into the mail! Choir's going great and Jen's conducting. Justin and I in

Perth 8th-9th for a childless weekend, but can't have sex all the time ;-) so can you do Sunday brunch?

Poppy laughed as she read the words, able to hear Sarah's voice in her head, and a fizz of anticipation bubbled inside her at the thought of seeing her. They'd shared some laughs at choir, the pub and at their respective houses and it would be wonderful to kick back over a leisurely brunch and hear all the Bundallagong news.

Matt sold his house and is in Samoa doing work for Lisa's Way. Still no replacement surgeon here and we miss your bossy but motivating ways.

A leaden feeling settled in her belly, overriding the excitement. She hadn't done anything fun since she'd got back to Perth. With shocked surprise, she realised exactly how much she missed Sarah and Jen's company.

You miss Matt.

You know you miss Matt. Every. Single. Day.

A fresh wave of pain washed through her. *Call him.*

The idea had her reaching for the phone but as her fingers started dialling she dropped the handset back into the cradle like it was on fire. Exactly what was she going to say? 'I miss you.' But then what? Nothing had altered; the impasse still stood. At least this time she'd found out before getting married that the man she loved wanted to change her.

So why are you so miserable?

Distracting herself, she shoved the choir's CD into her computer and while it loaded she read the last bit of the note.

Hope Perth is worth it. Sarah xx

She pushed the note aside and then pulled it back, her gaze fixated on five words. *Hope Perth is worth it.*

Deep in the recesses of her mind a small voice asked a question. *Are you sure this job is what you want?* The question scared her witless and she stomped on it hard and fast. *Of course it's what I want. I can depend on it.*

OK, if you think so. But the reply didn't sound all that convincing.

The CD finally started playing and her throat tightened as the choir's voices filled the air. She closed her eyes and Bundallagong moved into the office. She could smell the dust and the salt, see the smiling faces of her staff, visualise the old choir hall and feel the camaraderie of the women. She heard the pride in their voices and she knew how much more than just music the choir meant to its members; how much it had come to mean to her. An aching lethargy came over her, dragging at every muscle like flu. She ached for the connection she'd shared with the women.

You ache for Matt.

And she couldn't deny it. She pictured him lying in her bed with his arms around her, sitting at the kitchen bench, listening to her talk about her day and offering advice, and laughing as they swung Lochie between them.

But he wanted you to give up something that was vitally important to you. She bit her lips to stop tears spilling. She loved him but, like her father and Steven, he just didn't love her enough.

Get fresh air and coffee. Coffee will help. She pushed back her chair and left her office, walking across the road to the park and the coffee vendor. Families sat under trees, having picnics, and children on school holidays charged around kicking footballs.

She joined the queue, enjoying the sunshine on her skin after too many weeks of being inside. *You saw more of the outside world in Bundallagong.*

Yeah, red-dust dirt.

Walker's Gorge was red dust and dirt but it had a rugged beauty.

'Poppy, good to see you.'

With a start she pulled her attention away from memories of Bundallagong to the present, and the outstretched hand in front of her. 'Oh, Alistair, you're still in Perth?'

She'd met Alistair Roland once, soon after she'd returned, and she'd assumed he'd gone back east. 'Sorry, obviously you're here and not in Sydney.'

He laughed. 'We moved to Perth lock, stock and barrel five months ago. So, how's the new job and workaholic William treating you?'

She scanned his face, looking for signs of resentment that she'd got the job over him, but all she could see was genuine interest. She thought about the punishing hours. 'You know, like any new job, it takes a while to get a handle on it.'

'The surgery's the easy bit, right?'

She blinked at his insight and relaxed. 'I have days I want to hide in Theatre and not come out in case there's another manila folder on my desk.'

He nodded in understanding. 'You're lucky you're single.'

Irritation and sadness buffeted her. 'Why do you say that?'

A boy ran over. Alistair stretched out his arm and the boy snuggled in against him. 'Hey, Dad, can I have a strawberry smoothie?'

'Sure.'

'Thanks.' The boy tore off again.

Alistair shook his head, his expression full of affection. 'That streak was Jake and…' he pointed to another boy chasing a football '…that's Lucas. My wife Deanna is reading under the tree. They came down to meet me for lunch because I had a cancellation, and that's the beauty of Perth over Sydney. Lifestyle.'

'Exactly.' This was what she and Matt could have had if he'd been prepared to leave Bundallagong. 'It's just what I was trying to explain to someone not that long ago and it's great you've been doing this sort of thing since you arrived.'

A light frown creased his forehead. 'The whole time I was working for William, I hardly saw the boys.'

'Oh, why was that?'

'Seriously? You're working for William as Chief of Surgery and you're asking me that? How many evenings have you been home since you became Chief?'

None.

But that's because I want to be busy.

Not totally.

Alistair nodded, taking her silence as an answer. 'Which is why that job defeated the point of us moving here. Deanna's amazing but she didn't marry me to become a sole parent and that's what was happening. I want to be involved in my kids' lives.' Passion and love shone on his face. 'The stress of trying to do the job and be a dad and a husband, well, it was crazy stuff so

I pulled out of the running. Only a single surgeon can do that job.'

She stared at him, stunned. 'Wasn't it hard to walk away from the sort of job you spent your entire career aiming for?'

He gave a wry smile. 'You know, I really thought it would be, but at the end of the day I realised you can't have the one hundred per cent best career and a real family. So I'm not Chief but I get to see my kids most evenings. It's all about balance.'

If we go to Perth you'll disappear into that job and it will kill us.

Her gut rolled with nausea and she almost gagged. Alistair Roland with a supportive stay-at-home wife had walked away from the top job to protect his family.

'Poppy, are you OK?' Alistair looked concerned.

She tried to rally as her head swirled with thoughts and she managed a sort-of smile. 'Nothing a coffee won't fix. So what are you doing job-wise now?'

He moved up with the queue. 'It's been a huge step but I've gone into private practice and it's giving me the flexibility with the boys I could never have as Chief of Surgery. Being a parent is one big juggling act and I guess it's always going to be a work-in-progress but Southgate's given me operating rights and I'm really hoping you'll approve my application for City.'

Somehow she managed to nod, give her assurances that she would support his application and then finished the conversation with a promise of meeting his wife at a later date. Somehow her legs carried her back across the park to the reflection room at the hospital. In the cool quiet of the sanctuary, her heart thundered loudly and her stomach sizzled with acid that spilled into her throat.

Give me some credit, Poppy. I know how much time it takes to make a relationship work.

But she hadn't, she hadn't given Matt any credit at all. She'd seen his love and care for them as a couple as a direct attack on herself, and had lumped him in with her father and Steven. But Matt was nothing like them. He hadn't been trying to change her. Not wanting her to take this job hadn't been lack of support at all. He'd been trying to create the opportunity so they could try and have it all—love, marriage, career and a family. And she'd let her past control her and had completely messed it up.

Her head fell into her hands as everything she'd thought she believed in came crashing down around her. She'd risen to the top of her career ladder in the job of her dreams and she had absolutely nothing else. Five months ago it wouldn't have mattered that work was all she had, but William was right. She'd changed. Bundallagong had changed her. Matt had changed her. Being Chief of Surgery was no longer enough.

She wanted more.

She wanted Matt.

She'd put her trust in the wrong basket and made the most horrendous mistake of her life. She'd been so deluded, so busy playing the blame game, but it was all her own fault she was alone and miserable—she'd brought it on herself.

So stop whining and do something about it.

For the first time ever, her father's words actually helped.

She pulled out her phone and hesitated. She might be risking everything for nothing.

Just do it. Deal with any regrets later.

* * *

Matt sat contemplatively in the airport lounge at Perth airport. His flight from Apia had been late, making him miss his connection to Bundallagong, and now his only option was to sit out the two hours until the next flight. He texted the new flight details to Sarah, who was now on the Lisa's Way board, explaining his delay, and then let out a long sigh. The funny thing about travel was that the moment the date for returning arrived, the brain raced ahead and took up residence at home while the body still had to undertake the journey.

Home. He shifted in his chair. He didn't actually have one.

He'd sold the Bundallagong house fully furnished, as he'd planned to do before he'd proposed to Poppy, and had stowed a few boxes in storage before heading to Samoa to set up Lisa's Way. Two months later, with a fantastic young woman on the ground in the village, and the connections in Australia all set up it was time to go back to Bundallagong or even think of working somewhere else.

Perhaps he'd look at the jobs online while he was waiting but first he'd finish up his Lisa's Way financial report. Using the wireless internet in the lounge, he checked the foundation's bank balance and saw with pleasant surprise a new and sizeable deposit. He read the transfer note. Stanfield PCFR.

Poppy.

Stunned to see her name, he stared at the cryptic PCFR, trying hard to work out what the other four letters meant. His brain finally clicked in. Perth City Fund Raiser.

His heart beat faster. He couldn't believe that despite everything, despite how much she'd hurt him and the harsh way they'd parted, Poppy had organised a fundraiser.

Did it mean anything?

His wounded heart said, *No. Don't even go there.*

He ordered a coffee and a Danish pastry then turned his attention back to the financial statement and the rows of figures.

'Here's your coffee.'

Thinking that being in Perth was really doing his head in because the voice sounded just like Poppy's, he looked up abruptly. Ice and heat tore through him as his gaze met those unforgettable vivid blue eyes.

'Hello, Matt.'

She handed him a coffee and he noticed she held a cup, too. A thousand thoughts sprinted though his head but his anger won, coming out as sarcasm. 'It's a Wednesday morning. I would have thought you'd be at work.'

She shuddered slightly and he watched the movement roll down her body. *Irreconcilable differences.* He didn't regret for a moment that he'd just highlighted the reason they'd parted so acrimoniously. If she thought she could just sit down and 'chat' like old friends, she was wrong. Very wrong.

He caught sight of a familiar red suitcase and things fell into place. 'Ah, it's conference season.'

'Here's your pastry, sir. Sorry for the delay.' The smiling attendant put down a plate and looked at Poppy. 'I brought you one as well as a thank-you for helping me out back there with the coffee disaster.'

Poppy smiled warmly. 'No problem.'

As the attendant walked away, Poppy turned back to Matt, her hand creeping towards the silver P. Half of him wanted to pull her hard against him but the other half demanded he stay cool and aloof so that there was no danger of his heart ever being battered by her again.

'Can I sit down?'

He shrugged. 'Suit yourself.'

She sank onto the couch and crossed her long legs. 'Sarah said you've been in Samoa.'

Her perfume enveloped him, threatening to take him back to a time when he'd thought they'd be together for ever. He fought the memory by flicking the collar on his shirt. 'Two months. I'm on my way back to Bundallagong.'

'How's Lisa's Way going?'

He sighed. 'Poppy, do you really want to make polite chitchat?'

She rolled her lips inwards. 'I'm enquiring about it because I'm a contributor and a friend.'

'You're a *contributor*.'

She flinched at the harshness in his voice but he didn't care. Did she really think she could sit there next to him in her tailored black suit and pretend they hadn't shared anything? Did she think he'd overlook the fact that she'd put a job ahead of everything? A job she'd left him for?

The black heart of his pain spluttered.

She gave a grim smile. 'Matt, I don't—'

He held up a hand. 'I don't want to argue, either. I don't think I even want to talk to you. I'm not going to ask you how the job's going because I'm not interested.'

She breathed in, seeming to hold her breath. 'I've quit.'

Shock made him gape. 'You've what?'

'I've quit and I have a new job.'

His gaze returned to her red suitcase and he immediately recalled the prestigious job he'd seen advertised soon after she'd left. It carried more kudos than the job she had, and Poppy didn't like to lose. He couldn't keep the bitterness out of his voice. 'Ah. St Stephen's in Sydney. Of course, that makes total sense.' He couldn't bring himself to offer congratulations.

'Ah, no, not St Stephen's.' She twisted her hands in her lap in an unusual display of unease. 'The last decision I made as Chief of Surgery was to appoint a permanent surgeon to meet the needs of the growing population of Bundallagong. I have firsthand experience of how much one is needed.'

Every word she spoke reminded him of what they'd lost and he struggled to sound enthusiastic. 'Well, that's good news for the town. Who is it?'

'I'm the new surgeon in Bundallagong.'

Her words slammed into him and a glimmer of hope sprouted in a sea of pain, but the memory of how much she'd hurt him made it struggle.

Poppy watched Matt, knowing this was the moment of truth, and it petrified her. Everything about him, from the strands of his long hair to the tips of toes shod in leather boat shoes, emanated anger. Had she really been so naive as to think he'd welcome her with open arms?

You hurt him so much. From the moment she'd got Sarah's text telling her Matt was in the airport lounge, and from the second she'd seen him, she'd wanted to throw her arms around his neck and tell him what a fool she'd been and beg for his forgiveness. But she had to do it this way and now she was dying inside, waiting for him to speak.

He sat perfectly still, his body almost as rigid as a statue, and the only movement was the complex map of emotions on his face, with hurt shining the brightest. When he finally spoke his voice sounded strained. 'Why?'

She swallowed hard, knowing this conversation was never going to be easy, and tried a touch of levity. 'Because Bundallagong needs a kick-ass surgeon.'

Not even a hint of a smile hovered on his lips but his eyes sought hers. 'Is there another reason?'

This time she went for honesty. 'Yes. I love you.'

A flicker of something flared in his eyes and faded. 'You once said you loved me but you left me, putting a job ahead of us.'

She swallowed against the lump in her throat. 'I know and I'm sorry. I got it all horribly wrong.'

'Yeah, you did.'

His ice-cool voice made her heart hammer hard against her ribs, and she could hear the tremble in her voice but she knew she was fighting for the most important 'job' of her life. 'I was scared. I thought you were trying to make me a different person, just like my father and Steven, trying to make me more like Lisa, and my fear got in the way. I let it screw everything up.' Her hands twisted together. 'I now know you weren't trying to change me. You were making sure we'd make it by creating a wonderful life for us. You saw what I couldn't see, that being Chief of Surgery would consume me and destroy us.'

His expression gave nothing away. 'And yet you didn't believe me. Exactly when did you work this out?'

His quiet but drilling words made her sweat and she pressed her damp palms against her black skirt. Everything she held dear rode on her explanation. 'I missed you every day like a part of me had been lost.'

His jaw tensed. 'I find that hard to believe. You didn't even call.'

The accusation stung but she wore the pain like a badge. 'I know. I've made a mess of everything. When I first came back to Perth I thought I was returning to my life, slipping back into a familiar and secure groove. But it didn't feel right, and it isn't a life I want any more.'

She gulped in a breath and pushed on, exposing her heart like she'd never exposed it before. 'I came to Bundallagong thinking it was a waste of my time, but without me realising, it changed my life. *You* changed my life. I'd always believed that work kept me safe and gave me everything I needed but then I met you. You opened up my world, showed me that life is to be lived, not hidden from. No job, no matter how much I sacrificed to get it, is worth it if I lose you.'

He swallowed hard and his voice wavered. 'The Poppy I met when she first arrived in Bundallagong would never have admitted she was wrong but I need to ask you one thing. Are you absolutely certain this is what you want?'

She nodded. 'It's what I want most in the world. I want to be a surgeon, not an administrator. I want time with friends and girls' nights out. I want a family, but most of all I want you.'

Extending her hand, she let it hover between them. Trying to hold back tears, she sent up the wish of her life. 'I know I need to prove to you that I've changed, and I know at times I can be difficult and that I'm nothing like Lisa, but I need to ask you one thing. Do you want me?'

Matt's fingers bypassed her hand and cupped her cheek. 'Lisa was the love of my boyhood and what we shared will always be part of me but, Poppy, *you're* the love of my manhood. You're my future.'

She fell apart, tears streaming down her face. He pulled her into his arms, burying his face in her hair. 'I want you because you're you. Passionate, giving and full of wonderful flaws, just like me.'

She sniffed. 'I can be stubborn with workaholic tendencies but I'm working on that. I'm going to block out non-work time in the week and stick to it, plus having a new surgical registrar is going to help.'

Surprise lit his face and he grinned. 'The last chief of surgery at Perth City *was* very proactive for Bundallagong.'

She laughed. 'Someone has to look out for rural communities.'

He stroked her hair. 'I hate shopping and housework and I can't cook, but I'll pay Lizzie to keep the freezer full of healthy meals and I'll grill on the weekends.'

She snuggled in against him, pressing her hand against his heart. 'Who's cleaning the house?'

'Mrs Ferguson.'

'I can live with that.'

'And I can't wait to live with you.' He smiled, his face radiating love. 'So you'll want a year in the job before we start a family?'

Her heart swelled with so much love and adoration that it almost burst. He'd always known work was important to her and he still did, and she couldn't believe how she'd almost lost him. 'You're forgetting I've already had three months in the position and with an experienced registrar starting next week I think he'll be able to fly solo in about nine months.'

The delight on his face mirrored her own. 'I can't wait to start practising.'

'Will you marry me, Matt Albright?'

'I most certainly will, Poppy Stanfield.'

She grinned and ran her fingers through his hair. 'How do you feel about keeping this longer?'

His eyes took on a familiar smoky hue that made her weak with longing. 'Ms Stanfield, do you have a thing for guys with long hair?'

'No, just for you.'

He cupped her face and kissed her long and hard, his lips infusing her with his love, support, caring and passion.

'Passengers on Flight 273 to Bundallagong, your flight is boarding now. Please make your way to gate seventeen.'

Matt stood up and extended his hand. 'Let's go home.'

Home.

To the red dust of Bundallagong with the man she loved. She couldn't wait.

* * * * *

THE DOCTOR'S REASON TO STAY

BY

DIANNE DRAKE

First published in Great Britain 2011
by Mills & Boon, an imprint of Harlequin (UK) Limited,
Eton House, 18-24 Paradise Road, Richmond, Surrey TW9 1SR

ISBN: 978 0 263 88600 9

Harlequin (UK) policy is to use papers that are natural, renewable and recyclable products and made from wood grown in sustainable forests. The logging and manufacturing process conform to the legal environmental regulations of the country of origin.

Printed and bound in Spain
by Blackprint CPI, Barcelona

Now that her children have left home, **Dianne Drake** is finally finding the time to do some of the things she adores—gardening, cooking, reading, shopping for antiques. Her absolute passion in life, however, is adopting abandoned and abused animals. Right now Dianne and her husband Joel have a little menagerie of three dogs and two cats, but that's always subject to change. A former symphony orchestra member, Dianne now attends the symphony as a spectator several times a month and, when time permits, takes in an occasional football, basketball or hockey game.

Recent titles by the same author:

FROM BROODING BOSS TO ADORING DAD
THE BABY WHO STOLE THE DOCTOR'S HEART*
CHRISTMAS MIRACLE: A FAMILY*
HIS MOTHERLESS LITTLE TWINS*
NEWBORN NEEDS A DAD*

**Mountain Village Hospital*

Dear Reader,

Welcome to **New York Hospital Heartthrobs,** a trilogy about coming home. And, I'd like to introduce you to Rafe Corbett, Jess Corbett and Rick Navarro, three real heartthrobs who have their own ideas about home. When I first learned I was going to write these books, I knew instantly that I wanted a theme about the place to which we are all connected—home. But I wanted more than that. I wanted to write stories about what compels people to want to go home and binds their hearts to that special place. In this group of stories, it was the love of a generous woman who touched countless lives…a woman much like your own mother, grandmother or aunt.

Cherished memories…that's what home is to me, and that's what home becomes for the heroes and heroines of **New York Hospital Heartthrobs**. Of course, going home isn't always the easiest thing to do. Just ask Rafe Corbett, in *The Doctor's Reason to Stay*. He hasn't been home for thirteen years, and has no intention of staying once he's attended his aunt's funeral. But it seems that a five-year-old girl named Molly, and a Child Life Specialist by the name of Edie Parker, have other plans for Rafe because, for some reason, he just can't get away, even though he's trying. Somewhere in his struggles to escape, though, Rafe finds a brand new definition of home. The question is, can he trust that home is truly where the heart is?

I hope you enjoy Rafe and Edie's discoveries in *The Doctor's Reason to Stay*. Then please, come back to see what doctor-turned-firefighter, Jess Corbett and nurse/paramedic, Julie Clark, are up to in my next **Heartthrob** story. And, as always, I love hearing from you, so please feel free to email me at Dianne@DianneDrake.com

Wishing you health & happiness!

Dianne

CHAPTER ONE

WHOEVER said you couldn't go home again was right, in part. He was home in the physical sense now, sitting in an old wicker chair, sipping a tall glass of lemonade, with his feet propped up on the white rail separating the porch from the masses of purple and pink flowering hydrangeas traversing the front and both sides of Gracie House. Emotionally, though, Dr. Rafe Corbett was distanced from this place. Distanced by miles and year upon year of memories and pain yet so acute that more than a decade of separation felt like mere seconds. Distanced was the way he wanted to stay, however. But it was hard to do that right now, when half the population of Lilly Lake, New York, expected something of the family prodigal finally returned home.

"I see you," he said to the child sneaking up behind him. Molly Corbett, not any blood relation to him but his aunt's ward, was truly alone in the world now, and his heart did go out to her.

"Do not," she said, a little too shy for the usually outgoing girl.

"Do too," he replied. "You're wearing a red dress." Rafe flinched, thinking about Molly, then thinking about his aunt. Grace Corbett been the best person in his life, and the fact that she was gone now really hadn't sunk in. Logically, he knew she'd had a heart attack. Emotionally, he wasn't ready to deal with it. Wasn't ready to cry, or grieve, or even miss her yet, because some part of him expected her to walk through her door, tell him it was all a big mistake, maybe even a scheme to get him home to Lilly Lake. God knew, she'd tried everything she could think of these past thirteen years, to no avail.

"It's yellow, silly," she said.

"That's what I said. You're wearing a yellow dress." But, then, there was Molly, to remind him. Big, sad eyes. Clingy. His heart ached for her. She was five, and he didn't know what she understood, or didn't understand. And he, sure as hell, wasn't the one who should be trying to relate to her.

"It's not a dress," she countered, not giving over to the giggles like she normally had when Aunt Grace had brought her along on her visits.

Sighing, Rafe thought about his aunt, a larger-than-life lady who'd squeezed every last drop out of every last day the good Lord had given her. Horsewoman, humanitarian, entrepreneur, philanthropist…and what he was going to miss the most, something very simple—her chocolate-chip cookies. Once a month, come rain, shine, or any other adversity in the universe, she'd met him somewhere on neutral ground, somewhere other than Lilly Lake, and given him a tin of her cookies. Had every month for thirteen years. He'd always looked forward to it…to the cookies, but most of all to his visit with his aunt. And they'd never missed a month, until this month.

"I didn't say it was a dress. It's yellow pants."

"No, it's not," Molly said, stepping up right behind him.

"Shoes."

"No."

"Socks."

"No."

He'd been trying to draw her out the whole time he'd been here, without any luck. Oh, she'd respond when she had to. But that was all. Flat, polite responses. No emotion. Only rote words. "Hat. Purse. Hair ribbons."

"Shirt. It's a yellow shirt." Said with polite impatience. But who could blame her? She missed Aunt Grace, at least as much as he did. Maybe more, as Grace had been all the child had ever had, ever known.

Damn, he was going to miss his aunt. The ache of not having her around any more was starting to knot inside him, threatening to choke him, or double him over with grief. But Molly couldn't see that. She needed to see strength right now. All he could muster for her. All he could fake for what he was about to do… to give her away. "And that's exactly what I said. A yellow shirt. I saw you sneaking up behind me in your yellow shirt." Over the years, Aunt Grace had taken in numerous children. She'd raised them, tutored them, fostered them, cared for them, or simply given them shelter when they'd needed it—all ages, all races and nationalities. None of it had mattered when a child had been in need of a home or even a bed for a few nights. "So, Miss Molly-in-the-yellow-shirt. Are you hungry?" He asked even though he was pretty sure she was not. She'd barely eaten a thing these past few days. As her short-term, stand-in guardian, he was concerned for her well-being. As a doctor, he was worried about her health. So much grief at such a young age wasn't good. "Can I fix you something to eat, Molly? Maybe get you an apple, or a glass of milk? Anything you want."

She stepped around to the front of the chair and stood directly in front of him, but at a distance. She always kept her distance. She shook her head, the way she'd done every time he'd asked since he'd been here.

"Are you tired? Do you need a nap?" She hadn't been sleeping well either.

She shook her head again.

"Are you bored? Is there something you'd like to go play with? Maybe there's a toy you'd like for me to buy you?"

This time Molly didn't even bother shaking her head. She simply stood there, staring at him with some kind of expectation that made him uneasy because he couldn't interpret it. Her big blue eyes were practically boring through him, telling him he should know something, or do something. But what?

That was the way it had been since he'd arrived for the funeral, four days ago, and nothing was changing except the way he felt. Molly was making him more nervous by the day. Making him feel the inadequacy he knew she was seeing. Maybe even making him feel guilty for the way he was going to have to upset her life more than it was already upset. It was something he truly hated doing, as Aunt Grace had dearly loved this child. But what he had to do was clear. He couldn't keep her, couldn't raise a child, couldn't give her the things she needed, so he'd find her someone who would.

But Rafe's heart did go out to Molly in ways he

hadn't expected. She'd only lived in Aunt Grace's world, that was all she'd ever known, and now it was going to be taken away from her. She was young, though. As cute as any kid he'd ever seen. And smart. So surely some nice family looking to adopt and adore a child would be anxious to give Molly the good home she needed, the one he wanted for her. He was sure of it. Although he was also sure that being ripped from her home, the way she was going to be, would break her young heart.

That, alone, had cost him a couple nights' sleep, trying to figure out how to prevent it from happening. Problem was, there wasn't a good solution to this bad situation. He couldn't stay in Lilly Lake, and he couldn't take Molly home to live with him in his world. Neither way would work—not for Molly, not for him.

"Do you have to go to the bathroom, Molly?" he persisted, not sure what he'd do if she said yes. But much to his relief, she shook her head again.

"Look, sweetheart. You're going to have to tell me what you want. If you need me to do something for you, or get you something...*anything*...I will, but I have to know what it is." He was losing patience. Not with Molly, but with himself for not being able to connect to her. He, of all people, knew what it was like to be alone, to feel that deep-down kind of isolation. But he didn't know how to deal with it, or overcome it—not in Molly, not even in himself. On top of that, he was sure Molly wasn't totally aware of what was really going on. Maybe she had some understanding of Aunt Grace's death. Maybe she had a sense of what that meant or, perhaps, she'd guessed that it was a bad thing. But he didn't believe she truly knew that her life was about to change in big ways, ways that made him feel pretty damned guilty.

Having the proverbial rug pulled out from underneath you was never good. His own rug had been pulled out so many times he couldn't even remember most of them any more. *Or tried not to remember them.* Anyway, what he did recall was Aunt Grace always being there for him, being the one to save him and love him and protect him each and every time that rug had been yanked. The way she'd done with Molly when she'd been literally thrown away, abandoned at birth in a trash can in a bus station.

Except Molly didn't remember that, of course. What she would remember, though, was the day Aunt Grace had gone away and never come back, and changed her life for ever.

It was a sadness he shared with Molly, something they had in common. A starting place for the two of them that neither one could quite reach. It was also a terrible pain he was only now beginning to feel, one that Molly shouldn't have to deal with. But he didn't know how to protect her from it. "Does your tummy hurt?" he asked, continuing to grapple for what was bothering her.

In answer, she sighed, which made him feel even worse for not knowing. This was when he would have asked his aunt what was wrong with the child, and she would have known instantly. Except he was on his own here. Everyone had finally gone home. Summer Adair, his aunt's nurse, had returned to her old life, whatever that was. Mrs. Murdock, the housekeeper, was with her sister for a few days. His brother, Jess, had returned to his life in New York City after the funeral. Even

Johnny Redmond, the man who looked after all Aunt Grace's horses, and ran her equestrian rescue charity, was keeping to the stables. Meaning it was just Molly and him now, and one of them was at a total loss.

"How about we go for ice cream? Would you like that?"

"Can I see Edie, please?" Molly finally asked.

Edie…a name he didn't recognize. "Is she one of your little playmates? Because you're welcome to invite her over. Or I could take you to her house to play, if that's OK with her parents."

No response from Molly. She simply continued standing there, staring at him, causing the tension between them to rise to the point that it was giving him a dull headache. One little girl inducing more pressure than he'd ever felt when he was in surgery. Truth be told, it was grinding him down. Besides losing sleep, he'd lost his appetite. Of course, that could also be the effect of coming home to Lilly Lake, where bad memories infused the very air he breathed. But Rafe had an idea Molly played a big part in his queasy feelings as he truly didn't relish the idea of what he had to do. So finally, in desperation, he said, "Look, Molly, why don't you run up to your room and play for a little while so I can make a phone call? After that, we'll figure out what to do with the rest of the day." Other than simply hanging around, staring at each other, not having a grasp on how to remedy the situation. "OK?"

On impulse, he held out his hand to Molly, and she grabbed hold quickly. Clung tightly as the two of them made their way through the house, now emptied of all its guests, and parted company when she continued on upstairs and he didn't. Rafe watched until Molly turned the corner, then he continued standing there until he heard the sound of her door shutting. "What am I going to do, Aunt Grace?" he asked her portrait hanging over the fireplace mantel in the parlor, on his way to the study to put out a distress call to the man most likely to know what to do. "It's a hell of a mess you've gotten me into, so the least you could do would be to tell me how I'm supposed to get myself out of it and do what's right for Molly at the same time."

Rafe actually paused for a moment, like he expected an answer from his aunt. Then, when he realized how absurd *that* was, he continued on his way, thinking about how really alone he was in this. It was him, no one else. Jess had his responsibilities elsewhere, and his own private hell to wade through every waking minute of every day. Then after Jess, there was…no one. Absolutely no one. Sure, Rafe could have easily turned and walked away, and let Aunt Grace's attorney handle the remaining affairs for him. One of those being Molly. But that wasn't the kind of person he was. He was…dutiful. That was what Aunt Grace had always said about him. Jess was sunny, Rafe was dutiful.

Except these days Jess was sad and Rafe was…well, he wasn't sure what he was. But he sure as hell was sure what he was not, which was daddy material!

The dutiful tag, though, was the thing causing the tension to quadruple in him right this very minute, as finding Molly a new family seemed almost cruel at this particular time. But she needed love, and that was something he knew nothing about. More than that, had no earthly desire to learn about. Love caused pain, and he'd had enough pain to last a lifetime. That attitude probably made him selfish, but so be it. He'd loved his aunt, he loved his brother. But no one else. It was a hard choice, but he was OK with it, for himself. Molly stood a chance at better things in this world, however, and she needed the kind of love he simply didn't have in him.

So with the resolve firmly in place that he was going to find that perfect adoptive situation for her, Rafe stepped into the study to phone the man he hoped would do most of the solving for him and shut the door behind him, grateful for the thick wooden walls that had always felt so safe to him when he was a child. All those nights when his dad had been drunk, or bellowing for the sake of bellowing, this was where he'd found his sanctuary, in Aunt Grace's study right across the street from his own private hell. In the red leather chair behind her desk, where she'd let him sit.

He ran his fingers over the back of the chair, picturing himself as a little boy, feeling so safe and important there. For a moment, when he sat down, he could almost see Aunt Grace standing across the desk from him, telling him to take a few deep breaths to help him calm down.

"Calm down," he said to himself, taking those few deep breaths, noticing, for the first time, a small, custom-made desk in the corner of the room. An exact replica of Grace's massive mahogany desk. Next to it, an exact replica of the leather chair. For Molly. The way it had been for Jess and him, and countless others.

"I don't suppose there's a simple way out of this, is there?" he asked Henry Danforth. Henry was Aunt Grace's confidant, her lawyer.

"Do you actually believe your aunt would have

made things simple for you, son? She left this world the way she lived in it day after day…and you know how that was."

He did. In a word…complicated. "So tell me, what am I going to do about Molly?" Glancing at the big leather chair, then the smaller replica, he felt the first real knot of emotion constrict his throat. *I'll do my best, Aunt Grace. I promise, I'll do my best.* "And do you know where I can I can find her little playmate called Edie?"

"Shall I let him in?" Betty Richardson, Edie Parker's secretary, asked from the door separating her office from Edie's. "He's not on the appointment list, but he said he's here about Molly, so I figured you'd want to talk to him."

Rafe stepped up behind Betty, expecting to find little Edie's mother, ready to plead his case to her, but Edie, as it turned out, wasn't so little. And she wasn't anything close to the kind of friend Rafe expected Molly to have. In fact, his first impression was that Molly's friend was a very curvaceous friend indeed. Stunningly so. "You're sure that's Edie Parker?" he asked Betty, simply to make sure.

"That's Edie," she confirmed, stepping out of Rafe's way.

One without a wedding ring, he noted at first glance as he looked around the ample figure of the secretary. He also noted the long blonde hair, the blue eyes, the impeccable smile. Edie Parker, or Edith Louise Parker, as it stated on her name plaque, shoved her desk chair back and stood, staring straight at the man who hadn't waited but had followed her secretary through the office door. Yet before she could speak, Molly shot around him and ran straight into Edie's arms. "Edie," she squealed. "I was afraid I'd never get to come see you again."

Edie scooped her right in. "You know I'd have come out to Gracie House to see you," she said, holding on to Molly for all she was worth. "I've missed you. We've all missed you."

"I don't like it there any more, Edie. It's too…quiet."

Edie glanced up briefly at Rafe. "Then we're going to have to see about you coming back to work here, at the hospital, as soon as possible. We have a lot of things for you to do. Janie, in the gift shop, needs someone to straighten her shelves. And André, in the kitchen, needs some help getting his pantry rearranged. Oh, and Dr. Rick mentioned, just yesterday, that he needs someone to help him pick out what kind of fish he's going to put into the new aquarium in the front lobby."

"I like yellow-striped fish," Molly said, almost shyly. "The ones with the blue stripes."

"Then that's something you and Dr. Rick should talk about."

For a moment, watching the exchange between Edie and Molly, the only thing that came to Rafe's mind was the phrase from an old song…something about the mother and child reunion being only a motion away… That was what it looked like he was witnessing right now, not just on Molly's part but on Edie Parker's as well. He was surprised how well they connected. Pleased, actually, as he hadn't observed that kind of emotion in Molly since he'd been here, and he'd worried about it. But witnessing Molly with Edie, he was pretty sure there was nothing to worry about. For the first time, Molly appeared a perfectly normal little girl. "I, um… Molly wanted to see you," he said to Edie, somewhat awkwardly. "Didn't mean to interrupt anything, but I didn't know what else to do for her. It's been pretty difficult these past few days."

Glancing up from her embrace, Edie answered him with a soft smile. "That's fine. I've been worried about Molly, and she's always welcome here. I'd thought about stopping by Gracie House, but I didn't want to intrude on your family at a time like this, though, so I've stayed away." She tried pushing back from Molly a bit, but the child clung ferociously. "But I am sorry for your loss, Dr. Corbett. We all loved your aunt. *Dearly.* She was a kind, caring woman. Full of compassion. She's already missed."

Yes, she'd been all that, and more. "I appreciate your sentiment, Miss Parker."

"Please, call me Edie," she said, her voice so collected and reassuring it reminded him, in a way, of his aunt's voice.

He smiled. "I appreciate your sentiment, Edie. It's been a difficult few days for everybody, and I'm not sure any of us have even begun to feel just how much she's going to be missed."

"If there's anything I can do…"

He saw sincerity in her eyes. Saw genuine affection for Molly, too, and wondered… "Maybe there is. Molly hasn't been eating well, or sleeping. I thought that spending some time with one of her playmates might help, but obviously you're not a playmate. Maybe, though, you can point me in the direction of one of her playmates."

"Actually, in a way, I am a playmate. I'm the

hospital's child life specialist, which does entitle me to play with the children, along with a few other more professional-type duties." She laughed. "Although I'll admit to a real fondness for the play aspects of the job."

"Child life specialist. Isn't that a position you'd be more inclined to find in a pediatric hospital, or a hospital with a large pediatric department?" A position about which he knew nothing at all as he kept himself locked away in the orthopedic surgery for half his practicing life, and in his office for the other half.

"Usually, but Dr. Navarro, our Chief of Staff, has plans to enlarge our pediatric ward here, and your aunt wanted me on staff before that started, to serve as an advisor for the expansion." Pushing back from Molly, she straightened up. "Oh, and in case it wasn't clear, Molly has been my *assistant* for the past three months. She's very important to the child life program we're setting up." She smiled, not at Rafe but at Molly… "An advisor."

"I have!" Molly agreed eagerly.

Rafe noted the animation in her, pleased to see it. Something about Edie Parker was causing that in Molly. Of course, as pretty as Edie was, something about her would probably cause that kind of animation in any man, including himself, fortunate enough to be around her for very long.

"When Aunt Grace comes here to work, I get to help Edie sometimes. And sometimes I get to help other people here, too, because I have lots of jobs. So, when Aunt Grace comes back, I'll come back and help again. Won't I, Edie? Just like I used to before she went away?"

Rafe and Edie exchanged troubled looks, Rafe's

twisting from troubled into downright panicked. He didn't know what to say, didn't know what to do, and that must have shown quite clearly on him, as Edie jumped in for the rescue.

"Look, Molly," she said. "Right now, what I need you to do is go and help Betty. She's in the middle of a very important project, and she has a job for you." She held out her hand to Molly, and took her to the reception area, where Betty put the girl to work rearranging the boxes of toys Edie kept on hand for the kids she worked with. A very important job, in Molly's estimation. "Also, make sure nothing is broken, and if you see any toys in there that aren't clean, give them to Betty to sanitize." Edie turned to Rafe, then winked. "Molly knows how important it is to keep our toys clean."

The wink definitely caught him off guard, but so did the way Molly went right at her task, separating the toys into three boxes, one for boys, one for girls, and one for everybody, being careful to inspect each and every one. For the first time since he'd returned to Lilly Lake, he was actually seeing Molly smile. More than ever, that was a sure sign that he had no business taking care of a child. He didn't know what it took to cause her to smile, even though he'd made awkward attempts. Didn't know how to assess her needs. In fact, everything he did felt wrong. And that feeling of inadequacy was only emphasized by Molly's absence of response to his feeble attempts. The fact that even after he'd told Molly that Grace had died, her lack of understanding merely underlined his ineptness, which told him that even though he felt miserable disrupting Molly's life so much, what he had to do was the right thing.

"I figured she'd have some problems coping with my aunt's death," he said, once Edie shut her office door, "but I had no idea she didn't understand it at all. I'm sure you've already seen how much I don't know about kids."

"Don't worry about it, Doctor. Children adjust in their own way, in their own good time. Right now, Molly's just processing what's happening to her. For a child, it's difficult. But give her a little while to work through it. I'm sure she will, but if, for some reason, she doesn't, we'll try approaching it a different way, something she's better able to cope with. And that's all it's about at her age…finding that one special way that will help her cope. Because, honestly, I do think she understands. It's more a matter of her trying to figure out how to handle what she knows. That's most likely where Molly's still confused, which is why it's easier for her to ignore everything that's happened and simply return to a time when it was easier for her." She reached out, and laid a reassuring hand on his arm. "However it happens, Dr. Corbett, we'll work through it."

He glanced down at her hand, surprised by the sensation running up his arm. A tingle? "Please, call me Rafe," he said, sounding just the slightest bit unsteady.

"Rafe," she replied, gesturing him to the chair across from her desk.

He opted to stand next to the door, however. Ready to escape, maybe? Ready to throw in the towel and admit that he was totally out of his league here, and it bothered him because he was used to being the one in charge? "So, in your experience, how long does this processing take?"

Edie sat down behind her desk, folded her hands patiently and precisely in front of her, then stared up at him. "You really *don't* know a thing about children, do you?"

"It shows that much?"

She laughed. "You might as well be carrying a sign broadcasting it. Meaning I think you're going to need a lot of help. Probably more than you know."

Suddenly, the tension in him melted away. He liked Molly's friend, and he was certainly glad she wasn't a *little* playmate. In fact, he was very glad about that. "Do you like horses, Edie?" he asked impulsively, as the urge to ride hit him. He hadn't done it in years. Had put it away as part of a past he'd never wanted to revisit. Now he wanted to ride, probably the only thing that had ever made him truly happy when he'd been a kid and, more surprisingly, he didn't want to ride solitary the way he'd done more often than not back then. In fact, he could almost picture the three of them on the trail together—him, Molly, Edie. Odd, the picture of it developing. But pleasant. And totally unexpected.

"Real horses, toy horses?"

He chuckled. "Real horses. Leather saddle. A ride in the country." An idea with growing appeal.

"Horses are OK, I guess, from a distance. Why do you ask?"

"I've just decided to take Molly on a ride out to the lake later this afternoon for a picnic, and I was wondering if you'd like to come with us, maybe give me my first lesson in everything I need to know about children. Assuming that when you told me I needed help, you were also offering it."

She thought about it for a moment. Frowned, then

asked, “And the horse thing…is that negotiable? The only horse I’ve ever ridden was a mechanical one on a carousel, and once it started going up and down, I jumped off and sat on the bench seat, the one reserved for the cowards and elderly couples who wanted to ride and reminisce.”

Rafe laughed out loud, something he hadn’t done in a while. Being stuck in Lilly Lake for the next few days didn’t seem as bad now as it had only a few minutes ago. Actually, he was beginning to look forward to it.

Yes, he definitely liked Molly’s friend.

CHAPTER TWO

WHAT in the world had she done? Had she really accepted a date with a total stranger? Maybe even instigated it a little?

In a sense, Rafe was familiar to her. Grace had spoken about him so often she almost felt like she knew him. Well, some of him. And he was, after all, Molly's…well, she wasn't really sure what he would be called. Temporary guardian? Honorary uncle? Adopted cousin? Soon-to-be father? That was the one she hoped for. But however Rafe defined himself in that relationship, it was a difficult situation all the way round, and the day Grace Corbett had asked her to look out for Molly, she hadn't anticipated just how difficult it was going to get, or how much looking out she might be called on to do.

"I have a medical condition," Grace had said. *"Don't think I'm going to have much more time here, and I want you to promise me that you'll help Molly through this. I want Rafe to be her guardian and I'm going to need someone special, like you, to make sure my nephew does all the right things for her. He's got to be taught that he can take care of a child, Edie. And that he can love her. Rafe's a good man who doesn't*

know he has that potential in him, and I want you to guide him to that potential, to that place where he knows he can be what Molly needs, because he needs Molly as much as she's going to need him. But he's got to discover that for himself, with some gentle nudges from you."

That was why Grace had hired her, as a matter of fact. For her abilities as a child life specialist primarily, but also for those gentle nudges. Sure, the hospital pediatric department was expanding in new directions, and having a child life specialist on staff was a smart move, especially in the initial stages of the new services. But hiring her months in advance, even before the changes were to start… At first, Edie had thought it was simply good fortune, or being in the right place at the right time. But when Grace had come to her, that was when Edie had known her being there was as much about taking care of Molly as it was taking care of the children who would come to the new pediatric ward.

Funny, but in a way Grace had reminded Edie of her mother. Strong, compassionate women, both of them, always putting the needs of their children first. Edie missed her mother terribly, missed Grace, too, and, in a way, felt that maybe the two of them had connected in some karmic fashion to guide her life to this place and time, even though her mother had died years before Edie had even met Grace.

Grace had taken a big chance hiring Edie straight out of school, with no real work experience in the field except what she'd done as a student. In fact, Grace hadn't batted an eye when Edie had walked into her office that day and explained how she'd been delayed in her education, which was why she was graduating at the age of thirty-two rather than a full decade earlier, as most people in her position did. None of that had mattered to Grace. She'd hired Edie almost immediately. So now, for the unusual opportunity Edie had been given, she owed it to Grace to fulfill her most fervent wish. Yes, she'd teach, nudge, or otherwise encourage Dr. Rafe Corbett in the many ways he should care for Molly. Of course, loving that child was something Rafe was going to have to do on his own. Edie certainly couldn't force that. But Molly was easy to love. So very easy…

A knock on her office door jarred Edie's attention. "Are you busy?" Dr. Rick Navarro asked, opening the door several inches and poking his head in.

"Not really. Just trying to figure out why I got myself into a horseback ride later on, considering how horses scare me to death."

Rick chuckled. "Riding a horse is like riding a bike…only bigger, and bumpier. Horses do have a little more personality than a bicycle, though. But, trust me, once you mount up, you're going to see there's nothing else like it in the world. It's an amazing feeling, being on the back of a horse. Nothing you can duplicate with anything else. Think of it as a great big bike with legs instead of wheels, and you'll do fine."

"You have horse experience?" she asked.

"Not so much lately. But when I was a boy…my mother was housekeeper for a man who had a stable, so I got to ride just about whenever I wanted."

She could picture Rick on a horse, actually, sitting tall and rugged in the saddle. Not anything like the way she could picture herself…hunched over, shaking, holding on for dear life. "Suppose I was to tell you I've never learned how to ride a bike? That they scared me, too." As had so many things in her young life. Truth was, she'd never really had a *young* life. Most of the time it didn't matter. Sometimes, it did.

"Then I'd say you should plan on calling in sick tomorrow, because you're going to be too stiff and sore to get out of bed. And my prescription for that, by the way, will be a nice, long soak in a tub of hot water."

She really liked Rick. He was not only a great hospital administrator, he was an amazing doctor. He cared. Took time with his patients. Treated his staff with respect. Unfortunately, there were rumors floating around that he might leave now that Grace was gone and her two nephews had inherited the hospital. She was keeping her fingers crossed, though, that the rumors weren't based on fact. Lilly Hospital needed Ricardo Navarro. He brought the heart and soul to it that so many other hospitals lacked. "Well, I think maybe I'll stop by Physical Therapy later on and see if they've got any other advice for me. Or put in my reservation for one of their traction machines, since that's probably where I'll be spending the next few days…in traction."

"Cervical or back traction?" he asked, chuckling.

"Both."

"You could stay off the horse. Admire it from afar, but stay away."

Easier said than done, if she wanted to go on that picnic with Rafe and Molly, which she really wanted to do. Probably more than she was even going to admit. Her life had never really afforded her much in the way of picnics, playtime, holidays or simply relaxation, and she was looking forward to this outing. To most of it, anyway. "Or tie myself to the saddle once I'm there."

"You could also ask for a horse with short legs. The trip to the ground isn't as far and it's less painful that way." His expression sobered. "Look, Edie, getting back to work, we're admitting a boy through Emergency right now. Keith Baldwin. He has a ruptured appendix, and he'll be going to the operating room in about thirty minutes. I need you to go down to Emergency, explain the surgery to him, make sure he understands everything that will be happening while they prep him, as well as what happens during the surgery, and especially what to expect afterward. He's awfully worried about playing baseball this summer, so talk to him about some timelines for his return, and what his recovery might entail."

It often still amazed her, all the responsibility she'd been given in this hospital. It's what Child Life Specialists did, though. They were advocates for the children, acted as the intermediaries between them and the medical staff, explained the procedures, did the reassuring, held the hands, got involved in a lot of the hugging…the best part of her job, as far as she was concerned. And she loved every second of her job. Couldn't imagine doing anything else with her life. "How old is he?"

"Eight."

"Well, luckily, I know more about baseball than I do horseback riding, so I think we'll be fine." She grabbed up her clipboard and headed to the door. Then added, "I met Rafe Corbett, by the way. He stopped by with Molly. He seems very nice."

"He's your horseback date?" Rick's words came with a scowl. A very deep scowl, in fact.

"Molly is. She's having some trouble adjusting." She noticed the frown, but it wasn't her place to ask why. She barely knew Rick and didn't know Rafe at all, and judging from Rick's reaction to the mention of Rafe, she thought it best to simply ignore the obvious friction. Still, she wondered about it, especially as both men seemed so nice, so easygoing.

Rick drew in a stiff breath then let it out slowly, deliberately, as if trying to quell something inside him. "Well, you tell Molly for me that she's welcome to come back to work any time she's up to it. We all miss her, and would love having her back at the hospital again. And I'm worried about her, Edie. As close as she and Grace were…it makes me worry about my son, and what would happen to him if…" He shook his head. "Anyway, tell Molly we all miss her."

Edie wondered about Molly's future. Maybe even worried about it. What would happen to her if Rafe *didn't* do well taking care of a child? Or, worse yet, if he turned out to be the one person in Lilly Lake who didn't love Molly?

What would happen to Molly then?

It was something Edie didn't want to think about… Molly going out to the foster-care system and being put up for adoption. She herself had endured a lifetime with that fear, living with a mother who'd had so many medical problems, a mother who often hadn't been able to care for herself, a mother who had skirted death for such a long time. At times, it had seemed like the child protective services had perched just outside the door, waiting to take Edie away to some other circumstances, waiting to put her into what they viewed as a better home.

As a child, even as a teenager, it had always scared her. She'd had nightmares about being taken away from her mother, and had spent so many fearful years peeking out the front window, making sure nobody was coming up the steps. Sure, her life with her mother had been difficult, at times even back-breaking. But she'd loved her mother dearly and wouldn't have done anything differently. Even now, though, when she remembered all those times someone had talked about taking her away…

What they hadn't understood was that being with her mother, no matter how sick she'd been, no matter how poor they'd been, had been for the best. There'd been no neglect, no abuse. Only love. And Molly needed that now. What she didn't need, or deserve, was the awful dread that came from the knowledge that she could be ripped out of the life she knew at any moment. No child needed that. So, one way or another, Edie was determined to make sure Molly's future wasn't filled with the things she'd lived through.

Of course, her own immediate future didn't seem so bright, not when she thought about climbing up on that horse.

"She needs a good adoptive family. Actually, she *deserves* a good adoptive family. She's a sweet child and I want her to be in a normal situation. *My* situation isn't normal, there's no room for a child in it." Twenty minutes after he'd arrived home, Henry Danforth confronted Rafe, in person, with the one solution for Molly that Rafe was not going to accept. Keep her, adopt her.

"Well, then, if that's your final decision, all I can say is that we're working on it and we'll do our best. In the meantime, the county child services agency doesn't see any reason to remove her from the only home she's ever known, and stick her in foster-care. Which is what will happen if you don't look after her for now. And just so you'll know, the closest foster-mother they have is half an hour outside Lilly Lake, and she already has six children, plus three of her own. Molly would literally have to be squeezed in. So, is that what you want for her, son? To be squeezed in? Or maybe I should ask if that's what Grace would have wanted?"

He was the one being squeezed here, and Henry was so good at it. Almost as good as Aunt Grace had been. *Of course* Rafe wanted to take care of Molly in the best way possible. *Of course* he wanted her in a better situation where she wasn't going to be one of the many foster-children. "So what are you telling me, Henry?" As if he didn't already know.

"That if you want to do the *right* thing, you're either taking Molly with you when you go home to Boston, or you're staying here at Gracie House to take care of her for the time being. Which is probably what's best… letting Molly stay in her own home." He shrugged. "I mean, there aren't a lot of other good options here. I'm sorry about that, but your aunt loved that little girl something fierce, and would have adopted her if the courts hadn't said she was too old. And here's the thing. She set up a sizeable trust for Molly. You already know about that, but what I haven't told you yet is that Grace made you the permanent trustee…at least until Molly is twenty-one."

"Without telling me? Could she do that?" He was

surprised yet in a way he wasn't. His aunt had always expected more of him than he expected of himself.

"Yes, she could, and that's what she did, son. You were the *only* one she wanted."

"So, let me guess. She thought I'd refuse if she'd simply asked me, so she locked me in this way instead?"

"She *knew* you'd refuse. But Grace always got what she wanted, one way or another. Didn't mean to surprise you like I did, but that's the way Grace wanted it, too. Didn't want you having time to think about ways to back out of the arrangement."

Rafe chuckled. "I guess I should have seen it coming." He could almost see the smile on his aunt's face while she plotted this whole affair. Damn, he missed her! "So, OK. For now, that's fine. I'll serve as Molly's trustee. But I'm assuming that once she's adopted, that will change."

Henry shook his head, fighting back an obvious, devious smile. Henry was a burly man. Big, soft, with tons of gray hair on his head. And a pair of hazel, very astute eyes that missed nothing, including the fact that Grace Corbett, God rest her soul, had won this round. "The responsibility's still yours, even after she's adopted, son. Which in itself is going to be a problem, because finding placement for a child who comes with Molly's substantial financial means isn't going to be easy since there are going to be a whole lot of candidates lining up who'll want her only because she's a wealthy little girl. Of course, everything could be settled right now if you'd simply adopt her. Or at least let me write up the guardianship papers for you."

"That sounds like Aunt Grace's argument." Rafe

shook his head in frustration. "But I already told you, I'd make a terrible father. And guardian. I don't have time, I don't have experience. Maybe my aunt thought that tangling me up in all these arrangements would make me want to be an instant father, but it's not happening, Henry. I care about Molly, but my focus is on my work. No serious relationships and especially no children. So it's up to you to find Molly a family who wants her because they love her, not because she's wealthy. And when you're convinced that Molly is in the absolute best situation, you can see about changing the terms of Molly's trust…phasing me out as trustee and giving the responsibility to her parents, because that's the way it should be. Or I'll have my attorney do it if you won't. Bottom line, I'm going to make sure Molly gets the best. Personally oversee the interview process. But I'm not going to keep her."

Henry listened, still smiling and nodding as if he was *really* listening, which Rafe knew he was not. He'd known Henry since he was a child. Nice man. Devoted to the Corbett family. As easy to read as a child's picture book. In fact, Henry's *pictures* were so obvious, it wouldn't have surprised Rafe the least little bit if he'd already had Molly's adoption papers stashed away, ready to sign, with the name Rafe Samuel Corbett at the bottom. "I mean it, Henry. I'm not going to step in as Molly's father."

"I know you mean it, son. And I'm sure everything will work itself out for the best in due course. But that could take a little while. So are you willing to take care of Molly until we get it figured out?"

"Of course I will. And I'll do it right here, at Gracie House, so she won't have to be disrupted." He did have several weeks of vacation time saved up, and a host of medical partners who could take his place, so stepping out of his practice wasn't going to be a problem for a while. "But she needs her new family sooner rather than later, because I don't want her getting attached to me, then being pulled away. So work on it, Henry. Don't put it on the back burner, thinking that the slower you do this, the more I'll be inclined to keep her. That's not going to happen. And in the end Molly's going to be the one to get hurt if that's what you do." The last thing he wanted was to hurt her.

Henry nodded again, then continued like he hadn't heard a word. "I'm not going to hurt that child, son. I'll promise you that. I have only her best interests at heart." He crossed his heart. "So, let me go get started, and in the meantime I'd suggest setting up more opportunities to let Molly and Edie Parker be together. Edie's good with children. Especially good for Molly, and Grace respected that woman in a big way."

"She's not married, is she?" Rafe asked, surprised to hear the words coming from his mouth. Why did he care? Why did the image of an empty ring finger flash through his mind?

Henry wiggled his shaggy eyebrows. "Molly has good taste in friends, doesn't she? Very pretty lady. And, no, she's not married. As far as I know, not even involved. She's only been here about three months and, from what I've seen, she keeps pretty much to herself. But like I said, Grace really respected her. Took to her right away. Admired the way she worked with the children in the hospital." Henry's smile broadened. "Did I mention she's very pretty?"

"You mentioned it." And Rafe didn't disagree. Edie

was pretty. Distractingly so…obviously, since that was all he had on his mind at the present.

"OK, then I'll let the child services here know you're going to stay here and take care of Molly instead of putting her in a foster-home. It's a good decision, son, one you won't regret. And you *are* doing the right thing for the child."

As Henry lumbered through the front doors at Gracie House, Rafe thought about the child who was, right now, sitting in Grace's office, trying her hardest to be a small replica of Grace. So maybe it was a good decision to stay here after all. And maybe he wouldn't regret it. But it wasn't fair to Molly. None of it was, and Molly shouldn't have to find out just how much. That was something he couldn't prevent, though. At best, he could only ease the transition because, God only knew, he didn't have anything else inside him. At least, not what Molly needed.

But Edie had it all. Everything Molly needed… It did make him wonder.

She'd spent most of the afternoon trying to avoid the obvious…her pseudo-date with Rafe Corbett. When she thought about it in terms of spending time with Molly, she felt better. But when Rafe's image entered her mind, it turned into butterflies in her stomach. He was tall, broad-shouldered. Short brown hair, dark eyes she assumed were also brown, deep tan. And a dimple in his chin. She had to admit a certain weakness for dimples, thanks to the old Cary Grant movies she used to watch with her mother on the days her mother hadn't been able to get out of bed. Butterfly-makers, for sure. And here she was, primping in front of the car's rear-view mirror, getting herself ready to go. If she had a list of her top ten most frightening things to do, riding a horse would take a solid place at number five, right after climbing a mountain, jumping out of an airplane, going to the moon and getting involved with the wrong man again.

Thinking about Alex Hastings made her shiver. Wrong man, bad marriage, regrettable decision. More than anything, a huge waste of precious time. One year in, one year out, and almost every day of it filled with regrets for the time she couldn't get back. But she'd been alone, scared, confused, and he'd been the easy port in her storm. Water under the bridge now. Regrets, yes. Huge ones, not really. Fond memories, not one.

OK, so she'd lived a sheltered life, and done dumb things because of it. She'd admit it, embrace it and, hopefully, learn from it. That was, quintessentially, her… Edie Parker, always behind, taking bad detours, slow to arrive at her life. Well, she'd finally traversed the biggest bumps and arrived. Now, no more detours. She needed to advance herself. Take graduate courses, move along even further in her career. Avoid the bumps at all cost. Or, most of them, since this little horseback excursion promised an afternoon filled with literal ones. But she was looking forward to the time with Molly. Even with Rafe. So that was the price. But the horse?

She had nothing against horses in general. In fact, she loved animals…all animals. Horses, though, only from a distance. And this seemed a good distance, sitting at the end of the driveway of Gracie House, looking well past it to the paddock full of horses, trying to convince herself she'd survive the afternoon reasonably intact.

"You accepted the invitation, so do it," she said, sucking in a nervous breath through her teeth as she turned into the drive. She drove at a pace slower than an elderly snail, all the way up to the house. Horses... Rafe Corbett...all at once? This was precisely the time when she should have been asking herself what she had done because, honestly, she didn't know.

"What the hell is she doing?" Rafe asked under his breath, watching Edie coming up the driveway, her car creeping slower than he thought a car could go.

"Looks to me like she's avoiding something," Johnny Redmond commented.

Well, Rafe knew that feeling. Aversions and avoidances. He was the master of them. Practiced them to perfection. Could write a book on all the various techniques. "Look, will you bring Donder around for me?"

"You up to that?" the stable manager asked. "He's got a lot of spirit in him, especially now that Grace hasn't taken him out for a while. Your aunt liked it, didn't want it broken down."

Rafe smiled. Donder wasn't the only one with spirit around here. Even if the spirit stepping out of the car right now was fairly tentative, it was there, as big and bold as Donder's. But with a heart equally as big. "No, I'm probably not up to it," he told Johnny. "But I want to give it a try anyway. Nothing ventured, nothing gained. My aunt subscribed to that philosophy." But Rafe wasn't sure if he meant Donder or Edie.

"Good thing you fix broken bones," Johnny said, on his way to Donder's stall.

But Rafe barely heard the words, he was so focused on Edie's approach. She was stunning. "I'm not convinced you really want to ride," he called out to her long before she was near the stable, startled by how excited he was to see her again yet not willing to admit to himself that he'd thought about her more than a time or two that afternoon.

"That makes two of us," she called back. An old-fashioned wicker picnic basket swung from her left arm, while she clasped a red plaid blanket to her chest with her right. "I wasn't sure what kind of food you were bringing, so I threw together a few things…fried chicken, fruit salad, freshly baked croissants, chocolate-chip cookies…"

"My aunt's chocolate-chip cookie recipe?" he asked, hopefully.

"My own. I had a lot of time to cook, growing up. Chocolate-chip cookies were one of my favorites to make."

Well, she had mighty big shoes to fill in the chocolate-chip cookie department, he thought. "So, you fixed all that food this afternoon?" How could anyone look so downright girl-next-door and sexy at the same time? Even the way her ponytail swished back and forth captivated him.

"I took a few hours off work this afternoon…time left over from the last holiday I didn't take. Haven't really done much cooking for a while, and it was fun."

"Better than the peanut-butter sandwiches I was going to go slap together." Everything about her took his breath away—her blue jeans and white cotton tank top, her white athletic shoes. Simple, nice and natural. Not like the sophisticated, polished women who moved in his social circles in the city. Yet seeing Edie, he did have to admit there was a little emotion trying to creep into a place where he hadn't felt any in longer than he cared to recollect. Was it…excitement? Could he actually be a little eager over the anticipation of spending some time with her?

No, that couldn't be it. He didn't get excited. So it had to be a mild case of relief as Edie was here to stand in as the buffer between Molly and him. *Relief.* Yes, that made perfect sense. Still, seeing Edie with her hamper full of food, looking the way she did…

OK, maybe his pulse had sped up a beat or two. But, hell, he liked home-made fried chicken. Hadn't had it ages. That alone was worth a couple of extra beats. And the cookies… "Anyway, how about we find you a ride? Any kind of horse you're particularly drawn to? We've probably got just the one you want."

"Or I could walk," she ventured.

Molly stepped into the conversation at that point, went straight to Edie's side and leaned into her the way an affectionate cat leaned into a person's leg. "You could ride Ice Cream, Edie."

"Ice Cream?" both Edie and Rafe asked together.

"Aunt Grace let me name her. She was really sick when she came here to stay, and she wouldn't eat anything. But I brought her a bowl of ice cream…vanilla. And she loved it. Aunt Grace said that's what made her better again, so I thought it was a good name. And when I'm big enough to ride on my own, Aunt Grace is going to let me keep Ice Cream as my very own horse because she's so gentle."

"I think it's a perfect name for her," Edie said, slipping her arm around Molly's shoulder. "And I'd be honored to ride Ice Cream."

It was a natural gesture, Rafe noted. Not forced. Not even thought about. From where he stood, it looked like they could have, maybe should have, been mother and daughter. For a moment, he wondered if that could happen. "I think I saw her smile a little when you said her name."

"Because she still likes ice cream, silly," Molly said, giggling.

It was such a relief, seeing her act like a little girl her age should act. Rafe knew it had a lot to do with Edie, also with doing something normal from her life before all this tragedy. Unfortunately, it had nothing to do with him, for which he felt a little guilty because he felt…well, he wasn't exactly sure what it was. Left out, maybe? But that was what he really wanted, wasn't it? Not to be part of Molly's permanent situation, not to let her get too attached to him. So, in a way, he was getting exactly what he wanted, yet it didn't feel as *right* as it should have. In fact, it felt pretty darned bad, and he hadn't expected that. "Well, I think Molly has picked you the perfect horse, Edie. Care to saddle up and give her a try?"

"Me, saddle up? Sure, I'll give it a try, but first you've got to tell me which end of the saddle would face the front end of the horse?"

He chuckled. "OK, I get the hint."

"Not a hint. A blatant statement that if you want to get this picnic under way, you're going to be the one doing the saddling, while Molly and I go up to the house and make lemonade for the picnic. And I brought the lemons, just in case you didn't have any."

"I'd rather help with the saddles," Molly offered, almost shyly. "Aunt Grace let me do that sometimes, and I know how. And in case Rafey doesn't know where all the tack is kept…" She stepped away from Edie. "Do you need some help, Rafey?"

"Rafey?" Edie said, fighting back a laugh.

Molly nodded seriously. "That's his name. *Rafey.*"

A look of undiluted sheepishness, along with a fierce, red blush, crept over Rafe's face. The name *Rafey* wasn't exactly the manly image he wanted to portray to Edie, or even to Molly, for that matter. But that machismo delusion was certainly shot all to pieces now, leaving him wondering why it even mattered. Because it shouldn't. Yet it did. "That's what Aunt Grace called me when I was a boy. She tried to stop when I was high-school age, figured it embarrassed me. Which it did. But it slipped out of her every now and again, and that's probably where Molly heard the reference."

"Uh-huh," Molly piped up. "Aunt Grace *always* called you Rafey."

"Rafey," Edie repeated, smiling. "Well, it's kind of cute, I'll have to admit. Rafey… Rafey…" she repeated a couple of times, as if trying it on for size. "Has a nice ring to it. Dr. Rafey Corbett…lacks sophistication and pretense." She grinned. "But it's good."

"Maybe it's good, but only when you're five years old," Rafe said, as the embarrassment dissolved into good nature. "Not when you're thirty-five."

"So, then, what you're telling me is that I *can't* call you…" She liked the way his discomfort gave way to ease. Rafe was trying really hard to fit in, to relate to Molly, which gave her hope. It wasn't a natural fit on him, but he was working on it and, at this point that's all Edie could ask. For now, probably all Grace would have expected.

"What I'm telling you is that you *can't*." Rafe gave his head a crisp shake in emphasis, and Edie couldn't help laughing. Rafe Corbett was a big man sitting in the saddle who was saddled with a little boy's name. It was so endearing and, for a moment, she saw some vulnerability there. A little bit of softness clouding his eyes over a nickname, perhaps? Or maybe he was only reminiscing about something nice from the time when Grace had called him Rafey. Whatever it was, it made him less stiff. Not enough to be considered loose or relaxed, but he was definitely not so starchy now. Definitely working on it, too.

"You *can* call him Rafey," Molly piped right up. "Aunt Grace did."

"*Molly* can call me Rafey," Rafe interjected. *"Only Molly."*

He said it with a little twinkle in his eyes. Or was that a challenge? Either way, it melted Edie's heart just a little bit, as Rafe clearly wasn't comfortable with the name, yet he was going to put up with it from Molly. That was just plain sweet of him. So, maybe, just maybe, her job to help him realize that he did have all kinds of father potential wouldn't be so difficult after all. She hoped so, because Rafe was a little awkward about it right now. Yet given some time, along with some good coaching…who knew? And in the future, well, who knew about that one either? Possibly, with some luck, Molly would be able to call him Daddy sooner than Edie had hoped for. That would be nice, Edie decided. What Grace would have wanted. But for a moment her heart clenched when she thought about Rafe and Molly together, just the two of them. No one else in that picture. It's what she had to do, and that was what she'd have to keep telling herself. Getting *the two* of them together was what she had to do. What she'd promised to do.

CHAPTER THREE

"COULD you two slow up a little?" Edie called from behind them. She was lagging back quite a way, not because she wanted to but because it was the best she could do. Rafe and Molly were doubling up on the lead horse, with Molly riding in a pink tandem saddle right behind Rafe, hanging on to him with her face pressed to his back. From Edie's position, it was cute. But she wondered if Rafe was bothered by it, because he looked…uncomfortable. He seemed too rigid in the saddle, even to an untrained observer such as herself. Yet Molly looked happier than Edie had seen her looking in days. Possibly because Rafe had made her happy. Or it could have been about her honest need to hold on to someone strong for a while…something Edie understood better than she cared to, given the way the first time she'd really held on to someone had turned out. Of course, everybody needed that extra jolt in their lives at some time, didn't they? Strength from someone else. Someone to support them on the journey, to guide them when they were lost.

She'd certainly had those moments in her own life… moments with her mother, moments with Alex. Good and bad. Going down the right path, going down the wrong one. Rafe wasn't the wrong path for Molly, though. He didn't know that, of course, even though Molly obviously did. Most likely, he'd never thought of himself in terms of any kind of course for Molly, which was something Edie certainly intended to change.

But the path Edie was on today had nothing to do with any of that. It was all about the path she was taking on the back of a very gentle horse named Ice Cream—a horse, as it turned out, who was absolutely perfect for a beginner to ride. Vanilla in color, she was mellow, plodding along in no hurry to get anywhere, and if it could be said that a horse was stopping along the way to smell the roses, that was what it seemed like Ice Cream was doing. Smart horse, taking in her surroundings—the path, the sky, the flowers. It wasn't a bad way to go through life, Edie supposed. Too bad more *people* couldn't take a lesson from Ice Cream.

"So, when do we get to stop?" she called out, when they rounded the bend and she saw the lake ahead. "Right now, I hope, because this is a perfect place." At least, that was what her aching backside was telling her.

Like he'd been reading her mind about stopping, Rafe brought Donder, a well-muscled, brown and white Appaloosa, to a halt, then turned in his saddle to face her. "It's only another five miles," he said, without cracking a smile.

"Five?" Pulling Ice Cream up alongside him, she looked square at him and saw, up close, his very stern expression, but also saw the corner of his mouth twitch up imperceptibly in a fight to keep from smiling. "Then why don't you go on ahead, take part of the picnic food with you, while Molly and I stay here and have *our* picnic at the lake. Is that OK with you, Molly?" His eyes were dancing now. Beautiful. Mischievous. Unnerving. But she didn't look away. It took everything she had in her to stay eye to eye with him, and keep a straight face at that. She managed it, though, with some struggle. "We'll have our picnic right here, just the two of us, while Rafe goes on ahead and finds his own place to picnic."

Very straight-faced, Molly said, "You can't take the lemonade with you, Rafey. It's two against one. We get to keep it here. But you can come back and have some when you want it."

"I think you've been thoroughly told," Edie remarked.

"I think I've been charmed by the two most beautiful women in Lilly Lake," he replied, slipping down out of his saddle then lifting Molly to the ground. Heading straight to Ice Cream, he steadied the horse and held up his hand to help Edie. And in that instant, when the silky skin of her palm slid across his, if there wasn't a visible spark, there sure was an unseeable one, felt by both of them, because Edie and Rafe both pulled back in that moment of extraordinary awareness, and simply stared at each other. Speechless, almost to the point of dumbfounded. Edie wasn't sure how long it was, but the intensity couldn't be questioned. At least for her. As for Rafe…he was still holding tight to her gaze when *she* finally had to break it or become completely lost in it. "I, um…thanks," she finally said, letting go of his hand. "For the compliment, and the help."

His answer was to arch his eyebrows. Then he turned away. Unaffected? Edie didn't know about Rafe, but she surely knew about herself, and at that moment there was nothing in her, from her head to her toes, that wasn't affected. Not one little bit of her anywhere. And try as she may, she couldn't shrug out of the mood, or even shake herself hard out of it. Not after a minute, not after five minutes. Which meant she might be in deep trouble.

"So tell me about yourself," Rafe said, as he spread the blanket on the ground. Molly was a hundred yards away, wading in water up to her ankles, looking for goldfish and bullfrogs, expressing a wish to find a whale and an octopus, too, while Edie and Rafe were laying out the picnic food. "Other than the fact that you're a child life specialist and that my aunt thought highly of you…so does Molly, by the way, that's about all I know."

"There's not much to tell. I've been in Lilly Lake for a few months now. I work, I like to read, I have a cat…" She shrugged. Getting personal wasn't easy for her because she'd spent most of her life trying to stay guarded. On purpose. One little slip of the tongue and the social workers had been on the doorstep, one misspoken word to her teacher that could be perceived as something wrong in her life and everything had gone crazy. The possibility had always been there that she could be snatched away from her mother, thrown into a foster-home where nobody loved her, and her mother forced into a nursing home until some kindly lawyer made it all better, or her mother died. Grim reality then, bad memories of it even now. "I'm from New York City originally. Born and raised there. Went to school there, didn't ever have any call to wander very far away until I took this job in Lilly Lake. And I'm not married now, but you already know that."

"Not married *now*?"

"Well, there were a couple of years in my life when I was. You know, naive schoolgirl meets big charmer. He wasn't what I needed, I wasn't what he wanted and in the end we didn't even make any memories, good, bad or otherwise. So, *you've* never been married, have you? Your aunt told me you…"

"She told you I avoid it like the plague. Right?"

"Something like that."

"Well, she was right about that. I do avoid it, maybe not so much like the plague as I do like an entanglement I just don't want to deal with. The thing is, Aunt Grace harped at me for my lifestyle, for being single. Yet she never married, and she never considered that a lack in herself."

"But she considered it a lack in you?" Edie asked.

"I don't honestly know."

"Maybe she just wanted to see you have a shot at something she missed."

He thought about that for a moment. Frowned. "She never seemed lonely, never really struck me as someone who wanted a permanent relationship in her life."

"Yet she was surrounded by so many friends, and she took in children all the time. She kept herself busy, Rafe, and she was devoted to the people in her life, but maybe, at night, when she went to bed, there were times when she would have preferred not going alone. It could be she didn't consider your lifestyle a lack so much as she didn't want you to go to bed alone every night either. I'd say that's someone who truly loved you."

"I was lucky," he said.

"More than lucky. Blessed."

Rafe was quiet for a moment, his eyes fixed on something far off that wasn't really there. Then he cleared his throat and drew in a deep breath. "So, what else is there to know about you?"

"Not much, really. I'm taking some online classes in preparation for getting my master's degree. I like gardening. Oh, and I'm thinking about getting a kitten to keep my other cat, Lucy, company, when I'm away."

Even to Edie, all the explanations sounded like uptight chatter. Nothing too significant, nothing too revealing…pretty much the way she'd trained herself to chat when people had insisted on it. It was all laid out, evenly rehearsed, rarely off the script. Reverting back to old habits was what she did when she was nervous. Rafe made her nervous.

"No family?" he asked. "Parents? Brothers or sisters?"

She shook her head. "Not any more. Maybe some distant relatives I've never met but, basically, it's just me now. And you?"

"Just Jess. And we're not really too close. We talk occasionally, see each other whenever I get to New York City…he's a firefighter there."

"I thought Grace said he was a doctor."

"He is…*was*. Trauma surgeon. But he experienced a loss in Afghanistan…his fiancée died in his arms, and he left medicine. Took up a more risky life. Don't know why, and I'm not going to argue with him about it."

"Even though you think he should go back to medicine?"

Rafe laughed. "Am I that transparent?"

"In ways."

"OK, I'll admit it. I think he should go back to medicine, but I don't really have a say in his life. And he's pretty blunt about telling me it's none of my business."

"But he's part owner of the hospital, isn't he? Along with you?"

"According to the papers. But we're not sure what we're going to do with it yet."

"Keep Rick Navarro on, I hope."

Rafe flinched at the mention of Rick's name. "Probably. I hear he's pretty good."

"Better than pretty good. He's exactly what that hospital needs, and it would be a shame to get rid of him. But I've heard rumors…"

Rafe held up his hand to stop her. "No hospital talk today. OK? Jess and I have some serious issues to address, and we're not ready yet so, in the meantime, I'd rather not get into it."

"But you'll consider my recommendation about Rick?"

"Why? Are you and Rick…?"

"No!" she snapped. "We're colleagues. That's all. Anything else wouldn't be…professional." She chanced a long look at Rafe when he glanced over at Molly playing in the lake, and what was that she saw there? Relief? Was it because she *wasn't* involved with Rick?

No, couldn't have been. Because that would have suggested something she didn't want suggested. So, like Rafe, she fixed her attention on Molly, who was thoroughly enjoying herself in the water. Too bad adults couldn't enjoy themselves that way, too. But life got in the way too often.

"I think too many people take their families for granted. You know, ignore them. Or treat them bad because they're *just* family and they know that, in the end, family will or should forgive you. Then one day they're gone—died, moved away, just drifted off—or you're so estranged from them that you might not be able to find your way back. And being alone…it's not good. Your aunt knew that, I think. But if you have family, you don't have to be alone, because being with your family is the one place you should always feel welcomed, embraced…safe."

She could hear the words just pouring out. Couldn't stop them. Didn't know where they were coming from. It was almost like she'd stepped totally outside herself to watch the delivery. "And if you have family and ignore them, or have the opportunity to have a real relationship and you don't do that…it turns into a really lonely life, Rafe. And it's not just about having someone to go to bed with, it's about having someone to sit on the porch and talk to, and call in the middle of the night when you need to hear another voice. It's about having someone who knows you so well that you don't have to say how you feel because they know. Friends, acquaintances…that's one thing. They'll stick with you, but only so far. Yet family…" She took a deep breath, forced herself to stop. "Look, I'm sorry about that. I have some strong feelings, and sometimes I just…"

Rafe chuckled. "No need to apologize. What you were saying was…was right. There's nothing wrong with having strong feelings. I've been known to have some pretty strong feelings about family myself. Just not feelings that go in the same direction as yours…

unfortunately. But it doesn't matter, because I enjoyed watching you finally relax. You've been pretty tense since you got here, and it's nice seeing some of the real you getting through."

"Horses make me nervous," she confessed. "Never been on one before today, never been anywhere near one, and I've kicked myself a thousand times since I accepted your invitation because I'm usually more cautious than that."

"So, is your first experience turning out to be a good one? If it's not, I can call someone to come get you so you don't have to ride back on Ice Cream."

He looked genuinely concerned, which touched her. "I'll be fine riding Ice Cream when we go back. She's a gentle soul, and I think she understands me." And, to be honest, she was enjoying spending time with Rafe.

"The horse? The horse understands you?"

Edie nodded. "Sure she does. As well as I understand her. She's had a lot of pain in her life, and she doesn't want to cause pain to someone else. It's pretty simple, really. Ice Cream has found her place in the world. She knows she's loved, she knows she's respected for who she is, and she's happy. Ultimately, Ice Cream has found that one place where we all want to be."

Rafe thought about that for a moment. Thought about the way Edie had connected to a simple horse. He also thought about her passion for family. She looked at life differently. Looked at it in ways he'd never considered. Gentle ways. And optimistic. Edie Parker was an extraordinary woman, and one who frightened him a little, with the way she connected to things so quickly. It was a natural ability, and one he didn't understand, coming from a life where connecting simply meant opening yourself up for more pain. Even though he was well past those days, he tried hard to be the opposite of Edie. She wanted to be connected, and flowed into it easily. Whereas he fought hard to keep his emotional distance and build up those barriers around him. He wasn't sure what to make of that.

An hour later, after they'd eaten their meal, and Molly was dozing peacefully on the blanket, curled up with Edie, who wasn't asleep but was lying there, holding Molly in her arms and simply staring up at the sky, looking as contented as he'd ever seen anyone look, he recognized that connection there again, and it rattled him to the core as it surrounded him, coming so close to touching him. OK, maybe he did envy that a little. Maybe when he'd been a boy, he might have been open to it or, perhaps, even wanted it. But that had been so long ago he didn't exactly recall all the emotional aspects of those days. Or maybe he'd just put them away, never to be brought out again.

Except, of course, Aunt Grace had been the difference, the memory that mattered. His connection. And he missed it, still needed it. Thinking back, he knew she had been his only real link to a better life, to a life where someone really did care. And now here he was, sitting on the opposite side of the blanket from Edie and Molly, totally unlinked. Totally left out. His choice, of course, and not the first time in the few hours he'd known Edie that he'd nearly regretted his choice. But even though the wounds were old, they felt more acute here, in Lilly Lake, than anyplace else. Wounds he didn't want opened again. And Edie would be the one to open them. Edie, or Molly. Not intentionally, but more as a fallout from the things he couldn't allow himself to have.

"Look, I'm going down to the lake," he whispered. "Care to come with me?"

"I'd like to, but I don't want to disturb Molly."

She connected with horses, children...probably even the ants sneaking their way up to the blanket in search of picnic crumbs. *Could be trouble,* he thought as he wandered down to the water's edge by himself. Big, *big* trouble, if he wasn't careful.

A huge part of him was on the verge of wanting to turn around and look back toward the picnic blanket, at Edie and Molly, but he knew he shouldn't. Just one look right now would change the situation from casual into something he wasn't even sure he could put into words. And he didn't like these feelings coming over him. Didn't like the mellowness, or the slender thread of longing that came along with it. Not at all!

So, he chalked it all up to this being the effect of coming home, and hoped that would take care of him until he got the hell out of there. These were old insecurities returning to haunt him, leftover emotions that apparently hadn't ever quite resolved themselves after his father had died. Damn, he hated the old man, even after a dozen years. Maybe hated him more now than ever, because those feelings his dad had burned into his soul wouldn't let go. Wouldn't even be put aside, it seemed.

After all these years being away, convincing himself he was over it, convincing himself he was well beyond the dark cloud his former life had cast over him, he despised the fact that he'd been so wrong about it, despised the fact that all the emotions had been hiding close enough to the surface that they'd simply popped out to strangle him when he let down his guard the least little bit.

But that was what was happening. Same feelings, same anger. He could feel it in his gut, feel it in his heart. And this time he didn't have his aunt to help him through it. It was just…him. No family, no friends. No one!

Unable to resist, he stole a quick glance at Edie and Molly, again seeing that easy connection between them. Even though he did envy them a little, he almost resented them for it, too. Almost resented them for something he couldn't feel. Yet, when he glanced back again, he realized it wasn't resentment he was feeling. It was…emptiness.

For a moment he caught himself wishing he could be curled up on that blanket, too, with Edie and Molly. But he knew better. If there ever was a lesson his old man had taught him, it was that he definitely could not go home. Not now, not ever. Home meant pain, and that, above everything else, was the reason Rafe spent the next half-hour standing on the shore, alone, skipping rocks.

"It's been a long time," Rafe said, extending his hand to Rick Navarro, not sure whether or not Rick would take it. To his credit, Rick took Rafe's hand right away, and greeted him with a hearty shake. But there was no sense of friendliness in his eyes. Nothing warm, nothing welcoming. Not that Rafe expected there to be. In fact, he wouldn't have been easy with it if there had been, as he didn't deserve it.

"It has been, hasn't it?" Rick said. His steady, wary

gaze met Rafe's straight on. "So, welcome to Lilly Hospital… I'm assuming you and Jess are going to continue to call it Lilly Hospital."

"Actually, we haven't really talked about what we're going to do. But I don't anticipate changing the name."

Rick nodded. "Grace liked the name. She thought it sounded warm and nurturing. After she bought the hospital, the board wanted to call it after her—Grace Corbett Memorial, even Grace Memorial, but she wouldn't have it. Said it was too pretentious, that the hospital was about the town, not about her." He chuckled. "She threatened to dismiss the entire board if they went through with it. Joking, of course. But that was Grace, wasn't it? Always getting her way, one way or another."

"The hell of it was, her way was always right," Rafe said, forgetting the tension between them for a moment. "She knew it, and she had the most subtle ways of convincing other people to see it like she wanted them to. Never browbeating. Never nagging. Just…"

"Friendly persuasion," Rick offered. "She did that better than anybody I've ever known, and I respected Grace probably more than anyone I've respected in my life." He paused, drew in a deep breath. "Look, I'm sorry for your loss, Rafe. Grace meant the world to many people, including me, and we're already missing her. She always treated me fairly, when…"

Rick paused. Didn't say the rest of the words. Words Rafe knew so well in his heart. Words to which Rick Navarro had a right. "I miss her. She was one amazing lady."

That was something about which the two of them

could agree. Common ground, after all these years. "She *was* an amazing woman," he said. "And I respect her decisions about the hospital, Rick. Respect her decision to make you Chief of Staff. So let's get this awkward moment out of the way, OK? While Jess and I haven't really reached a decision over what we're going to do with the hospital, the one thing we did agree on is that we want you to stay here, in your same capacity. We don't want to make changes that will disrupt anything…not the way the hospital operates, not people's lives in general. Jess doesn't even practice medicine any more, and I have no intention of staying in town, so we're not going to interfere with anything you're doing here. Grace trusted you to run her hospital and as you're who Grace wanted, you're who I want. Can you deal with that…deal with staying on in your same capacity for now, maybe even taking on more responsibility in the future?"

Rick didn't even hesitate before he answered. "I can deal with it. But I'll need the terms laid out for me, considering…"

"Considering how badly Jess and I treated you when we were young?" His mother had been their maid, and they'd taken every opportunity they could get to bully Rick because of it. Jess hadn't done it so much. More like stood off on the sidelines and watched. But he himself… He cringed, even thinking about what he'd done to Rick.

"You did," Rick stated. "You made my life a living hell all those years, and I know people change, but I haven't gotten over all of it, Rafe. And you've got to know it. Out of sight, out of mind works, but now that you're not out of sight, I'm having a hard time separating myself from the way you and Jess treated me. Bad memories returning to haunt me. But I'm trying to chalk it up to youthful pranks. And hoping my own son, who's six now, doesn't have such a rough time of it growing up."

"You have a son? Aunt Grace never mentioned it."

"It's a long story. Wife who sidestepped the responsibility and gave it all to me. Son caught in the crossfire. Dad with full-time custody. Christopher's a great kid. Smart, full of life. Best thing that ever happened to me. Which isn't what we're talking about here. I mean, I know what your old man did to you, Rafe. He was wrong, and I'm sorry about what he did. My mother used to tell me to be patient, that you and Jess…particularly you…weren't really such a mean boy, but looking at you through my eyes…it was tough, and there are parts of me that still resent the hell out of both you and your brother, even though I'm a man now, and I can understand where you were coming from. So you've got to know how I feel, and I'd understand if you two decided to get rid of me and hire someone else to run the hospital. This is going to be awkward for all of us, maybe for some time to come. Maybe for ever, who knows? But in my defense I can do one hell of a job for you if I stay, because I truly care for this hospital, and care for the people who work here. But like I said, you have to know how I feel about you and your brother, *personally*, before we go any further with this discussion as you may not want somebody in charge of what you own who has the kind of feelings for you that I have."

Blunt, but honest. Rafe admired that forthrightness. Respected it, even. Especially considering that Rick had a good right to his opinion. He and Jess *had* bullied Rick when they'd been kids. Kids' stuff, most of it. Unrelenting kids' stuff. But kids damaged so easily. He knew. He thought about it now, more than ever, because of Molly. Back then, he'd been a damaged kid, too, who hadn't really gotten over it yet. So he understood Rick's position. "Look, I want to apologize. Accept it or not, it's up to you. Truthfully, I don't expect you to forgive me because there was no excuse for the things I did to you." The way he couldn't or wouldn't forgive his own father. "But I am sorry for the way I treated you. It was wrong. I was wrong. And I'm not going to hide behind youthful stupidity, or give you any excuses, not even the most obvious one that I was a bully because my dad was a bully, because that doesn't cut it. Doing that would diminish my apology to you, Rick, and I don't want it diminished, because I am deeply sorry for what I did. I'm also sorry it's taken me so many years to step up and apologize." So many years to face up to the fact that he'd been just like his father. There weren't any words to describe how that made him feel, other than sick to his stomach.

"I appreciate that," Rick said, stiffly. "I do. So give me some time, OK? Let me work it out. I teach Christopher that he should accept an apology when it's offered, but doing that's harder than it sounds, I'm just now finding out. But we're good for the time being."

"Better than I expected," Rafe said. "I know that a few words aren't going to take away the impact of the way my brother and I treated you. We were wrong. Like I said, there aren't any excuses, and I don't expect that my apology is going to change much between us. But I hope I can earn your respect over time. And I do want you to know that Jess and I are aware of what you've done for the hospital and we're hoping you'll stay on."

"If I do, how will it work? How does my staying here to run the hospital really work, when you and Jess will have all the power?"

"That's just it. We don't want all the power. It's not in the best interests of the hospital. *You are*. Aunt Grace knew that, and she trusted you. Because of that, so do my brother and I, and next time he's back in Lilly Lake, he'll tell you the same thing." At least, that was what Rafe hoped. But Jess was on his own course of avoidance these days, so who knew?

Rick gave his head a skeptical shake. "Well, just so you'll know, I've already been packing up my office for the transition. I have a couple of offers I'm looking at. Nothing firm, but the possibilities are there."

"Can you unpack? Turn down the offers and stay here...hopefully for a long time. But if you can't make that commitment right now, at least long enough for all of us to figure out what we're going to do?"

"I can, but I'm a cautious man, Rafe. I have a son to think about now, and his needs come first. We've been happy here, and I want him to stay happy, but part of that is about me being happy, too. It's sort of a reciprocal relationship. So I'll have to think about it. Is that fair enough?"

"That's fair," Rafe said, pondering how the father-son relationship was a reciprocal thing. He'd never seen that in action in his own father-son situation, but there were hints of it there in Molly. In some ways she did reflect his moods, which wasn't good as he wasn't going to be her father. "Think about it for as long as you need. And for what it's worth, you should have kicked my butt from Lilly Lake all the way over to Jasper for the way I treated you. I deserved it. Jess and I both deserved it."

Rick actually chuckled. "Is that an open invitation?"

"If that's what it takes to keep you here, it's an open invitation."

"I appreciate your honesty, and your apology," Rick said, just as his cell phone vibrated. He turned away, took the call, then turned back to Rafe, who was already half way down the hospital hall, on his way to the door. "Hey, Rafe. Care to see how we operate here?"

"As in?"

"Got an orthopedic patient coming in. A child. Probably a surgical case. I've got my surgeon on call, but if you'd like to see how things work in your own hospital, now's as good a time as any."

"Sure. Any idea what it is?"

Rick shook his head. "He fell out of a tree, so it could be anything. I'd suggest you go get our child life specialist. The kid's only seven, and this is where Edie is worth her weight in gold."

"You're working?" Edie asked Rafe several minutes later.

"Apparently. And so are you."

She grabbed up her clipboard and headed to her office door. So efficient, he thought. He'd seen Edie in a lot of ways, but this professional look at her was new. He liked it. "He's seven, victim of a tree…or rather the ground, when he fell out of the tree."

"And he's a surgical candidate?"

"Possibly. So, how do we do this? I've never worked with a CLS before."

"It's pretty simple. You take the lead, do the exam. I follow your lead, try to figure out what kind of emotional support the child is going to need, deal with the parents, address any behavioral issues that might arise."

"In other words, you compensate for my lack."

She stopped, and turned to face him. "You lack only because that's the way you want it to be."

"We're talking about Molly now, aren't we?"

"Are we?" she countered.

"And that's supposed to be you, questioning my guilty feelings over something I've already told you isn't going to happen."

"You're right about part of that. It is your guilty feelings." With that, she turned down the hall leading to the emergency department, and shoved through the double doors before Rafe had time to articulate a comeback. Or a defense. All he could think, as he watched her disappear into the ER, was, *Wow.*

CHAPTER FOUR

"THREE ribs, one ulna, one tibia, luckily no surgery. But he's got a long recovery ahead of him." He spun away from the X-ray viewing-box to face Edie. "And since this is the third time he's fallen out of the tree, I'm going to prescribe cutting the tree down."

She laughed. "Or maybe a simpler solution, such as putting a lock on his bedroom window that he won't be able to unlatch."

"Which is why you're the CLS and I'm not."

"Trees and kids…big temptation. Bobby's just doing what any normal little boy would do when presented with such exciting temptation."

"But this temptation is going to get him killed if his parents aren't careful."

"I'll talk to them and if better locks aren't the answer, I'll bring up your idea." She smiled. "But with kids, simpler is usually the best course of action. And I have an idea that since Bobby's going to spend the next couple of months being sidelined from pretty much everything, he might not be so inclined to *escape* again."

"Ah, the optimism of a girl who probably never climbed a tree. Maybe next time we go out, I'll have to teach you to climb. Seeing the world from that high up… Definitely our next date." Pulling the X-rays off the viewing-box, he stuck them in an envelope and handed them over to the waiting ward clerk, an older woman whose scowl betrayed her obvious disdain for non-professional chitchat on the job. "Will you see that these get into the proper file, please, Wilma?" he asked the woman, reading the name on her name tag.

She cleared her throat critically, grabbed the envelope and marched from the room.

"Wilma's a stickler for professional protocol," Edie said, laughing. "And it doesn't matter if the person who's not following it *does* own the hospital."

"Then she's an asset to her job. So, about climbing that tree…"

"Never have, never will."

"Then it's not a date?" he asked, faking a sad frown.

"The only date I have is with Bobby Morrow's parents, after you talk to them about Bobby's injuries."

"Another stickler for professional protocol."

"No. Just someone who's trying to get away from the man who wants her to climb a tree. Look, you go do what you need to do with Bobby, and I'll be in there in a couple of minutes to talk to his parents. In the meantime, avoid Wilma. She'll report you to the Chief of Staff." In a flash, Edie was gone, leaving Rafe alone in the designated viewing-room, wondering why the only thing on his mind was climbing a tree with Edie.

Because he was crazy, that was why! Crazy, and borrowing trouble he didn't need.

But the image of her clinging to a tree limb, him shinnying up to rescue her… Shaking his head to rid himself of that rather nice daydream, he cleared his throat and headed back to Exam 3, chiding himself that this flirtation, even though most of it was in his mind, had to stop. Edie was Lilly Lake, he was not. The twain that would never meet.

"So, by—" The words were barely out when Bobby's body nearly shook off the table in a huge convulsion. The first thing that came to Rafe's mind was a bone fragment broken lose and moving, or a blood clot. Instantly, Rafe pushed the emergency button on the wall near the door, then flew to the child's bed and wedged himself between Bobby and his mother, who was practically in the bed with the boy, trying to shake him into a response.

"Doctor!" she cried helplessly. "Bobby…what's wrong with him?"

"Please," Rafe said, trying to move the mother aside. But she wouldn't be moved, and when Rafe looked at Bobby's father, he seemed to be in some kind of a trance. "I need room…"

"Mrs. Morrow!" Edie called from the doorway. "Please step back from the bed."

"But my son—"

"Dr. Corbett will take care of your son, but you need to give him room."

Rafe, who was struggling to take a pulse, managed to diagnose tachycardia, meaning the boy's heart was beating too fast. "Did you give him any medication, or is there a possibility he got into something prescribed to you?" he asked the woman.

"No!" she screamed. "Nothing!"

"Nothing at all?" Rafe persisted.

"He fell out of a tree, now this…"

But what he was seeing didn't seem connected to the broken bones, and Bobby's symptoms didn't appear to be a bone fragment or blood clot broken loose. "If he took something, I have to know what it was," he said, his patience wearing away as quickly as Bobby's life seemed to be ebbing. "Tell me, Mrs. Morrow, Mr. Morrow!" he shouted, as his patience finally snapped.

"Nothing," the woman cried. "Nothing!"

Rafe sucked in a sharp breath, then turned his back to the couple and spoke to the nurse in charge. "I need this boy treated with activated charcoal, stat. And get a crash cart in here. We also need oxygen, and get an IV in him."

Mrs. Morrow grabbed hold of Rafe's arm. "Please, you've got to help him," she begged, but he removed her hand so he could focus on the child.

"Could somebody please see that Bobby's parents are made comfortable while we take care of their son?" he barked at the crowd of people now amassed in the room—nurses, interns, lab techs, respiratory therapists…the full emergency team at the ready.

"No," Mrs. Morrow cried, as a nurse stepped forward. "I won't leave here. This is my son, you can't make me—"

"Mrs. Morrow, you must leave so Dr. Corbett can help your son!" Edie's voice was gentle but firm. Taking the woman's arm, Edie physically pulled her all the way to the hall outside the exam room, then came back and did the same with Mr. Morrow, as one of the nurses rolled the red crash cart into the area and immediately began the efforts to save Bobby's life. Oxygen, IV, heart monitor, intubation tube just in case… Rafe led the way, calling the shots, the other medical personnel responding.

About two minutes into the procedure, Rick

Navarro appeared, but rather than throwing himself into the mix he took his place alongside Edie. "What happened?" he whispered.

"When I got here, Bobby was having a convulsion. Rafe was handling it, but the Morrows were getting pretty…let's just say in the way. So I got them out of the room, which is a good thing because Rafe also diagnosed tachycardia, and, well…" She glanced out into the hall at the Morrows, who were huddled together, and her heart went out to them. Too often, she'd been the one looking in the tiny window, watching the doctors frantically trying to save her mother's life. She knew what it felt like to be left out at the moment the person she loved most in the world needed her. "Look, they shouldn't be watching this, so I want to get them out of the area, unless you need me…"

"Go," Rick said. "Take them to the doctors' lounge, do what you have to."

She looked at Rafe, who caught her eye at the same time then smiled at her. He was so…in charge. Larger than life. Confident. Maybe, just maybe, she *would* like to go and climb that tree with him some time after all.

"It may have been an aspirin overdose," Edie whispered to Rafe, who was looking at the test results of blood drawn from Bobby.

They'd stabilized him for the moment. Treated the tachycardia and convulsions, splinted the broken ribs, and Rafe was in the process of getting ready to set the broken arm and leg. Overall, the kid was in bad shape, part of it caused by the fall, part of it because of what had happened afterward. "Aspirin?" he said, going straight to the result for the serum salicylate levels.

Sure enough, the indication was there. "Then it's a good thing I got the charcoal into him. It was a shot in the dark, but it seemed..." He shrugged.

"Logical?" she asked.

"Kid gets hurt, he's in pain...in Bobby's case, excruciating pain due to so many injuries. And the parents' first reaction is to help ease that pain. I've seen it before. Give the child aspirin, maybe in a panic give them too much. A lot of people think that baby aspirin isn't strong enough so they load the child up and, essentially, overdose them."

"And you spotted that?"

"I suspected it. But you've got to look at a whole list of other complications, too. Especially with children. There are so many childhood conditions that mimic something else, so you've got to be careful."

"Careful, as in suspecting it could be poisoning of some sort and treating for it before you have the lab results back?"

"Time is critical. You don't want that aspirin, or other painkiller, being absorbed into the system, because then you could be looking at a whole boatload of other complications—metabolic acidosis, renal shutdown, respiratory problems..." He shrugged. "How did you find out it was aspirin? When I asked, they wouldn't say a word."

"I told them that having the best doctor in the hospital wouldn't do Bobby a darned bit of good if that doctor didn't know what he was working with. Then Mrs. Morrow admitted giving him a couple of baby aspirin, and Mr. Morrow said it was more than a couple."

"Well, now we know what we're dealing with, so it'll be easier for us to treat Bobby. Thanks for getting it out of them because I sure as hell didn't have the silver tongue to do it."

"Maybe because you were too busy saving Bobby's life."

"Or maybe I lack the people skills."

"Aren't you being a little too hard on yourself?" Edie asked.

"What I'm being is honest. Nothing else intended. I treat conditions of the bone, it's what I do, it's who I am. The rest of it doesn't matter." With that, Rafe spun away and returned to the treatment room, ready to finish the process with Bobby Morrow and his parents. It wasn't his intention to be rude to Edie, or to even shut her off, but he didn't like compliments, didn't like anyone glowing over his work. He did what he did, and that was all there was to it. Oh, he liked being an orthopedic surgeon. Actually, he loved it. But he didn't want, didn't need accolades, and as sure as a new day rolled around every twenty-four hours, Edie had been on the verge of accolades. So it had been easier to leave. But he felt a little rotten about it. She'd done a masterful job of getting the information out of Bobby's parents. It probably wouldn't have hurt him to lay a few accolades on her. Hindsight, he thought, as he walked through the door to Bobby Morrow's treatment room. It was a kick in the rear end. Too bad he hadn't used a little foresight.

"I come bearing a peace offering," Rafe said, setting the cup of hot tea down on Edie's desk.

She looked up at him. "For what?"

"I was pretty rude to you earlier. Didn't mean to be,

but that's how it happens with me sometimes. It just slips out."

She hadn't taken it personally, though. He'd been a little abrupt, but not so much that she'd been offended. "A real apology would have included a vanilla bean scone with the tea," she said, pulling the cardboard cup over to her, "but I appreciate the thought."

Rafe laughed. "You're a tough one, Edie Parker."

"No one's ever accused me of being tough before. I think I like it."

"Look, sometimes I get…preoccupied with my work, and…"

"And you don't take compliments very well."

"That, too."

"Well, how about a hand signal? Maybe a subtle salute, or a half-wave? That way, it's not a real compliment, but you'll know one was intended."

"Tough, and relentless. Not a bad combination, actually."

"No one's ever called me relentless either. Normally I was the gushy one, the one given to the biggest emotions, the one who sort of got shoved to the wall when the room filled up and I didn't know how to fight my way to another spot. But I appreciate the description. I aspire to being tough and relentless."

"Would you aspire to grilled cheese sandwiches and tomato soup from a can tonight? I promised Molly her favorite meal, figuring I'd be ordering take-out pizza or something, and that's what she wanted. So I'm going to be donning my chef's apron and whipping up a culinary masterpiece later on, if you'd care to join us."

She laughed. "A man who cooks? How could I refuse?"

"Actually, I have ulterior motives. I'm pretty sure I can handle opening the soup cans, but grilling the actual sandwiches may be well beyond my culinary capabilities."

"What do you do back in Boston?"

"Eat at the hospital cafeteria, or order in."

Edie shook her head. "Bet you don't do your own laundry either."

"As a matter of fact…no." The way her eyes twinkled when she laughed caught him off guard. He really didn't intend to stare, but he couldn't help himself. She had such depth. More than that, she had a spirit like he'd never seen in anyone before, and he was pulled in by it. Edie was a woman who generally cared about everybody. She couldn't help herself. It's what she was about. And, honestly, other than his aunt, he'd never known people like that existed. "But I do bundle it up and haul it down to the laundry myself. Even sort it."

"A man who sorts laundry and opens cans of soup…"

She gave him a salute, *and* a half-wave. But the thing that caught his heart most was her smile. He was already addicted to it, and even though that should have worried him in a big way, it didn't. The fact that he wasn't worried didn't worry him either. Actually, he spent the rest of the day enjoying the lingering results of something as simple as Edie's smile.

"And for dessert, I have a surprise," Rafe said, setting the silver-domed platter on the picnic table on the patio. Soup and sandwiches had gone down well and Edie and Molly had done all the preparations while he'd stood back and watched them interact. It had occurred to him, more than once, that Edie would be the perfect parent for Molly. Their genuine affection for each other showed, and they had a natural rhythm together, one that would cause anyone looking on to see them as mother and daughter. That, plus the fact that they simply looked the part.

Could it work out? It was a thought, maybe even a good one. And somewhere, in the back of his mind, he'd even considered that if he did manage to make it happen, he might be able to keep himself on the fringes of the relationship. Seeing Edie again…he wouldn't mind that. Wouldn't mind having some insignificant part in Molly's life either. "And I'll have you know that I spent all afternoon in the kitchen…" He whisked the lid off the dome. "Arranging these vanilla bean scones on the platter."

"What are they?" Molly questioned.

"The perfect accompaniment to hot tea," Rafe answered.

Molly wrinkled her nose. "But we're not having hot tea."

"No, but Edie did earlier today, and the person serving her the tea neglected to get her the scones so he's trying to do a make-good."

"And succeeding very admirably," Edie commented. She turned to Molly. "When I was a little girl, there was a tea room a few blocks from my house."

"What's a tea room?" Molly asked.

"It's like a restaurant, only every afternoon they serve tea and little sandwiches or scones. You get all dressed up to go there because it's a very special place, and once a month my mother and I would put on our best clothes, catch the bus, and go to the tea room.

She liked the little sandwiches with her tea…they had fillings of cream cheese and cucumber."

"Yuck," Molly said.

Edie laughed. "My opinion, too. I loved the scones. Sometimes they were lemon, sometimes butter toffee. Always delicious. So, now, when I have tea, I like to have a scone with it."

"Do you and your mother still get dressed up and go to the tea room?" Molly asked.

"No. My mother went…well, she went to the place Aunt Grace is now."

"So you have to have your tea and scones all alone?" Molly's face was deadly serious when she asked the question. "Because I'll come with you, Edie, so you don't have to go by yourself. But I don't want those yucky sandwiches. I think I'll have the scones, too."

Rafe shut his eyes, shut out the emotion of the moment. Dear God, his aunt had done such a good job with Molly. It touched him, the way it had just touched Edie, who was brushing tears from her eyes. He knew what he had to do. The only thing was how was he going to do it? More than that, how was he going to do it and *not* get involved himself?

"Not good enough," Rafe told Henry Danforth. "The Simpsons seemed too preoccupied with image, the Walcotts weren't concerned enough with a proper education, and I don't know how you slipped the Bensons on the list because the only reason they wanted a child was to have an indentured servant."

"You've turned down seven perfectly good families, Rafe," Henry said, his irritation clearly showing. "I pre-interviewed each and every one of them myself, had my investigator do an exhaustive background check, and I can assure you these are all good families for Molly."

"But not good enough!"

"So who is it you really want? Because I'm sensing an agenda."

"My agenda is doing the best thing for Molly. And who I really want…?" He hadn't said it aloud. Hadn't even let himself think it in a couple of days because if he had, and Edie wasn't agreeable, he wasn't sure what he'd do. She was the perfect mother for Molly. In his mind, the only perfect mother. The thing was, she hadn't said a word about wanting to adopt Molly. Sure, Edie's agenda was to get him to keep her. Aunt Grace wouldn't have manipulated it any other way. But Edie knew that wasn't going to happen. He'd made himself perfectly clear. So, to be honest, he was a little disappointed that Edie wasn't stepping up because from everything he'd seen between her and Molly, she should have been.

Of course, from his detached perch, maybe he wasn't seeing this the right way. It was a distinct possibility, but one he didn't want to admit. Not yet, anyway. "Who I really want is the person who wants Molly the most. But she…or he…has to also be the person Molly most wants."

"Which wouldn't be you," Henry snapped.

Actually, that didn't sound so good to him any more. It was still his reality, though. Maybe a more bitter one than he'd expected. "Which wouldn't be me."

"Fine. Let me go and break the hearts of all the people I've interviewed so far, then start over."

"I'm not wrong here, Henry. None of these people have been right for Molly."

"And if they're not right for her, and you're not right, who is?"

"Edie Parker," Rafe finally confessed.

"Edie?" That seemed to catch the old lawyer off guard. "Have you talked to her about it?"

"No, because she's involved in this and she knows Molly is—"

"Up for grabs?" Henry interrupted.

"She's not up for grabs!" Rafe huffed an impatient breath. "And you know that!"

"What I know is that you're ignoring the obvious and if your aunt were here, God rest her soul, she'd be drumming, kicking or pounding some sense into you right this very minute."

But good sense didn't involve adopting a child who needed so much more than a man who didn't have it in him to love that child the way she needed to be loved… the way he'd never been loved. When it got right down to the most cutting truth, he *was* his father's son. He'd read to the end of the book. He knew how *that* story turned out. He wanted better for Molly. "If my aunt were here, she'd be the person Molly needs most. But since that's not going to happen, we have to do our best to find the person who has all the qualities to replace my aunt. Those are some mighty big shoes to fill but, for Molly's sake, we've got to fill them." And Edie was the only one. But what would happen if he asked, and she turned him down?

"Then I'll ask Edie."

Rafe shook his head. "No. She needs to ask us. Edie needs to be the one who realizes she wants Molly without us asking her." For the sake of two people who really did belong together, he firmly believed that.

"In the meantime, should I line up more interviews?"

On one hand, if Edie did say no, then they'd be back at square one, which meant he'd have to prolong his stay in Lilly Lake to reopen the search. That part didn't matter so much, but Molly's emotions did, and that was what had him worried. She needed to start her new life…her real life…now. Without delay. Yet he couldn't even think in terms of someone other than Edie raising her. "No more interviews for now," he finally said.

"Then you've changed your mind, and you're going to ask Edie?"

Rafe shook his head. "Edie's going to ask me."

"You're that sure of it?"

Truth was, he wasn't sure at all. But he hoped, like he'd never hoped for anything else in his life. "I'm not sure of anything, Henry. Not one damned thing, except that Molly needs to be with Edie."

Henry cocked a bushy eyebrow then exited the den, smiling. And whistling.

"I'm *not* going to be the one to keep Molly," Rafe shouted after him. To which Henry did not reply.

"It's not as easy as it looks," Edie said, looking at Rafe in the mirror. "First, you divide her hair into three sections, then your job is to alternately cross each outer section, one at a time, over the center section. And make sure it's consistent." She was demonstrating braid technique on her own hair for him. "I mean, you're a surgeon, you've got good hand technique, so how hard should this be?" He was cute, actually. All thumbs and frowns. She liked the vulnerability she saw in Rafe when it came to Molly. He tried so hard to please her, which gave Edie hope that Rafe might be reconsidering his position.

"Let's just say that by the time I got through with her, she was in tears. This party tonight is important to her, and she's set on having her hair braided."

"Then I'd say that if you're not up to it, take her to one of the salons in town. While you're at it, does Molly have a new dress to wear?"

"She has a closet full of clothes."

"But a new dress for the party?" He was such a man! She didn't mean that in a bad way, but Rafe was so…oblivious. Definitely oblivious to little girls, probably to women as well. "And shoes! She has to have new shoes to go with her new dress." With a couple of twists, her hair turned into a perfect braid, and she spun around, smiling at him. "See, not that difficult."

"Then maybe you could braid her hair tonight. And take her shopping for a new dress and shoes."

"Or maybe you could," Edie suggested. Sure, it would have been easy enough to do that for Molly, and having a girls' afternoon out would have been fun. But that was something Rafe needed to be doing. He was the one who had to get closer to Molly, who had to see how much fun she would be in his life. He was also the one who had to discover, for himself, that Molly was the person he most needed to fill out his life. In other words, open himself up to her. She could see the signs, see Rafe's willingness to do anything he thought was necessary for Molly, see how he tried hard to be responsive. But she also saw the way he kept himself distanced. It was like he was going through the motions yet not letting himself fully invest in them. An hour in a beauty salon could help that. Watching Molly try on ten or twenty pairs of shoes definitely would.

"With a woman's touch?" he asked. "Would you come with us? I'll do what needs to be done, but if this party is so important to Molly, I think you being there to help in her decisions would be a good idea. Especially as this is the first time she's really ventured out since…"

Well, Rafe had her on that one. Maybe Molly did need the extra emotional support. God knew, she'd needed it after her mother had died. Needed it in ways she hadn't seen coming. In fact, she'd needed it so desperately she'd pretty much jumped straight into a bad marriage on her first time out, and while Molly certainly wasn't at risk of that, Edie did understand the emotions involved in moving on. "I'll go, as long as you're not backing out of this."

"Not backing out," he said, on an obvious sigh of relief.

"Oh, and just so you'll know, we should pick out the dress first so Molly can have co-ordinating hair ribbons. Things like that are very important to the total ensemble." Was that panic creeping to his face? Actually, it looked adorable there, and she really wanted to laugh at his discomfort over such simple little-girl things, but she wouldn't. Rafe was trying hard to do the right thing for Molly, even though he was that proverbial fish out of water. "It's going to be fun. Just relax. Enjoy yourself."

"Fun? Back home, I have a shopper. She's a nice lady who has a thriving business going, shopping for people like me who find it easier to pick up a phone and tell her what I need rather than going out buying it for myself. And I have a barber who makes house calls. These people do what they do for me, first, because they're making a good living at it and, second, because for me, shopping and going to the barber shop *isn't* fun. It doesn't make me relax, and I never enjoy myself doing either!"

"Well, it *could* be fun, if you were doing those things with the right person." Did he ever allow himself to relax? Even in something as simple as shopping, Rafe kept himself distanced. In a way, it was sad he limited himself the way he did. It almost seemed like he was afraid to let himself go even a little.

"Well, *you're* the right person for Molly. I want to make this fun for *her*."

"But not for you?"

"What I want for me is to make sure Molly gets what she needs to make her happy. That'll be sufficient for now."

It wasn't exactly what she'd wanted to hear from him, but somewhere in his words lurked a pure motive. It was better than nothing. "Then I say let's go down to the stables, get Molly, and see what kind of power shopping we can get ourselves into."

"Power shopping?" Rafe actually moaned aloud. "I thought this was about a dress, a pair of shoes and a perfect braid."

Laughing, Edie whisked around him and headed to the door. "It's never just about a dress, a pair of shoes and a perfect braid."

Prophetic words, as it turned out. Because three hours later, with no less than five dresses, six pairs of shoes, and more accessories than Edie could count, and a pair of cowboy boots Molly just had to have, the three of them stumbled into the beauty salon ready for the next part of the adventure. Or, as Rafe would put it, ordeal.

"She'd like…" Rafe started to tell the beautician, but Edie laid a hand on his arm to stop him.

"She can do that," she whispered to him. "Part of this needs to be a teaching experience, too."

"Maybe you should make me a list, telling me everything I should know, because I'd have never guessed that a hair appointment could also be turned into a teaching experience."

He dropped the shopping bags on the floor then slid into one of the chairs lined up along the wall. It was pink, rather undersized for him. He looked awkward, but cute, she thought. In the past three hours, her estimation of Rafe had grown about a hundred times more. He was patient, considerate…not very adept at little-girl things but trying harder than anybody she'd ever seen. "With kids, everything can turn into a teaching experience. The thing is, they don't have to know that's what it is. Right now, Molly's involved in a huge decision that's going to affect the outcome of her evening. All those books the beautician is taking to her…they're full of different hairstyles suitable for a child her age. Molly's going to get to choose."

"But I thought she wanted a braid. Isn't that pretty simple?"

Edie laughed. "I'm afraid you've just wandered into a very complicated world, Rafe. There's nothing simple about a braid. I'm mean, there are so many types… French braids are one of the classically most popular. It's where hair is woven in small chunks on top of the main braid, which lies close to the scalp. The final result is a tidy and very sophisticated look. Maybe a little too old for Molly, but who knows? Then there are herringbone braids, which are thin, layered braids that use a number of small intertwined pieces of hair. And lace braids, which are simple braids that crown the head of the wearer in a half-moon shape, like a tiara. Personally, I think that would be a lovely choice for Molly. But she might like cornrows or Dutch braids, or…"

Laughing, Rafe held out his hand to stop her. "OK, so when you said there was some teaching value here, I didn't know I was the one being taught. So, a braid is not a braid is not a braid."

"You're catching on."

"Just like a party dress is not a party dress is not a party dress."

"Has it been that awful for you?"

"Not awful so much as…exhausting. She tried on that pink dress three times then bought the blue one instead."

"And she might still change her mind and want to exchange the blue one for the pink one. That's a woman's prerogative."

"My world's a whole lot simpler. You just—"

"I know. Call your shopper, and wear what she picks out. But where's the fun in that? I mean, think about it, Rafe. What would happen if you took Molly out shopping for you? You might discover that there's more to life than gray dress slacks and blue dress shirts."

"How do you know that's what I wear?"

"You're predictable. Sure, you're in jeans right now. But you're out of your element. What happens when you get back into your element…your rut?"

"I wear gray and blue, which suit me just fine, thank you very much!" He said this almost defensively.

"But what if Molly found you a pink shirt or, heaven forbid, navy-blue slacks? Could you handle that?"

"It's just colors. What's the big deal?"

"The rut's the big deal." She didn't know if he liked his rut, or if it was just easier for him being stuck in it.

"So, when is a shopping trip *not* a shopping trip?" he asked. "When it's meant to show me just how much I need to be a father?"

"I'm not denying it," Edie said.

"And I'm not buying into it," Rafe argued.

But he was, hook, line and sinker. She knew it. And an hour later, when Molly hopped out of the beauty chair, her hair done in a pretty lace braid, the look Edie saw on Rafe's face only confirmed how much he was truly buying into everything.

"She's beautiful," he whispered, his voice full of emotion. The emotion a father would have for his daughter.

It was such a touching scene, it brought tears to Edie's eyes, and she turned her head quickly so Rafe wouldn't see.

"Rafey," Molly called out. "Can we take the blue dress back and get the pink one?"

Rafe laughed out loud. "Of course we can." He gave Edie a gentle nudge, then held out his hand for Molly. "I wouldn't have it any other way."

CHAPTER FIVE

IT WASN'T like she was a schoolgirl out on her first date yet somehow that was exactly how she felt. A little bit giddy, a little bit nervous…all of it probably owing to the fact that she hadn't actually been out on a *real* date with Rafe yet. Or, for that matter, any kind of date for some years. Occasionally, there'd been casual coffee at the corner coffee house or lunch with a casual friend… Casual, casual, casual…that was about as far as her life had gone in the dating department since her one and only venture into the real relationship world had sent her running for shelter before the ink had barely dried on the marriage certificate. She took the blame… all of it. She hadn't been ready to be out in the world on her own let alone tied into a relationship. But marriage had seemed stable, and she had been at a place in her life where she'd wanted stability. Alex, though, he'd wanted a real marriage…something she hadn't been able to give him even after the hasty vows had been pronounced at the county courthouse. Oh, she'd playacted for a while, fashioned herself in the role and given it her best effort, but her best hadn't been good enough. So after that, no men, no dates until now.

The thing was, Edie wasn't even sure that this

qualified as a date. As they were exchanging Molly's blue dress for the pink one, a mention of dinner had slipped into the conversation, barely without noticing. Then the next thing she knew, she was home worrying, primping and worrying some more. Admittedly, she was attracted to him. What woman wouldn't be? Big, rugged, handsome. The kind of man who brought a sigh to her lips…lips she'd tried to keep *those* kinds of sighs away from for a long time. After all, what was the point? She'd dipped her toe into that pool once and found she didn't like getting wet. So why bother with the sighs when she wasn't willing to allow anything more?

Except with Rafe those sighs seemed inevitable now, even when she fought them off.

Well, she'd just have to deal with it, wouldn't she? Keep her distance, as well as a good, hard bite down on her lower lip. "Besides, it's just a silly little dinner," she chided herself, looking at her reflection in the mirror. "Food, conversation. A way for Rafe to kill a couple of hours waiting for Molly to be finished at her party."

But who was she kidding? She *was* nervous. No avoiding it. Suppose they got on too well, or discovered they didn't get on at all? How would either way affect her quest to win him over to adopt Molly? What she did, or said, could have such a strong bearing on Rafe's intentions with Molly, and that was the thought that pestered her for the next ten minutes, until the doorbell rang.

"Rafe, it's so nice to see you," she said, trying not to sound breathless when she opened the door to him. Her first look at him nearly took her breath away, though. Casual jeans, tight. Boots. Close-fitting T-shirt showing off a nice expanse of chest. Leather jacket. Everything about him impeccable. Not bad at all, she decided as he helped her into her wrap. Actually, very good…his look, her reaction. Because she was still focused on her mission in spite of Rafe's incredible good looks. This was about Molly, not about her. So, it was all under control, she decided as Rafe took her arm and led her down the walkway to his car then helped her in. *About Molly*, she kept telling herself the whole way to Mama Bella's World Famous Pizza.

"You don't mind casual tonight, do you?" he asked, holding open the restaurant door for her. The hostess, a jovial, matronly woman with short red braids who spoke with a fake Italian accent, showed them to a secluded table for two, probably the table considered to be the restaurant's most romantic, even though the tablecloth was red-and-white-checked vinyl.

"Excuse me?" she asked, biting back a smile as he was pulled out the chair for her.

"Casual. You don't mind making this a casual evening, do you?"

"But doesn't the candle on the table automatically make it romantic? Most of the other tables don't have candles." The candle was a drippy red thing, burnt down to a stub, stuffed into a used wine bottle.

In one swoop Rafe grabbed up the candle and put it on the floor. "There. Casual."

In a way, that was disappointing, not that she'd expected a romantic evening with him. Or even wanted one. But to dismiss it so quickly…to just whisk the candle off the table the way he had, was, oddly, a letdown she hadn't expected. *It's about Molly,* she reminded herself. "There, casual…" she said, picking the candle up off the floor and handing it to a passing waiter. No more hints, no more reminders, no more awkwardness…at least, on her part. "OK?"

"Well, it occurred to me that I should have mentioned what I had in mind for this evening, so you could dress appropriately."

"I'm not?" she asked, suddenly self-conscious. She was wearing black slacks, a simple powder-blue sweater, something that should have covered both worlds—casual or dressy. Even romantic. Damn, did he actually think that was what she thought? Now she felt awkward again.

"And I've gone and said the wrong thing, haven't I?"

"It shows?" she asked.

He smiled. "You don't hide yourself very well, you know. Everything shows on you. But it's nice. Very nice."

"So what you're saying is that I wear my heart on my sleeve?" This wasn't the first time someone had told her that. In fact, that was what her mother had always said.

"And a very nice heart, and sleeve, they are. Oh, and before I put my foot back into my mouth, let me just say that you look beautiful this evening. That's what I was trying to say a minute ago when I went so horribly wrong."

"Not *horribly* wrong. Just a little wrong. And you're forgiven."

He laughed out loud. "Beautiful and brutally honest. No wonder my aunt liked you." Settling in, Rafe stretched back in his chair. "Look, Edie, let *me* be brutally honest here for a minute. I don't…don't date. Don't do relationships."

"And you think that's what my accepting your invitation is about? That I'd want a relationship…with *you*?" She could already feel the flush rising in her cheeks. "That I'd accept a date for pizza and expect a side order of commitment to go with it?"

Immediately, Rafe went rigid in his chair. "I feel my foot wedging in my mouth again."

"Both feet," she snapped. Sure, she was angry. And humiliated. Embarrassed, too. So much so that she tried to shove back her chair so she could stand and muster the dignity to march out of there. But Rafe stood first, caught her by the wrist on her way up, and had the decency to look a little embarrassed himself.

"Could we just start this over?" he asked.

"There's nothing to start over," she said, not sure whether she wanted to sit back down or stand all the way up and leave, the way she'd planned.

"I was trying to explain myself, Edie. That's all. Trying to tell you a little bit about the way I am… which, as you can see, is pretty damned pathetic."

Admittedly, he did look pathetic. Which was why she sat back down. She *was* curious about Rafe, was interested in hearing what made him tick. "OK, tell me. But it had better be good, Rafe Corbett, because so far I'm not impressed with your dating manners."

"Neither am I." He let go, then sat back down. "Which is why I need to explain myself. The thing is, Edie, I really don't date, don't get involved. For a lot of reasons I don't want to get into this evening, it's easier that way. So I'm rusty."

So this *was* a real date in spite of what he'd said! Not a romantic date, but a date nonetheless. Suddenly, she was nervous again. "Trust me, you don't know rusty.

That's my middle name. But, in my defense, it's fine. I don't date, per se, either. Bad marriage aside, dating's scary."

"Ah, yes, the marriage thing. You don't seem like the type who would un-commit once you've committed."

"Well, I'm probably not, under normal circumstances. But it was a low point in my life. I was desperate, afraid of being alone, he seemed…nice. And he was. But not for me. So my mistake cost me a lot of time, but I suppose you could say I came out of it wiser."

"Let me guess. You're older and wiser, and you've taken some kind of vow against marriage. You're never going near it again."

Edie laughed. "Well, maybe I won't go quite that far. But I did take a vow that the next one has to be the right one. The one and only. And my list of qualifications going in is pretty long, and stringent."

"You have a list?"

"That's the only way to do it these days. You decide what you want, and—"

"And go shopping with your list." A fake frown covered his face. One that gave way to an amused grin. "I think you're on to something, Edie. Maybe I should make a list of my own."

"Starting with?" she asked.

"Hands down, this is the list topper. She has to make me laugh. Everything else is negotiable."

"Then you're pretty easy to please. Some lucky lady's going to find you irresistible just for that alone."

"*That* alone?" He faked a wince. "That cuts to the core of my ego. A man likes to live in this delusion that he's irresistible in *other* ways. You know, that list thing. Most men do have their lists."

And Rafe's was a very long list. In fact, there was practically nothing about him that wasn't irresistible. Which was turning into a big problem. "Well, in the defense of some men, maybe it's not a delusion. Of course, maybe the list isn't as long as they think it is either. But I suppose irresistible is in the eye of the beholder, isn't it? And depending on the beholder, that list could be very long, or very short. So, if your only real requirement is that she has to make you laugh… " Edie leaned across the table to him. "I won't say this too loud since you apparently don't want to get caught, but you could be a sitting duck if you want to be. Look around you, Dr. Corbett. The world is full of women just waiting for the snap of a finger."

He leaned even closer to Edie. "The thing is, Miss Parker, I'm probably the hardest man to please you'll ever meet because I don't laugh."

She pulled back then folded her arms across her chest. "But you do, Rafe. All the time. Especially around Molly."

"So to *you* that means that Molly is the one who's supposed to catch me?"

"So to me that means you don't know yourself as well as you think you do."

"And *you* know me better than I know myself?"

Edie didn't answer that. She didn't have to, because the answer was obvious. At least, to her it was. In this matter, she *did* know him better. Which meant her biggest task was to introduce Rafe Corbett to Rafe Corbett. Unfortunately, that was easier said than done. More than that, she wasn't sure how yet.

The next fifteen minutes passed in a nondescript blur of inconsequential small talk—weather, current events, hospital—over a frosty pitcher of beer and, finally, a pizza. "Aunt Grace used to bring me here," he said, as the server made a tableside production of cutting the pizza into slices. "Lilly Lake's done a lot of growing since I've been gone, but this place…nice memories. Not much change either. Especially here," he said, taking Edie's plate and holding it up for the first slice.

"It is nice," she agreed. Nice ambiance, the smell of the pizzas was wonderful, the servers all friendly… she felt good here. Felt like she belonged, which was something she hadn't felt since her mother… "We used to have a little deli down the street. It was a lot like this place. Not fancy, but nice. You felt welcome, and sometimes, when my mother was feeling up to it…" She smiled, fighting back the memory. They hadn't been able to afford the deli, but Mr. Rabinowicz, the owner, had never turned them away.

"You mother was sick?"

This wasn't the topic of conversation she'd hoped for over dinner, but she'd started it, after all. "Sometimes… most of the time. But we managed…" She smiled sadly. "Most of the time."

"Care to talk about it?"

"There's not a lot to say, really." She stared down at the slice of pizza on her plate. Didn't want to see his expression, didn't want to see his sympathy, or pity, as the case may be. She'd seen that too often in her life, didn't want any more of it. "My mother had pernicious anemia. It was diagnosed when I was seven and lasted until, well…" She didn't have to say the words. He was a doctor. He knew the consequences of a condition where, in even the best cases, survival was measured in remissions and relapses that never stretched out into a normal life span. "Mum had good days as well as bad ones in the early years then we hit a mid-point where the doctors thought she might be achieving some sort of remission. False hope, of course. But it was nice while it lasted. Then came the relapse, and as the disease progressed to its end stage, the bad days started outweighing the good ones. That's the nature of the disease, as you know, and the more debilitated my mother became, the more I took care of her. Consequently, I had more responsibility at home than most girls my age did." Finally, she gained the courage to look at his face, and what she saw there was so compassionate it brought tears to her eyes. He wasn't pitying her, or looking at her as some kind of martyr. He was simply understanding her words, maybe even understanding a little bit of her heart. Which scared her in ways she didn't understand, in ways she didn't want to understand.

"And you wouldn't trade those years for anything, would you?" he asked.

"No, I wouldn't. My mother was this wonderful fount of so much knowledge and love, and I never saw her frown, never even saw her get angry. I mean, she went through the worst, things you can't even imagine, and she did it with so much grace and strength. She had a tough life, raising me alone, not much money coming in, always up and down in her health, but she never complained, never felt sorry for herself."

"No father?"

Edie shook her head. "He left before I was born.

Didn't want the responsibility. The only thing my mother ever said about him was that he didn't have the heart for it."

"Kind words for a man who didn't deserve them." Rafe said, not even trying to hide the bitterness in his voice.

"Maybe he didn't, maybe he did. I'll never know, because he was killed when I was a toddler. My mother always said that he was a sad man who didn't know how to follow his heart, and that's how I like to think of him…as a sad man. And the thing is, even though I never met him, what I learned from him is that people don't follow their hearts the way they should. They get so caught up in what society expects or dictates, or whatever other trappings are out there ready to grab them, they forget to follow their hearts. But every day my mother showed me how much that mattered, showed me how to do just that, no matter what else was going on."

"She sounds like she was an amazing woman," he said, as sadness washed down over his face. "I'm sorry she's gone now. Sorry I'll never have the chance to know her."

"She *was* amazing, and I'm sorry about the way *your* father treated you. Grace told me some of it, and there are rumors…it was horrible, Rafe. You deserved better. But you had your aunt…" She reached across the table and took hold of his hand. "Grace found me when I was pretty lost, you know. Sheltered life, failed marriage, fresh out of college a decade later than I should have been and totally without a clue, and there she was, a great big miracle in a tiny, feisty package, crooking her finger at me, telling me to follow her."

She paused, swiped at a stray tear that had found its way down her cheek. “I’m glad I did, because what I have found in Lilly Lake is…everything.” Her path finally restored. “I’m happy here, and I’m sorry you can’t be.”

“It’s that obvious?”

She shook her head. “Grace warned me.”

He chuckled. “It seems my aunt was the prognosticator of a great many things.”

“And a good judge of pizza,” she said, picking up her slice, glad for the opportunity to change the subject. She held it out to touch it to his slice in a toast. “To Grace Corbett,” she said. “A woman of influence and perfect insight.”

“To Grace Corbett” he said, smiling fondly. “A woman who knew her heart.”

“She did, didn’t she?” Edie asked.

He nodded. “Not only did she know her heart, she knew everybody else’s.” With that he took a bite of the pizza.

Edie filled up after one huge slice, and Rafe went on to eat three before he was feeling the need to loosen his belt. One last swallow, and one final sip of beer swigged, and he pushed his plate and beer mug away, then settled back in the chair. “So, what’s next?” he asked Edie.

“As in?”

“As in, are you planning on staying here? Settling down, making Lilly Lake your permanent home?” It was occurring to him that if he succeeded in persuading Edie to adopt Molly, it might be good to give her Gracie House, so Molly wouldn’t have to be uprooted.

“Maybe. I haven’t really thought about it in the

long term. In the short term, I love my job, I'm renting a nice little cottage…it's good. I don't really have a reason to go anywhere else."

"But if better job opportunities came up?"

She frowned, clearly puzzled by this line of questioning. "What's this about?"

"Just curious. I mean, I do own the hospital, so I have a vested interest in what you do since…"

"Since I work for you? Have you turned into my employer now?" Said in quite an irritated voice.

"True, I own the hospital. That's all paperwork and legalities, nothing to do with the actual operating of it. But I was just curious about you. Future plans, hopes, dreams…"

She eyed him suspiciously. "Future plans—keep on working. Hopes—keep on working. Dreams—get an advanced degree and keep on working. Is that what you wanted?"

OK, he was doing it again. Opening mouth, inserting foot. He hadn't meant to. In fact, he'd hoped to settle back into a nice, relaxing conversation and approach the subject of Molly's future. But he'd put her on edge….*again*. Which meant any talk about Molly wasn't going to be met with the most receptive attitude. "What I wanted was to start a nice after-dinner conversation with a lovely lady. But the lady seems to be taking it the wrong way."

"Or the gentleman seems to be starting it the wrong way. Look, Rafe, I like you, but this…this so-called date isn't really a good idea. We did better when our mouths were full, but now that we have to actually sit back and talk to each other…"

"And you wonder why I don't date," he huffed.

"It's not you. It's both of us. I have my agenda, you have yours…"

"What if our agendas overlapped?" he asked. "Would that be common enough ground to keep us on this date for another few minutes? Because, as bad as I am at it, I don't want it ending so soon, Edie."

"Why?" she asked, trying to mask all emotion in her face.

But he saw the emotion…the warmth in her eyes, the way the corners of her mouth turned up ever so gently. She couldn't help but care, couldn't help but put herself out there for someone who needed her. And while he wasn't about to admit that he needed her, he would freely admit that Molly did, and that was what this conversation had to get on to. Molly. "Because I like being with you," he said, kicking himself for those misspoken words before they were all the way out. He should have told her it was about Molly. Had meant to tell her it was about Molly. Then he'd gone and said he liked being with her. Another kick to the head. "And I have a bad habit of shutting out the things I really like. Over the years, I've developed this uncanny way of letting in only what I want to let in, and shutting the rest of it out. It keeps things in good balance that way, and my old habits aren't yielding very much this evening, for which I truly am sorry, Edie."

"There's no need to apologize for you being you. But what I have to wonder is what happens if you shut something out that really would have been nice to let in?"

"Do you mean Molly?" he asked.

"That's not where I was going with this, but we

could turn this into a conversation about Molly, if that's what you want to do."

"Maybe we should, because Molly's my priority, over everything else, and I'm counting on you to help me with her. The thing is, I'm not shutting her out. I'm opening new doors for her. Or trying to." Trying hard to open Edie's door and, so far, failing miserably.

"Opening her doors, shutting your own at the same time. Isn't that what you're doing, Rafe? Because I wonder what would happen if you could keep *all* the doors open for a little while…yours and hers. Give it some time, see what happens, instead of being so…so stubborn about it. You know, forget the open doors for now and try being open-minded for once."

He arched amused eyebrows. If there was only one thing he could say for Edie, it was that she was fierce in her loyalties. Of course, he was glad he didn't have to say only one thing because that list she'd mentioned earlier, the one with her stringent qualifications… well, he had a list, too. And it all concerned Edie. But nothing on it was stringent. More like, it was a list of attributes…lovely to look at, nice to talk to, wonderful to just sit back and watch… "Did you know you fairly glow when you're impassioned?"

"And *you're* condescending when I'm impassioned. This is a serious discussion, Rafe. Don't deflect it by telling me I glow."

"OK, so maybe I'm deflecting. I'll admit it. Talking about Molly's future is difficult. But, Edie, you've got to understand, I don't have many doors in my life, open, shut, or otherwise. I'm all about structure. I live by it. I'll die by it. Everything in my life is so damned structured it's like I stay on a very linear, very narrow path, and I can't get off it. But I don't want to get off it because it works for me. Me. Alone. Nobody else involved. I accomplish what I want to, have everything I need, and the thing is, I *do* want what's best for Molly, which is *not* my life. I wish it could be, because that would be the easiest thing to do. I genuinely care for that little girl. But she needs more than I can give her, more than I can be for her." More than his own father had ever been for his sons.

"And you can't adjust your life just a little to accommodate her? I mean, how do you know that if you haven't tried?"

"I know it because…hell, it's complicated." He shifted in his seat. "Look. I am who I am, and while I may not be the person you want me to be, I have the good sense to know my limitations. Getting involved with someone else in a way that matters…that's my limitation. It's not an excuse. It's a fact."

"But what if there's something else inside you, Rafe? Something you're not seeing, or something you're trying hard not to let get through?"

"Yeah, the Rafe Corbett who's just waiting to be some poor little girl's daddy. Well, that's not me. And if that's what you're seeing, you'd better look again." He huffed out an impatient sigh. "Look, I'm sorry. I wanted this to be a nice evening, but with Molly's situation hanging between us… I feel horrible about what I've got to do, Edie, and you're seeing the fallout from that."

"Then the simple solution is not to do it."

"Easy to say, impossible to do. Sometimes we don't get what we want, no matter how hard we try to make it work. That's just a fact of life, like it or not." Tonight he didn't like it one little bit, because he could almost see himself staying in Lilly Lake, settling down, raising Molly, maybe even he and Edie… No! He blinked it out of his head.

"But sometimes we do get what we want. It might be a struggle, or it might be a battle like we've never fought. My mother always told me that if there was something out there I wanted badly enough, I'd find a way to have it. And I believed her. I mean, look at me. Who knew I'd ever get this life? I started late, messed myself up before I hardly got started, yet I'm here. And before you go and tell me something like what I wanted was simple, and what you want isn't, don't. I never had simple in my life. Not for one minute. What I had, though, was desire, and that's what got me through."

"And I'm happy for you, Edie. I know it wasn't easy, and I know your dream wasn't simple. But you had a dream. That was a starting point."

"And you don't?"

"What I have is a function. I like being an orthopedic surgeon. I'm good at it. I take great satisfaction in helping people. But is it a dream? Or have I ever had a dream?" He shook his head, trying to remember a time when he'd had a dream. And came up blank. Well, almost blank. Because for the first time in his life he was feeling some regrets. Which meant there must have been some kind of a dream in there somewhere. As further proof, when he looked over at Edie, his heart clenched. So he blinked away from her in an instant and set about the task of blinking away what had just happened to him.

"But why can't you embrace what you have and, at the same time, try for more? You're a talented doctor, but can't you define yourself some other way? Something that isn't about your function but about your…your heart?"

"My heart? It beats, Edie. It's a biological necessity to keep it beating if I wish to continue living. Which I do. But the rest of it…the romantic notion that my heart can dictate something in my life? I don't buy into it. Which is precisely why I can't be Molly's father. She needs someone who subscribes to the whole theory that the heart is more than an organ in the body. And don't go looking all sad on me now that you know you're not going to win this argument, and get Aunt Grace's way."

"My way, too, Rafe. Molly is meant to be with you. When I was younger, I chose to go one way. Then when I got a little older, I made another choice. We can make those choices in our lives, but we have to take the first step, which is admitting we want that change. So why limit yourself, or even stop yourself where you are, if you want more? And I think, deep down, you do. Otherwise you wouldn't be so torn up about finding a family for Molly."

He didn't have an argument for that. No comeback, no response. Edie was right, of course. But how could someone who was so full of love understand someone who was not? In her rose-colored world, love took care of everything. In his world, love didn't exist. It was easier that way. It didn't open him up to be hurt. And he was better at being alone than anybody he knew. So why change it, and take the risk?

And why bring someone else, like Molly, or even Edie, into his misery, if he took that risk, and failed? *You're just like your father, Rafe.* Just like his father. How many times had he heard that throughout his life, and how the hell could he wish that on anyone? "Care for another beer?" he asked Edie, more with the intent of grappling for conversation to clear his head of the dark thoughts rambling around in there rather than offering an actual beer, which he was pretty sure she would refuse as she'd hardly touched her first one.

"One's my limit," she said, pushing away her still half-filled mug. "I'm full. Good pizza, good beer, interesting conversation…"

So, this was it? The end of the evening? A little conversation, a little food, then what? Rafe wasn't even sure this warranted a circumspect kiss at the front door when he dropped her off. Which, in the end, turned out not to matter, as Henry Danforth called before they made it to the car, telling Rafe that he'd brought Molly home from her party, and she seemed a touch under the weather.

"Probably nothing," Rafe said as they headed out the door. "Kids pick up bugs all the time." Yet only two hours ago, all decked out in her frilly pink dress, she'd seemed fine. No symptoms, no nothing. Just a normal child with an exciting evening ahead of her.

"Want me to come with you?" Edie asked. "I know you're the doctor, but she might need…"

"Mothering?" A chance to see how much Molly needed Edie.

"A woman's touch. And if you could see the look on your face right now…"

He bent down, took a look in the rear-view mirror, saw the worry mixed with stress, tried pretending it didn't exist. "Looks normal to me," he lied.

"Looks nervous."

He chuckled. "OK, so maybe I'm a little over-anxious. But I've never had a kid to care for, and I don't really know much about them."

She climbed into the car, and Rafe shut the door behind her then went round to the driver's side. "Good parenting is a lot about good instincts. Don't over-think it, Rafe. It's all really pretty simple. Give her the basics—food, shelter, clothes, education, add love and support and some wise guidance along the way, and she'll turn out to be amazing."

Maybe so, but not for him. "Guaranteed?"

Edie laughed, then reached over to squeeze his arm. "With Molly, yes. Guaranteed."

His inclination was to kiss her now, before the evening turned crazy. But she fell back into her seat too quickly for that to happen, fastened the seat belt almost instantly, and pretty well sent out some very strong body language…all of it negative. Naturally, he didn't blame her. He hadn't handled this evening well. Thank God, Edie was good-natured about it, because any other woman would have left him before the beer arrived. But Edie…she was different. The more he got to know her, the stronger his conviction became that she would be perfect…for Molly.

For some lucky man, too. Edie and another man…a thought he shoved right out of his head.

"I think she's feverish," Henry Danforth explained. He had almost leapt out the front door to greet them, he was so anxious over Molly's condition. "I thought about taking her straight to the hospital, but seeing you're a doctor…"

Rafe laid his hand on the man's shoulder to reassure him. "You did the right thing. I'll go take a look, and if she needs something I can't do for her, I'll get her admitted in a few minutes. But most times these things turn out to be nothing."

"I was worried I might have done something wrong. When I got the phone call…by the way, her little friend's mother called me because Molly said you were on an important date tonight and couldn't be disturbed. Anyway, Grace always told me I was like a bull in the china shop when it came to children, but I never took her seriously. And when I got the call, I wasn't sure what to do. Maybe I should have…"

Rafe silenced him with a squeeze, gently nudging him toward the door. "I'll call you later. Go home, relax. And don't worry about it, Henry. You did the right thing, bringing her home, putting her to bed, and calling me."

"She's a little flushed, Rafe," Henry said on his way out the door.

"And I'm sure she'll be better in the morning."

"Well, call me, one way or another. You know how I care about that child."

Everybody did. Which made Rafe feel guilty, as he was the lone hold-out, the one who couldn't care enough. "I'll call. Now, go home, go to bed." As it was to turn out, his "next morning" prognosis was a little off. Molly had a good case of flu. The two days in bed type, Rafe feared, once he had a look at her.

"And now we're exposed," he said to Edie, who was already placing cold compresses on Molly's forehead. "Sorry about that."

She laughed. "I work with children, get exposed to things every day. I've got pretty good immunity built up. Haven't caught a thing from anyone yet. In fact, one of the reasons I chose to work with children is that I seem to have a high level of immunity, at least from the common, everyday ailments like colds and flu. Kids are living, breathing, breeding grounds for bacteria and viruses, and my stamina has come in handy. So, do you want me to spend the night?"

An offer he wanted to accept in a different way, one having nothing to do with taking care of a sick child, but, having her here to take care of Molly would have been nice. But having her here would have also been too cozy, and he was beginning to think of Edie in terms of someone *other* than the woman he wanted to be Molly's mother. Those feelings, in fact, were springing on him much faster and stronger than he could have ever expected. Not good.

Rafe reached out and took her hand, pressed a set of car keys in them. "I appreciate the offer, but we're good. How hard can it be, taking care of a sick kid? Keep her hydrated, keep her rested…"

Edie laughed. "Bet you won't be saying that tomorrow. When kids are sick, they have this way of getting really—"

"Annoying?" he asked, smiling.

"More like rambunctious, needy, lots of whining. Their energetic little bodies aren't meant to be sidelined, and while the wise doctor in you will know that Molly needs more rest for a full recovery, Molly's going to be telling you, and showing you, the very opposite. So, call me when you're overwhelmed, because I have a few sickbed tricks up my sleeves." She held up the car keys. "Thanks for the ride. I'll bring it back tomorrow."

"No hurry. I have an idea I won't be going anywhere for a couple of days."

"Then maybe I'll stop by with a care package after work. Are you *sure* you can take care of her by yourself?"

"Guess we'll find out, won't we?" He walked with her to the front door then opened it. "Look, Edie. I'd like to do this again before I leave Lilly Lake. Another night, no flu. Maybe something other than pizza. Do you think we can manage that?"

Another date? He was actually asking her out on another date? She was sure they could manage it, but with the way her pulse was racing, she wasn't sure she should. "Let's wait until we see what this strain of flu holds in store for us, OK?"

He chuckled. "Well, I've got to give you credit for one thing. That's the most original turn-down I've ever received."

"Not a turn-down, Rafe. I'd really like to go out with you again. And for two people who basically don't date, or get involved with anyone else, that's a pretty big step. But you're not going to be here much longer, and with Molly's needs to see to, I'm not sure that the two of us getting together is really a priority. Plus, I'm betting you'll probably be sick with flu in a couple of days. So…"

"So it's a maybe?"

"*Possible* maybe."

"And if I don't start showing any flu symptoms in a couple of days?"

"Then I'll upgrade the prognosis to a probable maybe." She stood on tiptoe and kissed him on the cheek. "I had a nice time this evening, Rafe. Thank you."

He frowned for a moment then shrugged. "As I don't know if we're going to get to do this again, I might as well go for it."

"What?" she asked.

But he didn't answer. Instead he pulled her into his arms and lowered his face to hers. "Incubation time for most common viruses is one to three days so I could already be infectious. There's still time to back out."

"But I've got good immunity," she said, tilting her head back as all willpower flew right out of her. "Great immunity, and..." And she wanted this. Didn't kid herself that it could be a one and only, because for them that was most likely their destiny. But she wanted this almost as much as he did, and she was ready to take the step that crossed the line of no return. Knowing what she did, that nothing could or ever would come of this, the prudent choice would have been to step back, but there was nothing prudent in her as she pressed herself hard against his body. "Just this once," she whispered, staring up into his eyes. "Because we know who we are."

But looking led to touching and more senseless ideas than she could deal with. His hands splayed on her spine, working their way down from her shoulders to the hollow curve at the small of her back. His body, hard with an arousal she couldn't explore, crushed unrestrained to hers. Her attraction level was crazily out of control now. Sure, she'd admit it. She was attracted to Rafe in ways she hadn't known attraction could exist. The other aspects of his life, of her life, though... the ones that were invading her mind...that was the real problem. Except at this moment she wouldn't allow the problems to beat them.

"You're sure?" he asked, his voice so low she barely heard it.

She nodded, tried to speak, but there were no words as Rafe pushed her hair aside, pulled down the neckline of her sweater, but only enough expose the skin over the tender place where her neck and shoulders met. Then he kissed her there. Tender kisses in a row, leading to her jaw.

Edie tried to steady herself, tried willing herself to be calm, tried thinking of this as only a kiss, but as his lips first touched her flesh, her knees nearly buckled underneath her, causing her to hold on to Rafe for dear life, lest she slide to the ground at his feet. As her arms reached up to entwine themselves around his neck, rather than saying or doing anything that would spoil this perfect moment, Edie simply breathed out the longest, most satisfied sigh she'd ever sighed, and let the tingle of his lips trailing down the back of her neck take over.

"Maybe we should stop," she finally managed, when it was obvious he was ready to start yet another exploration. She didn't want to stop, though. Not anything. But common sense was the only barrier between her and a broken heart and she was just coming to realize that Rafe was the first man, the only man, who could break her heart.

Suddenly, all the need in her turned into trepidation.

"You're not enjoying this?" Taking over with his fingers, Rafe kneaded her shoulders then started down her back.

Enjoying it? She was enjoying it more than he would

ever know. "It's not..." His hands skimmed over her ribs and came to rest in the small of her back, eliciting an involuntary moan from her. "Not right." Breathless words. "We're not supposed to be..."

"Not supposed to be what?" he whispered in her ear as he placed a kiss there.

It would be so easy to get lost in this, to forget that he didn't ever commit, that she wasn't ready to commit again, but... "Mmm..." she mumbled, as his hands descended ever so slightly lower, nearly, but not quite to the round of her bottom. Her eyes flew open as the pressure of his slight squeeze jolted her out of the moment. "Rafe, we can't." She tried forcing conviction into her voice, but she couldn't do it. It simply wasn't there to be found.

"Fine, if that's what you really want..." As he spoke the words, though, his hands continued their journey, not down but to her hips. Which was where he stopped. Which was where he pulled her so roughly into him that there was no question what came next. Not now, not in the next hour or two.

"It isn't," she forced out. "What I want is..." she whispered, "is one moment."

Rafe cupped her chin in his hand and tilted her face up to his. "Only one moment?"

Edie swallowed hard as his gaze fell to her mouth. She could feel his heat, feel the sparks arcing back and forth between them, feel everything... "Maybe two or..."

Before the rest of her words were spoken, Rafe lowered his lips to her. Kissed her hard at first. Kissed her out of pure frustration and raw want. But the kiss melted into tenderness as his tongue slid back and forth across hers. His mastery of such a simple thing sucked the air from her lungs and caused her to forget that they were standing on the front porch of his aunt's mansion, caused her to forget that this was only a moment and there might never be another one. In that time, there was *only* that moment, *only* that tangle of emotions she so desperately feared.

Her kiss to him came on a moan as she pressed herself even harder against him and snaked her left leg around his right. Rafe groaned with pleasure, a heady sound she enjoyed almost as much as she enjoyed the taste of him—the tantalizing reminiscence of pizza and beer. Shamelessly, she ground herself into him, found his erection, and nuzzled it into her belly, then rocked back and forth into him, into his arousal. Then she gave herself to his hand pressing underneath her sweater, seeking out her breast…the ache of pure, sexual desire cresting in her in a way she'd never before felt. And would never feel again.

Reality, in all its ugly manifestations, came crashing down. They couldn't do this. Nothing about them was about…*them*. Except that one new feeling she had. And she truly didn't know what to do with it, or about it. So, she stepped back, took a firm hold of his car keys, and prayed her legs would take her all the way down the walk to the car.

When she got there, after she'd managed to get the door open, she finally allowed herself a look back, to see if anything about Rafe looked the way she was feeling. But he was gone. The porch light was still on, and the front porch was totally, completely empty.

CHAPTER SIX

"RAFE, I need your help." Rick Navarro's voice came over the cell phone.

He'd barely had time to check on Molly. So far, she was sound asleep. Resting pretty comfortably, actually. Now he was sitting in a chair, staring out the window at the night sky, hoping for sunrise, hoping for a new day to begin, seeing that he'd gone and messed the old one in ways he didn't even want to think about.

It could have been a simple kiss, should have been a simple kiss… Hell, who was he kidding? He'd wanted Edie like he'd never wanted another woman in his life. Hence the topic of his current thoughts. *Why had he wanted Edie like that?* He wasn't kidding himself about the answer. It was about a lot more than just the physical urges. A whole lot more.

The thing was, he wasn't finding an answer. Or maybe he didn't want to find one. But now it didn't matter. Rick was on the phone, saying something about needing him.

"I can't come. Molly's sick," Rafe said.

"That's what Edie just told me. So I've got Summer Adair on her way over to look after Molly. She was your aunt's nurse."

He'd talked to Edie? How was Edie sounding? he wondered. Just as confused as he was? "What's the emergency?"

"Accident. We have casualties…multiple car pile-up out on Route 9. Roberts Turn. Small van full of children involved."

Children involved. Suddenly everything else in his mind was pushed aside. "Any other information?"

"Not yet. I'm on my way to the scene. We've got firefighters on the way, and I've called some extra staff into the hospital. Don't know what to expect, though. Reports from the scene are pretty spotty."

"OK, I'll be there as soon as your nurse shows up. I'm probably twenty minutes out once I hit the road." Without a car! Or ten minutes by horse. As soon as Rick hung up, he called the stable and asked Johnny to saddle Donder. The way it turned out, Johnny was ready to ride with Rafe by the time he reached the stable.

"Just keeping track of the horses," the older man said.

"Or keeping track of me," Rafe said, climbing up into the saddle.

"I'm not saying that you're out of practice or anything, but it's been a while since you've had a good hard ride, and I just want to make sure nobody gets hurt."

Rafe smiled. "Me or the horses?"

"Your aunt did love her horses, son. But as far as I could tell, she loved you, too. Don't expect she'd have wanted either you, or her horses, getting hurt none."

Taking the reins, Rafe turned Donder toward the stable doors, wondering how often doctors made house calls on horseback these days. In a way, he liked it. "Giddyup," he said, nudging the stallion in the side.

Donder whinnied, snorted in a deep breath, then Rafe was off. Black horse, black night. Somehow he felt exhilarated, felt more alive than he had since… since he couldn't remember when.

Too bad it was Lilly Lake doing this to him, he thought, turning just short of the pine grove beyond Gracie House and heading down the trail leading to the back door of Roberts Turn. Too bad, because he liked the way he felt. Could almost imagine himself living here, doing something like this more often.

But it was Lilly Lake. And that was always the bottom line.

"Seven children, five adults involved," Rick shouted in greeting as Rafe climbed off Donder and handed the reins over to Johnny. "We've assessed a couple of specific orthopedic injuries. Stabilized them for the time being, but we may need to send you back to the OR to take care of them if we can't get hold of Dr. Wallace."

"Who's Wallace?" Rafe asked, practically running alongside Rick.

"Our orthopedic surgeon. We share him with the clinic in Jasper, as well as the hospital in Beaver Dam and the one in Redbird."

"I didn't realize that resources were stretched so thin here."

"Well, doctors don't really want the small-town life so much these days. So you have to make do. We're pretty good at it."

That was not what he wanted to hear. Until he and Jess decided what to do with the hospital, its operation was their responsibility, and no way in hell did he want it staffed inadequately. For sure, it was an issue to address with Rick in the very near future. But in the meantime he was just another of the doctors in the field. A fact he became acutely aware of as he got closer to the accident scene, close enough to see the need but also close enough to be stopped by the firefighters.

There was a crush of mangled metal ahead of him. Somewhere in that carnage, there were also injured children. He thought about Molly for a moment as he made his way forward, trying to push past what had turned into a wall of firefighters.

"Sorry, sir. You can't go any farther," one of them yelled at him.

He did stop, did try to obey the order. But when he saw the first injured and bloodied child being pulled from the van, and when he saw that child's parents rush forward, crying and frantic to get to their little boy yet being pushed back like everybody else, that was when the coldest chill he'd ever felt in his life hit him. No, Molly wasn't one of the children involved in this mess, for which he was incredibly grateful, but the utter dread of having your child involved in something like this and not knowing...*that* was the cold chill he felt. The one that told him, in this instance, he knew exactly what it felt like to be a father.

"We've got everybody out of the van now except one child, a little girl, and the firefighters aren't going to let us in until they have it better secured," Rick called to Rafe from across the commotion of several dozen people doing several dozen different things. Lights were being set up, boundaries being laid out to keep the growing crowd under control. Various medics and rescuers were working with patients in all sorts of different conditions. People were taking pictures, others were videotaping. A helicopter overhead was shining a spotlight down. Attempts were under way to get down a cliff to the car perched on a ledge below. The passengers inside were phoning that they were OK, but the frenetic effort to rescue them was still under way, and the growing concern that the car could easily topple on down sobered the thoughts of everybody on the scene.

All Rafe wanted to do was shove everybody back so he could go get that little girl who was still trapped in the van. But on his second and third attempt to get through, he was still being pushed back by the firefighters. "Look, Doc, I know you want to get at that child as much as we do, but right now we can't do it. Site's not stable enough yet, and you don't have any rescue experience, do you?"

Rafe swallowed hard. He'd criticized Jess for giving up medicine to become a firefighter. Criticized him more than once. But now he wished to God he had his brother's rescue experience. "Do you know anything about her condition?"

The firefighter shook his head. "Other than she's not conscious, and she's trapped…her arm, I've been told. Sorry I don't have anything else for you. But as soon as we think it's safe…"

Not the words he wanted to hear. Not the image he wanted in his mind, because he was thinking about Molly, seeing her as the child trapped inside, wondering what the trapped child's parents were doing, thinking, feeling right now.

Damn, he wished Jess was here. No way in hell his

would brother have stood here, waiting, wondering. Jess was about action. Sometimes it was action Rafe didn't like. But that was who Jess was now, and Jess would have been down on his belly, crawling to get in there, no matter what anybody said. Of that, he had no doubt.

On impulse, he phoned his brother. "OK, so I know there's nothing you can do from where you are, but talk me through it. I'm going in, don't give a damn what they're telling me to do or not do. I can't stand here and wait while that kid might be dying, so I need some common sense shouting at me before I do it."

"Are you sure?" Jess asked. "Considering *everything*, are you sure you're the one who should be going in there? I mean, none of that has changed about you, has it?"

Rafe drew in a ragged breath. "No, none of that has changed. I'm still claustrophobic as hell and I expect that once I get inside that van I'm going to experience claustrophobia in a way it's never been experienced before. But somebody's got to get that kid out of there, Jess."

"Then my best advice to you is to get someone else, big brother, because if you get in there and panic…"

"No one else, Jess. It's just me." Because he wasn't going to be stopped by the things that could happen, when the thing that *had* happened wasn't being attended to as fast as he wanted it to be. So, maybe he was impatient. Maybe he was totally wrong. But if that was Molly in there, he'd be ripping through chunks of steel with his bare hands to get at her no matter what anybody else was telling him to do. For somebody else's little girl he could do no less. "And I'm going in, so give me the condensed version of how to do this, or I'm going to have to figure it out on my own."

"Damn it, Rafe…" Jess heaved out an impatient, audible sigh. "I hate heroes."

"No, you don't," Rafe said softly. The love of Jess's life—she had been a heroine. And Jess, himself, was a hero. "And I'm not going to do anything you don't tell me to do. So, are you with me?"

"You have to tell me everything," Jess warned. "And if you feel a panic attack coming on…"

His brother referred to all those times when their old man had locked him in a closet. It had been the one underneath the front stairs. No room to stand, no room to stretch out. Basically, a cubbyhole with a padlocked door on the outside. He'd crouched in there, his muscles aching and cramping, scared to death of the dark and the creepy, crawly things he imagined in the dark, crying quietly, while his brother sat outside, talking to him, reassuring him that he wasn't alone. It had happened so many times Rafe had lost count, and the result was a bad case of claustrophobia. Jess knew, and Rafe appreciated his brother's concern. But he was going in anyway.

"And you don't know what to expect?" Jess asked, breaking Rafe away from his childhood flashbacks.

"Arm's trapped. She's unconscious."

"Can you do a field amputation in there, if you have to?"

He could, but he didn't want to think about it. "Yeah, if I have to. But it's the last option. So just get me in there so I can see what needs to be done. OK? I'll deal with everything else once I get to the girl."

"Fine. Have they popped out all the glass yet?" Jess asked.

"As far as I can tell, yes."

"Good, then click me off some pictures on your phone so I can see it."

"Don't have time," Rafe growled.

"Take the time anyway, Rafe. You're not going in blind, and if you think you are, I'm going to hang up on you right now and call the fire department and ask them to put you in restraints."

Rafe actually chuckled. He knew his brother, and that was exactly what Jess would do. "Fine, some pictures coming at you." From a distance, he clicked shots of the three sides he could see then sent them on to his brother. It only took a minute for Jess to assess the situation and respond.

"Disclaimer first. You should be leaving this to the professionals. But that van's positioned to go over if you're not careful, Rafe."

"They can't let it go over because there's another car down on the ledge below it. People trapped."

"OK, then they're going to have to take it apart piece by piece."

"With the kid inside?" Rafe asked.

"No. The kid's got to come out, one way or another. And, Rafe, they're not going to wait too long on this since they have survivors down below."

"Meaning?"

"Meaning huge chance of field amputation. Get yourself ready for it if you do get in."

"You mean *when* I get in."

Jess laughed. "Cut from the same cloth, brother."

"I guess we are." And there were apologies to be made to Jess. But later. "So, tell me how to get in."

"Windshield. Whatever you do, keep to the left. Passenger's side. If you go to the right, the van's going to shift, and the integrity of some of the anchor ropes could be compromised. From what I see, the van looks stable enough right now, but when you add your weight and motion...anyway, stick to the passenger's side and you should be OK for this first part. Oh, and, Rafe, if you do anything dumb, like get yourself killed, just remember that the first person you're going to meet up with in heaven's probably going to be Aunt Grace, and she's not going to like seeing you there."

"Trust me, I have no intention of having a face to face with Aunt Grace today."

"You're not going in, are you?" Edie exclaimed.

"You've been eavesdropping?"

"Enough to know that you're joking about getting yourself killed."

"Nobody's getting killed. But I *am* going in." He held up his phone. "I've got good instruction. Jess is going to be with me."

"And you're not a firefighter, Rafe! They're still telling us to wait."

"But I've got a patient inside who can't wait." He held the phone back up to his ear. "Look, you'll hang on, won't you?"

"Not going anywhere," Jess said.

"Rafe," Edie cut in, "we've got plenty of injuries for you to deal with over there." She pointed to the triage area, where the accident victims were being staged according to the degree of their injuries. "Rick asked me to tell you they need your help."

He looked, saw the medical flurry. "Tell Rick I'm working on another patient right now, that I'll be over there as soon as I can."

"You tell him," Edie snapped, pulling a helmet on.

"What are you doing?" Rafe asked.

"Going in with you to get April. That's her name, by the way."

"No way in hell!"

Edie looked up at him, stared him straight in the eye, then spun around and marched straight to the van, forcibly shoving back the firefighter who tried to grab hold of her. Once there, she turned and waited for Rafe.

"You're not doing this, Edie!" he shouted, catching up to her and trying to wave off two firefighters coming his way.

"And you're not stopping me."

"I am," one of the firefighters said, stepping in front of Rafe. The name on his jacket identified him as Chief Will Brassard. "I'm stopping both of you."

"No, you're not," Rafe said patiently. "I've got a child trapped in there who could die, and you're not going to let that happen to her, are you? If you let me go in, it's *not* your responsibility—if you do, it is. Simple choice, in my opinion, Chief." He held up the phone. "You know my brother Jess? He's going in with me."

"You're as persuasive as your aunt was," Brassard said, stepping back.

"I'll take that as a compliment." Rafe rushed round the man to get to Edie's side.

"Or a curse," Brassard muttered. "Here's the deal. If we cut through the metal, it's going to take a while, and it may undo what we've done to stabilize the van.

Also, because the kid's head is positioned so that cutting around her is going to be a risk, that's pretty much the last thing we want to do. That, plus the fact that she's coming to, and I'm not sure she's going to hold still for what we'd have to do. One of my men tried getting her out, but she was lodged in there tight. There's not much room to do anything."

"Did he see bleeding?"

"Some. Not excessive. He couldn't tell where it was coming from, and he was afraid to start probing and risk more complications."

Tamponade, where blood flow was stopped by a constriction created by an outside force. It was the first thing that came to Rafe's mind, and something he couldn't shake off as he prepared to go in. A tamponade could be a lifesaver but, if dislodged, could be a killer. Somehow, in such a serious situation, with a lack of blood…

"Look, Corbett, you're aware how dangerous this is. And I don't like the fact that you're not experienced in field rescue. But we may not have too much time left for this kid if we don't get something done fast, and if we need a field amputation—"

"Last option," Rafe interrupted.

"Or first, depending on what happens. Which is why I'd rather put a doctor in there on that than one of my firefighters. We're going to keep trying to get at her from out here, but in the worst-case scenario, we have an emergency…you're going to have to take her arm and get her the hell out of there fast. No time to argue with us. You'll just have to do it. Understood?"

Rafe nodded.

"Good. I'll give you your shot at this, but if you

can't make it work, we're going to have to take that van apart piece by piece so it doesn't fall down on that car below here. Those people trapped down there are at risk, too. Meaning five minutes in and you amputate if you don't have another solution. So you've got your timeline. Five minutes, then we're pulling everybody out. And at that point, if the kid is still stuck, I'm putting one of my medics in to take her arm if you haven't already done it. So it's going to be your rescue, Doc. And also your choice." He tossed his helmet over to Rafe.

Five minutes. He was already feeling sweat drip down his back. Five minutes wasn't a lot of time to wait, but those five minutes could be precious to that child trapped in there. Especially as more than five minutes had already ticked off the clock since he'd been here, and at least thirty minutes beyond that. "I'm going in," he said to Edie.

"And I'm right behind you," she replied, then thrust out her hand to stop him from arguing with her. "You're not stopping me, Rafe. If April wakes up..."

Edie was good at what she did. Brilliant, actually. But putting her into this kind of situation? "You'll do what I tell you," he warned her. "Your job...your only job...will be to keep her calm, and if she's not conscious, I want you out of there. Do you understand? You can't get in the way because I may have to..." He paused, swallowed hard. "May have to amputate her arm. You understand that, don't you?"

"I understand," she said. "And I'll do whatever you tell me to."

"Then let's do it." He held his phone back to his ear. "I'm going in. I'll keep this line open, but if something happens…" He didn't finish the sentence, didn't even wait to hear his brother's response. Instead, he got down on his belly and wormed his way through the broken-out windshield.

"What can you see?" Edie asked, wedged in tight against Rafe's back.

"First thing I can see is that there's no way in hell I'm going to fit in here. Second thing I can see is that her arm is pinned in tight, and it's basically caught up in the mechanism of the seat that was in front of her. I don't see any blood so I want to get a blood-pressure reading, but I can't move." The forces of his own private hell were beginning to close in around him already. He was basically on the interior roof of the car, lying on his side, wedged in between two dislodged seats where there was barely enough room for his large frame to fit. Maneuvering in this tight space was nearly impossible. Catching his breath in the tightness closing in on his chest was nearly impossible as well. "Can you take a BP reading? I think we're going to have to trade places so you can do it, as there's no maneuvering room in here for a man my size."

Edie drew in a sharp breath, heard Rafe do the same. "Sure, I can do that," she said, already backing away so Rafe could scoot himself out and let her go in first.

"April," Edie said, on her way out. "Can you hear me?"

The child murmured a faint "Uh-huh."

"We're here to get you out, so don't be afraid." As she brushed by Rafe, she whispered, "Talk to her. Reassure her. The words don't matter as much as the fact that she's not alone here."

"How is it in there?" Rick called from outside.

"Tight," Edie yelled. "Her arm seems caught almost all the way to her shoulder, but it's hard to tell, and she's trapped at a difficult angle. Rafe's too large for the space." She glanced back in, aimed her flashlight into the interior dark space and saw Rafe talking to the child as he slid himself out.

"Well, once you get back in there, maybe you could…" Rick held out the blood-pressure cuff she needed, as well as an old teddy bear. "It used to be Christopher's."

"I think she'll be glad to have it," Edie said, dropping back to her knees, waiting for Rafe to make his exit.

"I'll be right back, April," Rafe reassured the child in a voice so tender it nearly broke Edie's heart. Somehow she had to make Rafe understand what an amazing father he'd make for Molly. She could see it so clearly. She thought Molly probably could, too. Rafe was the only one denying it, and she didn't know why. It bothered her, though, because where there could be so much happiness, Rafe was bound to a path that seemed like such a waste.

"Four minutes," Brassard stepped in and warned.

Rafe nodded, but didn't acknowledge him in any other way. "She's brave," he said to Edie, "but we're going to have to get her out of there pretty soon because I don't know what else is going on with her, and she's been pinned too long. Have you ever taken a blood pressure in somebody's leg before?"

Fear, icy cold and blinding, hit her. "No, but I can do it. Um…Rafe? Since *you* can't get in there, you won't expect me to…to amputate, will you? If that's what it comes down to, I won't have to be the one…?"

"It's not going to get to that," Rafe said. "I promise, Edie. We're going to find another way to get her out of there."

Reassuring words that didn't reassure her as much as she would have liked because her hands started to tremble and she couldn't stop them. "Rafe, I…I'll do what I have to do. But I'm not sure…"

He reached out and took both her hands into his. "That's the last possible alternative, Edie. To save that child's life, if that's what it comes down to, I know you *can* do what you have to do. And I'll be right there with you. But we're going to look at other alternatives first. I'm not going to take that little girl's arm without exhausting every other possibility. I promise you." Ever so gently, he brushed a strand of hair back from her face. "I'll be with you, Edie, no matter what happens."

His voice was so calm, so reassuring she wanted to believe him. Something in Rafe inspired her to be more than she was, to see capabilities in herself more than she had. "I know you will," she whispered, fighting hard to keep the trembling out of her voice. "But I'm not sure if I can."

"My aunt trusted you with the ominous task of turning me into the father she thought I could be, and that speaks volumes. Actually, it shouts volumes."

"You know about that?"

"Of course I know about that." He tilted her face up to his. "I trust you to help me, Edie, not because my aunt trusted you but because I trust you. You can do this…we can do this. But I won't force you to go back in there with me if you don't want to."

"When you get back in there, you've got three minutes," Brassard reminded them.

This time Edie paid no attention to the fire chief. "I'm going in *with* you, Rafe," she whispered, her voice still shaky. This was nothing she'd ever prepared herself to do, but Rafe gave her confidence. And that confidence grew as she felt Rafe right behind her on her way in. "Hi, April. My name is Edie, and I've come to help get you out of here. I know you're scared, so I brought you a little friend to hold on to while Dr. Rafe and I take care of you." April took hold of the bedraggled teddy with a fierceness that told Edie she was a tough little girl. "So, what I need to know first is where you hurt the most. Can you tell me?"

April nodded. "My arm. It's stuck. And there's something in my tummy, on the side."

Edie rolled a little to her left, wedged herself back against another of the seats that had broken loose, and aimed her flashlight at April. That was when she saw it…something wedged into the child's side, just above her waist. Maybe part of the metal bracing broken off one of the seats?

"Two more minutes," someone outside shouted.

"Rafe," Edie said calmly, trying not to alarm the child, "April has a tummyache. I think I can see the cause of it."

"Where?"

"Left side, just above her waist. Metal bar of some sort, I think. Wedged in, can't tell how deep." She waited for his response, waited for him to tell her what to do, but what she heard instead was an utterance of profanity under his breath. So she continued to talk to April. "Can you wiggle your fingers, April? Just your fingers, nothing else." Edie shifted the position of her flashlight so she could watch April's reaction, and what she saw for a moment was a child putting forth every effort she had—frowning, biting down on her lip, squeezing shut her eyes to concentrate.

"A little," April finally said, with great effort. "My thumb a little, and I think my first two fingers. My others feel…yucky."

"How yucky?" Edie asked instinctively.

"Like they're not there."

Edie cringed inwardly, and Rafe gave her a supportive squeeze on her shoulder. "Are they sticky?" he asked April.

"Some."

"And cold?" he continued.

"Yes. And they hurt all the way up my arm."

"Pain is a good sign," Rafe murmured into Edie's ear, then continued, "When we get her loose, we've got to stabilize the metal bar in her side before we move her out. Just make sure we don't bump it or dislodge it somehow."

Those words sent cold chills up Edie's spine, almost as much as Chief Brassard's one-minute warning did. "Let me get her BP before we do anything else, and maybe you can figure out how to take care of her arm in the meantime." She wedged herself in a little closer to the girl. "April, I've got to check your blood pressure. It's going to pinch a little, but it only lasts a few seconds. The reason we do this is so we know how well your heart is sending the blood flowing to all the places in your body it needs to go."

"So you can fix me up when I get my arm out?"

Edie felt a knot catch in her throat. That was what

she wanted, what she was praying for, but the two things she'd never do were offer false hope or lie. Which was why she chose her words carefully. "So we can give you the best care when we get you out of here. OK?" The knot almost choked her as she spoke, but she was going to hold on to hope…because of Rafe. He would do everything possible to help this child, and to assure the best outcome. She believed that with all her heart.

"OK," April agreed. "But I'm getting sleepy. I want to go home."

Sleepy meant shock. With her limited medical training, Edie knew that, and it worried her. "Soon, sweetheart. We'll get you home as soon as we can. In the meantime, just try and hold as still as you can, and be very quiet, because I've got to listen through these." She held up the stethoscope, then impulsively placed them in April's ears and placed the bell on her own heart. "Can you hear it beating?"

"Yes," the girl said, almost mesmerized.

"That's what I'm going to be listening for in you, only in a different place. I'll bet you didn't know that there are places all over our bodies where we can either feel your heartbeat or listen to it."

"Will you show me?" April asked, almost timidly.

"When we get you out of here, and after the doctors at the hospital have had a look at you, I will definitely show you. So…" She held a shushing finger to her lips then twisted slightly to look back at Rafe, who handed her the blood-pressure cuff.

"You're doing a good job," he whispered, as she took it from him.

She hoped so, hoped that wasn't just Rafe trying to

be encouraging. "How do I do this? I know how to take a reading in the arm, but not in the leg."

"There's not much difference. It's all about the positioning. What you need to do first is bend the knee of her right leg, and try keeping her foot flat, without twisting her abdomen. Actually, let me move over a little so I can work with her foot."

He scooted back, brushing against her, and even in his slightest touch she felt his strength rush through her. Edie hoped her shiver was imperceptible to him, even though to her it was massive, shaking her down to her very essence. "So I strap on the cuff next?" she asked.

"Make sure the bottom is about an inch above April's ankle then put the stethoscope on the dorsalis pedis artery. Find that by placing your finger halfway between the inner ankle bone and the Achilles tendon. Let me know when you're there."

Knowing such a little thing may have seemed simple to Rafe, but to Edie his knowledge was awe-inspiring. "I feel it," she said, when she'd finally located the pulse.

"Good. Now listen. Most of the time you'll be able to hear it pretty easily. Sometimes, in about two to three percent of healthy people, the sound can't be heard in one or both legs, though. Pump up the cuff like you would in the arm, and listen."

Which was exactly what she did. "Ninety-four over fifty-six," she said, then heard an audible sigh of relief from Rafe.

"Time's up. Everybody out!" Brassard yelled.

Edie and Rafe both ignored the warning. "A little low but, all things considered, not bad," he finally said, as he reached over Edie and took the cuff and equipment. "Now, the next thing we need to do is pack some gauze around her abdominal would to make sure nothing moves." He handed several wads of gauze over to her. "Just be gentle. Build up enough around the metal bar so we reduce the risk of bumping it when we finally pull her out of there, then tape the gauze into place."

"I said, get out!" Brassard yelled.

"I like my job a whole lot better than I like yours," she said, placing the first of the gauze. Her fingers trembled, her gut churned. She bit down on her lower lip, concentrating so hard she could taste her own blood. "How will I know if it's good enough?"

Rafe gave her a little squeeze on the arm. "It'll be good enough, Edie. Trust me, you'll do a good job." His squeeze was a squeeze of triumph, maybe of relief… whatever it was, it caused her confidence to soar. Rafe was definitely in charge here, and one way or another, he would make things work for April.

"Get the hell out of there!" Brassard yelled again. "Right now, or I'm sending in one of my men!"

They both ignored him again. "Well, I think I've got as much gauze taped in as I can. What's next?"

"What's next is that I'm going to go out and let Chief Brassard know he can't start cutting. Not the van, not…" He nodded toward April. "I'm going to persuade him to give us more time. You going to be OK in here for a minute?"

"We'll be fine," Edie said, wiggling into a more comfortable position, grateful she wasn't spooked by cramped spaces, because this was about as cramped as she'd even been in any space. Cramped and now dark.

"What's it looking like in there?" Rick asked even before Rafe was all the way out.

"Child's stable. Talking. Scared, but Edie's handling that. Haven't been able to evaluate her arm yet, but she does have some kind of a rod stuck through her belly, and as there's no significant bleeding to go with it, I'm thinking tamponade."

A diagnosis that caused Rick to suck in a sharp breath. "Well, I'll get the OR ready for that one. And her arm…"

Rafe shrugged. "Don't know enough to give an educated guess at this point. But what I need for you to do is hold off the fire department for me. Don't know how, don't care, but there's no way in hell I want them taking that van apart, not when I've got a kid in there with a rod through her belly. And she's too alert to take off her arm, especially when I don't think it needs to come off. We need to find a way to get her out without jostling her, and while I know the guys out here are doing the best they can, there's got to be another way."

"Done," Rick said. "Anything else?"

"More light, if we can manage it."

"Done," Rick repeated.

Rafe would have asked for more space, but it didn't matter. For now he was stuck with a good case of claustrophobia, and there was nothing he could do about it. "Oh, and while I don't see anything to indicate it, prepare for crush syndrome, just in case. I have an idea we may get lucky with that one, but I don't want to get everything else right and have that go wrong on us." A smile twinkled in his eyes. "Oh, and if you have to cite crush syndrome to the fire chief as a reason why we *can't* rush getting April out of there, do it." Crush syndrome was where an extremity or other part of the body that has been trapped for a long time could start causing other problems throughout the body with the release of dangerous chemicals at high levels. Shock at the immediate release was almost always a given. Kidney failure could result, as well as death. It was a little devious using that because he was fairly certain April didn't have it, but any excuse in a storm. And crush syndrome was a good excuse. "Also, since I have every confidence that you're going to buy us more time, I'd like to get an IV started in April before we do *anything*." A tall order for a limited space. It was going to be a challenge.

"I'll get the supplies ready to go in. Oh, and Jess called. He hadn't heard from you, and his phone clicked off. Said to call him when it's over." He started to turn away from Rafe, but turned back. "I thought about it, by the way."

"What?"

"The apology, the offer."

"Now's a hell of a time to bring it up," Rafe said. "Especially if you want to negotiate something."

"No negotiation. Accepted. All of it."

In response, Rafe arched his eyebrows. "Light sedative, too," he said, then spun round and went straight back to the van.

"I think we need a better vantage point," Edie called out to him. "The extra lights are good, but I think we need to have a look at her arm, and do it from somewhere between the seat and the floor?"

"Then that's what I'll do," he said, gritting his teeth, knowing that he was going to have to shove himself into an opening where he didn't fit. "Look, Edie," he began once he was back in the van, "there's something I've got to tell you…something I hope to God doesn't cause any problems here." He paused a second, then continued. "I'm claustrophobic."

"A lot of people are."

"Not like me. I'm claustrophobic to the point of panic attacks. My old man used to lock me in a closet. Made me spend hours there. On a couple of occasions, days. Most of the time I'm OK dealing with it, but in tight spaces…"

Edie rolled over and squeezed Rafe's hand. "We'll deal with it," she said.

And that was all she had to say, because he knew they would. Together.

"It feels like the walls of hell are closing in on me," Rafe panted, slithering his way into a tiny space at the back of the seat. He couldn't see, didn't really fit, was sweating in a way he'd never sweated before, and holding his breath in such long spurts his lungs were beginning to hurt. His lip was bleeding from biting down so hard, his muscles already aching from extreme clenching, and the panic headache pummeling him had such a loud, thumping beat to it he was surprised Edie couldn't hear it. But after five minutes he'd cut away significant snippets of seat, and for that he was relieved. April was still doing well. Sleeping now, with an IV anchored in her leg, and a small amount of sedative to keep her relaxed.

"You OK?" Edie asked for the hundredth time.

"I'd rather be eating a baguette at Le Pain Merveilleux in Paris. But as that's not an option, I'm doing fine."

"You've been to Paris?"

He reached up to cut away another strip of seat vinyl then rose up and shone a light down into the seat's exposed innards. "Twice. The first time was all work, no play. Medical conference. Second time I decided that all work really wasn't the best thing to be doing in Paris, so I indulged in some of the finer things…the wine, the museums, the food…"

"The women?" she asked.

He chuckled. "As lovely as the women of Paris are, and they are some of the most beautiful in the world, I decided to make it an adventure for one. It's easier that way. No one to fight with over where to go or what to do. No one to tell me when to take a nap if I wanted one, or not to drink so much wine, if that's what I had a mind to do. Doing Paris as a single really wasn't so bad," he said, pulling himself into a better angle and fighting off the panic that wanted to slap him down the instant he realized he was stuck in there as tight as humanly possible, with nowhere to go, or even move, unless he wanted to back out. At this point, he was in so tight he wasn't sure he could even do that.

"But wouldn't it have been wonderful to do Paris with someone you loved, someone you could share the adventure with, who didn't care about your naps, or drinking too much wine?"

"Maybe," he said, feeling an increase in his heart rate, feeling the tightening of his muscles, as each and every one started clamping down on him in some kind of conspiracy. No air to breathe… He tried, sucked it in greedily. Shut his eyes, tried to focus. "If that person… existed. But she…doesn't. At least not…for…me."

"So you're an avowed bachelor?" she continued. "I

mean, I understand the no-dating thing. But no nothing? Not ever?"

"Something like that," he forced out, sounding winded.

"But wouldn't an avowed bachelor still like some consistency in his life? Maybe not in the form of a wife, or even a permanent adult relationship, but what about a child? They keep you young, you know. Change your focus. Give you balance. Make you more giving, I think."

Why the hell was she prattling on about this now? He was in the throes of a damned panic attack, and she was starting up on him adopting Molly.

"Can you even imagine the sense of accomplishment you could feel once you've raised that child, and she's turned out to do something huge, like invent the drug that will cure cancer, or teach the world how to achieve global peace? I mean, one little child, in the right home situation, with the right parent, could do so much…"

He shut his eyes for a moment, reined in his anger. She had him trapped—now she was doing the hard adoption sell. "I can't raise Molly, if that's what this is about. I've told you that. I can't…*won't* do it."

"Even though you're bound to be desperately lonely in your old age, considering the way you isolate yourself?"

"My choice. I isolate myself because that's what I choose to do."

"And who knows how you'd feel if you opened up a little, took Molly in, raised her as your daughter? She's a wonderful little girl, Rafe. Give yourself some time to get to know her, and I promise you'll see how fantastic she is. She'll make you better in ways you've never thought could happen."

He glanced down into the seat parts and saw…was that April's hand? Quickly, he shifted slightly and repositioned the flashlight for a better look. "I know she's a wonderful little girl, and I know that adopting her is what everyone wants me to do, but…" He pressed himself tighter into the seat until the edge of it nearly cut off his breathing. "I see it," he said. "Her hand, her arm…I can see the whole thing. And… Thank God for small miracles. Her arm is fine. It's only her hand that's trapped, and I think… Hand me the oil, Edie."

She handed him a bottle of lubricant that had come in with several other medical supplies then positioned a flashlight from her place down below. "I've got the IV steady, and I'm holding on to April, supporting her belly so that metal rod doesn't move, so do what you have to do."

Which was what he did. He maneuvered April's hand out of its trap. Gently released each of her fingers, one by one, then moved on down the hand until he'd finally extricated her wrist. No words spoken, no whispers, no gasps. Simply swift efficiency when it was clear what was required of him to assure that April Crowley's life was going to go forward beautifully, after a fair amount of reconstructive surgery and rehabilitation.

Five minutes after extricating April's arm, he handed her out to the waiting medics, the metal bar still holding its place in her belly, then crawled out himself and collapsed on the ground, grateful to inhale unobstructed breaths, grateful for all the open space around him.

"You OK?" Edie asked, plopping down beside him. For a moment they were two people lying flat on the ground, staring up at the night sky, while the rest of the medical emergency whirled on around them. The only two people…

"Fine," he said. "You?"

"What we did in there, Rafe…I can't even…"

"No words to describe it?"

"No words."

But actions spoke louder than words as he reached across and took hold of Edie's hand, then simply held it for the next minute or two. Or for an eternity. It all seemed the same right then. And it all seemed very good.

CHAPTER SEVEN

OK, IT WAS only a kiss. Well, maybe a little more than a kiss. Or something on the way to becoming a whole lot more. He'd kissed plenty of women in his time, no big deal. But two days after the bus accident, two grueling days of taking care of a sick little girl who didn't want to stay in bed or follow doctor's orders, and that kiss was still on his mind. That made it a big deal, didn't it?

The heck of it was he didn't know why. Or maybe he didn't want to dig deeply enough to find out why. Either way, he was grateful for the routine his life had settled into in the interim. Take care of Molly, rest, take care of Molly. For someone sick, she sure had a lot of energy. Even though Edie had warned him, he hadn't expected it, didn't know what to do with it and, in so many profound ways, it scared him. This child needed so much, and in ways he couldn't even begin to fathom.

In his defense, amidst his obvious lack of parenting skills, he hadn't run short of patience yet. That surprised him. But some of that had to do with Edie, who stopped by before work every day, and had spent the evenings there after her workday had ended. She'd cooked, read to Molly, played games. It was a sight to behold, a glimpse of life he'd never before seen. Family life at its best. Which simply reaffirmed to him who needed to be a family. At times, though, when he caught himself observing that family life too closely, his realization turned to cold chills. Could this be what he really wanted?

Reality always slammed back. This *wasn't* his life. Couldn't be. He wasn't going to let himself buy in to some ridiculous delusion that he could ever have it, because that wasn't meant to be the case. He was his father's son, after all. Corbett blood at its very worst. No getting around it. "French toast?" he asked Edie. "Is that what you're fixing?"

"Molly requested it, along with fresh strawberries."

"Do you think she might be taking advantage of this situation? I know she's been sick, but that doesn't necessarily mean she should be wrapping you round her little finger."

"And if she is, does it matter?" Edie arranged the strips of toast on a plate, then put the plate on a serving tray. "We all need to be indulged sometimes, Rafe. Too bad most of us only get it in some kind of a crisis. And as far as being wrapped round her little finger, I don't think that's really possible if you enjoy what you're doing for someone."

"Well, I'm not sure being overly indulgent is the best thing to do. Most of us never get it at all. But then the other side of that coin is who really needs it? It spoils us for something we can't have all the time. Or in some cases won't have ever again. Why put yourself through that emotional mess"

"Emotional mess? How do you consider that being indulged a little leads to an emotional mess?"

"Because being indulged leads to expectations, most of which can't ever be met. At least not on practical or consistent terms. So call it pragmatism if you want. Or pessimism. Either way, the result is the same. I mean, what's the definition of indulgence anyway? To take unrestrained pleasure in? To gratify? If you want it, do it. It's just that easy. Well, guess what? You don't have to depend on someone else to do it for you. In fact, why bother? They may not meet your expectations or needs, so just go and indulge yourself."

"Sounds like someone needs some indulging himself," Edie responded. "Did you get up on the wrong side of the bed this morning?"

"What I need is my life back. Not this pseudo-domesticity." Because the closer he came to domestic, the more he wanted it. And the more he wanted it, the more he knew he couldn't have it. Which was why he was grumpy this morning, the side of the bed on which he'd woken up notwithstanding. Seeing Edie in the kitchen, fixing breakfast for Molly, seeming so happy in that place…all he wanted to do was shove his fist through the wall. Which proved that his old man could get through any time, any place. With so little provocation, too. "I need to find Molly a family then go home and get back to doing what I do best. It's as simple as that."

"Is it really that simple, Rafe? Giving up a child seems anything but simple to me. In fact, I think it'll be the hardest thing you'll ever have to do…if you really intend to go through with it."

"Oh, I intend to." He drew in a deep, steadying breath in the hope of warding off some of the agitation that seemed to be filling him up. "And, Edie? Just so you'll know, what's simple is the desire. The rest of it is getting pretty damned complicated."

"Then uncomplicate it. Adopt her."

"Well, isn't that just a wealth of insightful advice. Adopt her and do what? Tell me, Edie. What, exactly, should I do with Molly once I adopt her? I won't have time for her. So maybe I can shuffle her off to boarding school. And I don't have experience with children. So maybe I can hire her a full-time nanny, governess, tutor or whatever other kinds of child-care specialists money can buy to raise her the right way. Are either of those acceptable solutions? Because they're all I have. And just so you'll notice, neither one of those come with a full investment of me, because I'm really not adding much of myself to the deal." Damn, he didn't mean to snap at her, didn't mean to be so grumpy. And he certainly wouldn't do any of the things he'd just said. But he couldn't get Edie to see the situation for what it was. And right now, existing so close to everything he truly wanted yet wasn't able to have was taking its toll on him. Two days of playing father had made him realize he wanted it probably more than anything he'd ever wanted. But two days had also reminded him why he had to back away. And fast.

"I was right. You do need some indulging."

He'd expected another fight from her, but got sympathy instead. He wasn't sure what to do with that. Wasn't sure he wanted to find out. "Look, I'm sorry for snapping. I'm sorry for being so disagreeable. But this whole domestic thing…it's not working for me."

"Or it's working too well. Have you ever considered that?"

He stared at her for a moment, amazed by the insight

and annoyed by it at the same time. To have someone read him the way Edie did made him feel so vulnerable he was almost shaking. He wasn't going to be vulnerable, not to anyone, for any reason. That was the way it was, the way it had to be. "Look, you need to get to work. How about I take this tray up to Molly so you won't be late?"

"You really work hard at keeping people at arm's length, don't you?" She handed him the tray. "I don't think it comes naturally to you, Rafe. I think you want to let people in, but once they get close, you get scared."

"So, with French toast I get psychoanalysis, whether or not I want it?"

"Point taken. It's none of my business."

She was right, though. He did keep people at a distance. Even people he wanted to let in, like her. "Look, Edie. I really appreciate all the help you've been with Molly these past couple of days, and I'm sorry about my rotten attitude. It gets away from me sometimes."

"It's not as rotten as you think, Rafe. More like, it's honest. I don't necessarily agree with you, pretty much in most things that concern Molly, even in some of the things you think about yourself. But we're all welcome to our opinions, aren't we? No matter how right or wrong they may be."

He chuckled. "And that implies that my attitude is wrong?"

She tossed him a cheery smile. "It implies whatever you want to make of it. Now, go and take care of Molly."

She'd shooed him out the kitchen door before he could respond in a semi-intelligent way, but there was something about being around Edie that caught him off guard more than he wanted to be. And by the time Molly had eaten as much of her breakfast as she cared to, Edie appeared upstairs with another tray bearing a plate of French toast and a bowl of strawberries. "Rafey needs someone to indulge him," she said to Molly, who was already involved in a video game.

Molly looked up at him. "Do you?" she asked, as if she totally understood what that meant.

"What I need has nothing to do with being indulged," he said, "and as you get older, and have more experience in life, you'll understand how meaningless it is. The indulgence lasts a minute, maybe two, then you're right back where you started, with a couple of minutes you'll never be able to get back again. And a longing that may never be satisfied."

"But it has French toast with it," Molly argued. "And Edie makes the best French toast ever!"

Something in Molly's simplicity struck a chord with him. Or made his position seem awfully rigid. "So, do you think I ought to go indulge myself?" he asked.

Molly nodded. "But only if you like French toast."

In a way, it made perfect sense to him. And as he crossed the room to take the tray from Edie, she shook her head.

"Not here. This morning you get breakfast in bed. The ultimate of all indulgences."

"Why?" he asked, clearly puzzled by the attention.

"Because you never have. Because it's time."

She was right. He'd never had breakfast in bed. There was no reason to when a quick cup of coffee and a muffin from one of the hordes of coffee shops would suffice. "Why is it time?" he asked, intrigued.

"When I was young, I loved making breakfast and serving it in bed to my mother. Especially when she wasn't sick. I think it made her feel like she was special, like she really mattered. Like she wasn't a burden to me. And it always seemed to bring us a little closer. Taking care of other people does that, Rafe. It's who I am. So, which bedroom is yours?"

"You're serious about this?"

"I sliced every one of these strawberries myself. That makes me pretty darned serious, don't you think?"

Serious, and sexy, and more frightening than he'd bargained for. Because, for the first time in his life, he wanted that breakfast in bed, wanted to be indulged. Maybe because he knew it was a genuine, generous offer and not one that could come back to bite him in some unknown way.

Leading Edie to the bedroom he was using, he stopped short of the door and turned to face her. "My father would offer a cookie, or a candy bar, or some other thing that a little boy would truly want, then he'd tell me to come and take it from his hand. 'Come on, Rafe. You can do it. Just take this cookie…' Sometimes he'd give it to me, and sometimes he'd hit me. The hell of it was, I never could tell what he was going to do. After so many years of his abuse, you'd have thought I could figure it out, but…"

"But you were always that little boy who hoped his dad would hand him the cookie and never hit him again. I'm so sorry…"

He shook his head. "It made me stronger."

"And less trusting."

"But don't *you* have a motive with this French toast?

Be nice to me, indulge me a little, and maybe weaken my position on what I'm going to do with Molly? You may not slap me, Edie, but what's the difference?"

"The difference is, sometimes a nice gesture is just that…a nice gesture. I'm sorry you got slapped, Rafe, but I wasn't the one who slapped you." She shoved the tray at him. "I think maybe I shouldn't come back any more. When Molly's allowed out of the house, I'd like to spend some time with her. Not like this, though." She turned, and walked out the door. In the hall, however, she stopped, and turned back to face him. "Sometimes French toast is just French toast, Rafe. And yours is cold now." Then, spinning on her heel, she marched away.

It hadn't been a good parting and, truthfully, she missed him. Missed Molly, too. But she'd stepped over the line. Gotten involved where she shouldn't have, and now she had to live with the outcome. Meaning she'd let Grace down in a huge way. She should have stayed detached, shouldn't have kissed him, or made him that silly French toast. But she had, and that was that. No going back. Rafe was going to do what he wanted and she was no longer involved with any of it. Or with him. In fact, this morning, when she'd mustered the courage to call him, he hadn't even bothered answering. Or returning a call later on. And now, at the end of the day, she was no longer jumping on each and every incoming call, hoping it was him.

"Why the glum expression?" Rick asked, in passing. "Your day's over. I'd think you'd be happy to leave here."

"Just reflecting on all the mistakes I've made in my life."

He chuckled. "Well, after you've reflected on yours, if you need a few more to work out, come see me. I've got a pretty long list, topped by a couple of whoppers."

"The thing is, when you're involved in the act that ultimately turns out to be a mistake, you can't see that it's a mistake. You go into it clear-headed, plunge all the way through it, and it's only when you come out on the other end that you realize what you've done. Good intentions aside, wouldn't it be smarter if people didn't get so involved in things that didn't concern them?"

"Smarter, maybe. But wouldn't it be a dull life if we didn't get involved, from time to time, where we shouldn't? It's a growing experience, Edie. Sometimes good growth, sometimes difficult growth."

"Well, maybe I'm not in the growing mood."

"Then you should stay locked in your office. Text or email only when necessary and, for heaven's sake, don't answer your phone."

In spite of her bad mood, she laughed. He was right, of course. "Look, I didn't mean to dump my problems on you."

"In case you didn't notice, I was the one who commented on your glum expression. You know, getting involved in a place I probably don't belong. But on the off chance that I might be able to help you work out this mistake you think you've made, can I?"

"Maybe the better question is, can I?" Could she simply walk up to Rafe's door, tell him she would back off? Tell him that Molly was his decision and she was no longer going to interfere?

"Well, whatever you do, tell Rafe to call me. I need

to finish up some paperwork about his involvement in the rescue the other day, and get him to sign off on it. But he's not answering his phone."

"Not for you, either?"

"Rafe…he's the big mistake you're talking about, isn't he?"

"What makes you think that? We're barely friends. I hardly know him." Even as she said the words, she felt the blush creeping to her cheeks.

"And you wear your heart on your sleeve, Edie. That's what makes you so good with the kids. You care, they see it, they feel it. There's nothing hidden. Which goes for Rafe, too. Nothing hidden."

"It's not what you think."

"Or maybe it's not what *you* think. Look, at the risk of getting involved in a place I shouldn't, let me just tell you one thing. Years ago I took my shot at it. The timing was bad, my self-esteem shot all to hell, and I went in a direction I later regretted for more reasons than I've got time to tell you about. But out of that confusion, out of that bad place in my life and all the mistakes I was making, I got my son, and he's my constant reminder that there's nothing that can't be fixed if we want to fix it. Rafe and I…we've had problems in the past. Rafe came to me, apologized, and I was the one who wasn't ready to deal with it, wasn't ready to let those mistakes…his and mine…pass. Yet when I go home at night, and see Christopher…" He smiled, shook his head. "The best things in life can happen when you're least expecting them. Even in the midst of what you think is the worst mistake you've ever made. Like I said, you wear your heart on your sleeve. That's not a mistake, Edie. So, tell him to give me a buzz when he has time."

"He's not easy, Rick."

"Want to see the scar on my shin to prove it?" he asked. "Of course, if you ever notice a little nick on his right shoulder..." He grinned. "In the meantime, I've got a pizza date with a very demanding little guy who rocks my world. No mistake, Edie. In the whole scheme of the universe, definitely no mistake."

So maybe it wouldn't be a mistake, dropping by to see Rafe and Molly. That was the resolve that got her all the way up to the driveway. But the rest of the way, from the road to the door, after her resolve had dissolved, she doubted herself in every way she possibly could. She didn't want involvement, yet she did. She craved it while she pushed it away. Denied it while she dreamt of it. One way or another, she had to get her head straight. Get him totally out of it, or find a way to deal with how he was totally in it. She didn't know which, didn't want to know why she didn't want to know. It was all too confusing. And the plan had been so simple. Show Rafe that he could be Molly's father.

Well, in that, she'd failed. If anything, her insistence had caused more of a gap between them, pushed Rafe even further away from Molly than he had been before. Now it was time to see if she could fix it. Yet, as she rang the doorbell then stood there chewing away nervously on her bottom lip, waiting to be let in, she didn't have a clue in this world how she was going to accomplish that.

Step one foot inside, she told herself. Then take another step after that. And another, and another. That was all her brain would allow and she hoped against hope that her brain would come up with the second part of the plan once the first part was under way. Otherwise she'd be adding another mistake to her list, but with no good outcome in sight.

When the door opened a crack, Edie was prepared to meet Rafe eye to eye. But it wasn't Rafe there to let her in. "Edie!" Molly cried, practically jumping into her arms.

"You're looking better," Edie said, bending down to hug her. "Are you feeling better?"

"I have to, since I'm going to be a nurse."

"Nurse? That's a very good thing to be," she said, stepping inside and looking around. "In a few years, when you're old enough…"

"Not then. Now! I have to be a nurse now."

"Why now?" Edie asked.

Molly pointed to the kitchen. "Rafey's at the kitchen table, taking his nap. I think he's sick."

Suddenly Edie was alarmed. Darting around Molly, Edie ran straight to the kitchen where Rafe was, indeed, slumped over the kitchen table. His face in his arms, breathing, thank God. "Rafe," she said, laying her fingers to the pulse in his neck.

"I'm alive," he muttered. "Wish I weren't, but I am."

He looked up at her through bloodshot eyes, and his features were hardly noticeable under a two-day growth of beard. Sexy, actually. Would have been sexier if he hadn't looked so darned sick.

"Would you mind making me some French toast?" he continued, his voice gravelly to the point it was beyond recognition. "I think I need someone to indulge me."

"Flu?" she asked, nudging him up, out of the chair.

Getting a steadying arm around him, she guided him to the stairs.

"The worst flu anybody has ever had," he muttered, slumping into her as hard as he could without knocking her over.

Edie laughed. So she wore her heart on her sleeve? Well, if she did, the man leaning on her sleeve, maybe even drooling on it, was the man she loved. She wasn't sure what to do about it, except put him to bed.

"It's juice," Molly piped up. "You have to drink it. Edie said so."

Rafe glanced across the room, caught sight of his face in the mirror, and moaned. This was the first time he'd been sick in years. He hadn't caught so much as a cold, but look at him now. He was pale, emaciated looking, his eyes looked hollow. And Edie was loving every minute of it.

Actually, the part about Edie being here to take care of him wasn't all that bad. She was taking a few vacation days from the hospital to play nurse. It was nice. Domestic in a way that felt good. Probably too good, because he wasn't in much of a hurry for this little illness to come to an end. "Tell Edie I said thank you. And thank you, too, Nurse Molly." She was cute, carrying her play nurse's kit, dispensing him candy pills every hour. Edie had bought those for her, and managed to find a nurse's cap and surgical mask at the hospital, which Molly hadn't taken off for two days.

Oh, he was pretty sure it was all part of Edie's plot to get him to keep Molly, but the more he got to know the child, the more he knew she needed the best life she could possibly have, and parents who weren't…him.

At times, though, he did catch himself wishing it could be different.

"Edie said you have to get out of bed, get dressed and go and sit outside on the veranda for lunch. That your in-in…"

"Indulgence?"

She nodded. "It's over."

No wonder everybody at the hospital loved Molly. No wonder his aunt had. She was a real charmer.

Thirty minutes later, Rafe descended the stairs, showered but not shaved. "It's a look," Edie said, fighting back a laugh. "Beard's good, but the sad look on your face sort of spoils the rugged effect."

"You're enjoying this, aren't you?"

"Not enjoying it so much as being entertained by it."

"My inconvenience is your entertainment?"

She shrugged. "Just a little. Oh, and so you'll know, it's only going to be the two of us for lunch. Johnny Redmond stopped by, and he's taken Molly with him to pick up a neglected pony out near Jasper. She was getting pretty restless being cooped up here, and I thought the fresh air would do her some good. Plus Johnny as much as promised her the pony would be hers once the pony is in better shape. Grace was in the process of trying to get this particular pony when she… Anyway, I guess it's a gentle thing, and there was no way Molly wasn't going out with Johnny to get it. Oh, and your brother called. He was surprised you were still here, and when I told him why, he said to say tough luck, but he's not coming back until you're over your flu."

"My family has an uncanny way of avoiding the things that really shouldn't be avoided."

"You mean the decision about Molly?"

"I mean decisions about a lot of things." His life, the hospital, Edie. *Molly.* "Look, would you like to take a walk with me?"

"Are you sure you're up to it?"

"I'm fine. More humiliated about my illness than anything else."

Edie laughed. "Just proves you're human, like the rest of us. You had the same flu as Molly, who came through it in good spirits."

"Children take things better. They don't have as many preconceived ideas of how they really should be feeling."

"If you say so."

"And illnesses usually run a much less serious course with children."

"Anything you say, *Doctor.*" Smiling, she turned to face him. "But keep in mind I'm the one who works with sick children, so if it's me you're trying to fool…"

"Not trying to fool, Edie," he said, suddenly serious. "In a way, that's what I've been doing. But I can't do it, not any longer."

"Fooling me about what?" she asked, stopping dead on the porch. "What's this about, Rafe? Molly?"

He nodded. "About adopting Molly."

"You're going to do it? You've actually decided to go through with it?" She was so excited she was almost jumping up and down.

"Not me, Edie. It's never been me, and I've said that all along."

"Then who?"

"You. I want you to adopt her. She loves you, you love her…"

Edie held out her hand to stop him. "No," she choked. "I can't do that. Grace wanted you—"

"And Aunt Grace isn't going to get everything she wanted. I'm sorry about that, and nobody wishes more than I do that it could have turned out differently. But I'm not the answer to this situation. You are. Which is why I want you to adopt Molly."

"But you, Rafe…"

He laid a hand on her arm. "Just listen to me for a minute, OK? Then maybe you'll understand why I can't do it. And believe me when I tell you I've given this a lot of thought. Lost sleep over it. Weighed it from every angle. Always came to the same conclusion."

"That I'm the one?"

"That you're meant to be Molly's mother. It makes sense. When I watch the two of you… Edie, my old man…" He paused for a moment, and stared off in the distance, at the property directly across the street. "We lived over there. Nice house. Big. Our house was actually nicer than Gracie House, if you go by size and furnishings." Except now it was a meadow. Trees, grass, several of Gracie Foundation's horses turned out to graze. For which he was very grateful. Land where so much hatred had been rooted deserved to be reclaimed for something good and decent.

"When the old man died, Jess and I burned it down. Didn't want to see it, didn't want it cluttering up the landscape as an ugly reminder. So we torched it… legally. Funny thing is, the town turned out and most of the people were shocked by our sentiment. Shocked that we would dare destroy the residence of the venerable Dr. Lawrence Corbett, but for us it was liberating. And what I discovered that day was that sometimes you have to dive into the fire in order to come out tempered on the other side. When I walked away, I didn't look back, didn't come back."

"No one ever knew, or suspected, what he'd done to you?"

"There weren't any visible scars to show anybody. Anything other than that was my word against his, and who the hell would believe a kid? Especially when that kid's father makes a point of telling everybody how bad his kid is."

"But your aunt?"

"She knew. But every time she threatened to turn him in to the authorities, he told her she'd better make sure she came out on top because if she didn't she'd never see Jess and me again. That was the one threat that always beat her, because if she had waged the battle and lost, I don't know what would have happened to Jess and me. Maybe the old man wouldn't have gone through with his threats but, then again, maybe he would have. Who knows?

"And whatever the case, Aunt Grace did what she had to do to stay involved in our lives. That's why she built her house across the road from ours. It wasn't so much that she wanted to live in Lilly Lake but she wouldn't live anywhere where my brother and I couldn't get to her whenever we needed to. And there were so many times…" He stopped. "But that's not why we're out here, is it? This is supposed to be about going on a nice walk, relaxing, thinking positive thoughts. About me telling you why I think you're the perfect mother for Molly."

But what positive thoughts could there be when every time Rafe stepped out the door he saw *the house*, even if, quite literally, it wasn't standing there any more? It looked like an innocent, peaceful lot, but the more Edie stared at it, the more she could see the house, see the scared little boys inside. For the first time, Edie truly understood why Rafe couldn't stay here. Memories adjusted, and they found their rightful place, but some memories didn't fade. To Rafe, the house was as real right now as it had been when he'd been a boy. All she had to do was look at the sadness written all over his face to know that, to understand it.

Perhaps it was when she studied the lines of that sadness that she realized she couldn't stay here and have him, too. The thing was, it was too soon to be thinking this way. She was only now discovering who she wanted to be, and the journey was good. Difficult, sometimes frustrating, but ultimately very good, and she wasn't ready to trade it in for anything else. Except maybe for motherhood? And perhaps for the slim chance at a life with someone who didn't have a clue where his own journey was taking him?

"I do love Molly," she confessed.

"Which is why I want you to take Gracie House. Adopt Molly, live here with her, give her the life she deserves."

So, this didn't come with Rafe after all. He was bargaining for his escape without taking anyone with him. And here she'd been, ready to make a commitment he had no intention of making himself. What a fool she'd been. An utter fool!

Still, she couldn't deny that stirring inside her. Couldn't ignore it either. Because it was now infused with heartbreak…something she would never let him see. Which was why, when Rafe took hold of her hand

and they headed toward the trail that led to the lake, she clung to him like her life depended on it yet didn't say a word. After all, what was there to say? Except… "No. I can't adopt her, Rafe. I'm sorry, but I can't adopt her."

Not because she didn't want to, because she did. With all her heart. But because Rafe was using her as his easy way out, and if he didn't have *her* to fall back on, maybe he would be the one to adopt Molly. With the way her heart was breaking, it was the only thing that made sense. The only thing she could do.

CHAPTER EIGHT

"I APPRECIATE you doing this for me. I'm usually a pretty good judge of character, but as this is about Molly, not me, I want your opinion of these people, too. Molly needs the best and I think you're much better equipped to handle that than I am."

Even before she entered the den where prospective adoptive parents Wallace and Betsy Cunningham were waiting, Edie felt a cold chill. She hated doing this. Hated, loathed, despised it. Couldn't believe he was actually going through with it. Somehow she'd hoped for a change of heart. But that wasn't the case. Rafe was actively interviewing prospective parents now, and the only thing she could feel was…nauseated. "Let's just get it over with," she said grumpily, on the first thud of what she knew was going to turn into a pounding headache.

"OK, I get it. You're not happy about my decision, but I still think it's best for Molly. She needs a real family. Needs the stability of parents who know how to raise a child, and that's not me. Apparently, not you either."

"That's not fair, Rafe. This was never supposed to be about me, and you know that!"

"What I know is that you turned me down, so I had to move on to the next plan."

"And do what? Hope that I'll back down and agree to take her when it looks like you're getting close to making a selection? Is that what this is about?"

"It's about moving on, Edie. We all need to do it, I think."

She'd peeked in at the Cunninghams a while ago. Peeked in at the Bensons as well as the Farleighs. They all seemed nice. Henry Danforth had put them through the initial wringers, so to speak, and she'd even read the background checks. All suitable candidates was what Henry had said. But Molly didn't need a suitable candidate. She needed a parent, or a set of parents.

The thing that bothered her most, though, was the air of indifference Rafe was trying to put on. It wasn't working on him. She saw that, but she didn't know how to get through it. So maybe it was time…time to make the next move. She'd thought about it for two days now. In fact, that was all she'd thought about. Being Molly's mother. Even now, as the words floated through her mind, they made her smile. There was no downside to the situation. Not the way Rafe saw the downside, anyway. She loved Molly, and that was really all that mattered.

But it did feel like such a betrayal. Except the one thing that kept coming back to her was how Grace's only concern was that Molly have the best chance at a good life, with a good parent. So maybe Grace had miscalculated a little. Maybe what she had seen in Rafe simply wasn't there. The only thing was, Edie saw it in him, too. In those unguarded moments when he took hold of Molly's hand, when Molly walked next to him and tried to match his steps and Rafe would slow his stride just for her, in the way he watched Molly when he thought no one was looking…the big gestures didn't matter so much, but she saw Rafe's feelings for Molly in the little gestures.

She didn't know what to do, though. Not any more. "Yes, I think we all do need to move on," she finally responded.

Expelling a frustrated breath, Rafe turned away from the door to face Edie. "Look, I'm not going to argue with you about this. I thought it was going to be easy, finding her a family. In my mind, the perfect family would magically materialize, and Molly would get her happily-ever-after. I want her to have that, Edie. I *really* want her to have that."

"Yet you can't be the one to give it to her? Because she's getting attached to you, Rafe. I see it more and more every day. Molly adores you, and her attachment is growing."

He shook his head. "I see it too, and it scares the hell out of me. But, no, I can't be the one to bring her up. I know that makes me look terrible, but it's not me. I don't have what it takes to be a good father, and at least I have the sense to know what I'm *not* capable of doing. I wish it was different, but it's not."

But he wished he could raise Molly. Edie could see it in his eyes. Rafe truly wished he could, and something was stopping him.

"So, let's just get this over with, OK? Henry has one more set of prospective parents to send over later today, and by tonight I really intend on deciding which ones will get Molly."

"Which ones will *get* Molly? Will *get* Molly? Oh,

my God, Rafe! Could you be any colder about it? It's like you're having a contest and she's the prize. Step right up, put your name in the hat, let me pick a winner!" OK, so she was shouting. She couldn't help it.

"Now you're being ridiculous," he hissed.

"I'm being ridiculous? Look in the mirror, Rafe. Take a good hard look then come back and tell me who's being ridiculous. Molly needs you, you need Molly, and I don't know why you can't see that. Everybody else can."

"Everybody else sees what they want to see, and you…you're the queen of it, Edie. But guess what, you're not seeing everything. You're not seeing why—"

"Then tell me, Rafe! Tell my why you're refusing to keep Molly. You keep saying that it's not your lifestyle, that you don't have room in your life, but I don't buy it. I've seen the way you and Molly are with each other, and there's nothing in you that *doesn't* scream father." Her voice softened, and she reached out to squeeze his arm. "Rafe, please…"

He shook his head.

"Then I'll adopt her." She didn't want it to sound like she was accepting the consolation prize, because as she said the words, her heart skipped a beat. In the blink of an eye, she'd become a mother…Molly's mother. And suddenly she was excited. "I'll adopt her!" she said, the enthusiasm rising in her voice.

"You're sure about his?" he asked, sounding more relieved than anything else. "I've always thought it was the perfect solution, but I don't want to force you…"

"You're not forcing me, Rafe. I *do* want to adopt Molly. I want to be her mother, want to give her the home she needs. More than anything else, Rafe, I want to be the person who will help her develop into everything she's meant to be." The way *her* mother had done for her in spite of so much adversity. "I was lucky. I had a perfect mother who showed me life in so many wonderful ways. That's what I want to be for Molly. What I want to do for Molly."

"Then Molly's going to be a very lucky little girl. From the moment I first laid eyes on you, I considered you perfect for Molly. She lights up around you…"

"She lights up around you, too." It was exciting, but in a way sad, because with the feelings she'd been harboring for him, the only thing he'd been harboring for her was the desire for her to adopt Molly. Foolish in love, once again.

"And she can't wait to see you, to talk to you, to play with you."

"The way she can't wait to see you, to talk to you, to play with *you*."

"What's this about?" he asked.

"It's about adopting Molly. That's all." About giving Rafe one last chance, about showing Rafe what he was going to be missing. About trying, one last time, to do what she'd promised Grace she'd do. She *had* to do it. Never giving up was also a big part of who she was.

"But I get the impression you're still trying to convince me I should be the one."

"You should, and…" She placed her hand on his chest, her palm pressed flat to his heart. For an instant she felt a little jolt. Felt it so much she nearly pulled back. But it had to be static shock, that was all. "And if you'll let yourself, you'll feel it in here, Rafe. You *are*

Molly's father, meant to be. I know it. Grace knew it. Molly knows it."

He pulled back. Stopped for a moment, and simply stared at her. Stared hard, stared deep, then spun and walked away.

Suddenly, the whole idea of adopting Molly scared Edie. What was she thinking? That somehow the three of them could turn into some kind of real family? She loved Molly, she also knew Rafe did. Molly loved both of them back. But the rest of the dots didn't connect, and Edie startlingly realized what she was afraid that Rafe was feeling—that this was a trap meant to either stall the inevitable adoption so she'd have more time to convince him, or to slowly pull Rafe into a place he clearly didn't want to be.

She should have thought it through more carefully. Truthfully, all she'd thought about was Molly. "It's not what you think, Rafe," she called as he headed to the front door. "I'm not trying to back you into a corner here. I only want what's best for Molly."

He stopped for a moment, but didn't turn back to face her. "And how many times do I have to tell you, that's *not* me?"

"Because you don't want to?" Edie cried. "Because you really don't want to? Tell me the truth, Rafe. I know we've argued this over and over but tell me the honest truth now, and I won't say another word." She watched him turn toward her, and saw agony written clearly on his face. It was excruciating, it broke her heart. And in that moment she knew for sure that she loved Rafe Corbett more than life itself, no matter how he felt about her. His pain was so acute to her that his suffering was taking root in her very being.

But through the pain, she saw the heart of the man she wanted to be with for ever. A good heart. A kind heart. But a troubled heart. "Tell me, Rafe. Please…"

"It's about loving someone. I can't. Can't love them, don't want to be loved back. Sure, I can do the right things for Molly. Outwardly, go through the motions. But she'll know the difference. She'll see that I don't have that real capacity in me to be anything more than an authority figure, and she needs better than that. I needed better than that, and I know what it's like to be raised by someone who can't, or won't, give you what you need. I was. And now I see so many of my father's traits in me. I look in the mirror and see my father's son. I'm *just* like him, Edie. I was abused. In turn, I abused Rick Navarro. I *am* my father's son and there's nothing I can do about it. His heredity beat me." He spoke his words—words filled with the emotion of an anguished man. Then he was gone.

Edie stood alone in the entry hall, not sure what to do next. Run after him? Leave him alone? Give him his space then go to him?

She didn't know, and as she brushed back the tears on her cheeks there was nothing inside her that could reason this through. Nothing at all. So she left. Went home, sank down in her favorite cozy chair, and wished desperately for her mother. Or for Grace. Or for Rafe.

It was a beautiful evening. Clear black sky, millions of stars, the sound of the bullfrog in the distance croaking out some kind of mating call to his lady love. He'd always felt balanced here. Balanced, accepted, safe. Maybe it was the only place he'd every truly felt that balance, and being here again brought so many memories rushing back. Mostly the good ones, though. And there had been some good ones, especially with Jess. Coming here together, camping out, making plans for their future like nothing was wrong in their lives. Yes, some good times, and he missed those. Missed his brother. Missed that youthful optimism that tried so hard to come through even when everything else was going so wrong. "When I was little, I used to think that when I looked out over the bluff, I could see the edge of the world," he said.

"Is that where it is?" Molly asked innocently. "Over there, where you can't see anything else?"

"No, sweetie. The world is infinitely large. You can't see the edge of it." Even though right now it felt like he was about to fall over that edge. He'd done the right thing, though. He was sure of it. Molly would have everything she needed now. And he would have… nothing more, nothing less than he'd come with.

"But what's on the other side of where you can't see?"

"A world full of possibilities. Things that will make you happy, things that will help you in your life, things you don't even know about that are waiting for you to find them."

"What kind of things, Rafey? Maybe toys and a kitten?"

"Maybe toys and a kitten. Maybe more people to love you, and for you to love."

"And candy?"

Chuckling, he tousled her hair. "And candy." The innocence of a child…it was magical. Molly was magical, and he was already beginning to miss her. But he'd made the decision and there was no turning back. In his heart of hearts he knew Edie was Molly's mother. That was the only consolation in this. Edie was Molly's mother, and he'd seen that so many times over these past few days. Even seen himself in the father spot, too. Except that couldn't work. "And anything else that makes you happy. It's all out there for you, Molly."

"You, too," she stated seriously. "Except the toys. You're too old to play with toys."

This was tougher than he'd expected. When he'd been young, Hideaway Bluff was where he'd come to make things simple in what was, otherwise, a very complicated life. Yet there was nothing simple here tonight. Not for him, certainly not for Molly. "You're right, I'm too old for toys. But I do have equipment."

"What kind of equipment?"

"Medical equipment. The things I use to help make people feel better."

"Then maybe there's medical equipment out there for you, so you can make lots of people feel better." Sitting on a craggy rock shelf, protected from the elements, Molly snuggled into Rafe's side and laid her head against his chest. "Whatever kind you want, Rafey. Like whatever kind of toys I want."

"And candy," he said wistfully, staring into the campfire he'd built. "Look, Molly, there's something I need to tell you." Instinctively, he put his arm around her shoulders. "It's very, very good."

"Aunt Grace is coming home?" she cried. "When? When is she coming?"

Dear God. He hadn't expected this. Not at all. And he didn't know what to do, what to say. Somehow he'd just figured Molly knew. Granted, everybody had pretty much tiptoed around the subject of Grace's death when Molly was around, but he'd truly thought she understood, and that she was simply taking her time to process it in the way a child would.

He needed Edie here. She was the one with all the right words for children. She was the one with the empathy, the one who instinctively knew what to do. And he was the one who didn't have a clue. Not a single, solitary clue. So maybe it was time to douse the fire and head back. Put this off until he could get to Edie.

But Molly wasn't to be put off. "When, Rafey?" she persisted. "I want to tell her all about Ice Cream, and about my new pony, Lucky. She's beautiful, Rafey. Black and white. And Aunt Grace is going to love her. She always says I can't ride by myself until I'm eight, but with Lucky maybe she'll let me ride by myself when I'm six. Do you think she will, Rafey?"

To break a child's heart…this wasn't the reason he'd come here. In his mind, it should have been a very simple thing. Take Molly to the place he most loved in the world, let her share that feeling with him, then tell her about the wonderful new mother she was about to have. It should have been a good evening, but now this. And he couldn't wait for someone else to take care of it. Molly needed honesty, and understanding. *She needed it from him*—the least likely person in the world to do this.

Rafe drew in a shuddering breath, bracing himself. "Molly, we need to talk about Aunt Grace. And you have to listen to me very carefully, because what we have to talk about isn't going to be easy for you."

"Can we have a party for her? She loves parties, and a nice, big party will make it all better for her. We can have cake and ice cream…the *real* ice cream, not the horse. And maybe party hats."

He remembered those parties his aunt used to have…parties for all occasions. Big ones, little ones, private ones just for Aunt Grace and him. In his aunt's estimation, a party could cure almost anything, and she had been right. Her parties had cured so many ills, wiped out so much cruelty, eased so many pains, all because her parties had been about caring. About nurturing. "I remember the cakes she used to bake for her parties. My favorite was chocolate, with lots of chocolate icing."

"Mine, too," Molly agreed. "And with sprinkles, too."

"Especially with sprinkles." Glancing out over the vast night expanse in front of him, Rafe wished he could be somewhere out there, having a party with his aunt, listening to her tell the little boy in him that things were going to get better. But he couldn't. And it was foolish of him to think things could be different because there'd never been a moment in his life when he hadn't known who he was, and what he was about. Festive little parties hadn't changed that. "Aunt Grace loved baking those cakes, Molly, and she loved having those parties. Do you know some of the other things she loved, too?"

"Her horses. And you and Jess. She always told me how much she loves you and Jess, that you are her two favorite boys in the whole, wide world."

The lump in his throat hardened. "And you, sweetheart. Aunt Grace loved you more than anything in the world. From the day she brought you home to live with her, she loved you so much, and she wanted you to be her little girl, her daughter…"

"But she's too old," Molly chimed in. "I don't think she is, but the people in charge said she is."

"And they were wrong. In Aunt Grace's heart, you *were* her daughter, and she loved you more than anything."

"Will she again, when she comes back?"

Now the heartbreak. Molly's and his. "Her love for you will never change, Molly. In fact, it's bigger now. Bigger than anything you can imagine. For ever. But Aunt Grace can't come back to tell you how much she loves you. Not any more."

This time, Molly was quiet.

"She got very, very sick. Do you remember that?"

Molly nodded, but still didn't speak.

"She wanted to get better so she could come back and take care of you, and the doctors tried very hard to help her, but it was something the doctors couldn't fix, sweetheart. They tried so hard, and Aunt Grace tried so hard, because she missed you so much, but there wasn't anything anybody could do. Do you remember when she had to go to the hospital?"

Molly nodded. "Summer said it was to get her all better. That when Aunt Grace was better, she'd come home again. But she hasn't. Not yet."

Summer Adair, Aunt Grace's private duty nurse. Summer, herself, had a child, and Rafe knew that anything Summer might have said would have been with sensitivity. But it hadn't been Summer's place to explain the situation to Molly, and now he realized no one had ever taken up that responsibility. They'd simply assumed…too much.

"That's what everybody wanted, sweetheart. Everybody wanted Aunt Grace to get better and come home."

"But she couldn't get better?"

The beginning of the realization. The taking away of innocence. It hurt. "No, she couldn't get better." He paused, searching for the right words…words that wouldn't destroy Molly, words she would understand. Words that came so easily to Edie. "The doctors tried everything they knew how to do. Dr. Rick…he's a very good doctor. You know that, don't you?"

Molly nodded, but didn't speak again.

"Dr. Rick did everything a doctor could do to make Aunt Grace get better, but sometimes even doctors can't fix everything. And he was very sad…we were all very sad because we loved Aunt Grace so much. But she couldn't stay here any longer, Molly. It was time for her to…" He choked on the words, as the tears fell silently down his cheeks. "It was time for her to go to a place where she could be well again, and stay that way for ever. But well in a different way. Molly, sweetheart, Aunt Grace died. Do you know what that means?"

Molly was quiet for a long time, trying to process it. He didn't want to interrupt her, but he also didn't want her to be lost in a dark lonely place. Not the way he'd been for most of his life.

"It means you go to live in heaven," Molly finally said.

"It means Aunt Grace went to live in heaven."

"But I don't want her to go, Rafey! I don't want her to go!" Molly threw herself into Rafe's arms and sobbed…the great, racking sobs of a broken heart, of a child who truly did understand but whose heart was breaking anyway.

"It's OK," he said, holding on to her, rocking her, feeling her tears soaking through his shirt. Feeling his own tears spilling freely down his face. "It's OK, Molly," he soothed, over and over. For Molly, for himself. "Everything's going to be OK."

He said the words, but he didn't know how to make it OK for her. Dear God, he didn't know how. And tonight he ached for Molly the way he'd never ached for anyone else.

"Can I go to heaven, too?" she finally whispered in a tiny, broken voice.

"No, sweetheart. Aunt Grace loved you so much she wanted you to stay here and have the best life you could possibly have."

"But I miss her, Rafey. I want to see her again."

"We all do, Molly." He took a deep breath, sniffed, tried to brace himself…against what, he didn't know. But none of it worked. Right now the world was made up of just the two of them…two broken hearts who could do nothing but sit and hold on to each other. Clinging for dear life. It didn't seem enough, not for him but especially not for Molly. Yet maybe, in the grand scheme of things, this was all there was. "And we'll never stop loving her. But it's in a different way now. It's in here." He placed his hand on her heart, and took her tiny hand and placed it on his. "This is where Aunt Grace is now. She's in our hearts, in a very special place."

Molly thought about that then pulled herself out of Rafe's arms and pointed to the vast openness that extended farther than any eye could see. "She's out there too, Rafey. Where you can't see. You said that's where things will make you happy, where things will help you. And that's where Aunt Grace is."

"In a world full of possibilities," he whispered, gathering Molly back into his arms. "You're right, Molly. That's where Aunt Grace is."

CHAPTER NINE

"No, it's already scheduled. I've got my plane ticket and I'm going home the day after tomorrow. Henry will have all the legalities worked out by then, you can move into Gracie House any time you want, and life will go on."

"So that's it? I sign the papers, you hand Molly over to me, then you leave?" She had known this was what was going to happen, but she hadn't let herself believe it, or even think about it. On one hand, adopting Molly was the best thing she'd ever done in her life but, on the other hand, it was also the most difficult, because it felt like she was shutting all those doors she'd truly believed would open. She'd hoped for a miracle and while she had gotten one, it hadn't been the one she'd planned on, and Rafe wasn't shifting on this whole Molly situation. He was going ahead full steam with his plan, and she couldn't stop him.

"You're not your father," she said. She knew it with all her heart, but Rafe didn't, and there really wasn't a way to convince him. If his heart wouldn't budge, there was nothing she could do.

"Look what I did to Rick, and he's still pretty scarred from it. That's the way my father acted."

"But you were a boy, Rafe. A boy who was in horrible pain, lashing out. You were thinking with an adolescent's mind, reacting the way an adolescent would. You're a man now. A gentle, compassionate man who takes care of people. What, in there, makes you think you can't love Molly the way she deserves to be loved? The capacity to love isn't dictated by heredity, as you seem to think it is. It's dictated by your heart, and you have a good heart, Rafe. Good, but very scarred."

"In an ideal world, I'd have moved home to Lilly Lake, married you, adopted Molly, practiced at the hospital. But I've never lived in an ideal world, Edie."

"Married me?" she asked. "How can you throw that out there now, when you're two steps shy of stepping on the plane and leaving for ever?"

"I can throw it out there because that would have been my ideal world. We would have dated for a while, the two of us. And the *three* of us would have spent time together, growing as a family. Then..." He shrugged. "Then you would have suffocated. One day you would have woken up and realized I wasn't enough. That maybe I was too emotionally distanced. Or I simply wasn't the kind of support you need. Then where would that leave us? And where would it leave Molly?"

"So, you've got this little life scenario all planned out for us without even including me? How could you do that, Rafe? How could you *assume* us all the way from beginning to end?" They were sitting on the front porch, Edie in the wicker chair, Rafe on the swing. Almost at opposite sides, the way they'd been for days, during the adoption preparations. During those days she'd had the impression, more than once, that Rafe had been on the verge of regretting his decision. Now she knew it. This was what he wanted, but his scars were too tough, his walls too high.

"Just being practical. People don't do that enough. They don't lead with their heads…"

"Because leading with their hearts is so much nicer, Rafe. It takes you to better places, places your head would never allow you." Instinctively, she pushed herself out of the chair then crossed the porch and sat down next to him on the swing. "Your head kept you here, on the opposite side of the porch from me. But my heart put me here, next to you."

"It's not going to work, Edie."

"Why?"

"Maybe that's the question I should be asking you. Why are you fighting so hard for me?"

"Because you're not fighting for yourself."

"I don't need to fight for me. I have a good life, successful career, nice condo…"

"With a porch swing?"

"No!" he snapped. "Just stop it, OK?"

She was getting to him. She knew it, could feel it. So could he, but the feeling was so foreign to him he didn't know what it was. Or maybe loving someone opened you up to the fear of losing them…a fear she knew so well.

"Rafe, when I was a girl, I didn't have a life like all my friends did. My mother was sick, and she truly couldn't get along without me. I took care of her, spent practically all of my childhood taking care of her, and it's what I wanted to do because I loved her. But I lived with this horrible fear…actually, two horrible fears. The first was her death. The doctors were amazed she lived as long as she did, but I think it was because she didn't want to leave me. The second fear was that I would be taken away from my mother. The social workers tried so many times to do that. They thought I needed another life, needed another family...the way you think Molly needs another family. But all I needed was my mother, and everything she was, no matter how hard it got for us sometimes. Consequently I spent a lot of time scared to death they would come and take me away from the person I loved most in the world.

"All those years, that fear never went away. It was with me, day in and day out. And there were a couple of times when they did pull me out of the house and put me in a group home because it was in my own best interests. I know, Rafe, what it feels like to be wrenched out of your life and not be able to do a darned thing about it. But I always ran away, always ran back to my mother because she needed me. More than that, I needed her. Even in her sickest moments I needed her in ways no one could understand. I loved her, Rafe, the way Molly loves you. That's all there was to it. In spite of all the complications and hardships...and there were many hardships...I loved her. It was a simple thing, and nothing else mattered.

"But that love always had this overwhelming dread attached to it because I knew her time was limited, and because I knew I could be taken away from her. So I do know what it's like to have that fear surrounding something you love...*the way you do.* But I also know what it's like to simply let the love happen, no matter what else is going on."

"Then you have a bigger heart than I do," he said, his voice filled with sadness.

"Not bigger. Just one that's found out how to stay open." She twisted to face him and laid her hand on his heart. "Molly could do that for you, if you let her."

"Molly shouldn't have to suffer for my trials and errors." He laid his hand on hers. "Neither should you."

"So you get to make the decision for all three of us? Molly and I don't have a say?"

He pulled her hand to his lips and kissed it. "You see things in me that aren't there. I'm not sure why, but I thank you for it. It makes me feel like I *could* have what you offer…someday. But not now. It's too risky… for you. I'm too risky."

For Rafe, risky translated into not worth loving. She understood that, and it hurt her deeply. Here she was, in love with the man and ready to throw aside all her caution about not getting involved again or waiting until she had more life experience under her belt. All because she'd found the person worth changing for. And she was pretty sure now he loved her back, or else he wouldn't have so much conflict in himself. But maybe the problem here was that *she* wasn't enough. Maybe she'd been deluding herself into believing that all he had to do was believe and they'd have their happily-ever-after when she was the one who didn't have everything Rafe needed to make it come true for himself.

She'd always believed that love was enough, but this time she could have been wrong. Maybe it was time to count her blessings about having Molly in her life, and move on from there. "Life is about taking chances," Edie said, as the sad realization washed down over her. "Everything we do is about taking a chance. Sometimes it works out, sometimes it doesn't.

You're not like your father, but you're going to have to put yourself out there in ways that scare you to find out. I hope, someday, that happens for you." With that, she stood and headed to her car, leaving little pieces of her heart behind her. The fight was over. They'd been going round and round for days now, and ending up in the same place they'd started. Now it was time to move past it, time to look forward.

But it was tough to do when so much of what she wanted was behind her.

"I've never pretended differently, Edie. You know that," he called after her.

"Yes, I do know that," she whispered, but not for him to hear as she fought not to cry. This was what she should have expected after all. Rafe wanted a parent for Molly, and he'd got one. No regrets there. Maybe she should chalk it up to another reason to stay out of relationships and get on with it. If nothing else, it sure proved that she didn't know how to pick them. In fact, she was abysmally bad at it. It was so hard, though, because she'd pinned so many hopes on Rafe. And had trusted him to come round. Except she hadn't been enough to make him come round, and that was something she couldn't overcome. She wasn't enough for Rafe, wasn't who Rafe needed.

Well, the bright side was she had a wonderful daughter now, and that did make up for everything else.

As Edie climbed into her car, she fought the urge to look back at Rafe. What was the point? He was done here in Lilly Lake now, and he'd never come back. And she was only beginning here. That was all there was, all there could ever be.

Yet, she did glance back anyway and he was… slumped against the white support column at the top of the steps, leaning there, his head hanging down. He looked like a very sad man, a broken man, actually. But he'd made the choice that had caused that, and there was nothing she could do about it. Yet, in spite of everything, her heart ached for Rafe because he knew what he was losing. Because, like her, his heart was breaking, too.

"Want to go for a ride?" Rafe called through the bedroom door. He felt like hell, and he didn't want to stay in this house. He needed to get away, spend some last quality time with Molly and make sure she understood what was happening. When he and Edie had told Molly that Edie was going to become her real mother, Molly had been excited. But she hadn't understood why he wasn't going to be part of that family. They'd explained that he had to return to his real home, and Molly seemed to accept it. But who knew? Maybe she was still trying to process it. Or, in her young mind, ignoring it and focusing only on what she wanted. Whatever the case, he needed to spend some time with her. "Molly, did you hear me? Do you want to go for a ride?"

She didn't answer. He didn't blame her.

"We can saddle up Lucky, and you can ride by yourself for a little while." That was something he really did want to do for her before he left here—give her the thrill of riding solo on her very own horse. Or in this case pony. "You can use that saddle Aunt Grace had made for you. Molly?" He knocked again then pressed his ear to the door to listen. But he heard nothing. Not a sound.

"Molly," he said, twisting the knob and pushing the door open a crack. "Are you in there?" A chill of dread was creeping slowly up his spine. "Molly?" he said again, shoving the door all the way back, only to discover what he was afraid he'd discover. She was gone!

"Molly!" he shouted in a voice that resonated throughout the entire house. "Molly, where are you?"

She'd been there half an hour ago. He'd seen her go to her room, seen her start to line up all her dolls for a tea party. "Molly!" he shouted, over and over, as he ran up and down the second-floor hall, opening all the doors and looking in. To no avail. His downstairs search was just as fruitless. So he went to the stable, saw Johnny hand-feeding a new quarter horse arrival that was so emaciated it turned his stomach. Molly had to have known about this horse and she was down here somewhere, helping. That was it. She loved the horses as much as Aunt Grace had, and she was helping with this one.

"I need to talk to Molly," he told Johnny, as he caught a calming breath. "Is she in one of the stalls?"

"Haven't seen her all morning, Rafe. I was surprised that she didn't come down to help me with this beauty…" He stroked the horse's muzzle. "But with her big day coming up, I figured she was busy doing something else."

The words sank in, but slowly. "So what you're telling me is that she isn't here?"

Johnny shook his head. "Haven't seen her since you brought her down last night to say goodnight to Lucky and Ice Cream. Why? Is she missing?"

Panic started rising in him again. "Don't know yet. I thought she was in the house, but she's not. I'd assumed she'd be here."

"Maybe she is, and I haven't seen her," Johnny said. "I've been pretty busy with this one, trying to get her back on her feed. Have you looked around the paddock? Or maybe out in the other stable? I've got a couple of volunteers out there right now, working with some of our problem horses, so maybe Molly's gone out there to help feed or brush them."

"Without permission?"

Johnny shrugged. "Kids are kids. When mine were little, there was always this test of wills going on. Most of the time they did what they were supposed to, but sometimes they did what they wanted to do, no matter what. Molly's a good kid, and smart. When you catch up to her, don't be too hard on her."

"Like my old man would have been?" Rafe snapped, on his way out the rear door. "You were here in those days, so is that what you're telling me? Not to be like my old man was?"

"What I'm telling you is not to be like *any* child's old man who's in a panic over not being able to find his kid," Johnny shot back. "Parents have a way of overreacting when they're scared for their child. I know I did that on more than one occasion. But that's not about your father. It's about you. Be who you are."

Rafe heard the words, heard Johnny call him Molly's parent, and thought about them as he ran to the second stable, only to discover that no one there had seen Molly that day. "Where's her pony?" he asked one of the volunteers who came there as part of the Gracie Foundation.

"In the paddock," a fresh-faced, college-aged volunteer by the name of Ben responded. "We took her out there earlier, along with Ice Cream and a couple of the others. Thought we'd take them over to the pasture later."

But he'd gone by the paddock and hadn't noticed Lucky. Or maybe he hadn't looked thoroughly enough. So on his way back over to the main stable he took another look and Lucky was definitely not there. And Molly's saddle was not hanging in the tack room when he went to find it. "Johnny!" Rafe shouted, on his way back through the building. "Tell me you did something with Molly's saddle, that you hung it somewhere else. And that Lucky is already down at the pasture to graze."

Johnny's weather-beaten face drained of all color. "I can't, which means I think we have a problem here, Rafe," he said.

Rafe swallowed hard. "Can you saddle Donder for me while I go and make a couple of phone calls?"

"Consider it done," Johnny said. "And I'll be riding out with you too, Rafe. I feel terrible about this. I knew she wanted to go solo. She's been begging for days. I should have..."

Rafe squeezed the man's shoulder. "Not your fault. Nothing here's been normal for Molly for a while, and I'm hoping she just needed to get away, go someplace to think." Adult reasoning, he knew. But the alternative was that she'd run away, and he didn't even want to think about that. "Give me ten minutes, then I'll be back to ride."

His first call was to Edie. "You haven't seen Molly along the road somewhere, have you?" Stupid question. If Edie had seen her, she'd have stopped.

"Is she missing?" Edie choked.

"Looks like she might have gone for a ride on her pony. We're getting ready to go out looking right now."

"I'm not home yet. I'll turn round and be back in a few minutes."

That's what he'd counted on, what he needed. "I'm going to give Rick a call, in case Molly turns up at the hospital." He did that. "She's missing, Rick," he explained. "Took her pony and left here. I was hoping she might show up there as the hospital is one of the places where she feels safe."

"I'll alert the staff to be on the lookout. And, Rafe, you shouldn't be going through this alone. I'll be there in a couple minutes to ride out with you."

"I'd appreciate that, Rick," he said, as a knot formed in his throat. "I'd really appreciate that." After all these years Rick had found it in himself to become a friend. It touched Rafe in ways he'd never expected.

"I've looked everywhere, and she's not in the house," Edie called out to the group assembling near the stable door. Johnny was ready to ride, along with his small group of volunteers. And Rafe and Rick were ready to go, both of them looking downright handsome in the saddle, she noticed. In fact, the two of them, together, were breathtaking. She was glad, at least for now, that they were able to work together. "Is Ice Cream saddled for me?"

"You don't have to ride out with us," Rafe called back.

"She's my daughter, Rafe. What else am I supposed to be doing?"

"I'll stay here, in case she comes back," Summer

volunteered. "She trusts me, so we should be fine. I'll make some phone calls, and I'll call you if I hear anything from anybody." Summer approached Edie and pulled her into a hug. "I know we've never really spent any time together, but I'm glad you're going to be adopting Molly. Grace thought the world of you, and she'd be happy. And Molly's going to be fine out there. She's a smart, tough little girl. She'll know how to take care of herself."

"I haven't even signed the papers yet, and I'm feeling so…so…"

"So like a mother?" Summer laughed. "Welcome to a mother's world, Edie. It's a great place to live, and it can be more scary than anything you could ever imagine."

Edie climbed up on Ice Cream, patted the horse on the neck then looked down. "And to think that only a few days ago this was one of my biggest fears in the world."

"Grace taught her well, Edie. Trust that."

Summer stepped back then waved her off, while Edie turned Ice Cream in the direction of Rafe and Rick and looked up the hill at the house. Her house, to share with her daughter now. Life had changed so much, so quickly, her head was spinning. But her heart was breaking too, in more pieces than she'd ever known it could, and for the first time in her life she truly understood what her mother had felt all those times the authorities had threatened to remove her from the house, to give her to other people. There was no way to describe the anguish, no way to bear the shattered heart. To love a child…that was all there was, and she felt her mother there with her, guiding her through this ordeal. Felt her mother's strength and courage. That was what sent her to Rafe and Rick and allowed her to ride as hard as they did through the meadow and the hilly incline to the place where Rafe hoped Molly had gone.

"I told her that Aunt Grace was out there," he said, as they paused once to look for any visible signs that Molly had come in this direction. "That somewhere in the distance she could find all her possibilities."

Edie reached over and took hold of his hand. "That was a beautiful thing to say to her."

"But she's not old enough to come up here. It's too dangerous." He gazed up the side of the bluff. "Not steep, but if she doesn't know the way..."

"Nothing over here," Rick called from the far side of a copse of sugar maples. "No sign of a horse or Molly."

"I think I'm going all the way up, and you and Rick can continue around the base and see if you can find anything over there." He started to turn away, but Edie pulled Ice Cream in front of him.

"Rick's fine on his own. I'm going up with you."

Rafe shook his head. "It's too dangerous."

"Yet you took Molly up there?"

"With me. I took her up with me. On the back of my horse."

"But that's the best vantage point up there, isn't it?"

"Best one of the valley, and you can see at least half of the entire estate from there."

"Then I'm going. And you're not stopping me, Rafe."

He reared up in his seat and flagged Rick off in the other direction, then settled back down. "No, I guess I'm not stopping you, am I?"

"Look, this isn't your fault. I know you're blaming yourself, but—"

"You don't know half of what I'm thinking," he growled, nudging Donder around to head in the direction of the trail leading up, "so just follow me. OK? Keep a couple of lengths back, and you'll be fine."

"But will you?" she asked.

He twisted back in his saddle to look at her. "Do you ever give up?"

"Do you ever give in?"

Rather than answering, Rafe straightened in his seat and urged Donder forward. She knew Rafe was worried. More like scared to death. Blaming himself, too. She knew, because she was going through the same gamut of raw emotions. But at the end of this ordeal she'd have Molly, and Rafe would have… "I guess I don't ever give up," she said, pulling Ice Cream in behind Donder. Because she loved Rafe. When it was all said and done, she loved that stubborn man like crazy, and she wasn't going to give up on him. Not any time soon.

The ride up to the bluff wasn't as difficult as she'd expected, but once at the top her legs felt rubbery and her back was beginning to ache, so she was happy to slip out of the saddle while Rafe had a look around. "It's beautiful up here," she said, gazing out over the great expanse of land.

"Jess and I used to come up here when things got too intense at home. It always felt safe. Probably because I knew the old man was too drunk to come this far looking for me."

"Would he have seen beauty up here if he'd been able to get here?"

"What a joke! Lawrence Corbett see beauty anywhere? Not a chance in hell." He stepped up to the precipice outside the shelf where he and Molly had spent that evening, visored his eyes with his hand, then looked out over the valley below. "He was a miserable man, Edie. Rotten soul. Nothing fazed him, nothing touched him except the ugliness he chose to have around him."

"Yet he was a good doctor?"

"A brilliant doctor, technically. Don't know how he related to his patients, but no one ever complained, as far as I knew. So I guess he knew how to curb the demon when he was on the job."

"He must have been a miserable man."

"That much is true. He was."

"I mean miserable in his own skin. How could anyone live with himself, straddling the line the way he did? Good doctor, bad person?"

"Guess I've never asked myself that question." He walked over to Donder and pulled a pair of binoculars from his saddle bag. "Probably because I never gave a damn about anything having to do with my old man."

"So why not let him go now, Rafe?" She picked up a fist-sized stone and handed it to him. "This is your father. Throw him over the cliff and be done with him once and for all."

He studied the rock for a moment then tossed it on the ground. "I like the way you care, Edie. Shows me there's still good in the world. But it's not as simple as that. I can't simply hurl everything over the side of the cliff and put an end to the past thirty-five years of my life." He reached out and brushed his thumb across her cheek. "If it were that easy, I'd throw every loose rock up here over the edge. But that's not going to get rid of the one glaringly obvious problem—I am my father's son. I look like him and I act like him."

She took the binoculars and headed back to the edge of the overlook then began to scan below for any signs of Molly or her horse. "Personally, I like the look. At least he left you something good. But as far as acting like him…" She turned herself to face south, and continued looking. "Answer me this one question, Rafe, and answer it honestly. If you weren't afraid that you were like your father, would you keep Molly?" She knew the answer could break her heart, especially if it didn't include her, but she also knew it could be the best thing for Molly.

"Yes," he whispered. "I would."

A single tear clipped down her cheek. "Then you have to keep her. Because here's the thing…" She turned to face west. "Your father wouldn't have come up here looking for Molly this way. His heart wouldn't be ripping in two, thinking about the little girl being out here somewhere, lost. He wouldn't be putting Molly's needs before his own. You are not your father, Rafe. But you are Molly's father, the man who loves her and who would give his own life to protect her. And you would, wouldn't you? You would give up your very life right now if that's what you had to do to save Molly, because you love her more than you love yourself."

"Yes," he choked.

"Then it's settled. I'm not sure how we're going to work out the rest of the details, but for now we don't have to. All we have to do is find Molly." She swiped back her tears then turned to him. "Grace will be happy, Rafe." She'd done her job. Done the right thing. But the pain was unbearable as she didn't know if she would be included in what she'd just done. Rafe had overcome such a major hurdle in his life, but could he overcome another one? Or would it even be fair expecting him to, considering how difficult it had been to get him to realize his feelings for Molly?

Maybe that was as far as it could go.

Before Rafe could respond, his cell phone rang. "That was Rick," he said a moment later. "He said he hasn't found a single clue that would indicate Molly has even come out this far, so he's going to head out to Jess's cabin, regroup and get ready for a night ride. I think we should do the same thing. Meet Rick at the cabin and regroup."

She glanced up at the setting sun, the gold and pinks of the evening sky, and nodded. "Maybe we'll see something on the way there." She could only hope because even though Molly wasn't going to be her daughter now, that didn't mean the connection was automatically broken. She still felt so linked to that child, still loved her in ways she'd never believed she could love anyone. "I don't want to leave her out there in the dark, alone, all night."

"Neither do I," he said, stepping up to Edie and pulling her into his arms. "But I want you safe in the cabin while I go back out, because I'm not going to put you at risk the way Molly is."

"I can hunt along with you all night, Rafe."

"Maybe *you* can, but I can't do it. The two people I...I love most in the world...I can't have them both at risk."

She heard the words, and they scared her to death,

because she truly did want to believe them. Part of her, though, chalked them up to some kind of emotional reaction to Molly being missing, while part of her hung on to them for dear life. She didn't know what to do, couldn't figure it out right now. Maybe she was afraid to figure it out. So instead of over-thinking the moment, she simply sighed contentedly and stayed in his embrace for another moment. Then she gathered the resolve to push herself away from him. "How about I lead the way back down, and you can bring up the rear? That'll give you a better vantage point in case we've missed something on the way up." Oh, she knew what she'd missed on the way up. And now she was scared to death that she could lose it on the way down. Or lose it after Molly was discovered safe and sound. Or after Rafe came to his senses and remembered what he'd said in the heat of the moment.

But it was all good, she kept telling herself. She'd done what she was supposed to, what she'd promised she would, and the rest of it…well, the only thing she knew for sure was that she loved Rafe, loved Molly. For now, it was enough.

"At least eat something before you two go out again," Edie insisted, as she scanned Jess's cabinets for anything she could heat up. "Here…some soup. Will you have some soup?" She eyed the propane stove, not sure how to get it going. The cabin wasn't wired for electricity, but Rick had laid a nice fire in the fireplace, so that was good. She wouldn't have to sit alone in the dark once they went back out. And there *was* indoor plumbing.

"You heat the soup," Rick said. "While you're doing

that, I'm going to step outside and call my son. Say goodnight, maybe tell him a bedtime story."

What she wanted to be doing with Molly right now. What Rafe *would* be doing with Molly very soon. Or maybe what they'd be doing together.

"And I'm going to look around the cabin to see what Jess left behind in the way of flashlights and batteries. This could turn into a long night." He glanced at Edie. "And soup will be fine. Thank you."

"I'm going to fix a flask of it to take along, in case you find Molly. She'll need something to warm her up."

"You're going to make a wonderful mother," he said.

"Someday, maybe."

"She's your daughter, Edie. You can't deny that."

"And she's your daughter, too. *You* can't deny that."

For the first time in what seemed like for ever, he managed a smile. "You know I'm a work in progress, don't you? With a lot of emphasis on the work."

"Aren't we all?" she whispered, as she opened the first can and dumped it into a pot. And for the first time her optimism didn't outweigh her fears. It's what she wanted, of course, but now that she was so close to having it all, she was also so close to losing it all. But that was her fear to overcome, wasn't it? The one fear she'd never been able to get rid of.

A loud slam at the front door startled her out of her thoughts, and she looked up to see another large man step inside. One she vaguely recognized, but wasn't sure about.

"Where's Rafe?" he asked.

It had to be Jess. Same voice. Same eyes. "He's in the back room, looking for flashlights."

"And you're…Edie? I think I've seen you around."

"I'm Edie."

He studied her for a moment then smiled. "I always wondered what you'd look like."

"What do you mean?" she asked.

"The woman who could bewitch my brother. Wasn't ever sure it would happen, but I always wondered what she'd look like if someone did. Welcome to the family, such as it is, Edie."

"That's a little premature," she said.

Jess grinned. "I doubt it, but we'll see."

"What the hell are you doing here?" Rafe boomed from the doorway to the back room before Edie had a chance to respond to Jess.

"I came as fast as I could. Caught a helicopter up when I heard what was going on."

"Who called you?" Rafe asked.

"Wasn't you, big brother. It was Rick. Should have been you, but we'll take that up later on. In the meantime, are you up to some night riding?"

"Nothing could stop me, but, Jess, Rick's out there, getting ready to ride, too. He's been solid in this…in everything."

"I can deal with Rick." Jess stepped over to Edie and pulled her into his arms. But briefly. Then he stepped away. "My brother is certainly one lucky son of a…" He cracked a grin at Rafe. "Give me ten to get ready then we're out of here. But just for a couple of hours, if we want to be fresh for morning. And, Edie, if you could open up another can of soup, I'd appreciate it."

She watched the three men eat, and it struck her that they were all very similar. She couldn't explain how, but later, as they mounted up in the dark and she watched them disappear into the night shadows, she knew, for the first time, that they would find Molly. So much power, she thought. Rafe, Rick, Jess…so much power. When she settled down by the fire to wait, that was the thought she clung to.

"You've been to Hideaway Bluff?" Jess asked, as they headed down the west trail.

"Took a good look around a while ago," Rafe replied. "I took Molly up there the other night. It's where I think she finally came to terms with Grace's death, and I thought sure that's where I'd find Molly."

"Maybe she's still trying to find her way out there," Rick suggested. "We give Molly a lot of credit for being an amazing child, but she's only five so maybe that's where she's still trying to get to and she just hasn't made it there yet."

"Then we should go back there," Rafe said.

"Rick's right," Jess said. "In the city, when we do a search and rescue for a child, we always go to the obvious places first, then keep going back to them. Children are predictable. They want to go to someplace they know, someplace they feel safe…like you and I did when we were kids, Rafe. I'm betting that Molly is trying to get to Hideaway Bluff."

"Not in the dark," he gasped, thinking of how dangerous it could be. "She wouldn't…"

"She would," Rick assured him. "Christopher finds his refuge in the food pantry at home. It's large enough that he doesn't feel closed in and small enough that he feels safe." He chuckled. "That, plus he knows where I hide the cookies. But, seriously, Jess is right. Kids need that familiarity. If Molly feels a special connection to this place you call Hideaway Bluff, then the chances are she's still trying to get there."

The three of them rode silently back in the direction of the bluff, relying mainly on the moonlit night and stars to guide them, and with every pounding hoofbeat along the trail Rafe thought about his life, the way it had changed, the way it would change. It scared him, but he was ready to face the fear. But everything still boiled down to some basic questions. Could he live in Lilly Lake again, because it might come down to that? Could he really sit on the front porch of Gracie House, look across the street, and not see his old man there or feel his old man haunting him, trying to get under his skin?

The only answer he could find in himself was Edie. She believed, and because of that, he wanted to believe. No, he wasn't there yet, and it might take him a long time to get to where he believed on his own. But for now, maybe leaning on Edie's belief would be enough. It had to be, because he didn't want to lose her.

Of course, there was another consideration in all this. If he couldn't make it here, could Molly survive Boston? Could Edie? Because they were the most important parts of him now, the two essential parts of his equation. The truth was, he was already thinking of the three of them in terms of a family, which was putting the cart well before the horse because his work in progress really did need a hell of a lot of work. So, borrowing from Edie's optimism, they'd just take it one day at a time, the three of them, and figure it out from there.

"Molly's pony!" Rick called from off to the side,

closer to the tree line, interrupting Rafe's thoughts. "It's tied up over here."

Rafe and Jess immediately brought their horses around and stopped short of where Lucky was tied, rather loosely, to a sprawling mulberry bush. "Molly!" Rafe shouted into the night.

He listened, but heard only the sound of crickets.

"So she's on foot," Jess said. "Which means a couple of us need to be on foot, too." He slid off his horse at the same time Rick did. "I think, Rafe, that you should go on up to the bluff again while Rick and I cover this area down here. I don't think Molly's hurt, but she may be getting scared or a little woozy from dehydration, and she might not respond to us when we call so we're going to have to take it slowly. Look under all the bushes, behind all the logs and trees. But I think that if she did make it to the bluff, you need to ride hard to get up there, because she's got no business in a place like that, all alone, in the middle of the night."

"We used to do it," Rafe reminded him.

"But we had each other. That's the difference, big brother. We had each other."

And they still did, he was only now coming to realize. "Look, I'm sorry I've given you a hard time about becoming a firefighter. When this is over, Jess, we need to—"

"I know," Jess interrupted. "And we will."

"I'm glad you're here, little brother. I needed you." He glanced over at Rick. "And him, too. He's a good guy, Jess. We need to do something about him and the hospital. Make him a partner, at the very least."

"I'm glad I'm here, too. You couldn't have kept me

away. And about Rick, we'll work it out. Now, get the hell out of here, OK?"

That was exactly what Rafe did. He rode hard through the darkness for the next half-mile, until he came to the trail leading up to the bluff. "Molly!" he yelled, then listened. Nothing. So he dismounted. Taking a horse up there at this time of the night was crazy. By foot was the only sane way, even if it was going to take an eternity. "Molly!" he called again, as he began his ascent.

Every few feet he called again, facing disappointment and a rising level of fear each time when there was no response. Then finally, when he was in sight of the shelf where he and Jess had spent so many nights, he called out one more time, pretty sure by now that this was futile. "Molly, if you can hear me, sweetheart, please say something." It was a cry of desperation. "Please, Molly…" A plea ripped from his heart. "You're not in trouble. I want to make sure you're safe. So if you can hear me…"

"Rafey…" the tiny voice cried out in the night.

When he heard her voice, Rafe shut his eyes, said a silent prayer of thanks, and brushed the tears from his eyes. "Come to Daddy, sweetheart. Come to Daddy."

"She's sleeping peacefully," Edie whispered, tiptoeing from Molly's bedroom. "Exhausted, and glad to be home."

Rafe was sitting on the hall floor outside Molly's room, his back to the wall. He'd allowed Edie to bathe and dress Molly for bed, but he'd refused to go any further than that. "She said she wanted to talk to Aunt Grace."

"Because we were fighting, Rafe. She heard us, and it scared her because she knew we were fighting about her." Edie slipped down to the floor next to him and leaned her head on his shoulder. "We did that to her, Rafe. We scared her."

"I remember when my dad used to get so mean, and I couldn't get away, so I'd hide under the bed and hope he'd go away. Molly wasn't hiding under the bed but it's the same thing, and I know what it's like to be that scared." He took hold of her hand. "I'm going to stay here, Edie."

"In Lilly Lake?"

"In Gracie House. It's not about me any more. I mean, I'm not over all that mess in my past, but I'm moving forward. More than that, I *want* to move forward, and that's because of you."

"Because of Molly," she corrected.

"I would have never let Molly in if it hadn't been for you. And I never meant to hurt you, Edie. All the things I've said, all the arguments…I'm sorry."

"But I'm not," she said. "Because look what you've got. In the end, that's what got you to where you are now."

"You mean with Molly?"

"Of course I mean with Molly. I've always seen it in you, Rafe. Grace knew it was there, too."

"But you love her as much as I do. I always saw *that* in you."

"Loving someone…it's a gift, Rafe. There are so many people out there who are never lucky enough to find it, so when you do have a chance at it, you've got to grab hold and hang on. That's all I wanted you to do. Grab on to Molly and hang on until you found your way. I never thought I'd be part of that because I didn't trust myself enough to think I could. Even now I wonder if I'm everything you and Molly need…"

"Everything, and more."

"So that's the part of me that's *my* work in progress," she said.

"Something I'm going to love working on."

"It's funny, hearing you say that word."

"Love?" he asked.

"Love," she murmured.

"I think it fits pretty well. But I'm going to need practice."

"I think it fits beautifully, and practice all you want."

He stood, then took hold of her hand and pulled her up off the floor. As they walked together through the house, to check the door locks and turn off the lights, they stopped for a moment at the entry to the den to look at the portrait of Aunt Grace. As always, her watchful eye was on them, but tonight her portrait had taken on a glow that made it seem as if she was smiling. She was, Rafe knew. She absolutely was.

As they headed, hand in hand, up the stairs, Rafe scooped Edie into his arms. "I know what I'd like to start practicing, if you're interested."

"I thought you'd never ask."

EPILOGUE

"It is beautiful," Edie whispered, gazing out at the eternity of stars sprawled against the blackest sky. "Like nothing I've ever seen in my life."

"And full of possibilities," Molly added.

It was a perfect night up on the bluff, and the view stretched for ever, the way he always remembered it doing. It was the first time he'd been here with his family…his wife, his daughter. But it wouldn't be the last. "I think she always knew," Rafe said. "Aunt Grace. I think she always knew this was the way it would turn out for us. You, me, Molly…together as a family."

"Do you really think she chose me for you?" Edie asked, as she toasted a marshmallow over the fire Rafe had built. Rafe was refusing the marshmallows but munching away on chocolate-chip cookies. The best he'd ever had, he'd claimed. Even better than his aunt's, he'd told her. But Edie knew, as well as Grace had known, it was just the same old recipe off the back of the chocolate-chip bag. Love had been, and would always be, the ingredient that made them special.

"I'd be surprised if she didn't. That's the way she was."

"And she *would* have let me ride solo," Molly tossed in, still trying to get her way on the issue.

"You *had* your big adventure, young lady," Edie said. "We know you can ride solo, and you know the deal. You can do it only when one of us is there to supervise you. Your daddy or me. Or your Uncle Jess or Dr. Rick, or Johnny when he has the time. No one else."

In the years to come they were going to have their hands full with Molly because she was a strong-willed little girl. Full of life, full of adventure, ready to grab life in a big way. She was like Grace in many ways. Aunt Grace's daughter in every sense of the word. And their daughter too, for which he and Edie said their prayers of thanks every day of their lives.

"Can I have a kitten? And a puppy?"

Rafe slipped his hand into Edie's, and smiled at her. "How about a new horse? We're going out tomorrow to pick up a white stallion, and I have an idea he's going to need lots of attention to make him healthy again. Would that be OK with you? Having a new horse instead?"

"Can I name him Possibility?" Molly asked, looking out into the distance. "Then he'll remind me of where Aunt Grace is."

"I think that would be a very good name for him, honey," Rafe said, sighing the sigh of a contented man.

"A very good name," Edie agreed, handing her daughter the toasted marshmallow. Then she whispered to Rafe, "But we're not letting her name her little sister."

He placed his hand on Edie's belly. It was still their

secret, but not for long. "Mary Grace," he whispered back. "For your mother and Aunt Grace."

"Mary Grace," she repeated.

Tonight Mary Parker and Grace Corbett were very happy. Edie felt it, and he felt it too, because he was where he belonged. Rafe Corbett had finally come home. And he'd never, ever leave again. "Mary Grace," he whispered, pulling Edie into his arms.

* * * * *